Lessons for a
Sunday Father

Claire Calman

Lessons for a
Sunday Father

HarperCollins*Publishers*Ltd

Lessons for a Sunday Father

Copyright © 2001 by Claire Calman.

All rights reserved. No part of this book may be used or reproduced in
any manner whatsoever without prior written permission except in the
case of brief quotations embodied in reviews. For information address:
HarperCollins Publishers Ltd., 55 Avenue Road, Suite 2900,
Toronto, Ontario, Canada M5R 3L2

www.harpercanada.com

HarperCollins books may be purchased for educational, business,
or sales promotional use. For information please write:
Special Markets Department,
HarperCollins Canada,
55 Avenue Road, Suite 2900,
Toronto, Ontario, Canada M5R 3L2

First mass market edition

National Library of Canada Cataloguing in Publication

Calman, Claire
Lessons for a Sunday father / Claire Calman.

ISBN 0-00-639222-9

I. Title.

PR6053.A3915L47 2002   823'.92   C2002-902450-1

OPM 9 8 7 6 5 4 3 2 1

Printed and bound in the United States
Set in Trump Mediaeval

For my parents
—who separated
for the sake of the children

Acknowledgements

Thank you to everyone—adults, teenagers and children—I spoke to while researching *Lessons for a Sunday Father*, including those who preferred to remain anonymous, and especially the following:

Kevin Grout, Jane Ufton and pupils of Lady Joanna Thornhill Primary School in Wye, Kent

Joe Moran, Dominic Bergen and pupils of Walworth School, London

Trevor Dry, the Pied Piper of mackerel, with thanks for providing inspiration and fishing tips

Glass 'N' Glaze of Pluckley near Ashford, Kent, especially Jim, Thelma and Trevor Pearson

Dr Paul Barnett, Ned and Dan Brackenbury, Jordan Dry, Will Faulkner, Laurence Fegenbaum, Darren Peters, Oscar Russell, Mark Smithson, Igor Sprodnik, Ben Tansey, Honor Wilson-Fletcher

Terry Hill and Dave Watson for illuminating the mysteries of the male mind

James Barraclough, for early morning alarm calls

Jonathan Edgington, for advice on blokishness, vocabulary and swimming

My mother, Pat McNeill, for slogging through the first and second drafts and offering keen editorial insights as well as nice motherly encouragement

My late father, Mel, who knew that being a Sunday father is a full-time job

My sister, Stephanie, my one-woman cheerleader team, for her unfailing support

My agent, Jo Frank, for being so much more than an agent, and Vicky Cubitt for enthusiasm beyond the call of duty

My editor, Linda Evans, for having immense patience and a light touch with the red pen

... And Larry, a dedicated man, who really puts his heart into his work

Lesson One

Scott

Last night, I had precisely nil hours', nil minutes' and nil seconds' sleep. Take a tip from me—if you ever have a major ding-dong with your wife, girlfriend, cohabiting-type person, don't do it after midnight. If you're in the wrong, and believe me, you're bound to be—when was it ever *her* fault?—skip the excuses, skip the justifications and cut straight to the grovelling. Least that way you might get to kip on the settee. After a night like I just had, you'd be grateful for it. It's always like that on the telly, isn't it? There's a row and then the man, always the man, is dossing down in the front room—notice the woman never ends up on the bloody couch—and if he's lucky she'll chuck a pillow and a blanket at him. Cheers, I love you too.

Obviously, Gail's never paid enough attention or she'd have known that's how it goes. I should have filled her in: "No, Gail, this is where you banish me to the front room and you stomp upstairs and slam the bedroom door." Then it'd be cut to corny close-up of our wedding photo falling off the mantelpiece. But by that time I'm already on the wrong side of the front door, wishing I'd got my jacket and my mobile rather than a sodding tea-towel which doesn't look like it's going to be much use in saving me from freezing to death.

Thoughts whirled round my head like water going down a plughole, desperate thoughts and crazy thoughts and weird thoughts one after the other. I would have called my mate Colin, but it was after half-twelve by then and I could just picture his wife Yvonne standing there in her pink dressing-gown, nightie done up to the top button, saying it's no trouble, none at all, she just has to get out the step-ladder and fetch down another quilt from the loft, and offering me a coffee, not to worry she can unload everything from the dishwasher for a clean mug and they usually like to open the fresh pint first thing in the morning but she may as well open it now seeing as it's—goodness—already morning. I always feel I should give myself a good shake like a wet dog before I go in their house; she has this way of look- ing at you like she wants to put down a bit of plastic sheeting before you get too near her furniture.

I considered checking in at the Holiday Inn, but they know me there after we had that do just before Christ- mas. Especially after the unfortunate mishap that occurred with the sort-of accidental hurling of mince pies across the Churchill Banqueting Suite. Toyed with the idea of breaking into the MFI showroom on the ring road so's I could kip in one of their room sets. I even thought about ringing up a monastery to tell them I'd had the call from God and would be right round: "I've

4

spoken to Him Upstairs and He said you're to let me stay, but that I can skip all that praying, silence and head-shaving stuff, OK?"

No way could I stay at my parents'. I'd sooner have slept on a park bench. I'd sooner have slept on a park bench with a bag lady, come to that. Make that two bag ladies and a wino. And a dog with an itch. This is the point where Gail normally says, "Oh, come on, Scott, stop exaggerating. They're not that bad." Not that bad? I'd rather suck my way through a bumper size pack of frozen fish fingers than have a meal with those two. I'd rather eat school dinners for the rest of my life, soggy greens and all. I'd rather—oh, forget it. All I'm saying is, if Competitive Moaning was included in the Olympics and they signed up the parents, then Great Britain's gold medal count could be in for a stratospheric rise. My dad's specialist areas are, in no particular order: other drivers, foreigners—which of course includes people whose grandparents came here fifty years ago and, in fact, anyone who lives further away than Folkestone—appliances of all kinds because nothing's made properly any more nowadays—"they do it deliberate so's you 'ave to keep buying new ones ev'ry free weeks"—the government, the neighbours—oh, yes, and me. Mum's faves are the weather, the Russians (current affairs have kind of passed her by really), Gail's family, people with body piercings—"I don't know what they can be thinking of a metal stud right through her tongue it's not hygienic is it they must all be perverts they want a good smacking," the ever decreasing size of Mr Kiplid's exceediddly small cakes, the neighbours and—surprise, surprise—me again. In fact, as far as I can see, the only thing that's kept her and him together all these years—that's together as in not actually divorced and as in living under the same roof, not together as in this is the person they love and want to spend time with—is their shared paranoia about the neighbours and their disappointment in me.

Not exactly top of my list when it comes to looking for a cosy bed and a warm welcome on the spur of the moment then. I'd have been better off getting myself arrested so the police would lock me up for the night. I'd have had some sort of bed and maybe got Gail to feel guilty into the bargain, might be worth it. Then I told myself it'd all blow over and I'd only be embarrassing myself and I'd have looked like a total pillock for nothing.

So I went to work. I'm usually first in anyway, but it was very different arriving at night. Weird. Majorly bizarre. Bizarre with a capital "B," as Nat would say. I let myself in, fumbling for the light switches, hearing the familiar beep-beep, rushing to the alarm to tap in the code. There's a small reception area—just the counter where we take the orders and a couple of crap square chairs covered in scratchy dark brown cloth and, on the other side, a coffee table which is a pathetic apology for a piece of furniture and only has the right to call itself a coffee table because over the years it's become marked with overlapping coffee rings, so many of them now, they almost look like they're meant to be there and are having a go at being a pattern. Plus there's three plastic seats, the moulded ones you can stack. We have them 'cause most of our customers turn up covered in paint and plaster dust and we don't want them buggering up the so-called good seats for the occasional non-trade person who comes in for a special order or something. I know, I'm sounding like Yvonne, but it's not up to me.

I poke my head round the door of the workroom, checking everything's OK, then go into the office and sit at my desk, thinking maybe I should phone Gail to see if she's cooled down yet and knowing she'd hang up on me. I phone anyway.

"It's me."

She hangs up.

I make myself a coffee, over-filling the kettle so's it would take longer to boil. At least it gives me something to do, standing there in the squashed corner by the sink, trying to think and trying not to think. Then I lay down on the brown seats. They're pushed together but I still can't scrunch all of my body on and it's bloody cold too. I switch on the fan heater, but it gives out more noise than heat, so I have a hunt round for something to cover myself with. Take a dekko in the workroom. There's a few old blankets and dustsheets dumped in one corner, as there always are, but they'll all have fragments of flaming glass embedded in them and I'd rather be freezing than slashed to ribbons, thank you. It makes

7

me think of them Indian blokes who lay on a bed of nails. Gail would love that, thinking about me alone and shivering, every bit of me pricked and pierced by millions of tiny pieces of glass.

On the back of the office door, there's my mac that I left there about two months ago and keep meaning to take home. I curl up on the seats again, shivering under the mac, thinking about what I said and what she said and what I could do to make it all right and worrying in case I do drop off and the lads find me in the morning and what the hell I would say and how was I going to get a shave between now and then and I should have gone to the bloody Holiday Inn and so what if they did recognize me, bollocks to the lot of them. Then I get up again, put the mac on and go and sit in my chair and rest my head on my desk. Bugger, bugger, bugger. Bollocks, bollocks, bollocks. You are a grade A stupid twat, I tell myself. Now what are you going to do?

I open the desk drawer and have a poke round as if the answer might be written on a yellow stickie, but it's just the usual collection of loose paperclips and stray staples, the spare scissors that don't cut properly, a grimy rubber that leaves smudges and a couple of highlighter pens that are running out of juice. Anyway, after one hour and twenty minutes spent pretending to tidy my desk—I know because I take a look at my watch about every three minutes to see if the time can possibly be passing as slowly as I think it is—I get up and wander round the office, sliding the filing drawers in and out and poking about in the stationery cubbyhole just in case someone's happened to leave a thick quilt and a fresh doughnut in there.

Back in reception, I go behind the counter and flick through the special orders book for something to do. You can see the days when Denise has been in because she does these circles above her "i's," like little bubbles. And Maureen's writing, ever so neat the way Rosie does for homework, only with the letters all leaning at exactly the same angle like those dancers we saw at that show in the West End. Under the counter, there's a packet of chocolate Hob-nobs with a rubber band round them holding them closed. Denise's. I take it off and flick it across the room onto one of the brown chairs. Dead-eye Dick. Then I eat my way through the packet, telling myself I'd get some more tomorrow, or was it today, and knowing Denise will be right pissed off with me and I'll have to get her some more otherwise she'll "forget" to give me my messages.

Trailing crumbs, I return to the workroom, looking for something to moan about. Well, a blind man with his hands tied behind his back wouldn't take more than ten seconds to find a problem in that place, 'cause they're ruddy clueless most of them. Safety goggles on the floor instead of hanging up where they should be. A pile of broken glass just swept into the corner with the broom still on top. Dirty coffee mugs on the workbenches. Sometimes it's like running a ruddy nursery school. Half of them would forget to wipe their arses if someone didn't tell them.

OK, OK, I know. It's just, you see, I needed something, anything, to fix on, something I was allowed to be annoyed about, something that wasn't my fault.

Gail

Please tell me last night was only a dream. If I shut my eyes tight and pinch myself, I'll wake up properly. Tell me it was no more than a nightmare—to be kissed away, forgotten by morning. When he was a little boy, only about four or five, Nat used to have nightmares. He'd call out in the night and one of us—usually me, Scott could sleep through a brass band marching round the bed—would go through to him. I'd cradle him in my arms and whisper into the sweet softness of his hair, kiss his flushed cheek,

"There, there, it's just a bad dream, Natty, just a bad dream. All gone now. All gone."

I know last night wasn't a dream, of course, now standing here at the sink, concentrating all my attention on wringing out a cloth, wiping the already clean worktop. I know it wasn't a dream because afterwards I didn't sleep. How could I? After he'd gone, I heard him start the car and drive away. I ran upstairs and tiptoed into Nat's room at the front of the house to watch from the window, peeking through the crack in the curtains as if I was watching a scary film through my fingers.

The red of the car brakelights glowed bright as he slowed at the corner, then he turned left onto the main road . . . and he was gone. I stayed there a little while, thinking any second now he'll do a U-turn and come back. Or he'll go up to the roundabout and turn there. Any second now and I'll see the beam of his headlights swing round as he turns into our road. I'll run downstairs to let him in. He'll say it was all a mistake, a silly joke that backfired. He'll explain and everything will be all right again. I crossed my fingers and laid them on the windowsill. Touch wood. It was all just a mistake.

But the road stayed dark and still.

I turned round and looked at Nat, his limbs—so long now, he's grown so much—sprawled across the bed, the duvet all bunched over on one side. I pulled it up around him and bent to touch his hair. It's as much as I can do to get near him these days; you know what they're like at that age. He's just thirteen. Last week. Scott took him bowling with a bunch of his friends and they had a whale of a time, though Nat tried to be cool about it—it's not done to show you're excited at his age. What a great start to his adolescence. Nice timing, Scott. I dug my nails into my palms. Better—better to feel angry. Better to feel something at least, not this strange numbness, this nothing feeling like I've died and no-one's bothered to tell me. In the bathroom I looked in the mirror, telling myself in my head: *See? This is you, Gail, still here. This is you looking just the way you always do*. I stared at my image, thinking maybe the real me was in there, trapped behind the glass, and out here was just my reflection and that's why I couldn't feel anything.

"I suppose I better go to bed." I said it out loud. I wanted to hear my voice, check I was still there I suppose, that I was still real. Silly, I know.

I got into "my" side of the bed and lay there, stiff and straight as an Egyptian mummy, replaying what had happened, turning it over and over in my mind, inspecting it from all angles as if it were an unfamiliar object I'd come across by accident, wondering if I might suddenly spot something new, some vital clue that would make everything clear, something I could hold onto and understand. Maybe I'd just got the wrong end of the stick. Maybe I'd hallucinated the whole thing. It was a caffeine-induced vision or something. I thought again of Scott's voice, the things he'd said, his eyes avoiding mine. The quiet click of the front door, his face distorted and unfamiliar through the frosted glass, the face of a stranger.

Why aren't I crying? I thought to myself. *You should be crying, Gail*, I said back to me, trying to sound firm and positive like Cassie. *For goodness' sake, woman, don't bottle it all up. Have a good cry if you want to.*

I lay there, waiting for the tears to come, telling myself I'd feel better if I could just let go. But there were no tears. There was nothing. Surely I should be feeling more—something—more hurt, more upset, just more.

Then I thought, "This is stupid. I can't be wasting time lying here all night if I'm not going to sleep. There's plenty to do." So I got up and went downstairs again and got out the bucket and mop and started washing the kitchen floor.

Surely this wasn't my life? I thought, plunging the mop into the sudsy water. My life was simple, busy but uncomplicated, a predictable juggling of kids, work, shopping, cooking and cleaning, with not enough treats such as meals out, drinks in the pub with Scott or my best friend Cassie, or girlie nights in with my sisters, Mari and Lynn. But this *thing*—this wasn't my life. This was TV drama-land—people arguing in kitchens and lying and cheating and driving off at midnight. And I'm right in the middle of it, only I don't know what's going to happen next. I shoved the mop back and forth over the floor, the colour of it brightening at my feet. It's supposed to look like real quarry tiles, sort of terracotta-ish, but it's just vinyl of course, no more than a sham. A practical sham.

Back in the bedroom, the red figures of the clock said 2:13. Twenty-four hours ago, I was asleep in this very same bed, and Scott was right here next to me. Twenty-four hours ago, we were a normal family. Not perfect, not rich, just normal. But we were like children playing in a field where there's a hidden landmine. Twenty-four hours ago, I was content, secure, my biggest worry no more than what to cook for supper, where Rosie's gym kit had got to, and whether Nat might ever respond with anything other than "Mn?" I was still in one piece, twenty-four hours ago, the children were asleep in their beds, the house was still standing. But now nothing was the same. The landmine was already there, waiting to explode. I just didn't know it.

Scott

So in the morning, I have my croissants and coffee with cream in bed, brought to me by my adoring harem of exotic maidens, sink into a deep bath, mosey around in my silk dressing-gown, speak to my stockbroker, then have the chauffeur pick me up in the limo to take me to my first meeting of the day.

I am seriously going to have to do something about this. I can tell, the more miserable I get the more I tend to daydream. Gail says it's because I don't know what it means to be a grown-up. But that's crap—I earn a living to support my family, I pay my taxes and bills, I drive a car, so I'm a grown-up, right? Don't answer that.

Looked at my watch. It was twenty to eight. Well, I've no idea how that happened because I absolutely, definitely, 100 per cent did not close my eyes for a single second. So I'm there, sat at my desk with a grade A crick in my neck, stiff back and generally feeling like a load of old shite frankly. The lads are supposed to get in at eight but Harry and me aren't sticklers for timekeeping as long as everyone's in and stopped arsing about by 8.30.

Builders working out on sites often come in first thing, you see, and they usually wait and have their glass cut there and then. If there's no lads in, Harry or I do it. I like to keep my hand in anyway. I'm always in by eight to do the alarm and let the others in, but Harry's sometimes here first. It's Harry's company, well him and his wife's. Maureen comes in two, three days a week to "oversee" the paperwork, i.e. check on everything Denise has done because she doesn't trust her. Though, frankly Denise is too dull to be untrustworthy, you know? She hasn't got the imagination and I don't see how she could do anything dodgy anyhow—what's she going to do, sneak out some stock sheets under her coat? I mean, they're eight feet by four for chrissakes. And where would she sell them on—it's not exactly like offloading snide sweatshirts down the pub, is it? "Fancy some cheap glass, mate? Got plain, reeded or frosted." I don't think so.

Anyway, although Harry's the owner, he's not much of a manager type. Well, obviously—that's what he's got me for, though I'm not sure I'm much of a one either. But I'm better at smooching the private customers and chatting up business clients, offices and that. I'm the one with the looks and the charm—OK, only when compared to Harry, but I get by. Harry's been in the business since he was barely out of nappies, still carries round his grandad's diamond glass cutters as well as his new tungsten ones. He's sixty-one so I guess he might knock off for good soon, but I don't know what he'd do with the business. Their son lives in Australia and I can't see him being enough of a mug to leave behind the sun, sea and surfing to hide away on an industrial estate where the only excitement in our daily lives is the arrival of the sandwich van and wondering whether she'll have chocolate muffins or lemon drizzle cake. I know, sad, isn't it?

Still, the point is, twenty to eight didn't leave me a whole lot of time to get myself a shave from somewhere and find a clean shirt. But I figured Gail would have calmed down by now and I could call Harry and tell him I'd be a bit late in. So first I rang home.

"Gail? It's me. Look, I—" I was just going to go into how sorry I was and I'd make it up to her and all that, but I never got the chance, 'cause she hung up on me.

I rang again.

"What do you want?" Her voice was dead cold. Scary. Like I was a double-glazing salesman she was trying to get shot of.

"Gail. Come on, love. I need to come home. Let's not be silly about this."

"Let's not be silly? But 'being silly' as in sleeping with someone else is OK, is it? Perhaps you could draw up a sheet of rules, because I find your logic just a teensy bit difficult to follow."

"Sweetheart, I can tell you're still a bit upset—"

"A bit upset? Do you think you can just buy me a bunch of flowers and that'll be the end of it?"

"No, course not!" She wasn't all that far off actually, but I reckon there's a time and a place for honesty and so far telling the truth had done nothing but land me in serious shit.

"Scott, as far as I'm concerned, you are—" Her voice suddenly dropped to a harsh whisper so the kids must have been around, "—*never* setting foot past this front door again."

Bit over the top, don't you think? Women like a bit of a to-do in their lives, don't they? It's watching all that stuff on the telly, soaps and costume dramas, they're always chock full of women sobbing and fainting and generally getting their knickers in a twist. I was still pretty sure she'd settle down in a day or two—if I could just handle it right.

"Gail, at least let me fetch some things. I've not even had a shave . . ."

"Go to Boots if you want a razor. It'll take me a while to pack up all your stuff."

I knew she was just saying it to wind me up, so I bit my tongue and managed not to rise to the bait. I figured maybe it'd be best to lay low for a day or two, give her a chance to cool off. She got in a couple more digs but finally agreed to put a few things in a bag for me.

"Just my razor, a couple of shirts, pants and socks then. Maybe my light blue shirt and—"

"This isn't a telephone shopping line, Scott. I'll bring whatever's clean, I can drop it off before I pick up Rosie."

Rosie. What the hell had she told Rosie? "Your father's a lousy, lying cheating bastard and I've told him he's not allowed to see you ever again." "We've had a minor misunderstanding, love, but don't worry—everything'll soon be back to normal." I hadn't a clue. I was beginning to think maybe I didn't know my wife as well as I thought I did.

"And, and can you bring my mobile and the charger? And my thick jacket. I was sodding freezing last night."

There was a short, smug laugh from the other end of the phone. Cheers, Gail. Nice to think that the woman who vowed she'd love you for ever would one day hate you so much that she'd be pleased to hear you nearly snuffed it due to hypothermia.

"And Gail?"

"What now, for heaven's sake! I can't stand here all day while you itemize every last shoelace you want delivered."

"No, it's not that. It's just . . ."

"*What!*"

"Keep your knickers on—" Mistake. Big mistake. Not a good time to be mentioning knickers.

She laughed but it wasn't a ha-ha-aren't-we-having-fun kind of thing.

"What, like you, you mean?"

"OK, I deserved that. I'm just saying, keep it cool in front of the lads, eh? There's no need for us to have a scene here, is there? Put it in my old sports bag or something, yeah?"

Another sigh.

"Scott?"

"Mmn?"

"You're pathetic."

Nat

Are parents like totally clueless or what? Jeez. Mum and
Dad have had some kind of mega serious shit row—a no
holds barred, six rounds fight with a capital "F," but
we're not supposed to know. No-one ever tells you anything round here. I only know 'cause I heard them arguing last night. I mean, how stupid is that? They could've
woken up Rosie. I got up and crept out to the landing. I
couldn't hear properly, but then my mum went "—lying
bastard!" really loud. And I mean, my mum never
swears, like not ever, so I knew it wasn't just a normal
row. He must have done something really bad this time.
I think it was to do with another woman. That's what it
always is on TV. Then she said, "Ssh! The kids'll hear,"
so I ducked back into my room and they went down to
the kitchen and shut the door. Mum was just in her
dressing-gown and didn't have any slippers on, but she
kind of thumped downstairs as if she was wearing DMs.
I snuck down the stairs to listen, missing out the fifth
step 'cause it creaks. Mum says it's bad manners to
eavesdrop, but how else are you supposed to find out
what's going on? I was trying not to breathe so they

wouldn't hear me. I reckon I'd make an ace spy. I thought if they suddenly came out I could say I had a really bad stomach ache and had come down for some milk. I mean, I can't help it if I'm sick, can I? But then I heard Mum say about putting the rubbish out, so I sprinted back up the stairs and into my room before the door opened.

When I came down this morning, Rosie's at the kitchen table, spooning Rice Krispies into her gob and drivelling on about Henry the Eighth. Right. Is she sad or what? Get a life, Rosie. So I come in, whap a couple of slices in the toaster. No sign of Dad but he's usually out the door before eight anyhow. I look at Mum and she looks at me and I'm wondering if she knows I know and if she's going to say anything. I do my Man of Mystery look—you tilt your head forward then look up from under your eyebrows and you mustn't smile, not even for one second. It's pretty cool if you know how to do it right. Steve always starts laughing. Clueless. So I'm giving her the look, leaning casual like against the counter, then my toast springs up and makes me jump—which is not good for a Man of Mystery. Nothing should make you jump—not a police siren, not a gunshot, nothing.

I spread Marmite on one half of one bit of my toast and strawberry jam on the other. I could see Mum out the corner of my eye, watching me, biting her lip to stop herself saying anything. It was pretty revolting actually, the bit in the middle where the jam and Marmite met. It's not going to be up there on my top ten list of

23

favourite foods. Then she came closer and said "Nat" in a special creepy way and I thought here we go, she's going to tell me about what happened last night in one of those I'm-going-to-treat-you-like-a-grown-up talks. No thank you. And I'm up and on my toes like a spring and heading for the door.

I went back for an apple, then I shouted up to Rosie as I left: "Oi, Rozza!"

"What?"

"You know Henry the Eighth?"

"Not personally."

Rosie actually thinks she invented that joke. Still, she's only nine.

"Did you know he had VD? Put it in your project."

"He never! Did he really?"

"Yeah—Ask Miss Thing if you don't believe me."

Then Mum chimed in.

"Nathan! Please don't always do that! It's—"

"Bye, y'all." And I was out the door and heading down the path, a man with a mission.

Gail

I know I ought to have said something. I ought to have told Nat and Rosie. I kept steeling myself to speak. I was getting breakfast and making sandwiches for Rosie's packed lunch and all the time running things through my head, trying out what I could say:

Your dad's had to go away for a few days. For work.

They'd never believe it. Scott's only been away on business once in ten years and that was for all of two days at a trade fair and we all knew he was going weeks beforehand. He's not exactly some jet-setting executive who has to fly off to New York at a moment's notice.

Your dad's been called away. There's a family crisis.

Well, it could hardly be his parents, could it? What a tough pair—we call them the Gruesome Twosome. Granted, they're terrible hypochondriacs, the both of them—we've always a few like that down at the surgery, whose only pleasure in life seems to be finding some new bit of their body to moan about. But Scott's parents are never actually ill. Even if they were, like if someone had slipped rat poison into their tea or something—and just about everyone they know must have been tempted at some point—Nat would never believe that Scott had suddenly turned into the devoted, dutiful son. I thought of saying that Scott's sister Sheila was ill and that he'd dashed up to Scotland but the kids love her and I didn't want to upset them.

I even thought about just saying it straight out, as it really was: *Your dad's left. He's a cheating, lying snake and he's not coming back.*

I wanted to say it. I really did. But I stopped myself. I stood there, my hand shaking as I poured myself some coffee, the words running through my head again and again like an old scratched record. I couldn't think of anything else, couldn't focus for even a second. I kept opening the fridge then closing it again without taking anything out. I banged myself in the face with the cupboard door because I opened it so quickly. Knocked over the jam, saying, "Gosh, I'm being such a butterfingers this morning!" keeping my voice bright.

Rosie prattled away when I asked her what she'd be up to today at school, then she remembered she needed her gym kit and ran upstairs. Nat sat silently at the table, his legs stretched out awkwardly, so you'd have to step over them as you passed. Normally, I'd say, "Legs in, Nat!" Honestly, I get so sick of it sometimes, I feel like I'm a prison warder or a teacher, constantly trying to get him to behave like a normal human being. If he's really going to carry on like this till he's twenty I'll have to resign from the post of being his mother. The awful thing is, I see Nat the way he is and I remember how he used to be, then I look at Rosie and I know it's just a matter of time before she's demanding a clothes allowance and trying to sneak out the door in a top that shows her navel.

Anyway, God, I'm getting like Scott, going off the point. I didn't say, "Legs in!" to Nat because I felt so peculiar: sort of shaky and slightly sick, my own legs wobbly as a newborn calf. I still couldn't believe it, you see? Suddenly, I envied Nat, mooching around, leaving it till the last possible moment to go to school. I could have happily sat slumped in a chair all day with a gormless look on my face. Then he saw me looking at him and he stopped mid-chew, treating me to a view of half-chomped toast. And I knew that he knew that something was up. I hoped he hadn't heard anything last night. After the first flurry, we'd come downstairs and we had tried to be quiet. Well, I had. Of course, Scott's usually gone to work by the time Nat's down anyway, but Nat's no fool. I thought perhaps I better say something.

"Nat . . ." I started, without yet knowing what I would say, what I *could* say. The scrape of his chair on the floor. He shoved back from the table and got to his feet still holding his piece of toast.

"Gotta go." His eyes met mine for a second, then he looked away. I nodded and turned to the table, not bothering to say, "At least clear your plate, Nathan." What was the point? A bomb had just been detonated beneath our children's feet—now wasn't the moment to start nagging them about tidying up.

"You got practice tonight?" I knew he didn't, but I needed to say something, just to keep him near me for even another few seconds. Sounds silly, doesn't it? I can't explain it.

"Nah. Might go round Steve's."

"Do you want some food saved?"

He wrinkled his nose in that endearing way he has and shrugged.

"Well." I picked up the plates. "Whatever." I'm starting to speak the way Nat does. Scott does it too.

"Mn." He did one of his noncommittal grunts then loped away, doing his peculiar walk, his shoulders ranging from side to side like a cheetah stalking through the undergrowth. I suppose he imagines it's manly. Aah—*so* sweet.

I heard him pick up his bag in the hall and heft it onto his shoulder. He likes to get the bus in now, though with the traffic the way it is he'd probably be faster walking as it's not far. But Nat's like Scott—why walk when you don't have to? It doesn't make sense in Nat's case though because of all his swimming practice. He is so fit. But he takes the bus. You make sense of it, if you can; it's a mystery to me. Rosie's still at junior school, of course, and although it's no distance either, I drop her off on my way in to work. The roads are a devil and what with all these child abductions you read about practically every other day in the papers, I can't relax for a moment unless I know where she is.

"Bye then! Have a good day!" I called out to Nat as I

heard him open the front door. There was a pause, then he came back into the kitchen and walked past me over to the worktop. He picked out an apple from the fruit bowl and gave me a funny half-smile then, as he passed me again, he stopped mid-lope and gave me an awkward kiss on the cheek.

He did his silly Clint Eastwood face, like he's chewing tobacco, then he pushed up the brim of an imaginary hat.

"Take it easy now, y'hear?"

Well, it made me feel quite tearful. Nat's never been big on kissing, not since he was a tot anyway and in the last year he's made it more than plain he doesn't want to be kissed goodbye in the mornings and certainly not ever if his friends are around. He pulls away and wipes his cheek as if I'm a leper. Charming, isn't it? They're all like that at this age though. One minute, he's your own darling little boy, clambering up onto your lap for cuddles and wanting to be tucked in at night and have a story; the next they're walking several paces ahead of you in the street because they're embarrassed by your crumbly uncool presence and your clothes and your hair and the way you talk and they won't let you in their room at all, never mind to come in and kiss them night-night.

So, while on any other day I'd have been overjoyed to have Nat kiss me without having to be asked or it being my birthday, this morning it only made me feel worse.

For one moment at least, Nat must have felt sorry for me and I hated Scott for that, hated him for what he'd done to our children, what he'd done to *us*. I could feel myself welling up but I told myself to cut it out, cut it out right now. *You've no time for tears, I told myself. Pull yourself together!* Stay calm, take a few deep breaths. I'm fine. I *have* to be fine.

Dear God, I can't do this. If I could only go back, if I could just rewind the tape and go back to last night, maybe I wouldn't have said anything. I could have kept my suspicions to myself and life would have carried on as normal. Only now we've released this enormous boulder and it's started rolling downhill, getting faster and faster and more and more out of control and we don't know where it will end up. And now it's too late to stop it or ever bring it back. It's already too late.

Rosie

Dad wasn't there when I came down to breakfast, and he never said goodbye. Normally, if he leaves before we're down, he whistles like this—peep, *peep*—I can't do it, it's only air when I try, then he shouts up the stairs: "Bye-eee! See ya later!" Mum says it's bad manners to be shouting all over the house and if you want to speak to someone you should go and find them. My dad has to go to work early because he's the manager and he knows the code for the burglar alarm. He works in a place that is called First Glass which is meant to be a sort of joke—like First Class, to show it's the best. What they do is they put windows in for people, like say if someone broke your window with a football, then they would come and give you a new one. Dad knows how to do it, he's let me watch him, and he used to do it all the time but now he is the manager so he has to sit at his desk a lot or go and see the customers. They do doors and greenhouses and conservatories as well, and Tudor windows which have like teeny eeny-weeny window panes that are diamond shaped or square with lead all round them and they're all made by hand and it

31

takes sodding ages dad says and no-one likes doing them because they're a right royal pane in the arse (that's what dad says—"a pane—that's p-a-n-e"—that's a pun), and mum sighs and says will he please not use that language in front of the kids but we don't mind a bit. And they do pretend Tudor windows too, which are a lot cheaper but they are not pukka dad says. We are doing the Tudors with Miss Collins. Henry the Eighth had six wives but not all at the same time, and when he didn't like one he said "Off with her head!" and they chopped it off. He divorced two but it took ages and ages because they didn't have divorce properly back then but he was king so he could keep changing the rules as he went along, like when you play a card game with Nat. Now if you go off your wife you just get a divorce and then you live in two houses, like Kira's mum and dad. And Jane's. And Darren's, and Sheena's, and . . . There's loads in our class. Kira says it's quite good mostly because her mum and dad feel bad so they get her stuff like new trainers and give her money when she wants. Kira's got a stepdad who lives in their house and when he has a cup of tea he makes a big slurpy noise like you do when you get right to the very bottom of your milkshake and your mum says stop it now, that's not nice, but he is OK mostly. Her dad lives on his own but she thinks he has got a girlfriend because he started saying things like, "How would you feel if your old dad got himself a girlfriend, eh?" Uh-duh. So of course he's already got one. But, to wind him up, Kira said, "Don't be silly, Daddy. You're much, much too *old* to have a *girl*friend. It'd be so embarrassing. I'd die." So now he can't tell her he has one and Kira still gets him all to herself on Sundays. Well, not all to herself completely because she's got a little brother, Rory, who's only seven. Practically a baby. Kira calls him little squit when her mum's not listening.

My mum and dad have arguments sometimes but not like Kira's did. She used to get into her wardrobe and shut the door so she couldn't hear because they were shouting. Now it is better because they are in two different homes so they have to phone each other up when they want to shout. Kira's mum hates her dad so much that she tells Kira all horrible things about him and when he toots his car horn outside when he comes to fetch Kira on Sunday, her mum says "Oh, bugger him, why does he lean on the bloody horn?" then Kira runs outside and says, "Daddy, don't lean on the bloody horn!" and he says, "I'm only leaning on the bloody horn because she won't let me in the bloody house. And don't say bloody."

But my mum and dad are not like that because for a start they are not so loud. When they have a row afterwards my dad gives my mum a big kiss and puts his arm round her and says he's sorry so that she'll start talking to him again. Then he goes and gets a take-away so she doesn't have to cook and we have it on our laps as a treat and my best take-away is pizza but without all the yucky bits that Nat has on top of his. Then Dad goes all soppy and Nat says it makes him feel sick, all that snog-ging, but it doesn't really. He wants to snog Joanne Carter from down the road only he's too chicken to ask her out.

Mum was all quiet at breakfast and when I went and got the crisps and an apple to put in my lunchbox, she said, "Good girl, Rosie" like she used to when I was about six years old.

I wonder what Henry did with the heads after they got cut off. I must ask Miss.

Scott

It's just not possible. Half past eight in the evening and I'm back here at work again. See, the thing is, I was so sure that I'd be able to sort everything out—not that Gail would suddenly sprout a pair of wings and forgive me overnight, no—but that she'd have calmed down a tad and I'd be back indoors again. I mean, how are we supposed to talk about it if she won't let me in the sodding house? I'm not spending the rest of my life on my knees pleading through the letterbox.

I am not sleeping here again. Or not *not* sleeping here, to be precise. Sod it, I'm going to have to ring a mate. Right, let's look at the options. There's Colin, who's sort of my best mate, 'cept there's the slight drawback of the lovely Yvonne, she of the pursed lips and buttoned-up nightie. I can really see her welcoming me with open arms. There's Roger, who I've known for about a hundred years, but he's a rep and spends half his life on the road. Then there's Jeff, who lives on his own. No, it's not that he's a sad bastard who can't get a woman—actually, he *is* a sad bastard but that's only 'cause his wife ran off with his brother, so can you blame him? I mean, how crap is that? And, before she ran off, she'd been shagging the brother in their bed, Jeff's bed—once she even did it with him when he was staying over on the settee, and Jeff was right upstairs asleep.

Who else? Well, Harry, of course. Harry from work. That might be a bit weird, because of working together and that. Technically, he's my boss, you could say, because he owns First Glass, but it's never been like that, not for as long as I can remember. We're more like partners, like a family business, father and son type of thing. After school, I had a whole succession of jobs, in a clothes shop flogging suits, worked on building sites— I've done bricklaying, painting, tiling, bit of plastering; had a job in a fish and chip shop, behind the bar in a pub, killing chickens in a factory, telesales. Then I met Harry one night at a pool tournament in the pub. I was knocked out in the second round (you're impressed I got that far, I can tell), and he said hard luck, mate, and we got to talking about what he did and how he'd been a glazier since he was fifteen years old and I said I was good at DIY but I'd never done glazing but I wouldn't mind learning and he said come round and see him, have a chat, so I did and the next thing I knew I was working there.

It was Harry who taught me how to cut a piece of glass, how to measure so you're spot on, how to cut when you're working on site and there's no workbench; it was Harry who showed me how to handle a whacking great stock sheet so it doesn't crack on you; Harry who gave me my own set of cutters in a leather pouch so I wouldn't lose them. I'd say he's been like a dad to me, but that's not true. He hasn't—or at least not like my own dad, nothing like. Thank God. Harry's a good old bloke. The best.

We've always gone out for pints, Harry and me, had the odd bite to eat, been racing and that, fishing off the beach or the pier sometimes. I've taken the family round his place for Sunday lunch a few times, parties at Christmas and for his birthday, but . . . Well, that's not the same as phoning up and saying, "I've got nowhere to go, can I come and stay at yours?" is it? Don't get me wrong—Harry'd give me a bed like a shot. Harry would give you the teeth out his own mouth if he saw you having trouble chewing your steak. But . . . I dunno. Course, he'd never say anything but I'd kind of feel like I'd let him down somehow, and I don't think I could handle that. No.

This morning, after my night of blissful slumber at work, Harry got in just after eight. Well, he takes one look at me and he goes,

"You look a bit rough, mate. Been here all night?"

"You know me—can't keep me away from work." I laugh, keeping it casual. I told him our boiler had gone on the blink this morning so I'd not had a shave, but I was just popping back home for my razor.

I drove into town and bought a razor and some socks and pants. Back to work to freshen up, had a shave in the wash-basin. The lads were in by then so I stuck with the broken boiler story. Lee didn't believe it for a second, of course, suspicious bastard that he is.

"Scott's missus has chucked him out! Done a foul and the ref's given you the red card, eh mate?"

"Yeah, right, Lee." I didn't have the energy.

Gary said his uncle did heating and could maybe come take a look at my boiler. Lee was earwigging as usual, so I said,

"Yeah, go on then, give us his number. I'll probably be able to fix it myself tonight, but just in case."

The job book looked OK, healthy but not frantic, though it's always hard to tell because half our customers just turn up or phone wanting you to come fit them a new window yesterday. After all, you don't always know when you're going to break a window, right? And I had three appointments in town anyway—to recce and do a couple of quotes.

Anyway, had my shave and told Harry I was off. I stood in the doorway a minute, fiddling with the business cards pinned up on the noticeboard in the office. I wanted to tell him. I wanted to tell someone, someone who wouldn't laugh or take the piss. He looked up from the job book—he wasn't doing anything with it, of course, just leafing through it, being busy.

"You all right, eh?" His glasses had slipped down onto the very end of his nose, right on the tip they were. I wanted to step forward and push them back up.

Instead, I jangled my keys, my pathetic half-bunch of keys, now minus the ones for my house.

"Me? Yeah, fine. I'm fine." I tossed the keys high in the air and caught them left-handed. Not a care in the world.

Harry looked back down at the job book.

"See you later then. D'you want something from the van for lunch? Or will you be back by then?"

The van. The sandwich van. An oasis in our barren, humdrum little lives. The prospect of food and a little flirtation, what more could a man want? But, ah, the stresses the modern-day executive has to contend with: shall I have a chicken baguette? Tuna mayo on brown? A BLT? Cheese salad on a bap? So many decisions. It's non-stop thrills round here, I can tell you. She, the sandwich girl, lady, thingybob, comes round between half-eleven and twelve. She makes three stops on this estate and we all come pouring out like ants to a honey jar. She's always got a smile for me and is up for a bit of banter, but she doesn't dawdle long—a couple of times I've had to chase her down the road, so you want to get out there smartish soon as you hear her toot the horn.

"Dunno, Harry." I dig out some coins and put them on the edge of his desk. "Better get me a roll just in case. Cheese salad roll, yeah? And a cake. And an apple. That'll do. Cheers, mate."

"Cheers."

*   *   *

So I drive to the surgery where Gail works as a receptionist. She does four days a week, well, more half-days really. Drops Rosie off at school on her way in.

I stop outside the glass double doors a minute, watching her. She's standing with her back to me, looking through a filing cabinet. From the back you'd think she was only about twenty. She's very slim still and her hair's sort of light brown and shiny, shoulder-length. My stomach starts churning—no breakfast, or nerves, or both. I wonder how she'll look when I walk in—angry or icy or maybe her face will soften and she'll smile and I'll know it's going to be all right after all. I hang back, wanting to cling onto that hope, however crazy it might be, for a few more seconds. Then a bloke comes hopping towards the doors on crutches so I open it for him and then there's nothing but air between me and Gail at the desk and I've run out of reasons not to go in.

There's two people ahead of me, but I know she's seen me. The muscles in her face have gone tight, like they've been strained on wires. She's smiling at the woman in front of her, but her smile's too deliberate, too bright and her voice sounds high and unfamiliar.

"Please take a seat, Mrs Connors. Dr Wojczek is running about fifteen minutes behind." She turns to the man next, who's holding out a small piece of paper. "Repeat prescription only, is it? Yes, you can go straight to the dispensary—just along there, OK?"

A person watching her now would think how polite she was, how helpful, how concerned. Ha!

"Gail." I rest my hand on the edge of the counter and fiddle with the leaflets stacked in the rack. "Stressed?" it says at the top of one. Tell me about it. "Sexual problems?" says another. You could say that. "How's your heart?" stares back at me. Crap, thanks, but cheers for asking.

"What do you want?" She won't look at me and her voice is so quiet I can hardly hear her.

I shrug.

"To talk of course. Just to talk." There's something else I meant to say, something I'm supposed to say. What the hell is it? "And to *apologize*." She sits down at the desk and taps at the keyboard, eyes staring straight ahead at the screen.

"Did you have an appointment?" she asks in her nice, calm receptionist voice, then drops to a whisper, but it's a whisper with teeth and claws all over it: "What? You say sorry and you think you can come back now, as easy as that?"

"Course not." The very idea. What the hell else does she want from me? "I was thinking you could have me publicly flogged in the High Street."

"I'm glad you find it amusing." Her voice is cold, as though I'm a stranger bothering her on the street. "It must be lovely never to have to take anything seriously. Still, the answer is no, I don't want to talk to you. Probably not ever again." She turns away and bends down to riffle through a filing cabinet.

"*Gail!*"

41

She turns back towards me.

"Ah, about your *specimen*, is it?" She raises her voice and a couple of people look up from their magazines. Time to go, I think.

"I'll call you later."

This is not part of the master plan.

I phoned her later, at home, but she let the answerphone get it so I'm saying, "Hello? Hello? Gail, come on, love, pick up," talking to thin air like a total wally. Then I turn up at home, but she won't open the door.

"At least let me see the kids then. You can't stop me seeing the kids." I can see her face through the frosted glass panels. The pattern's called Arctic. It's all right but all the world and his wife's got it. I've been meaning to swap it for something unusual, etched glass maybe, sort of Victorian style.

"I can do whatever I like, Scott. You've forfeited any rights you may have had."

Well, that's not true, is it? She can't do that, can she? I'm not a wife-beater for chrissakes, though I'm thinking of taking it up. Joke. And I've certainly never laid a hand on either of the kids. I'm the last person on the planet to do that. She can't keep me away from them.

"You can't do this!" I'm shouting now.

She shushes me and tells me to listen.

"Scott, calm down a minute. You can't see them because they're not here. Nat's got late practice tonight and Rosie's over at Kira's."

"Can't you just let me in so we can talk?"

There is a silence. She's coming round. She realizes we have to talk, that she's just been making a mountain out of a molehill. She's going to open the door. We'll go into the kitchen and have a nice calm chat.

"No," she says, "I'm too upset to see you or talk to just now." She doesn't sound remotely upset to me, just cold and hard and horrible. "I'll call you when I'm ready."

"But what am I supposed—?"

"Just go away now, Scott. Please, just go away." Then she walks away and I see her shape retreating down the hall.

I think of going down the side path and banging on the door of the back porch, pressing my nose to the glass, making silly faces. If I can make her laugh, if I can only make her laugh, then she'll have me back, I know she will. But I haven't the heart for it. I can't bear the way she looks at me now, like she's never seen me before.

I sit in the car, wondering what the hell to do next. Then I drive up to the pub and go in and have a pint. I spread the paper out in front of me, but I can't read it. The words are just black bits on the page, like an army of ants frozen on the spot. I turn the pages, a man catching up with the news, dropping in for a quick pint on the way home to his wife and family, looking forward to a home-cooked meal and a warm house, having a well-earned break after a hard day. Is that how I seem? Or do I

43

look like a man who's managed to lose his wife, his kids and his home, with a ho-hum job, a crap car and nowhere to sleep tonight? And I'm sodding starving.

I pick up a burger and fries in town and eat them sitting in the car parked on a double yellow till a warden tells me you can't park here, didn't you see the lines, you'll have to move on now unless you want a ticket. Why do they say that? Who would *want* a ticket? Though in my case, frankly, it's the best offer I've had all day. It's the only offer I've had all day. Life not miserable enough? Have some rubbish food and scoff it down in your car in 30 seconds flat so you get indigestion and have a bit of an argy-bargy with a traffic warden. Another excellent plan from the man who just chucked his entire life down the toilet.

So I head back to work, stopping off at that petrol station on the way, the one with the jet wash. My car's filthy and God knows I've got nothing else to do with my life, I may as well kill time and wash the bloody thing. Least then I'll have a clean car. I'll still be a miserable sod, true, but at least I'll be a miserable sod with a clean car. It's important to have some standards, right?

I don't know if you've ever been on an industrial estate at night. Probably not. You're probably someone who's got a normal life that doesn't involve sleeping at work, having your spouse chuck you out on the street at midnight, or creeping about industrial estates after everyone else has gone home. Anyway, if you were thinking of trying it, I shouldn't bother. First Glass is on an estate a couple of miles outside town and it's dead creepy at night, not a soul to be seen. There's security lighting of course so the parking areas are all bright as a floodlit football pitch, but it's quiet as a graveyard. I manage a chirpy whistle and jangle my keys noisily to scare anyone off who might be lurking. Really scary that, a man jangling his keys. Is it a gun? Is it a knife? No, it's a man, fully armed with a set of . . . keys. Terrific.

I do the alarm and slump into my chair in the office. On my desk there's a cheese roll and an apple and a banana muffin. My lunch. Cheers, Harry. The burger didn't do much to fill me up so I chew my way through my late lunch and think about whether I'm going to phone Colin or Jeff.

Jeff's basically a decent bloke, but he's never grown out of playing air guitar to godawful old rock music and since his wife flew the coop the house is a bit of a pigsty. Jeff's one of those people who likes to leave the washing-up till later. Much later. Till it starts crawling towards the sink on its own it's so desperate for a wash. So I opt for Colin. Yvonne answers. Of course. Thank you, God, no chance of your playing on my side for a while, is there? If it wouldn't put you out too much. You know, just for a day or two would be nice.

"Yvonne! All right, angel? Is Col around?"

"Is that Scott?" How long has she known me? Unbelievable.

"Yes, it's me. How're you doing?"

45

There's a baffled laugh from the other end of the phone.

"I'm *doing* fine, thank you, Scott. And how are you? How's Gail and the kids?"

Go and get Colin, for chrissakes.

"Fine, thanks! We're all fine! Is Colin there?"

"No, he's round at his mum's. Won't be back till late."

"OK then! Not to worry!" My jaw aches from trying to keep a smile in my voice.

Jeff it is.

"—'lo?"

Cheerful as ever. This is going to be fun.

"Jeff mate, it's me. Scott. How ya doing?"

"'m OK."

I can feel my shoulders sagging just listening to him.

"Fancy a pint tonight?"

"All right." Don't get too overexcited now, will you?

"See you in the Coach & Horses in twenty minutes?"

"All right."

This is not my life. This is someone else's life that I've fallen into by mistake. I've slipped through a black hole or a time warp or something and I've become Mr Sad, ringing up his depressed friends so we can be depressed and drunk together rather than being depressed and stone-cold sober on my own, being chirpy and nice so's I can talk some other sad sod into letting me doss down on his settee for the night rather than trying to sleep on my desk or under my desk or on a workbench or just slitting my wrists somewhere and making an end of it.

So I meet Jeff in the pub, we both have more to drink than's good for us and I tell him my life's fallen apart and he says it's the women, always the women, and he'll never get over her, never, and do I know that she broke his heart, do I know that. And I say I do know that, Jeff, I do, and I silently hope to hell my life will never be as lousy as his because I wouldn't bother getting up in the morning. Then we roll back to his house and it's even worse than I remembered, but I'm so tired and also had just a little bit too much liquid refreshment maybe. But not drunk. No, I'm definitely not drunk. And he says course I can stay, I can stay any time, he'd do anything for me, his old mate, I can have his old bedroom, the one he used to—the one he and his wife—where they—he can't sleep in it any more, he's in the back room, course I can stay there, no probs, as long as I like, any time.

I have a slash, then blunder through to the bedroom. The quilt's covered in blue flowers and the chest of drawers has got one of them little china statues on it, a whatsit, a figurine. It's like a little boy sitting on a stool with his hands in front of his face and his head bent forward as if he's sobbing his little heart out, you know? Also, he's been dropped or chucked across the room at some point 'cause he's got these two ruddy great cracks

47

in him and been glued together again. If I had that in my bedroom, I wouldn't want to sleep in there either. Anyway, I pat the little fellow on the head and say, "Know how you feel, matey. Don't worry—things can only get better." Then I shed my clothes in a pile and slide under the quilt and the last thing I hear is Jeff stumbling about, cursing at the door, the wall, the toilet and anything else that gets in his way. I slip into sleep, telling myself it's all just a bad dream and everything'll be all right in the morning. When it's tomorrow, it'll all be OK. Roll on tomorrow.

Gail

If I let him back tonight, I wouldn't have to tell the children. I wouldn't be standing here with my insides churning away like a cement mixer, trying to think up fairy stories as to why their father's suddenly disappeared without trace. We could go to see a marriage guidance counsellor, talk to someone about his problems in an adult fashion. I picture it in my head—me, sitting legs-crossed and very calm, my voice low and reasonable. I am saying that he's betrayed my trust, and I feel as if I mean absolutely nothing to him. Also, as well as carrying on with another woman, he's irresponsible and leaves me to do everything plus I can't remember the last time we had a real conversation. I rest my hands, one neatly across the other, on my leg, and say we rarely make love and when we do, it's a routine, as predictable as loading the dishwasher: slot everything in their correct positions, add powder, close door, twist dial and push in. All systems go. He starts by nuzzling my neck, murmuring into my ear. Then he moves to my breasts; he tends to favour the left, because he's right-handed, I suppose, but then he might say, "Oh, and I mustn't neglect you, must I?" That's him, talking to my right breast. He does that, chats to them as if they're cute little pets. He keeps one hand on my breast, tweaking the nipple or cupping the whole thing in his palm as if he's trying to guess the weight of the cake at a village fête, while the other slides lower, following its inevitable route downwards as surely as a swallow heading south for winter.

I suppose I'm no better when it comes to our love life. We've found what works, more or less, so why change it? It's like once you've hit on how to bake a half-decent sponge cake, why bother to scout round for another recipe?

Next time he phones, I could talk to him instead of hanging up. Or I could phone him. That's what Cassie would do. She'd say I need to decide what I want and start taking control. Sounds so easy, doesn't it? Except I don't even know what I want.

We could work through this. People do. This happens to thousands of couples, millions probably. I tell myself that it's no big deal. It happens all the time. I bet that's what he's thinking—that everyone does it only he's just unlucky he got caught.

For the hundredth time today, the thousandth time, I think of last night. I had the weirdest feeling I was watching the whole thing on a cinema screen, like it wasn't really happening to me at all. Scott kept saying the same ridiculous things over and over again—pretending to be sorry and saying how much he loved me one minute, then trying to offload his guilt by claiming I'd pushed him into it because he'd felt so rejected and unloved. How pathetic can you get? That is so typical of him, he never takes responsibility for anything. Never. My own voice sounded cold and distant, as if I was only speaking a part that had been written for me by someone else. It sounded harsh and bitter, only I kept thinking I should be feeling so much more upset. But I just felt sick and strange and afraid and all I wanted was not to have to look at him any more; I couldn't bear the thought of looking into his eyes and not knowing whether he was lying.

Maybe I should make him tell Nat and Rosie, see how he feels when he has to tell his own children why he can't be at home with them any more. It's his fault, so why should I have to come up with an explanation that they can handle? But, if he tells them, he's bound to lie. He'd try to twist it all around, make them think I'm being unreasonable and unfair, that he's being punished for one small mistake. No, I have to do it.

I phone him on his mobile.

"Gail!" His voice is full of relief, I can hear it. He thinks I've forgiven him, that I'm going to ask him to come back. You arrogant little shit, I think, feeling real anger stirring inside me, making me come alive again. "I'm so—"

"Save it. I'm not ringing to exchange pleasantries." My voice stays calm, a model of control.

"But can I—?"

"No, you can't. I'm going to tell the children. Tonight. I'm just letting you know."

There is a silence. Scott's usually a bit of a babbler, so I wonder if his phone's lost the signal.

"Scott? Hello?"

"Yeah. Still here. Sorry. What are you going to say?"

"I think I should tell them the truth, don't you? They're not babies any more."

"Do you have to?"

Typical Scott, wanting to worm his way out of trouble.

"Well, I realize you may not prize honesty as much as I do, but I don't see why I should be expected to lie to my own children."

"No, course not. Not lie exactly. But can't you just . . . ?" His tone is wheedling, whingeing, like a child wanting its own way.

"Can't I just phrase it so you come out of it all smelling of roses? And you think that's a reasonable thing for you to ask, do you?" This is not the way I meant to sound. I was going to be calm, sensible and mature, but it comes out bitter and sneering. I sound like a schoolteacher, telling him off.

"No. I guess not."

"Fine, that's agreed then."

I wonder where he's sleeping. I wonder if he's staying with *her*. I bet he is, I bet he went straight there, fell into her bed and—, I'm not going to think about it.

"I'm planning to sort out your things in a day or two. Where are you staying?"

"At Jeff's. But Gail, we really need to—"

"You can pick them up one day next week, once the kids have gone to school."

"But what about the weekend? Can't I—?"

"No. I'm taking the kids to my parents this weekend."

"You can't stop me seeing them."

"Don't you dare tell me what I can and can't do!" My throat feels dry, dry and sour. I slump down on the stairs and lower my head, feeling sick and faint.

"When can I see them?"

I don't know, I don't know. I can't do this. I don't want this to be happening. I hate him for doing this to us. This isn't my life. I don't know how to do this.

"I don't know." I take a deep breath and clutch one of the banisters as if it might save me. I feel as if I've been thrown overboard and I'm lost, adrift and alone, with no hope of rescue. "Um, maybe next weekend. You know I wouldn't stop you seeing them. You're being ridiculous, trying to make out I'm being mean to you and that you're the victim in all this."

"I'm not. I just—"

"We need a few days' breathing space, that's all I'm saying. Please just leave us alone for a few days."

"Well, OK then. If that's what you want. And could you tell the kids—?"

"What?"

"Tell them I said—just tell them I said hi."

Scott

I suppose I ought to mention the event that triggered off my Great Departure. I didn't exactly leave of my own accord. Not entirely. Gail encouraged me to go. Yup, I guess locking me out on the front step in the middle of the night definitely counts as encouragement. Now, it's not quite what it sounds like, so bear with me. OK, it is what it sounds like but I know as soon as I confess that I slept with someone else you'll write me off and be thinking "Cheating slimebag—no wonder she chucked him out" and it really wasn't like that. I guess I should have filled you in properly before, but I reckon you're not stupid and it wouldn't take an Einstein to figure it out. Whatever. Anyway, the fact is that, due to circumstances beyond my control—i.e. being a man—my dick accidentally ended up in the wrong place at the wrong time. Or wrong person, more accurately. And Gail found out.

First of all, let me say I did not have an affair; it was barely even a fling—not so much a one-night stand as a one-hour stand and it's doubly unfair because I've never strayed before, not even once. I realize that doesn't let me off the hook but I just wanted you to know that I don't make a habit of this. I know it must sound like I'm trying to get myself off the hook—"Miss, Miss, it didn't count 'cause I didn't enjoy it." But it's like soggy chips—you feel you're wasting your—your sort of wickedness allowance because for the same fat and calories and what have you, you could have had really good chips and enjoyed being bad. But you've bought them now so what are you going to do but eat them and feel pissed off that you've used up your chips quota? Then you have to have a Diet Coke with them, to cancel them out. And maybe a doughnut after to have something properly bad to make yourself feel better because of the chips and to get rid of the taste of the Diet Coke.

I'll tell you about Angela later, the one who was the cause of all the trouble, the one who accidentally became over-familiar with the contents of my under-pants. Anyway, after our totally insignificant semi-shag, I'd gone back to work to fetch my stuff and then I went home. Now if I'd been more of a devious bastard instead of just a stupid fathead, I'd never have slipped up. But it's not like I carry a copy of *How to Commit Adultery—And Get Away With It* in my back pocket.

So I got back, kissed Rosie, said how ya doing. Nat was out somewhere, at swimming practice I think. Kissed Gail. This little frown crossed her face but I did-n't think much of it at the time and she didn't say any-thing. Maybe it was because Rosie was there, chattering away and telling us things, the way she does. You know, "Did you know that in sixteen-something-or-other, the

River Thames froze rock solid and they had a frost fair on it with people skating up and down and they lit fires and everything right on the ice?" That kind of thing.

We had our tea, some sort of chicken thing it was, then Rosie went up to do her homework and Natty came in and Gail went through to give him his food. We all watched a bit of telly then Nat went upstairs, supposedly to do his homework but probably to fool around on the computer as usual. It was all so bloody normal, do you see? An evening like a hundred others, a thousand others. Gail said she was off to have a bath and could I load the dishwasher and I said, "In a minute" and she said, "No, now" over her shoulder as she went up the stairs and I ignored her. I carried on watching this programme; it was one of those docusoaps, you know, where ordinary people suddenly get all famous from being on TV. I was stretched out on the settee wondering what it would be like if they brought TV cameras into work and who'd end up the star, whether it would be me as the manager, or Lee 'cause he's a cocky bastard frankly or Harry 'cause he's a real salt-of-the-earth type. Then I relived the day—well, mainly the bit with Angela—in my head like watching a video, replaying the good bit which was the anticipation and the moment we started kissing and pulling each other's clothes off and sort of rewriting the less good bit so that I lasted longer and took her to levels of ecstasy she didn't even know had been invented yet.

I stacked the plates on the counter, then thought bet-

ter of it and loaded them properly in the dishwasher and
rummaged under the sink for the powder. Why are these
things so fiddly? Jeez, by the time you've done all that
you could have washed them by hand. I locked up and
went upstairs.

Gail's at her dressing-table, taking off her make-up.

"Good day?" she asks, speaking to me in the mirror.

"Yeah, all right." I start getting undressed. "Just boring, usual stuff, you know."

"Did you remember to pick up my jacket from the
cleaner's?"

"Oh, bugger. Sorry. I'll get it tomorrow. Promise."

She sighs.

"You said that yesterday. It's not as if I ask you to do
much."

"I said sorry. You weren't planning to wear it in the
middle of the night, were you?" I take off my trousers.

"Scott?"

"Hmm?"

"Why are your pants inside-out?"

"What? They're not. Are they?"

"Apparently."

I look down. Oh, fuck. Fuckety-fuck.

I shrug. Stay cool. Don't get flustered.

"Must have put them on like that this morning. Getting more senile by the day. Soon be time to send me to
the Twilight Home, eh?"

Gail's voice is cold as ice.

"You didn't. I remember."

"What—did you carry out an inspection? Course I did. Must've done."

She turns round from the mirror then and stands up.

"I noticed your pants this morning because those are the ones with the hole on the left-hand side which you promised you would throw away."

"Hole? What hole?" Playing for time. I feel for the hole. Shit. It's now on the right. Remain calm. Make a joke of it. "What are you, Inspector Morse?"

"Who was she, Scott?" Her voice is calm and low. I can barely hear her, but I figure now's not the time to ask her to speak up a bit.

"Now come on! You've been spoiling for a fight all evening. What's all this about? If you had a crap day, then fine—just say so, but don't start taking it out on me. That's so typical of you. Just because a person's pants are inside out doesn't mean—"

"What does it mean then?"

Behind her, the mirror of her dressing-table catches my eye.

"Look, you must have seen me in the mirror this morning. That's why you thought it was on the other side. But they were already wrong, right?"

"Wrong. You're the one who's wrong. Right?"

It would have been better if she'd been shouting at me, crying and hysterical, then I could be the reasonable one concentrating on trying to calm her down. But she was already calm, which was much more scary. And I was running out of ideas.

"I remember now. I—I did take my things off after a job but only because—because I got a splinter of glass in my leg so I had to take my trousers off."

"And you removed your pants for what reason exactly?"

"Because there was this sharp bit. Look!" I stab at a point on my hip. "I thought I'd got a bit of glass right here, so I took them off in the toilet at work to check, but I couldn't see anything and I put them right back on. That was it. End of story. Ask anyone. Lee was there. Ask him. Ask Harry."

She just stands there, her arms folded, eyes cold and shining—like glass.

"*You're a lying bastard!*" Her voice is suddenly loud, the words snapping out like blows to my belly. "And you smelt of some awful perfume or soap earlier. You slept with someone else, I know you did!"

"I didn't. I swear I didn't." I'm going for calm with a touch of outrage. "I can see how you might have got that impression, but you're just wrong. Honestly."

"You swear?"

"Yes, I swear. I said so, didn't I? Now come on, love. You know I'd never do that."

"What on?"

*   *   *

Can you believe it? I mean, she's wasted as a sodding doctor's receptionist, she should be a lawyer. I was still going for the What—me? approach.

"Come on, Gail. Let's be sensible now. What do you mean, what on? What, like the Bible? I think you're getting things all out of proportion. When's your period due?"

Now, normally of course, I might think that but as I value my life, I don't say it. Nothing sends Gail into a strop faster than suggesting she has PMT and it's all down to her hormones. Don't know why—you think she'd be pleased to have an excuse. When I'm in a mood, it's just I'm being an awkward bugger and there's the end of it. But I thought it was a good diversionary tactic, like lobbing a hand grenade out the front while you escape out the back.

She doesn't rise to it though, just raises one eyebrow at me. Not a good sign.

"Swear you didn't sleep with someone else . . ."

"I swear. I didn't sleep with anyone else. OK?"

She shakes her head.

"Not good enough."

"I swear—look, I swear on my life. All right? Can we let it drop now? It's been a long day."

"No. Swear on Rosie's life. On Nat's life."

"What? You're being ridiculous now. I don't know what's got into you."

"Swear on our children's lives. Come on. You can't do it, can you?"

"Course. I—"

It's dead quiet. All I can hear is my own heartbeat, my breathing. I imagine I can even hear the blood rushing round my body, as if it's hunting in every corner of me for a miracle, a good excuse. It's only a lie. I can cross my fingers behind my back. I can say I don't really mean it inside my head, to cancel it out. I should just risk it. I'm not even superstitious for chrissakes. Come on, Scotty, what's the difference? Say it, for God's sake, man, just say it. I try it inside my head, saying it quickly, silently. I swear on Rosie's life, on Nat's life, that I didn't sleep with another woman. Even silent, the words crackle with danger, like they've sparked a deadly fuse—images flicker through my mind, in split-second flashes—Rosie cycling along the pavement on her purple bicycle—car taking the corner too fast—driver's face in shock, his whisky-dulled reflexes going in slow motion—mounting the kerb—Rosie's face, her little mouth falling open in a silent "O"—the sickening screech of tyres. And Nat—suddenly older—at a club— body so lean and tall, he looks like he's not yet grown into it, not ready for it yet—he steps back to let a girl pass, knocks someone's drink—a face, hot with hate, close to his—pushing—broken glass—the flash of a knife pulled from a sock—Nat's face, the surprise on it, his eyes as he looks down to see his own blood.

"I—"

* * *

Outside, a car suddenly revs up and we both jump. And then I lose it completely and start babbling:

"It was only the once. It really was. It was nothing, meant nothing. She doesn't mean anything to me—it wasn't what you think—it wasn't an affair, nothing like that—honestly—it just happened—it'll never happen again—I'll never see her again—I swear—I promise—you see, it—"

"Ssshh!" Gail says. "The kids'll hear. Keep your voice down."

"Sorry."

She snorts through her nose at my limp apology.

"Kitchen." She heads downstairs. "Put something on."

I pull my trousers back on over the treacherous underpants, and my shirt that I'd flung over the back of a chair.

She's sitting at the kitchen table, drinking a glass of water. I offer her coffee but she snorts again. Still, I need to do something with my hands, which won't stop shaking, so I fumble with the kettle, the coffee jar, drag out the business of opening the fridge, pouring the milk, slowly taking the lid off the sugar bowl, looking down into my coffee as I stir it, as if the answer of what to do next would suddenly be revealed in my mug. Wipe at the wet coffee ring on the counter and spread the cloth out to dry properly, showing her what a good husband I am. Pick up a tea-towel hanging over the back of a chair, clutch it for something to hold onto, as if it could some-how save me.

"I didn't realize our marriage meant nothing to you."

"It doesn't! It means everything, you know it does."

Gail shakes her head.

"Ssh! Fifteen years down the drain. Bit of a waste, I'd say."

"C'mon, love. Don't be like that. We can work things out."

"Like what? Don't you dare tell me how to behave. How dare you! You fucking little shit, you could have given me a disease, AIDS, anything!"

I flinch hearing Gail swear. I can't think the last time I heard her swear. She's normally really good about it, because of setting an example to Nat and Rosie. It's like hearing a nun swear or something.

"No, Gail. There's no need to worry about that. We used protection."

"Oh, I see. It was totally unplanned and you had no idea your wayward willy was going to lead you into some slag's bed but you happened to have a packet of condoms on you. Am I supposed to be grateful?"

You can't win, can you?

"They weren't mine. She had them."

After that, there's no stopping her, on and on she goes, one question after another, firing them off like bullets but still strangely controlled, like she's a quizmaster

63

reading them from an autocue: Who is this bitch? What's her name? How old is she? Where does she live? How did I meet her? Did I tell her I was married? Does she want me to move in? On and on. Nothing I say seems to make any difference.

"It's nothing like that, Gail. I told you, it was—"

"Oh, shut up, Scott. Just shut up. I haven't got the energy to be screaming at each other all night." I hadn't been screaming, but now wasn't the time to be picking her up on details. Then suddenly she stood up. "It's bin day tomorrow. Did you remember to put the rubbish out?"

"Er, no. Strangely, it slipped my mind." Still, it seems like a good sign, you know, that things are settling down and we're getting back to normal again. I start thinking, we'll sleep on it and she'll be better in the morning, we can have a talk and I'll explain how it was.

"Well, I can't do it. I've not got my slippers on."

I even feel grateful that I've got something to do. Something physical, something I could actually manage without making a total balls-up of it. I flick the tea-towel over my shoulder like a chef and shove my bare feet into my loafers from the shoe rack in the hall. Go round the side to get the bin. I hear the front door click shut. Put the bin out front then tap lightly on the glass.

"Gail?"

"Yes?" Her voice is cold, distant.

"Open up, love. It's cold out here."

"Who's there?"

Oh, great, we're going to play silly buggers, are we?

"Come on. It's me. Stop pissing about."

"I'm afraid you don't live here any more."

I squat down to talk to her through the letterbox.

"Gail!"

"Sssh!" Her eyes meet mine. "Don't you dare upset the children. I realize you've got no regard for my feelings, but I'd have thought you'd at least care about theirs."

"Gail. Sweetheart. I'm freezing out here. A joke's a joke, but that's enough now. Let me in and we can have a proper talk, eh?"

"A joke? Is that what this is to you? You just turn my entire life upside-down and throw fifteen years of my life away and you think it's a joke. Well, I'm sorry if I don't share your sense of humour. Try not to get in the milkman's way if you're planning to camp on the front step all night."

The hall light clicks off.

"Gail! For chrissakes. Look, let's all calm down now—"

"I'm perfectly calm. Yes, I seem to be. I'm quite calm."

"At least open the door to give me my car keys, Gail. You wouldn't have me walk the streets all night, would you?"

There is a silence. I stand up, seeing her shape move about through the frosted glass of the door. There's a jangling sound—my keys—what could be taking so long? I duck down again so I can peer through the letter-box and she nearly pokes my sodding eye out with the keys. She's taken my house keys off the ring, leaving just my car and work keys. Cheers, darling. Then she bends down and I'm staring straight into her eyes through the slot.

"I've taken off your house keys because you won't be needing them again."

"Gail, sweetheart, c'mon now, let's not get—"

Then she shoves the flap back in my face.

"Can I have my jacket then? Please."

"It won't fit through the letterbox."

I feel like Hannibal the Cannibal in *Silence of the Lambs*. You know, Hannibal Lecter and all his food and papers has to go through this slot otherwise he'll take a bite out of you as soon as look at you.

"Just open the door a crack." I figure if I can just get my foot in the door, I can keep her talking a bit longer, get her to see reason.

She's just the other side of the door. Then I hear her slam the bolt across and double-lock the door. I watch her through the letterbox, the backs of her bare feet as she climbs the stairs to our bedroom alone.

"Gail!"

Ha! She'll probably come down in ten minutes to let me in. She's just trying to get her own back, punish me by having me freeze on my own front doorstep. Still, what if she doesn't? Anyway, I couldn't stay out there all night. I get in the car and start the engine to warm it up, thinking what the hell do I do now? Where can I go, where can I go?

And that's how I ended up spending the night at work.

Rosie

Nat's a big, fat liar. He said that Dad's left us and he's not coming back, he said Dad never came home last night and Mum was lying when she told us he'd gone out with a friend and that's why he wasn't eating with us. Mum says it's wrong to lie. That time when I broke the yellow teapot and I hid all the pieces in the garden behind the shed and said I hadn't seen it, then Mum said you have to tell the truth and if you do everything will be all right. Nat tells lies the whole time. He says he's doing his homework when he's playing on his computer. He says he hasn't any money for the bus, so Mum gives it to him and then he walks to school and keeps the money. He says it is all right and not really like lying because he might need the money for the bus and anyway it is not hurting anyone.

Dad wasn't at breakfast this morning, and he didn't say goodbye again, same as yesterday.

When Mum wasn't looking, Nat kicked me under the table and said, "See?" He nodded at Dad's empty chair. I kicked Nat then tucked my legs up under me so he couldn't get me back again.

Then Mum told us we were going to Nana and Grandad's for the weekend. Nat made a face, but he likes it there really. Nana makes the best roast potatoes in the whole wide world and last time Grandad told us he had a picture of the Queen each for us behind the clock on the mantelpiece and when we looked there were two ten pound notes. Nat asked Mum if Dad was coming too. He took an orange out of the fruit bowl and started throwing it up in the air and catching it in one hand. Then Mum said, actually, no he wouldn't be coming and then her face went all funny and she sat down in a chair really quickly and said she needed to talk to us.

Nat turned round and dropped his orange.

"See, Rosie! I *told* you!"

"Nathan! Don't shout at Rosie."

"I've got to go."

Mum looked at the clock.

"You've got a minute. Please come and sit down."

"I'll stand."

Mum sighed, then she said that she and Dad had decided that they were going to have a little bit of time apart and so Dad wouldn't be living with us at home for a while. She said it wasn't because of us and we must understand that Mummy and Daddy both still loved us very much. Nat was standing to one side and he poked his finger in his mouth, like he does if something makes him sick.

Nat picked up his orange and dropped it on the table like a ball, as if he thought it would bounce.

"Don't do that, Nathan. You'll spoil it."

"So?"

"I realize you must be upset, Natty ..." Mum stretched out her arms, like she was going to give him a hug, but he stepped back away from her.

"I'm not. I don't give a toss what you two get up to."

Then he kicked his chair and went out into the hall.

"Wait, Nat! We really need to—" Mum started to get up.

"Got to go. You'll make me late." Then the front door slammed. Mum sat down again.

"Rosie? Do you understand what I've been saying?"

I tipped my bowl to get the last Rice Krispies onto my spoon.

"Are you getting a divorce?"

"No, Rosie love, nothing like that. We're just—your dad's just moved out for a little while, that's all. You know what it's like when you fall out with a friend at school and you get cross with each other? Well, it's a bit like that."

"Miss Collins says we have to make up and say we're sorry and if we don't we might as well be back in the Infants."

Mum started clearing the table and I got up to put my glass and bowl in the dishwasher.

"Yes." Mum said, and she gave a funny sort of laugh. "Well, I suppose she's right."

Gail

Cassie came over. I told her what happened and about locking Scott out and she practically choked on her Bacardi.

"And he was literally kneeling on your front step, begging? God, I wish I'd seen that. Can't get Derek down on his knees for love nor money, know what I mean?" She nudged me and cackled. She's got a filthy mind, has Cassie.

I picked up the bottle of rum and nodded at her glass.

"Just keep it coming," she said. "You must have scared the shit out of him. So, how long are you going to make him suffer? Hey—easy on the Coke. You don't want to drown it."

"Make him suffer? Hardly. He got off bloody lightly. I should have gone for his vitals with a cheese grater."

She gave a sharp intake of breath.

"Nasty. You quiet ones are always the most vicious. But you are going to have him back, right?"

I shrugged.

"Not necessarily."

"Oh, come on. You're kidding? But, Gail—seriously,

now." She took my arm and turned to look into my eyes. She even put down her drink. "I mean, after all these years, you don't want to throw all that away just for—well."

"Just for a meaningless fling, you mean? You sound like Scott. You're supposed to be on *my* side."

"I *am*. Of course I am."

"It's not meaningless to me. And anyway, just because he keeps claiming it was only a fling doesn't mean it was. I can't trust a word he says. He could have been carrying on with her for years, or screwing a different woman every week for all I know. We've been together over fifteen years. Surely that should count for something? But it's like it means absolutely nothing to him. Less than nothing."

Cassie was shaking her head and reaching for the bottle again.

"Come on, you know that's not true. The problem is you're thinking like a woman."

"Well . . . yes, strangely enough."

"See, what you're doing is imagining how you'd feel if you were to sleep with someone else. I bet you'd have to be madly in love with the guy, right?"

"I wouldn't do it at all. I never would."

"God, you're annoying. Don't you ever do anything wrong? Look, all I'm saying is, if you were to be unfaithful, it would mean that something pretty serious was going on . . ."

"Ye-es . . ."

". . . whereas with Scott—like most men if you ask me—it doesn't mean much more than he got lucky and he couldn't bring himself to say no."

"And that makes it all right in your book?"

"No!" She looked round. "Any more ice?"

"In the icebox. Finish what you're saying first."

"Right. All I'm saying is a lot of guys see no inconsistency in being in love with their wives but having a fling with someone else. They split it off in their heads, so it doesn't count. It's just fulfilling a basic need: you're thirsty—have a drink. You've got a hard-on—have a shag."

"So you think I should just forgive him and say, fine, you can come back now?"

"No. I'm not dispensing advice, just telling you how I see it. I think you should do whatever you want to do. Maybe you're happy to have an excuse to get shot of him. How the hell should I know? You do play your cards pretty close to your chest a lot of the time." She got up and went through to the kitchen to fetch the ice.

What did she mean by that, do you think? About having an excuse? It puzzled me at the time, but I didn't ask her, I don't know why. I'm pretty close to Cassie, closer than to my sisters really, but I suppose I don't tell her everything. I'm not one of these people who have to keep talking about how they feel the whole time. A lot of that's best kept to yourself, if you ask me. People say you should be open and express yourself, but half the time I

73

think that's just an excuse so they can offload their problems onto you or make out they're an interesting person when really it's just that they're bloody neurotic.

Cassie sees it differently because she was unfaithful to Derek. It only happened the once and she was pretty drunk, but I'm sure she regrets it now. She's genuinely sorry about it, not like Scott. Derek doesn't know, of course. I couldn't live with it, if it were me. I'd just be worrying all the time, wondering if he'd find out somehow.

"You know Scott loves you to bits. He's crazy about you."

"He's got a funny way of showing it."

"Well, that's men for you, the little darlings. Who knows why they act the way they do? Maybe Scott was feeling old or unloved? Mid-life crisis? How's your sex life? Maybe this woman offered—that's enough for most men. Bit of an ego boost. I'm sure it was no more than a stupid fling on his part. A mistake. Talk to him. Give him a chance to explain."

I shook my head.

"Why are you so keen to let him off the hook? He cheated on me and then he lied about it. End of story. *I* feel old and unloved all the time but I don't go around leaping into bed with one of the doctors, do I? If I talk to Scott, all he'll do is give me a whole load of excuses, make out it wasn't his fault in any way. He *never* takes responsibility for anything."

*　*　*

You see, that evening when I found out, I wanted to know if it had been going on for months, how serious it was, and all he kept saying was no, no, it wasn't like that. And I could just see, stretching ahead of me like some appalling endless road that leads nowhere, just years and years of this—arguing and excuses and lies. And then I just knew I didn't want it, not any of it. I wasn't going to let my life become that. I felt I'd give anything, absolutely anything not to get sucked into that. There was a sudden flush of energy through my body, so strong that I stood up as if a current of electricity had jerked me from my seat. I said something about the rubbish needing to go out—I just wanted not to see his lying face in front of me, even for a minute, you see. And then Scott went outside and I was standing in the hall. I looked at the front door and I thought, "I could push it closed with one finger and end all this right now." And, as I thought it, I watched my own hand stretch out in front of me, the very tip of my finger touching the door. He hadn't even put it on the latch. I didn't really have to do anything. Just one tiny push and that was it. The door clicked closed. It needn't even have been me. It could have been the wind—making the decision for me. Not my responsibility at all. And now I could just turn my back on him and start a new life for myself and the kids.

"OK, fair enough, make him suffer for a week or two. But surely you'll miss him after a while, right?" Cassie's voice was unexpectedly quiet. "I mean, I know you moan about him enough, but why have you stuck with him all these years if you're so ready to ditch him?"

I looked at her, her face suddenly sharply in focus.

"Do I moan about him?" I read the answer in her eyes. "I—I don't know, I always feel like I'm having to nag him, spur him on. Like I'm his mum or something. Honestly, sometimes, it *is* just like having another child to worry about. I'm so sick of having to be the grown-up all the time. Why's it *my* job? I know, I'm not making any sense." I covered my face with my hands. "I'm just *so* tired."

"Here." She topped up my glass. "Drown your sorrows."

I wish I could. How I wish it were that easy.

"Well, I'm sure you'll work things out." Cassie patted me on the arm, then gave me a squeeze. "If you want to . . ."

"Mn," I said, the way Nat does, so you don't know what he means—yes or no, or maybe or I'm not listening, just leave me alone. Leave me alone.

Scott

If I tell you about Angela, promise you'll hear me out, OK? I bet you anything you like that—if you're 100 per cent honest, hand on heart—you'll admit you'd probably have done the same as I did. I swear, a monk would have hoisted his habit and been up for it. A bishop—actually, that's not a good example. They're always at it, aren't they? Can't hardly open the paper without reading about yet another member of the God Squad who's taken a bit of a tumble from the Path of Righteousness. And they're such sodding hypocrites, that's what I can't stand. They never come clean and say, "She gave me the green light, so we had a quickie in the vestry." They always pretend to be all humble and start going on about how they see they have sinned but they felt moved by the Holy Spirit and were really just doing God's will—like God's got time to fanny about looking for nookie opportunities for the clergy when he's got avalanches and plane crashes to organize. I mean, what's all that about? Admit it, you were desperate for a shag and some sex-starved widow came to you for comfort and one minute you're saying, "There, there, the Lord loves you" and the next you've got your hand on her tit and are struggling to undo the buttons on your cassock.

Where was I? Oh, Angela. Right. So I'm in the office and suddenly Lee sticks his head round the door. Doesn't bother to knock, but what else is new? And he says someone's asking to see the manager. With a complaint. Course, what he actually said was, "Ere, Scott—'s a stroppy cow out front what wants yer bollocks."

Dunno what charm school Lee went to but I reckon he's due a refund. God knows why he's got so many birds after him. They're practically lining up, gagging for it. We get them on the phone, giggling so much they can't hardly speak. One time he was seeing four at once so we had to have a list by the phone of which ones he'd talk to. You know, it was like Melanie—Yes; Chrissy—Yes; Sandra—No; Laura—Don't even think about it. But we had to take it down because Maureen said she wouldn't be party to that sort of thing, thank you very much, and Lee shouldn't be getting personal calls at work anyhow. He thinks he is seriously cool but mostly he's just an arrogant smarmy git. You reckon I'm jealous, don't you? OK—I am a bit. He's a good-looking bastard, there's no getting round it, and he's got all the moves and the designer gear and that. He doesn't even have to try. Not like the rest of us.

Which brings me back to Angela. So I put my jacket on and go out front and there's this woman by the counter and you don't need a degree in psychology to see that she's not a happy bunny. She doesn't waste time with the niceties—hello, good afternoon—none of that, she's straight in: "Are you the person who passes for a manager in this . . ." she looks round at the scruffy seats and the dusty floor as if someone's just done a fart ". . . establishment?"

Not a smile in sight. And she's the wrong side of forty, at a guess, but not by much. She's nice-looking though—shiny hair and well-stacked up front, but I'm not about to hit her with the patented Scott special Combi-Smile-'n'-Raised-Eyebrow, 'cause I can see she's cross as hell and she looks like she'd have no qualms over killing the odd glazier now and then. Still, I'm not having anyone talk to me like that. I look all round and behind me at the floor, like I'm looking for something, then I say:

"Sorry, *Madam*—" really polite like, laying it on thick. "Were you speaking to me? I assumed from your tone that a dog must have come in."

But she doesn't miss a beat.

"We'll skip the pleasantries and the feeble attempts at wit, shall we, and cut to the chase? One of your—" she pauses, and gives a kind of sneery laugh, "—*boys* has made a complete cock-up of my doors and you are going to find me someone who actually knows what they're doing to sort it out right *now*."

I look at the clock on the wall. It's nearly five. I open my mouth to speak.

"—"

"No—*Not* tomorrow. *Not* in three days' time. *Right now*."

79

I'm thinking about saying I'll get the owner and letting Harry deal with it, but he's too soft and I reckon she'll chew him up and spit out the leftovers and he could do without the agg.

"What actually seems to be the—?"

"Frankly, I'm too angry even to speak about it. I want you to see it with your own eyes."

I sigh but I can't see any way of getting rid of her.

"OK, where do you live?"

High Firs. What a surprise. Poncy so-called exclusive so-called executive houses. Detached but a cat could barely slink through the gaps, you know? People who live there think they're a cut above, but the houses are nothing special. I knew a builder who worked on them and he says the walls are so thin you could spit through them. Anyway, I tell her I'll follow her if she wants to go outside and wait in her car a sec and I stick my head round the door of the workroom and shout at the lads:

"Oi! Which of you tossers did some doors over on High Firs?"

"Wasn't me, mate," says Lee over his shoulder, ducking down to look at himself in a bevelled mirror.

"Not guilty, Your Honour," says Martin.

I look at Gary who's apparently concentrating on cutting, frowning down at the glass on the workbench as if he hasn't heard me.

"Gary?"

"What?" He's still not looking at me.

"High Firs. Fucked-up doors. Ring any bells?"

His face goes red.

"What? I did a good job. Took me ages."

I shake my head.

"I'm going to sort it out now."

As I leave, I hear Lee taking the piss out of him, winding him up. Gary's only been with us a few months. First came to do work experience, and he was less clueless than the others we'd had. Quiet, just got on with it. He's slow but that's the best way to be when you start 'cause you make less mistakes. He's not overburdened with brain cells, but then if he was he'd be off at university or being a lawyer or something rather than rotting away here, yeah?

I grab my keys and jacket and tell Harry I'm off. No point worrying him with all this till I find out what the problem is. Ms Charming is standing outside, leaning against her car. It's a gleaming black BMW. New reg. Dead slick.

"Nice motor." I nod.

She doesn't bother to respond.

"You'll follow right behind?"

"Yes, Ma'am!" I say under my breath, thinking my car could do with a wash. And some new tyres. And a new engine. And a new chassis. That'll be a new car then. Some chance.

Course, it's five o'clock by now, or just gone, so you can imagine what a laugh and a half the ring road is. I turn up the radio and they're doing a run of oldies. I'm starting to get into it—"I Heard it through the Grapevine," Marvin Gaye—while I'm stuck in the traffic, and I'm singing away and having a bit of a groove in my seat, shoulders going side to side, head bobbing away, then I look ahead into Madam's car and I can see she's watching me in the mirror. She adjusts her mirror then and puts on some lipstick.

I feel like a teacher's told me off in class. You know what it's like singing in the car, same as when you're in the shower—you're loud, you can't remember the words, you can't carry a tune, but just for a few minutes you're hot, you're live, you're dangerous—and the world loves you. But, soon as you suss someone's seen you or heard you—usually I get a small clue at home 'cause they bang on the door and tell me to shut up and I'm sensitive about subtle signals like that—well you lose it and there you are, some sad old prick singing flat in a bathroom and feeling like a balloon with all the air gone out of it. It's weird, half the stuff I miss most is things like that, Natty banging on the bathroom door, I mean, shouting, "Oi, Dad, leave it out! I can't hear my CD!"

Anyway. So we get there and I park and we go in. Well, I've been in the business sixteen years but you don't need to be an expert to see what the problem is. It's a nice bit of workmanship actually. He's coming along, is Gary. Shame he's got less common sense than a hula-hoop. The fit's nice, yes; it's a neat job, yes; nice bit of beading, but—it's plain glass. Not normally what you want in a bathroom door, unless you're a bit of a perve.

"Ah," I say.

"You may well say 'ah,'" she says. "But can you sort it out? The other one's downstairs."

Downstairs, the glass panel in the back door is frosted. It's not a bad pattern, a bit unusual, sort of leaves and twiddly bits. It's called "Serenade," no idea why, probably thought it was better than "Leaves and Twiddly Bits."

"Marvellous view of the garden, hmm?" she says. You can't see a thing through it.

"I take it this is the one you wanted plain then?"

"Full marks. Have a gold star."

Actually, I can see what's happened. All the doors are the same size in these houses, see? Our clueless lad's come in, measured one bit of glass, sees it fits the panel in the first door, puts it in, then does the second one without thinking. It's the kind of mistake anyone could make. If they had soggy spaghetti for brains.

"Anyone can make a mistake," I say, "but we can sort that out for you, no problem."

"You better. Can you do it now?"

Thing is, I haven't got my tools on me. Didn't see the point without knowing what the problem was. Plus if I'd brought them I could tell she'd have had me there till midnight.

"Trouble is, I'm not sure if I'll be able to get it out in one piece. I can have a go but I can't guarantee it and I don't want to leave you with a draught blowing in on you when you're—when you're using the bathroom." She gives me a look then, a sort of assessing look. If I didn't know better, I'd say she was eyeing me up. "We might have to get new."

"Fine. So you can just drive back and get it now."

Unfortunately, it must have been a special order because it's not one of the most popular designs and it's toughened, so we'll have to reorder and start again and that's another two days minimum. She is not happy.

"But—" Harry says the customer is always right and we rely on repeat business. "One, I'll do it myself so you can be sure of a good job . . . And two, I'll make it half-price. Can't say fairer than that, can I?"

She sighs.

"OK."

She tells me to phone her the moment it comes in and I say I will and then when I'm at the door to go, she suddenly looks me right in the eye and gives me this dead sexy smile.

"Thanks. I'll see you soon then." Her eyes are sparkling and she pushes a strand of hair back from her face.

"Yes." I feel like I'm going red. Get a grip, man, for God's sake. "Very soon. Two days. Three at the outside."

I can feel her eyes on me as I walk back down the path. I don't know. One minute she's ready to tear me limb from limb and leave me out for the vultures, the next she's flashing me a come-to-bed smile and straightening her shoulders so her tits stick out more.

And, I have to admit it, I was intrigued. It's not that I never get offers. In our line of work, we've all had bored housewives coming on to us and, OK, I've been pretty tempted once or twice—who wouldn't be, so long as you still got blood in your veins, right? But you find a nice way to keep your distance and there's no harm done. Unless you're Lee, in which case he probably takes on all comers. But Angela was different. For a start, she was a career woman. Successful. A BMW but not a man in sight. Not the kind of woman that normally takes much notice of me, to be honest. And she was built too, you know? It's not that I'd gone off Gail. Gail's slim as a pencil though she goes on about her tummy like most women. But Angela was—well, on the large side if anything. Not just up front, but big hips, decent bum, something you felt you could really get a hold of. If you had the chance. I found myself thinking about her in bed that night. Besides, it's not like Gail was throwing herself on me the second I got home every night, saying, "Take me, take me, Big Boy!" Half the time even if I tried to kiss her she'd just give me a peck back like she was my aunty or something.

The next morning, I was on to Tuff-Glass first thing and begging them to make it a rush job.

*   *   *

And a couple of days later, when I go back, I know at once I wasn't imagining it. I'm barely in the door before she's falling over herself offering me teas and coffees, laughing at my jokes and giving me posh biscuits covered in chocolate an inch thick. No custard creams for her, that's for sure. So I'm thinking, "Ay-ay, what's occurring here?" I still can't figure it out, but I'm so pleased she's stopped biting my head off, it's possible that I go a tad too far on the smiling and flirting front.

Anyways, I crack on with the doors and I'm having a laugh with her, asking her what she does and can she get me a job 'cause if it comes with a spanking new BMW in tow then I don't care what it is but I'd like some of it thank you. And she says she's a marketing consultant and she's got her own company and she's doing OK, only she says it like this, "Actually, I have been doing r-a-a-a-ther well of late." Quite posh, like I told you before.

Then she's making me another cup of tea when she says, "Married?" Just like that. Only she's smiling in this dead sexy way as she holds out the biscuit jar.

I raise my eyebrows and delve slowly around the jar, taking my time, looking into her eyes.

"Does it make a difference?"

"I'd say you fancy yourself."

"Well, someone's got to."

Now all the while this is going on, there's another bit of my head—probably my brain, you know, the small bit—that's saying, "Here, hang on a minute, mate, where's all this heading?" Unfortunately, I'm not really listening to that bit. In fact, I'm kind of telling it to shut up because I'm doing just fine on my own and I'm not needing my brain at the current time.

Then she says, "I know it's an awful cheek, but you look like you might be a handy man with a drill and I've gone and bought this rather large mirror. I thought it would look nice in the master bedroom."

And I start thinking of various other things that I think would look nice in the master bedroom. I can see her blouse straining against her nipples.

"A mirror? And you never got it from us? Cheeky. Oh, go on then. Have you got a drill? Or mine's in the car." Never travel without a drill. You never know when it could come in handy.

She waves her hand around in the air.

"Oh there should be one somewhere. I've no idea. Possibly in the garage."

I get mine to save buggering about. I follow her upstairs, getting a good look at her bum as she goes ahead of me, and think about putting my hand up her skirt. I could just reach out and touch the back of her leg, my fingers sliding over her legs, moving between her thighs, making her quiver. Then she's at the top of the stairs and leading the way to the "master" bedroom. Why do they call it that? It's just estate-agent bollocks, right? Still, the bed's massive, queen size or king size or whatever.

87

Big anyway. It's so huge you can't ignore it, so I say, "Nice bed." I always was nifty with the quick one-liners. Still, at least it was short and to the point. She smiles and gestures at the mirror leaning against one wall.

I can't help myself now, it's like I've entered bad comedy zone and everything I say sounds like a come-on.

"Where do you want it then?" I smirk a bit at that 'cause I've given up all pretence of trying to be cool and I know she knows I'm interested but I'm not sure what to do about it. Well, we go through the motions of offering it up to the wall and dickering about, then I mark the wall with a pencil 'cept by now my hands are shaking and I'm wondering if I should take the risk and kiss her or if she'll give me a slap and phone Harry to complain. Then I'm holding the mirror and she's supporting the other side and I look at her reflection in the mirror and she's looking straight back at me. She doesn't look away. And then, without speaking, we put the mirror down, and I put my hand on the curve of her waist and pull her towards me and kiss her. Her arms loop round my neck and she kisses me back. She kisses me like she's not been kissed for a while and wants to make up for lost time. I let my hand on her waist sneak down a bit so it's on her hip, then round to her bum. I'd pull her closer but there's not a breath of air between us as it is and I can feel her pressing hard against my groin. I slide my other hand over her blouse, as if I'm interested in assessing the texture of the material for some reason, but then my hand's cupping her breast, thumb circling the nipple.

I hear a low moan then realize it's me. I touch her through the cloth of her skirt then I bend to hitch it up, my hand between her thighs just like I pictured it. I feel her hesitate a moment, wondering if she should stop me, wondering what she's doing, letting herself be touched up by some bloke she barely knows in the middle of the afternoon. Then my fingers find the satin of her knickers, slippery and getting damp. She jerks against me suddenly as my fingers cheat their way under the elastic, paddling in her flesh.

She pulls back for a moment; her face is flushed, her eyes glassy as if she's a bit tipsy. All traces of her lipstick have been kissed to oblivion, but her lips are red and full, her breathing hot close to my face. I start to unbutton her blouse with one hand, the other hand still busy beneath her skirt, moving her towards that vast acreage of bed.

"Wait a sec," she says, still pushing against me, her hand cupping my head as I nibble her neck. "I need to get something, you know."

I nod and reach down to tug off my socks, then undo my trousers. She comes back from the bathroom with a packet of three. At least it's a new packet. What could be more depressing than someone appearing with a packet of three, but there's only one left? That'd make you feel like you were walking on a well-trodden path, eh? Anyways, she whips off the cellophane, takes one out and pushes me, with one finger, onto the bed.

"I don't know my own strength," she says. She

reaches for me, her hand going straight to my cock. She's not shy, that's for sure. And I'm thinking I'm already just about ready to explode but I want to be inside her. She rolls on the condom, then lies on her side, her leg hooked over mine. I tease her for a few seconds, rubbing the tip against her, then feel her hand on my bum pulling me towards her—aa-aah, I thought I'd forgotten how to do it, but it's coming back to me now, oh yes. I bury my face in her cleavage, smell her skin, try to reach round her to undo her bra, hands clumsy with lust. She's grinding against me, getting more excited as I push into her, but suddenly, that's it—I can't wait. I want to, but I can't. I'm past the point of no return and I'm coming, feeling as if my eyes are rolling into the back of my head, but it's too late.

I shudder against her and collapse, my mouth hot and open on her cheek.

"Sorry. I'm really sorry. I meant to hold out . . ."

"Doesn't matter." She's trying to be nice. I ease out carefully, then gently start to touch her again.

"I want to make you come."

She smiles, then—can you believe it—my sodding mobile goes.

"Um . . ." I'm tempted to leave it but it's probably Gail.

"Perhaps you'd better answer that?"

"Won't be a tick."

The screen display says HOME, so I answer it and pad

out to the landing, away from the rumpled bed, away from Angela lying there with her skirt tangled round her hips, away from the scene of the crime.

"Hey there!" I say brightly, suddenly feeling very naked. I shuffle closer to this plant in the corner with whacking great leaves, trying to cover myself up a bit with undergrowth as if Gail could see me through the phone.

"Hi. Just calling to say can you pick up some wine on the way home?"

"Okey-doke! What colour?"

"White. Can you get that one we had before, with the blue squiggle on the label? Where are you now? Are you nearly through?"

You could say that. Christ, this really wasn't such a hot idea. Check my watch. Shit. It's after five already.

"Yeah. Just clearing up now. Gary only went and put the wrong glass in this customer's door—*clear* glass for a bathroom. He must have sawdust for brains."

"And can you pick up some crisps for Rosie's lunch-box tomorrow? Cheese-and-onion."

"Blue squiggly wine and crisps. Got it. See ya!" I press the end call button and stand there, naked on a strange woman's landing, holding the phone like I've never seen it before. What the fuck am I doing? What have I done? But I've not got time now to dwell on what a total prat I am.

Back into the bedroom. No sign of Angela, but the shower's running in the en-suite.

91

"Er, all right in there then?" I call out.

She says something back but I can't hear properly because of the water. I start picking up my socks and my shirt off the floor.

"Want a shower?"

Let's see—do I want a shower? On balance, I'd say probably a yes to that. Alternatively, I could go home drenched in the smell of sweat, sex and the tang of another woman. What a good idea.

She appears in a towel and smiles at me, but I don't have a clue what she's thinking. I smile back.

"Sorry it was a bit . . . speedy."

She shrugs and drops her head down to towel her hair.

"No sweat. Sounds like you'd better get going."

"Yeah. Guess so." I head for the shower.

I kiss her goodbye in the hall.

"I'll call you," I say.

"As you like."

And that was that. One brief shaglet equals one perfectly good marriage out the window.

Rosie

We went to Nana and Grandad's for the weekend, but Dad didn't come with us because him and Mum haven't made up yet. On Sunday, Aunty Mari came over for lunch as well and she and Mum were talking in the garden for ages and ages but when I went outside Aunty told me to run along and play as if I was about five years old.

Nat didn't hardly say a word the whole weekend and at lunch he reached right across the table for the potatoes and Aunty said, "Someone wants to start watching their manners, young man."

"Just leave it, Mari." Mum gave her a look.

Then Grandad said, "Come along now, let's not spoil a lovely lunch. Who'd like a drop more wine?"

Nat said he would and Mum said not on your life and I said I would too and everyone laughed but it wasn't funny. Then Nana poured me some lemonade instead and said, there you are, poppet, that's much better than wine and I said thank you but then Nat gave me a snotty look because he hates it when I remember to say please and thank you but it wasn't my fault he got told off in the first place.

I was going to ask Mum if Dad would be home again when we got back, but Nat said I was being a silly baby and I wasn't to ask her and he'd never talk to me ever, ever again if I did. I wasn't being a baby, I just wanted to know. Mostly on Sunday evenings, we all watch TV or a video. Mum sits at one end of the couch and Dad at the other and I go in the middle. Nat lies on the floor in the front. He doesn't like being on the couch with us because he says he likes to spread out and anyway he can never sit still and Mum has to tell him to stop fidgeting.

When we got home, it was all quiet and there were no lights on and Mum clapped her hands together the way Miss Collins does at school and then she said right, if you've any homework still to do, off upstairs and finish it now. I did mine then I went in Nat's room and he said, "See, told you Dad wouldn't be here. You'd only have made everything worse if you'd asked Mum."

"Why can't they say they're sorry and make up, then Dad could come home again?"

"Because they're both, like, totally clueless and if you haven't worked that one out by now then there's no hope for you."

So I stuck my tongue out at him and said he was a big horrible pig with greasy hair and I ran out and banged his door. I ran into my room and wedged the chair under the handle in case he tried to get me back. Then I went all the way along the shelf above my bed and shook every single one of my snow shakers. I've got seven altogether.

My best one is the one Mum and Dad got me when they went to France on their anniversary last year and Nat and me went to stay with Nana and Grandad. It's got the Eiffel Tower in it and it's supposed to be night-time but instead of snow it's got gold glitter in it. I gave it an extra shake then I knelt on my bed with my nose right up touching the glass so all I could see was the world inside it and I made believe I was in Paris all on my own with no Nat or Mum or Dad or anyone. I was doing pirouettes right on the top of the Eiffel Tower and there were lots and lots of lights and all around me was sparkly gold snowflakes floating down.

Nat

He's not coming back. I said he wasn't and he's not. All that stuff Mum came out with about it just being for a little while is total crap. It might work with Rosie, but she can't expect me to buy it. Some of his clothes have gone. I went into their bedroom and looked in the wardrobe. Before, his clothes were all on the right and Mum's were on the left. The clothes were all squashed up because Dad says Mum's got too many things, God knows why, she doesn't wear a quarter of them, he says. Now her stuff's all spaced out and there's a gap at one end, like his things were never there at all, like he never even lived here.

Mum told us we would see him next weekend and that we can phone him whenever we like. She said he'd phone Wednesday and we could decide what to do at the weekend. I won't be here when he phones. I've got swimming practice. My tumble turn's too slow. Jason sees his dad only on weekends. He stays at his dad's every other Saturday night and they go out and do stuff on Sunday.

* * *

I looked in the cupboard under the stairs. His fishing things were still there. He wouldn't leave without them. Maybe he will come back. There were his rods in their covers. The big green umbrella. That funny little tent to keep the wind off. It's not a proper tent really, no groundsheet or anything, but it's better than nothing when the wind's cutting along the coast or coming straight at you off the sea. We used to go a lot, Dad and me, down off the beach. I've got my own rod. Dad bought it for me one Christmas. The reel bit alone cost loads of money. It's a proper one, a grown-up one. Rosie's got a stupid little girl's rod because she's only come with us once or twice and then only so she would-n't feel left out and Mum said we had to take her and not to be a pair of spoilsports. She never caught anything except when Dad cast for her, so it didn't count. I got a couple of flatties last time, only small though, so I chucked them back. Dad promised that one day we'd hire a boat so we could go further out. Don't suppose he'll bother now. He shouldn't make promises if he's not going to keep them.

We used to go at night sometimes. You get there on a rising tide. We'd take like a kind of a picnic, Dad made it, not Mum, with soup or cocoa and sandwiches. But we'd always get chips as well once we were there. There's a chippie down this side street off the front. It helps keep your hands warm, holding chips. I started going when I was only six or seven. We used to take my sleeping bag in case I fell asleep. I remember Dad lifting me up, like I was a ginormous great caterpillar in this sleeping bag and laying me on the back seat of the car. Then at home, I'd feel him lift me out again. It was all dark but he'd carry me up the stairs, my legs swinging in the bag as he bounced on each step. Then he put me down on my bed, still in my clothes, and he'd pull the covers up over the sleeping bag, and the last thing I heard was him saying, "Night-night, Natty. Sleep tight," and then tiptoeing out again. And I'd say "Night-night" back, at least I always meant to say it, but by then I was too sleepy to speak. I thought I was saying it out loud, but I wasn't. It was just in my head. You do stuff like that when you're only a little kid.

Scott

OK, what's the worst-case scenario, I said to myself. Gail's always saying I'm too much of an optimist and that's why I keep being disappointed. But what's the point of carrying on at all if you think everything's going to turn out badly the whole time? Gail says it's best to prepare yourself for the worst then if things are only a bit crap you feel like you're ahead of the game. My words, not hers, but you get the gist.

I was still pretty sure she would come round and everything would be all right. I figured I'd be on the wrong end of some heavy-duty sulking and sarky remarks for a while and I'd get not enough nookie to keep a nun happy, but that I'd live through it. It's not like I'm not used to it or anything. If I was really unlucky, I reckoned she might make me go to one of those marriage guidance people. I've seen them on telly—d'you remember that series, with all the couples? Half of them you couldn't see why they'd ever got hitched in the first place, they never said more than "Pass the sugar." Hopeless. Yeah, like I can afford to be smug. Anyway, the marriage guidance bods, they're always like these really creepy blokes who sit there stroking their beards while looking at your wife's tits and asking nosy questions about how often you have sex. And the women counsellors are just as bad, all smiling and nodding and homely looking then—pow!—just when you're thinking maybe this isn't so bad, they stick the knife in and jiggle it around: "So it's been a long time since your husband's given you any pleasure in bed?"

Gail knows I can't stand all that stuff—like those couples that go on chat shows and talk about, well, everything: "Yes, I did find it difficult to maintain my erection, but Sue was very loving and we were able to laugh about it together . . ." Hilarious. What a giggle. Would you go on telly and tell millions of people you couldn't get a stiffy? Why not send cards round to all your mates while you're at it? Take out an ad in the paper. No need for an ad round here. They're so desperate for news, it'd probably make front page:

MAN AT NO. 36 CAN'T GET IT UP
Wife says council should support him

Anyway. That's another thing I do that drives Gail crazy—keep going off the point. How do I know it drives her crazy? You're thinking I must be some kind of expert on the subtle signals women are supposed to give out, right? Clearly, Gail never heard all that stuff about women being subtle. When I annoy her, which is like about fifty times a day, she starts gnashing her teeth and lunging at me with the potato peeler. "Is this all part of your feminine mystique?" I say, dodging out the way and flicking at her with the tea-towel. "I have an inkling you're a little bit upset about something. Tell me if I'm getting warm." Colin says when Yvonne's pissed off (when isn't she pissed off? I want to ask, but I'm too much of a gent), she goes into a sulk. Her mouth goes all pursed like a cat's bum and if he goes "What's up?" she says, "Nothing" which of course means "Everything, and you better start being sorry even if you don't know what it is." And it's always something minuscule like he forgot her mum's birthday or she's got on a new lipstick and Colin didn't notice.

Oh. Worst-case scenario. I remember. Well, I reckon the absolute worst, worst, worst-case scenario is if Gail doesn't let me come back for, say—well, ever. She couldn't stop me seeing the kids 'cause I've never been cruel or violent or whatever. So, absolute worst is—no Gail to cuddle up to at night ever again.

And I'd have to find a new place to live and support me and them for a lot more than I do now.

And I'd not get to hang out with Natty and mess around with the computer or go roller-blading or swimming or fishing whenever we want.

Or tell Rosie a bedtime story and kiss her good night.

So that'd be the worst.

Fuck.

*   *   *

Still, that's really, really unlikely. I mean, it was only a sodding fling, right? She'd have to have a screw loose to hold it against me for ever. It happens all the time. I read it somewhere: 50 to 75 per cent of men have at *least* one affair after they're married. So, looking at it logically, I'd be downright abnormal if I *hadn't* slept with someone else. It's obviously completely natural. Look at lions, for instance—you get one male with loads of females, don't you? I should find that article and send it to her. You know, to prove it. Then she'd see I wasn't so bad. We could start over, a clean slate, and I wouldn't go off the rails again. I mean, statistics might be on my side, but you don't want to push your luck, right?

I'd like to say I'm getting used to being on my own, that I'm enjoying this unexpected return to a bachelor lifestyle. I'd like to say that living at Jeff's house is a non-stop riot and that we have a load of girls over for drunken orgies every night. Ha! I wish. The joke is, I've turned into Mr House-Husband, spending half my evenings elbow-deep in suds or hoovering like a dynamo and tutting at Jeff when he leaves his cups and plates all over the house the way Nat does. With Gail, it was always moan, moan, moan that I didn't pull my weight round the house—if only she could see me now. Maybe then she'd stop looking at me like I was some slime creature who'd crawled out from under a rock.

At first, every time I attempted to have a sensible conversation with her about the Subject, she'd go into snide overdrive and things would spiral out of control and I'd end up wishing I'd never brought it up. But eventually, she agreed to have a talk, a proper sit-down talk as opposed to her slagging me off on the front step.

"Not because I think you've got anything to say that's worth listening to," she said. "But at least once I've heard you out you can stop going on about it."

I went through the whole thing again, and told her how much I love her and miss her, but nothing seemed to make any difference. I was being completely reasonable, I swear, and I pointed out that we'd been having our ups and downs and it wasn't all down to me—but she just went right off the bloody deep end.

"It's not that I'm trying to make light of it," I tell Gail, "but it really didn't mean anything, I swear." I *am* trying to make light of it, of course, but so far honesty seems to have been not the best policy for the King of Fuck-Ups. "I do realize how serious this is. I'm just saying that it's very, very common and we shouldn't let it get all out of proportion. This happens to lots of couples, but they manage to work things out."

"*This* as you so carefully put it, does not *happen* to lots of couples, Scott. Infidelity isn't an earthquake or a bolt of lightning and we just happened to be standing in the wrong place at the wrong time—it wasn't me, Miss, I was just lying there and this woman threw herself on top of my willy. It's pathetic. Take some responsibility for once in your life. Now that you're a big lad of forty you might try acting like a grown-up. Who knows? You might even get to like it. Many of us act like grown-ups every single day and come to no major harm."

"Cheers. I *do* take responsibility. All I'm saying is plenty of blokes—and women as well for that matter—"

"But not me."

"No, not you. I'm not saying that, course not. Where was I?" She always does that, throws you off so you lose your thread.

"Hunting for some sort of easy way out? Up shit creek without a paddle?"

She never used to talk like that. I don't know what's happened to her lately.

"My point is, Gail, lots of people have meaningless affairs—"

"So it was an affair? You've given up pretending it was a one-off mistake then? It's a good idea to stick to the same story once you've started lying, Scott. Do try to keep track. Perhaps you should keep a small notebook. So, are we getting some truth out of you at last?"

"No. Yes. No. I mean, I *am* telling the truth. No, it wasn't an affair, I told you. Look . . ." I rub my fingertips hard against my forehead; my brain is beginning to throb. "Can I just say what I'm trying to say for a sec?" She shrugs, then folds her arms, her expression a perfect cross between smug superiority and complete boredom.

"I mean—just 'cause someone goes off the rails once or twice, it's not as if it's really the be-all and end-all, is it? If someone makes one small mistake—which they really, really regret—it doesn't—"

She interrupts me. This is her idea of letting me finish. I just want you to know it's not all one way, that's all. She may make out she's the poor little victim but Gail can give as good as she gets. Better, even. I might as well have laid down on the floor, waved a white flag, and let her march straight over me on her way to conquer the rest of the planet.

"Scott," she says, spitting out my name like it's an insult. "You only 'really, really regret' what happened because you got caught. Otherwise you'd have been swaggering around thinking how clever you'd been. And your story still keeps changing. Was it once or was it twice? Surely even you must have noticed?—though I dare say *she* may not have. And if you don't call betraying your wife's trust and breaking your marriage vows and lying and cheating and letting down your children the be-all and end-all, then I'm afraid all I can do is feel sorry for you. You don't have the slightest idea of what it means to be a husband and a father, do you? I think you barely understand even how to be a passable adult. You're just a silly overgrown kid. Honestly, I might as well be a single parent half the time—I ought to have received extra child benefit for having you in the house."

I'm stood there, words lodged in my throat, trying to swallow, feeling my sodding eyes start to water. Bugger this, I am not going to cry, I'm just *not*. Nobody, but nobody, makes me cry. Not any more. But I'm not having her call me a sponger. No way. So I lost my rag completely at this point, but who wouldn't have? I meant to stay calm, I really did, but she shoved me over the edge because she gets off on being the mature, sensible one and making me look like the toddler having a temper tantrum. Well, good bloody luck to her. At least I don't go round looking like I've got a poker up my arse the whole time.

Gail

It was pathetic, of course, Scott insisted on having a talk, then all he did was trot out the same old excuses—how it was just sex and didn't mean anything, how lots of couples go through this and it didn't have to be a big deal. He even told me it wasn't very good and that she was a bit fat—as if that meant it shouldn't count. And men are always claiming that we're the ones who are illogical.

The worst thing was when he said, "It's made me realize just how much I really love you." Oh, well, that's fine then. Why not do it every week just to make sure? I came this close to hitting him, I really did. I wish I had done, I wish I'd really let rip and screamed at him, but I didn't. I was using all my energy to hold myself together, my voice getting more and more calm and controlled, every bit of my body tight and stiff. I had to. I thought that if I let go for even a split second, then I'd sort of explode inside-out and become this horrible screaming, crying heap. And then there'd be no Gail any more, just a raw red blob shuddering with rage and fear in the corner.

I pressed my toes down hard against the floor and pinched the skin on my arms.

"Honestly, Scott, you've had enough time to think about this. Is that really the best you can manage?"

And, get this, he even had the cheek to say, "But we were getting on so badly—" Well, there was no way I was letting him shift all the blame onto me. Typical Scott. He's worse than a toddler. If he breaks something, he never says sorry, it's always, "I don't know how that happened, it jumped off the shelf. I was nowhere near it."

"And sleeping with another woman was your idea of a miracle cure for our problems, was it?"

"No, course not," he said, looking all awkward, like a teenager. Like Nat, in fact. "It's just—I didn't know how to make it better."

"It's not exactly making an appointment with Relate, is it, Scott?"

"I'd have *gone*. You never *said*!"

Can you believe it? What is he, twelve years old?

"That's you all over, isn't it?" I practically screeched at him, while still trying to keep my voice down. "'*You* never said.' Why the hell is it *my* job? I suppose it's like the way it's *my* job to be cook, cleaner and general household dogsbody. Why is everything up to me all the time? And anyway—anyway, you're a pathetic liar. No way would you have gone for marriage guidance even if I had suggested it—and you know it."

"I might have."

I laughed then. I actually laughed. He seemed to be getting younger and younger. Before, he seemed about twelve. Now, he looked only about four years old, saying "I might have" trying to defy teacher with his bottom lip stuck out.

He sniffed.

"Well, you wouldn't want some nosy do-gooder asking personal questions about our sex life either."

"Why ever not? Unlike some people in this room, *I've* got nothing to hide."

Then I just felt so sick of it all, of him sitting there trying to make out that he was this poor, sweet, innocent boy who just happened to have made this tiny little mistake that any other woman would have forgiven without a second thought. He acted as if I was being a loathsome bitch trying to victimize him and it wasn't his fault that he'd cheated on me. He never takes responsibility, so he gets to be the one who's spontaneous and larks about the whole time, while look who gets stuck with having to be the sensible grown-up. So I made some dig about him being like a child, it was a silly thing to say, but it just came out and suddenly I thought maybe I'd gone too far. His face darkened, his jaw thrust forward as if he really was a little boy doing his best not to cry.

"That is well out of order, Gail. You really have crossed the line now." Then he started shouting: "I have *always* provided for my family—I've *always* worked—

you and the kids have never gone short—*never*—Jeez, you make me sound like some fucking sponger. How *can* you say that?"

I felt a bit bad, really I did. I hadn't meant it. I'd just wanted to hurt him, I suppose, make him feel useless and humiliated—the way he'd made me feel. And now it looked like I had World War Three on my hands.

"I'm sorry, Scott. I really am. I only said it because I feel so hurt and angry."

"Hurt and angry? *You*—hurt and angry! I'm the one living like a fucking gypsy out of a fucking carrier bag! How *dare* you make yourself into such a martyr—here you are in *our* nice warm house with *our* comfy settee and *our* proper kitchen and *our* big bed and *our*—repeat, *our*—children while I'm having to accept charity and live like a sodding student and be woken up by crap rock music at seven o'clock in the fucking morning. For fuck's sake—HURT and ANGRY? You haven't got a fucking clue."

Then he got up and stomped out and down the front path. I thought of going after him, to try to get him to calm down, but my legs were shaking and I couldn't move. I've never, ever seen him like that. Not about unjust parking tickets or the car being stolen or being gazumped over our first house. Never.

Scott

OK, I'll come clean—it *was* twice. With Angela, I mean. But you really can't count the first time. And the second time was only to make up for the first time being so godawful and anyway, I was already guilty by then, so it wasn't as if it was making anything worse. It's all water under the bridge now in any case, so what difference does it make? Still, there's no point in telling Gail it was twice, right?

The second time. I was driving practically past Angela's house. Well, near enough. So I thought I'd just call by, say hello, take a look at her doors and that.

"Oh hello." Angela opened the door a little way, with just her head in the gap. "Nice of you to keep in touch."

"Now don't be like that. I did call but I got your machine and I didn't know what to say."

"How about: 'Hello, it's Scott, are you available for shagging purposes?'"

I'm on the verge of blushing now. Still, she seems to be smiling, so I take advantage and edge a bit closer.

"You can't just turn up whenever you feel like it, you know. What if I'd had someone here?"

"You could say I'd come to check your garden door and other see-through items. It's only that I was in the area and—"

"Yes, I see. Come in anyway now that you're here. Coffee?"

"Cheers." I shuck off my jacket, casual, as if I'm a bit hot. Angela's wearing one of those wrap-round skirts. The sort where you undo one button and yee-har it's on the floor. The kind of women's clothing a man likes. I think about putting my hand on her thigh, sliding up under the material, but she's standing the wrong side of the jutting-out counter. Hang on a minute, matey. Don't rush.

"Sugar?" She busies herself making the coffee, fiddling with jars and teaspoons.

"One-and-a-bit. So, how've you been?" Slowly, I edge around the worktop.

"Oh, you know, moping by the phone waiting to hear from you." She looks at me then. "Not really, you idiot. I've hardly been here, actually. Got so much work on. I'm fine." She sighs. "Scott, I do know you're married. I'm not looking to get into some seedy affair or lure you away from your wife, you know. I had a good time," she laughs, hitching herself onto a stool at the counter. "Well, all right, I've had better but it was fine, and if we ever get it together again, that'll be fine too. But I'm not becoming the Other Woman. I'm not looking to be somebody's stepping-stone out of a hopeless marriage."

"But I haven't got a hopeless marriage. I love Gail to bits . . ."

"Yeah." She looks me straight in the eye. "You probably do, but you're at the mercy of your dick. You all are."

I shrug in what I hope is an endearing, oh-well-that's-us-lads sort of way and give her my best smouldering-but-sensitive look.

"You needn't worry, I'm not the sort to tell tales. I may have knickers with loose elastic but I'm not a bitch."

"I never thought you were. 's just . . ."

"Ye-e-e-s?"

"About the other day . . ."

"Other week, more like."

"I was a bit nervous . . ."

"So that's it!" She laughs, shaking slightly, perched on her stool. Her skirt comes open a little way and I notice she doesn't tug it back together again. I nudge a bit closer, spreading out my fingers on the worktop. "Scott. You're hilarious, you really are. Are you worried about your reputation? Good grief, you were fine. Still . . ." She eases herself down off the high stool.

"So then . . ." I stroke along her arm with one finger.

"Lord, we'll be here all day at this rate." She takes my hand and tows me towards the stairs. "Come upstairs if you're coming—I've got to go out at three."

Well, by now I've left my brain behind completely, it's

outside lurking in the driveway wondering what's occurring, saying tut-tut through the letterbox and hoping I'll come back to pick it up at some point. But I'm in no rush because I reckon I'm about to have a very good time. A very good time. If it was here, it'd only be in the way, muttering and criticizing—"What if . . . ? Do you think this is wise? What if Gail . . . ? You got away with it once, but—" Thank you, Brain, your services are not required at this time. Don't call us, we'll call you . . .

I bend to undo the button of her skirt, tugging at the cloth with my teeth, feeling her hand on my head, pulling me close. Her hairs curl round the sides of her silky knickers. I kneel down and knee-walk her towards the bed as I pull at her pants with my mouth. She pulls me onto the bed, feeling for the buckle of my belt, my zip, her hand hot on my skin, easing me out, holding me—pulling down my trousers, rucked around my knees—no time to take them off now—kissing—her hand driving me crazy—"Hang on, where's the. . .?"—fumbling in her bedside cupboard, one hand still encircling me—rips open the packet with her teeth—rolls it on smoothly, bending over me to kiss the tip—lying back now—her thighs spread—hand guiding—I hover on the brink, teasing her—her gasp as I push in—her flesh warm around me—legs holding me—good—God, I've missed this feeling—being surrounded—being held—so good—building now—getting faster—should I slow down?—is she . . . ?—mentally recite the names and phone numbers of our main suppliers—Tuff Glass 013—no need now, no need—her hips are ramming into mine—small urgent grunts—now high and breathy—our mouths open—too hot to kiss—gasping for air, for breath—shuddering—collapsing, her mouth wet on my shoulder, her hair across her face in sweaty strands.

I roll off her and we lie there for a few minutes, catching our breath. Then she levers herself upright.

"Better. A lot better. Have a gold star." She smiles and nods, as if to herself. "God, I really needed that." She pads towards the bathroom, calling back over her shoulder. "Do you want first shower or shall I?"

"You. Do you need me to come in and hold your . . . soap?"

"No thanks. I prefer to wash alone. Won't be long."

Then I had a shower, she gave me a kiss in the hall, said we'd best leave it for a while, and I left. When I turned to wave from the car, the front door was closed and she was gone. Then I went home—smelling of a different soap, it turned out, as Inspector Gail informed me later, that and the inside-out underpants, that's what gave me away—not knowing that my entire life was about to be tugged away from right under my feet.

All done in barely more than half an hour. I'd been married to Gail fifteen years. It took just half an hour to wipe out fifteen years of marriage. Half an hour. Jeez.

After the big row with Gail, when she'd said all those things, I thought, "Well, bollocks to you then—if you're going to treat me like shit and make like I'm the most evillest sinner on the whole planet, then why should I beat myself up about it as well and stay at Jeff's"—Mr Happy's Amazingly Cheerful Abode isn't exactly where you want to hang out if you're already feeling down, you know? So I drove round to Angela's. There's no answer when I ring the bell and I'm just hopping from foot to foot on the doorstep when she appears on the side path hefting her rubbish bin.

"Hiya!" Trying to sound breezy, casual, you know. "Let me take that. Where do you want it?" I give a little knowing smile at that last bit.

"Just passing, were you?" No hello, no squelchy kiss. This isn't going to be a pushover, I could tell.

"Yeah, sort of. Sorry I've not been in touch."

"I'd prefer it if you'd phone first, Scott. I might have had someone here." I try to peer in through the front room window.

"Sorry. Have you?"

"No, but that's not the point."

"Don't you like surprises? Come on—where's your sense of spontaneity? No-one does anything on impulse any more—no wonder the country's stuck in a rut."

"So that's Scott's solution to all global political and economic problems, is it? Be spontaneous?"

That's the way she talks. It's kind of hard to tell when she's joking. Also, I wasn't so sure about the being spontaneous thing. Well, look at the trouble it had got me in so far.

"No danger of being offered a coffee, is there?"

She nods me in to the house.

"Sure. Can't stand out here freezing on the front path. Besides, the neighbours might see you."

She's just kidding, right? Anyone'd think she was embarrassed to be seen with me.

We go in the back way, through the superbly glazed door—lovely bit of workmanship that, I pat it admiringly as I go in—and I perch on one of the stools at the breakfast bar.

"You OK?" she asks over her shoulder as she fills the kettle.

"Been better."

"Oh?"

I'm not sure whether to play it down, just say I've had a bit of a barney with Gail or whether to go for the full, woe-is-me, sackcloth-and-ashes bit. Play the poor-little-me card. What would you have done? Problem is with these things, you only get one shot, so if you're wrong you're stuffed really, aren't you? She shoves the sugar bowl along the counter at me, like a barman in a Western sliding that ol' whisky bottle down to the mysterious stranger at the far end. I spoon in the sugar in a mysterious stranger kind of way, stir it in and sit there looking down into the whirlpool in my mug, not knowing what to say.

"It's nothing to do with me, is it, Scott?"

I take a sip of my coffee to give me a moment more to think then immediately wish I hadn't because it's burnt my sodding lip and I jerk back as if I've been—well, burnt.

"Probably best give it a minute to cool, eh?" Angela smiles at me.

"Cheers. I think I know how to handle a cup of coffee now I'm a grown-up chappie of forty." Well, apparently not actually, given I'd just gone and scarred myself for life.

She shrugs and wrinkles her nose at me.

"Sorry. I was *trying* to show concern. Come on, what's up?"

"It's Gail. She found out about me and you—"

"Found out what exactly? Did you tell her that it really didn't mean anything?"

This was really making me feel so much better. Proper tonic, talking to Angela.

"Cheers, Angela. Course I tried to tell her that, but she wasn't listening. One minute she was having a go at me, and the next I'm stood on the wrong side of my front door with no jacket, no keys, no nothing. And saying, 'I really think we need to discuss this properly, darling' just didn't seem to be cutting it, you know?"

"Shit. I'm sorry. Really. But I guess you can't be all that surprised. I mean, what did you expect she'd do—

rap you across the knuckles and say try not to do it again?"

I shrug. Of course, at the time, you don't think about what to expect because you're not planning on being caught. If you knew you were going to be found out, you probably wouldn't do it in the first place, right? Still, I don't know why Angela was acting so superior. She wasn't exactly Miss Goody Two-Shoes in all this either.

"Thing is, it looks like she won't let me come back."

Realization dawns. Angela clunks her mug down hard on the counter.

"Oh no. No. I'm sorry, Scott, but you're not thinking for even a second that you might stay here?"

"Just for a couple of nights. I'll kip on the settee if you like. Just until Gail sees reason—"

"Scott, if you want to patch things up with your wife, do you really think staying with me is the best way to go about it? Use your head instead of your dangly bits for once, for God's sake. If she doesn't think we're having an affair now, she certainly will if you roll up here with a suitcase."

I start telling her about how I'd had to sleep at work, and hadn't managed to sleep a wink; I kind of made it sound as if I was still there, curled up under my desk in a sleeping bag.

"What about family? Friends?"

I peer down into the dregs of my coffee. Angela reaches over and gives me a playful shove.

"Oh, Scott—you're actually pouting. Surely you've got good mates who'd put you up?"

I think about Jeff and spending yet another night in that house with its dim light bulbs and its sadness, its stale, endlessly re-breathed air and stench of fag smoke. Jeff sleeps with his fags by the bed so he can light up first thing in the morning. And, instead of an ashtray, he's got this great big bowl, like a fruit bowl it is, with—literally—hundreds of fag butts in it, like he's saving them up to give to charity or something.

"S'pose so. Still, I do think you could stand by me a bit. I mean, I don't remember any reluctance on your part to get into my pants. You're my partner in crime really."

She folds her arms across her chest which I figure isn't such a good sign. I saw some documentary about body language once and they said it was a defensive posture, but I don't know. All I've noticed is that when women get cross the first thing they do is cover their tits up.

"Scott. Now let's just get one thing *absolutely* clear, OK? Yes, I had sex with you, but no, I am not your 'partner in crime' as you so winningly put it. I haven't done anything wrong. I've never even met your wife. She's not a friend of mine. I haven't betrayed her trust or broken any marital vows or anything. Your marriage is *your* responsibility and—frankly—*your* mess. I won't be roped in. Don't tell me for one second you thought I was in love with you or that you imagined I'd put my whole life on hold and was waiting in the wings for you to run off with me to the Bahamas."

She looks at me in a sort of weary way, like she's told me some long, elaborate joke and I haven't got it. I unstick myself from the stool and puff out my cheeks. Bugger. Still, I'm not going to beg.

She comes towards me then and gives me a kiss on the cheek.

"Best of luck, Scott. I hope you can sort things out with your wife. Perhaps she'll come round when she realizes it was just a fling, eh?"

"Yeah." I button up my jacket again. "You're probably right."

I trudge back to the car feeling like a heap of shit, frankly. Another night at Jeff's. Oh goody.

A spanking clean silver Merc pulls up just then and the electric window slides down on the driver's side, smooth as silk. Rich git.

"Excuse me," says this woman with one of those posh, would-you-mind-not-breathing-the-same-air-as-me voices. Classy looking, but she's not going to see forty-five again, that's for sure. "Is that your car?"

"Might be. What's it to you?"

I know, I know. Not a good start, but with the day I've had minding my p's and q's isn't exactly top of the agenda. Her mouth pinches together and her nostrils flinch as if I've farted in her jurisdiction.

"Well, if it is your car, perhaps you could move it? It's

blocking our drive, you see? Visitors and—" she pauses, giving my jacket the once over "—delivery persons etcetera are supposed to park over there."

"Oh, fuck off. I'm just going, can't you see? This is me, here, getting into my car and driving away from your stupid so-called exclusive sodding estate, all right? So don't worry—any second now me and my cheap jacket and my common voice and my crap car will cease to sully your fucking poncy driveway to your over-priced, rip-off executive home and you'll be able to drive right up to your authentic Tudor double garage—"

By this point, she's started to say, "Well, really—" but I'm on a roll by then. She probably figures I must be some kind of nutter and her protective window glides back up again.

"And another thing—" I bellow at her through the glass, as she starts to drive away. "Those would-be Tudor windows in your ponced-up house aren't even proper leaded lights. They're mass-produced crap with stick-on glazing bars and if you really had any kind of class you wouldn't be seen dead with windows like that!"

That told her.

Afterwards, I felt crap, I admit it. Really ashamed. I'm not the sort of bloke who goes around shouting at women just 'cause they've got a smug voice and a posh car. I realized I'd gone a tad overboard and I thought about going back, take her a bottle of wine or some flow-ers maybe to say sorry. But I reckoned she'd probably call the police or send her husband out after me with a shot-gun. When I got back to work, I just sat outside in the car for a while, staring at the wire fence through the wind-screen. I couldn't understand why I'd gone so ballistic. It wasn't like me. Two more days of this and they'd have to load me up with happy pills, cart me off and chuck away the key. I looked down at my hands then I pinched the flesh on the back of my left hand as hard as I could, till it made my eyes water. I don't know why. I think it was because I didn't feel real any more. And worse. It sounds weird, I know, but I didn't feel like me.

Rosie

Dad's coming on Sunday to take us out. He phoned last night and asked me what I'd been up to and what I'd done at school, like the way Nana and Grandad do. It was funny talking to him on the phone instead of sitting at the table with him or watching TV together. Normally, when we're eating our tea or having Sunday lunch, Dad talks a lot and Mum says he shouldn't talk with his mouth full because it sets a bad example. Dad says, "Yeah, right," but then he forgets.

I went to go in Nat's room. I knocked on the door first, he goes mad if you don't, and he said, "Mn" so I went in and he said, "I never said come in," so then I had to go out and start again.

I did a somersault on his bed. It was all messy, with the duvet all scrunched up at the foot end and things all over the floor. Nat never makes his bed and Mum says she's given up telling him, if he wants to live in a pigsty, then let him. She says that but sometimes she goes mad and tells him to tidy up his room, no, not later, right now. Then Nat says she's throwing a wobbly and she'll calm down in a minute, but he's just a copy-cat because that's what Dad always says. Nat picks up some of the stuff from the floor and throws it in the bottom of his wardrobe or hides it under the bed and he straightens the duvet so it looks not so bad and Mum says, see, that wasn't so very hard, was it, why couldn't he keep it like that all the time, why does he have to wait to be nagged same as Dad?

Nat was on his computer. He never turns round to talk to me but he says he can do two things at once, so I said,

"You know Sunday? With Dad coming and everything?"

"Mn."

"Dad said we could do anything. Whatever we like."

"Mn."

I wanted to go to the cinema and then go for ice-cream sundaes. Dad said he knows this place that does really big ones with lots of different kinds of ice-cream. But I thought maybe if Nat picked what we did he wouldn't be in a bad mood any more.

"We could go bowling. Like you did on your birthday."

I wasn't allowed to go. Mum and me stayed at home and Kira came round for tea and we had trifle as a treat because of not going bowling. Nat said I couldn't come because I was too young and would spoil things and anyway it was his birthday so it was up to him. Dad took him and his friends, but it was all boys except for his friend Kath and she's practically like a boy. Nat wanted to ask Joanne Carter too, but he didn't. Scaredy-cat Nat.

I unpopped all the poppers at the end of Nat's duvet, then started to repop them all closed again.

"D'you think Dad'll come back home soon?"

"Nah. Don't be stupid."

"Why's it stupid? Mum said they were just—"

"Don't you know anything? Grown-ups are always saying things like that, it doesn't mean anything."

Nat's always being mean and trying to make me cry. I used to, when I was little. Nat said I cried the whole time, but that's not true. I've got a trick now. You bite the inside of your cheek and think about something else or you say things in your head over and over. I do the colours of the rainbow: red, orange, yellow, green, blue, indigo, violet. Red, Orange, Yellow, Green, Blue, Indigo, Violet. When I think each word, I see the word in my head in big letters like it's standing in a field and I make it the same colour as it says. Indigo is the hardest, but I think that one as purple. Violet's like mauve. Mauve's my best colour. I have it for everything.

"I reckon he's not coming back ever and you better get used to it." He didn't even turn round from the screen, just kept playing his stupid game. He thinks he knows everything, but I know lots of things too.

"*I know*. Then they get a divorce and have two houses. Like Kira's Mum and Dad."

"Yeah, like them and like half our class practically. Jason says you've just got to learn how to play it right.

He says to make sure and get two of everything so you don't have to take all your stuff backwards and forwards and sometimes you can get two lots of pocket money."

"Are you going to ask Dad?"

"What?"

"About the pocket money. On Sunday."

"Mn. Oh, Rosie, you put me off. I've lost a life."

Good, I thought, serves you right. But I never said it out loud. I went back into my room and looked at all my things to see what I had two of already—not shoes and socks, I mean, where you have to have two, but other things like sets of felt-tips and hair slides and my animals and my posters and stuff like that. But some things you can only ever have one of, like Alfie-Bear, or they're all supposed to be kept together, like my snow shakers, so it's quite hard actually in fact.

Nat

He's turning up tomorrow to take us out, like that's supposed to mean everything's OK. Rosie won't shut up about it. She thinks I'm going too, but I'm not. They can't make me go. Mum tried to talk me into it and she said he phoned on Wednesday, but I stayed late at practice, doing tumble turns again and again and again until I got it perfect. It was good while I was doing them, I couldn't think about anything else just when to turn, waiting till you're just the right distance from the end, then gliding, tight into the turn, my feet finding the tiles, legs bending, one hard push, arms forward, pointing like an arrow, water rushing past my ears. Then there's only me and the water, see, and no thinking. Only when to breathe and my arms and legs moving, arms slicing through the water like knives, legs making the water boil behind me, head turning . . . NOW—to take in air, then face down again, ploughing forward, faster, faster, heading for the end.

When I came back, I felt tired and a bit spacey, I do sometimes when I've swum like that, on and on, the smell of chlorine still in my nose an hour later. Mum put my food in the microwave and told me Dad had phoned, wanting to know about Sunday.

I shrugged and opened the fridge to get some juice.

"He's coming at ten, OK? Do you want cheese on your pasta?"

"Mn."

"Well, don't stand there looking gormless. Honestly, Nat, there, top shelf. The cheese."

She came over and leant across me to get it. She says you're not supposed to lean over people, it's bad manners. I'd have got it anyway.

I swigged some juice from the carton.

"I'm not going."

"What do you mean, you're not going? Of course you are." She was grating the cheese like a maniac, going at double speed, like she was out to kill this poor little piece of Cheddar, really make it suffer. "You want to see your dad, don't you?"

"Why should I? *You* don't."

Mum sighed and leant against the counter then, like she couldn't be bothered to stand up any more.

"That's a bit different, Nat. Your dad and I—"

"It's *not* different. Why's it different? I don't want to see him and have to play at being happy families and going for ice-creams and pretending everything's OK. I'm not going and you can't make me. And if you've told him I want to see him, you're a liar and you can just forget it." I stirred my pasta all around and dumped a big pile of grated cheese on top.

129

Mum just stood there. I thought she'd have a go at me or try to talk me round or something, but she didn't. She just stood there, completely still, like she was a statue. It was kind of spooky. I almost wished she'd shout at me instead.

Then I fetched a tray and went and ate my pasta watching TV.

It's Sunday. Goody-good Rosie drove me mad yesterday. She spent like the whole afternoon practically packing her bag, taking everything out then putting it back in again.

"You're not going to live with him. You're only out for the day. What d'you need all that for?"

"It's just things," she said, folding her blue jumper all neat, the way Mum would do it. "Things I might need."

Then last night, Cassie came round again. She's Mum's best friend. She's older than Mum even, but she's OK. Not like most grown-ups. She swears in front of us and you can ask her stuff and she doesn't mind. Last night, she offered me a lager, I mean, like really casually, like it was normal. Still in the bottle, no glass, so I could swig it. I held it tight, then Mum came in and I kind of dropped my arm down by my side, so it wasn't so obvious.

"It's OK for Nat to have a beer now, right?" Cassie said.

"What?" Mum spun round and looked at me, clocked the beer straight away. "Cassie! I can't leave you alone for a moment! God, you're worse than—you're so bad. Honestly! He's only just thirteen."

Cassie took a swig. She did it all slow and lazy, just letting the liquid slide into her mouth. It looked really cool.

"Ah, come on, let him have it. It's weak as piss anyway."

Mum gave her a shove and went and got a glass. She held up the bottle to check how alcoholic it was.

"All right. You can have half a glass, no more."

I held out the bottle.

"Can't you leave my bit in the bottle?"

"What? Whatever for?" Mum took another look at Cassie. "Cassie, see what you've done? Now my children think it's cool and glamorous to go round drinking from the bottle like a down-and-out. I hope you're happy." Mum was doing her telling-off voice, but you could see she was joking, taking the piss out of herself. She's never joking when she tells me off. Still, she poured some into the glass and handed me what was left in the bottle.

"So-o-o-o-o," Cassie said, tipping a whole handful of peanuts into her mouth all at once. "Bring me up to date. What's the latest with that errant husband of yours?"

Mum nudged her and made a face. One of those children-in-room-alert-stop-saying-anything-interesting faces that grown-ups do and think you won't notice them doing it.

"Nat, haven't you got homework you should be doing?"

"Not really."

Cassie laughed. She's got this really loud laugh, even in the street. People turn round when she laughs, thinking she must be putting it on. But she isn't. It's just how she is.

"Go on, my man," she said to me. "Shove off and let us old bags have a girlie natter for half an hour. You can come back down for pizza."

"They've already had their tea."

"Mu-um."

"Fine, fine. You can have pizza, Rosie too. I don't know why I bother knocking myself out trying to bring them up properly and nag them to eat their vegetables, Cassie, if you're going to undo it all in two minutes."

Cassie hasn't got any kids. Mum said she had something wrong with her insides and she can't have any. Maybe that's why she's not like a real grown-up, I mean sometimes when you talk to her she seems like she's the same age as me. Or a bit older, like eighteen or something. Only then, if she's talking to Rosie, she's different again, almost like she's Rosie's age. One time, she went out in the garden with Rosie and skipped with Rosie's pink and yellow and blue striped skipping rope, while Rosie chanted some stupid playground rhyme. Then she taught Rosie an old one, like from when she was a kid. But it's good when she's around because

Mum's different. She laughs more and she doesn't get in a strop about little things like whether you've put your plate in the dishwasher or left your trainers on the kitchen counter. When Dad was here, Cassie used to come round sometimes with her husband as well. He's called Derek and he's got an artificial leg. He lets us stand on his foot. You can jump up and down on it even. It's his left leg, but when we were smaller, Rosie and me, we used to pretend we'd forgot which one it was and we used to jump on his other foot as a joke. Rosie still does it sometimes, she's still only a kid really, but he always laughs.

This morning, Mum kept dropping things at breakfast and she drank like a whole pot of coffee. She asked us if we wanted a cooked breakfast "to keep your strength up" like as if we were going to be running a marathon or something. I said I'd have a bacon sandwich and Rosie said could she still count as vegetarian if she had bacon and Mum said, well, not strictly, no, but she wouldn't tell anyone if Rosie didn't. When Rosie went upstairs after, Mum asked me if I'd managed to "have a think about going out with your dad," like as if I'd change my mind or something. I sat there, zigzagging brown sauce onto my sandwich, and said yeah, I had a bit and no, I still wasn't going. Then she put her hand over mine and went all serious and started calling me "Nathan," so I figured I'd had enough. She went blah-ing on about things being important and how I needed a male role model in my life, someone to look up to. I mean, explain that if you can. When he was here, she was always saying Dad was a bad example and we shouldn't copy him because he's got lousy table manners and he doesn't speak properly and he never does the housework and all that. And now she's saying I should be copying his every move. Anyway, when she turned away to load the dishwasher, I snuck out to the hall, grabbed my bag and jacket, then yelled I was off round Steve's and ran out the door before she could stop me.

Gail

I changed clothes twice this morning before he got here. As if I was going on a date. God knows why, I don't even want to see him. Not after last time, after that awful row. After he'd gone, I laid my head on the kitchen table. I could just lie like this for ever, I thought, but then I realized I had to leave in the next two minutes if I wasn't to be late for Rosie. *You can do this*, I told myself, *you have to do this. For Rosie, for Nat*. I haven't got time to have a nervous breakdown.

So this morning I wanted to show him how well I'm doing. *See, you've spoilt everything but life goes on, la-la-la, I'm doing fine without you*. Here I am, in my good black jeans and my clingy white top. I wanted to look attractive but not like I'd made any special effort.

"Dennis," I said, nodding.

Well, calling Scott Dennis, I haven't done that—other than to wind him up for a laugh—since, well, ever. A small flinch tightened his face. I could see him digging his nails into his palms.

He cleared his throat and looked down at his feet.

Hands in pockets. We attempted to chat for a couple of minutes, but it was hopeless. I kept looking for some sign of genuine remorse in his face, but I don't think he's even sorry. He said he wanted to talk, but what is there to say? Why should I sit there listening to him trying to come up with new lies and excuses?

Then he asked me to get Nat, but Nat had long since gone, sneaked out this morning with barely a word. I think he couldn't face it, so he went round to Steve's. Can't say I blame him really. Scott had a go at me about it though, as if I'd hidden Nat away or something. I couldn't believe it, specially when I'd been so bloody calm and civilized about the whole thing. I'd even tried to persuade Nat to go, for goodness' sake, told him I felt it was really important for him to see his dad. But of course, Scott being Scott wouldn't listen, just went into a rage and tried to make out the whole thing was my fault. Once he calmed down, he looked so young, not much more than a boy himself, a boy squaring his shoulders and pretending to be a man. And suddenly I felt sorry for him then, and said something about Nat just being a typical teenager, he'd grow out of it in time.

"Oh. Right. 'Course." Scott was full of bluff now and it made him seem even more pathetic. "Boys that age. Yeah. When I was thirteen, all I did was hang out with my mates. No time for old fogey parents, eh?"

I nodded and forced a smile. But Nat's never been like that and we both know it. He loved his dad like no child you've ever seen, used to trail after him round the garden and in the garage, copying him, the two of them standing there frowning at the car, with Nat barely big enough to see over the bonnet but, frankly, as likely to fix the engine as Scott was. Once I got into a terrible panic because I couldn't find Nat. Scott had just gone to work and this is about six, seven years ago, yes, Nat was only six. And it was before Scott had his mobile. So I was running round the house with Rosie toddling after me and me falling over her and trying to get her to play with her toys and keep out of my way, and Nat was just nowhere to be found. Under the beds, I looked, in the wardrobes, under the kitchen sink. I ran out in the street, expecting to see his little crushed legs sticking out from under a car, people gathered round, someone slowly shaking their head. I couldn't breathe. Then I thought maybe he'd been kidnapped, abducted or something, and I ran inside and rang Scott at work and babbled madly at whoever answered the phone that they must find him and tell him to come home at once. I was totally hysterical. Then Scott came on the phone, he'd just got there, and I was practically screaming by now, completely all over the place and crying, and Scott said,

"Hang on, sweetheart, hang on. It's OK. He's here with me. He's fine."

"What do you mean? How is he there?"

"I left the car open and he scrunched himself in the rear footwell under the blanket. I only found him just now when I got here."

*   *   *

137

I started to cry then, really cry, thinking of how lucky I was that Nat was OK and my God why had I ever had kids when they could do this to you, make you feel your whole life was over just by playing a silly trick for ten minutes.

I looked over Scott's shoulder and waved goodbye at Rosie sitting in his car, but I couldn't even see her face because the windows had fogged over.

"Have her back by six," I said.

Scott

I feel like I'm thirteen again. Nat's age. I'm thirteen and I'm loitering by the front gate plucking up the guts to walk up the path and ring the bell for my first ever date. Her name is Sally. Sally Harrison. I'm crap with names, but I'll never forget hers. No-one's called Sally any more, are they? It went out of fashion. In class, Sally wrote Sally Scott, Sally Scott all over the inside back cover of her rough book, surrounded by hearts and flowers like daisies. I wonder what would have happened if I'd married Sally? I bet she'd never have locked me out of my own house in the middle of the night. She'd probably be standing by the stove peeling the spuds for Sunday dinner and laughing at my jokes, whereas Gail would rather be peeling my meat and two veg if you get my drift.

I'm stood at my own front gate, but who knows what reception I'll get when I ring the bell. They're my own children, but they might as well be stir-crazy tigers I'm so nervous.

As I start to walk up the path, my nerves go because the front door opens wide suddenly and Rosie comes flying out as if she's been catapulted on elastic. Her hair bounces behind her in a ponytail; chunky trainers look comically large on her skinny girl legs. Then she stops dead right in front of me as if she's not sure whether to stretch up for a kiss or to shake my hand.

"Rosie!"

I open my arms wide and she jumps up at me and I catch her and she clutches on like a monkey, the way she did when she was only two or three years old, exhausted after a family day out, sucking her thumb and clinging onto her blankie for comfort.

"Gail." I nod as she appears in the doorway.

"Dennis." A smirk crosses her face, which she immediately tries to hide. Jury, please note my tremendous restraint in not rising to this obvious piece of provocation. No-one, except my parents and they're crumblies so they can't help but call you by whatever stupid thing they picked out for you in the first place, calls me Dennis. Would you call anyone you liked Dennis? Course you wouldn't. You'd give them a nickname wouldn't you? Or say "mate" or something. Everybody else calls me by my surname, Scott—I like it, it's a tough, stubbly, moseying-into-town, laid-back hero sort of a name. When Gail's being nice, say once in a millennium or something, she calls—called—me Scotty. I put Rosie down and tell her to go wait in the car.

"Good one, Gail. Nice to see you've not lost your sense of humour."

"Living with you has, of course, stretched it to the limits on a daily basis, but I do my best . . ."

Is she going to call Nat or what? I raise my eyebrows. She's not going to make me ask, is she? Bugger this.

"Well, entertaining though this is, Dennis, chatting with you cosily on the front step, I'm very busy. Loads of clearing and *chucking out* to do." She says this last with a slight grinding of her teeth as though she's a lioness who's spotted some defenceless bit of prey that doesn't yet know it's about to become a light snack.

"You're not going to be playing silly buggers with my stuff, are you? If it's under your feet, just stick it in the garage for now and I'll sort it out later."

"Bit late to be doing your Lord and Master act, don't you think? What makes you think you can boss me around? Anyway, I have absolutely no interest in wasting my time trawling through your belongings and attempting to decide which bits of rubbish you might regard as precious. Clearly—as I foolishly imagined a fifteen-year marriage meant something whereas you thought nothing of chucking it on the scrapheap—clearly we have rather different ideas of what constitutes rubbish."

Her tone is coolly polite but the frost on it's so thick it gives me goosebumps. Why can't she just shout and swear at me? Then I'd know what I was dealing with. This calm stuff gives me the creeps.

"How can you say that?!" I reach out my hand to

touch her arm but she jerks away from me. "You know you—our marriage—means everything to me—"

"And sleeping with someone else is what? A demonstration of your undying love for me?"

"If I could just come in a minute and—"

"No, you cannot just come in a minute and anything. I've got nothing to say to you other than I think you're a pathetic little prick and the less I see of your stupid arrogant face the better."

"Finished? Or shall I turn round so you can stab me in the back as well while you're at it?"

"Don't tempt me."

"Fine. Can you get my son now, please? We should be making a move."

"Oh, *your* son is he now?"

I sigh deliberately, childishly loudly. It's ten past ten in the morning and I feel like I've already had a long, hard day.

"*Our* son. Give Nat a shout, will you?"

"I can if you insist, but I doubt if he'll hear me."

I puff out my cheeks. This is getting annoying now.

"Well, if he's got his music up too loud, just—"

"He can't hear me, because he's not here."

And this is when I lose my rag completely. What restraint I had left is out the window faster than a rat from a sinking ship and I'm going all out from a standing start: How could she?—she's done it deliberately—I told her—we agreed—the time was her idea, to suit her—now she'd smuggled him out the way so I couldn't see him—my own flesh-and-blood son—I could just see it—bet she'd lost no time in bad-mouthing me—telling him I'm a liar and a cheat—not fit to be a father—did she even say I was coming?—did she?—just wait till he finds out I was here—I'd never have thought she'd sink so low—keeping me from seeing Natty—doesn't the past count for anything?—if not for me, then for him—he needs his dad like he always did, doesn't he? Doesn't he?

"Apparently not." She shrugs and folds her arms, infuriatingly calm. "Of course I told him you were coming. I said it was all arranged. But he refused to see you—"

"Can I phone him at least?"

"—or speak to you. Though it's nice to see how quickly you assumed it must be all my fault. How dare you try to blame me? I would never try to turn the children against you." She looks away from me then and down at her feet, then adds quietly: "Though God knows you deserve it."

I'm standing on my own front path, but it's not really me standing here. This is just the husk of my body, swaying slightly in the wind. Inside, somewhere in the pit of my stomach is a very, very small person huddled into a tight, scrunched-up ball, covering his head with his arms and wishing the world would stop punching him in the guts. Outside, I bite my lip and square my shoulders. Gail stretches out a cautious hand towards me but I flinch from her.

"I'm fine!"

"Sorry. I—he had something he was supposed to do over at Steve's. He's just being a teenager, Scott. He'll come round eventually."

Eventually? When's eventually? It's not listed in my diary. I could be dead and buried by then. I need to see him now.

"Yeah. Fine. Whatever."

Gail nods towards the car.

"You better go. Rosie's waiting. And Scott?"

"What?"

"Don't let her see how disappointed you are. About Nat not coming."

"I'm fine, I'm cool with it. I don't need lessons from you in how to be a good parent, thank you."

And I'm walking back down the path, hearing her voice behind me, saying she'll see me at six.

It's cold and the car windows are misted up. Poor Rosie, I hope she's been warm enough. I should have left the keys in so she could have the heater on. As I open the door, I see she must have leant over to draw on my window with her finger. It is one of those smiley faces kids are always doing. Only this one's smile isn't the perfect semicircle it's supposed to be. It's kind of a crooked line, the face of a smiley doing its best to smile—but not quite making it.

Lesson Two

Scott

I feel like I'm a babysitter. Or a nanny. Someone who's been given custody of a child and is supposed to be in charge of it for an entire day. Eight hours. How hard can it be? It's—*she's*—my own kid, for God's sake. But when Rosie opens the door—I hear her calling out to Gail from the hall, "It's Dad! I'll get it!"—I am suddenly filled with panic. Eight hours. What the hell am I supposed to do with her for eight whole hours?

"Hiya!" I say brightly, bending down to give her a kiss. She throws her arms round my neck and plays with my ears, folding the tops and lobes together so they meet.

"Hello." She gives me a shy smile, like I'm a new friend in the playground, and checks her watch. "You're nearly two minutes late."

"Hey! I was parking the car and combing my hair for my best girl."

Gail appears in the doorway and drops to her knees, imploring me to come home, saying she can't live without me.

*   *   *

OK, OK, fantasy time. Gail appears and composes her face into an expression of total contempt.

"Back by six o'clock." No please, you notice. No hello, Scott, how have you been keeping, dossing down in other people's back bedrooms?

"I'm fine, thanks for asking. And how've you been?"

And she says *I've* got no manners.

Last Sunday I made the mistake of being early—only by fifteen minutes, not enough to make the cover of the *Ashford Advertiser* (and God knows almost anything does—drop a gum wrapper on the High Street and it's FLOG THESE LITTER LOUTS SAYS TOWN). When Gail comes to the door, she looks me up and down from my hairline (which is undergoing something of its own mini-recession at the moment, that's stress that is, I should sue her for compensation) to my shoelaces (my second-best shoes—I remembered the look my old trainers got that first Sunday, I'm learning fast, see) and back again as if I were trying to sell her something at the door and no, she doesn't want any thank you and could I not lower the tone and use up the oxygen by loitering there.

She doesn't speak, just gives me the Braddon Look; they must get lessons in her family—her mum and sisters do it, too—if you had the four of them in a row looking at you, well, you might as well drop down dead on the spot and get it over with. That's her maiden name, by the way, which I notice she took up pretty sharpish after I'd left that first night—can't have reached the front gate before she was scraping off the gold-embossed Scott from her matching pen-and-pencil set.

So I'm stood there, getting the Look.

"Hello then," I say.

"You're early," she says.

Well, I knew I was of course, but like a dope, I say, "Am I?"

This only confirmed her belief that I'm irresponsible (high up on the list of Scott's Crimes, about Number Three I reckon. You're familiar with One and Two—I'm a cheat and a liar—and I can bring you up to speed on the other 437 later). Lesson One in Braddon Logic: Responsible fathers always know the exact time so that they aren't late (ah-ha, I hear you say, but you *weren't* late—but we are operating on Braddon rules here, so listen up and learn). If you're early, you can't be paying attention to the time so it's as bad as being late. Now here's the crowning cherry: except that it's *worse* because it means you might be trying to sneak an extra ten minutes with your own flesh-and-blood child—even though you already have a more than generous allowance of all day Sunday plus a phone call every other day. What other woman would be so spectacularly fair and decent about the whole thing?

Gail crosses her arms.

"It's important for you to turn up at the time when Rosalie's expecting you."

Nice, very nice. Blame the kiddy, why don't you?

"At least I'm not late." Mistake. Knew it as soon as I said it.

She snorted.

"Not like you were three weeks ago."

"That was only ten minutes."

"Fine. Be late if you like, if you don't mind letting down your only daughter."

"But I'm *early*."

"Oh, so you do know when you're supposed to be here."

You're beginning to see that I might not be the only villain of the piece after all, aren't you?

See, before this, before I left, it was easy. Being a dad, I mean. I didn't think about it from one day to the next. Specially not with Nat—it was just like hanging out with a mate, we'd watch a vid, go out on the bikes, down to the coast, fishing sometimes, roller-blading, stuff like that. I'd get in from work, shout, "Hiya! I'm back!" and make myself a cup of tea. Natty'd be up in his room on his computer or in the kitchen leaning against the furniture, he's always leaning against things or only half sitting on chairs so you think that he's going to fall over any second now. Any second now.

If he'd been upstairs, he'd shamble down and stand half in the fridge drinking milk or Coke, gulping it down like he's been in the desert for a month. And I say, "All right?" and nod and that's the cue for him to tell me what's occurring, what's gone on at school. Only Nat never says what he's learned, nothing like that, it's all like what's going down, what the teachers are up to, who's got in the swimming team, who thinks they're an ace diver but they're not, who's sucking up, who's clueless and who's cool. He does impressions, of the teachers mostly, but sometimes all the parts so it seems like you've suddenly got a whole class in the kitchen, with him doing the voices and the faces and the way they move, impersonating Miss Robson and the way she tugs at her pants when she thinks no-one's watching and bangs the board rubber down on the desk to get everyone's attention, and Mr Marks with the world's worst ties which he's always fiddling with, stroking the end, only when Natty does it, he puts on this creepy face like he's a lech, molesting someone, and it's dead funny.

Then I see Rosie's getting all antsy, sitting on her hands to keep herself calm 'cause she's more polite than the rest of us and thinks it's rude to interrupt. Which it is, of course. Even I know that. It's just I forget. A lot. Anyway, Gail's attempts to give the kids some manners seem to have rubbed off on Rosie at least. So I say, "And you, Rosie love? Good day at the office?" She likes that. Makes her feel grown up.

And so she tells me, well us, but Nat's not one of the world's greatest listeners and Gail's in the utility room, putting in a wash or taking one out or foraging in the freezer. Rosie says what she did and what she learned and what Kira said and what Josie said and who got told off and if she got a gold star and who's winning on the star chart, until Nat interrupts, teasing her, "Come on, Rozza, our ears are falling off, they're worn out."

Then Gail says we're having chicken or chops or spaghetti or stir-fry or it's only sausage, egg and chips because she's sick of cooking and why doesn't someone else take a turn, when was she ever appointed Official Family Chef, for goodness' sake, but seeing as how we all love sausage, egg and chips we can't see why she's making so much fuss and at least it's not pasta some-thing-or-other *again*, we've got pasta coming out our ears. She says will someone *please* set the table, and we can fight it out among ourselves, she's not interested, but will someone just make sure it's done, straight away *please*, that means *now*, and don't forget mats and glasses and God, you'd think we should know by now how to set a table without needing a list itemizing every knife, fork and salt pot. So I grab the cutlery and Rosie gets the mats and Nat tries to look as if he's helping but mostly he's slowly pulling out drawers and closing them again until Gail says, "Nathan! Glasses! In the cupboard!" And he gets out four tumblers and when we go to sit down Gail puts hers back and takes a wine glass to fill up from the wine box in the fridge and I swap mine for a bigger glass and get myself a beer and the kids have Coke or milk or squash depending, and we all sit down and sometimes we talk and sometimes we mostly just feed our faces and sometimes we squabble and sometimes we don't, but any which way I didn't mind.

Because it was us, you see, our family, and I like it that way. *Liked* it that way.

And now, every second, I'm thinking, should I do this? Should I do that? What do I do now? Nat won't see me, even speak to me, and I don't know what to do with Rosie. I can't bring her back to Jeff's to watch TV because the place is too depressing and anyway there's nothing on Sunday daytime.

See, there's this whole huge day to fill and I feel like I've kind of borrowed her or like she's been let out from prison or the zoo and I've got to give her the best treat day ever only I don't have a clue where to start and what if it's so awful she says she doesn't want to come any more? I look at her little face, with her sweet cheeks and her serious straight eyebrows, and I have no idea what she's thinking or what I should be doing, only I know whatever we do, Gail will hear about it and God knows I better get something right soon if I'm to have a hope in Hell—if we're to, well, if I'm to have a chance.

I'm just making it up as I go along, hoping no-one will twig, no-one will say, "What are you doing? Don't you know how to be a proper father? What on earth's wrong with you?" And I'd have to admit I don't know, I've no idea. And they'll know I'm an impostor, and so will I, still desperately trying to bluff my way, hoping I'll never have to show my real hand. Shit, there should be instructions for this, a manual or something: Lessons for a Sunday Father.

Rosie

On Sundays, my dad comes to pick me up for our day out. Usually, we go for a bike ride by the sea or round the reservoir and Dad says soon we will both be fit as athletes and can enter the Olympics. Last time we had races and whoever won had to let go the handlebars and you put your hands up above your head like this because you know you're going to get the gold medal. If we go on the road or the promenade, I have to wear my helmet, Mum says, but Dad says I can take it off at the reservoir or in the woods because it is a dirt track and Dad says it'll be OK if I fall off because my head will bounce and not go splat. Dad doesn't wear a helmet even on the road because he says it makes him look like a boiled egg. On the promenade, you get people roller-blading. It is boys mostly, like Nat. I've been three times with Nat and Dad, but that was before. Nat's the best but he always said Dad is not bad for an old guy. Dad was the oldest person there. Mum came one time to watch but she hasn't got skates and she said she hasn't got the least interest in getting any because she'd be bound to fall over and break her neck and having three daredevil kids in the family's more than enough to worry about and someone's got to be the sensible one. But there aren't three in any case—there is only Nat and me.

Nat doesn't come with us on Sundays and he keeps getting all cross and kicking things and Mum sighs at him and tells him not to, he'll damage the furniture and we can't be buying new things at the drop of a hat now. He acts like it's all my fault that he's missing out on everything but no-one said he wasn't allowed to go. I think he does want to come too, only now he's said he doesn't and he can't take it back without looking stupid. And, anyway, it *is* fair for me to have Dad all to myself because Nat used to go fishing with Dad loads of times and I only went twice because Mum said it was too cold and I'd catch my death and wouldn't I rather be all snuggly with her and stay up a bit past my bedtime than be huddled on a beach in the pitch black with the wind whistling through my bones? But Nat said he and Dad used to get chips and it was really brilliant and he caught loads of flatties but that it was right that I didn't go because it was too tough and I'd only cry and spoil things. But I wouldn't have.

Kira says I'm the same as her now, but I'm not. I'm different because my mum and dad are not divorced, only separated like Charlotte's and William's and Kelvin's. And there's Sara and Florence too, but they don't have dads at all, so they don't count. Kira said my mum and dad will get divorced because once your parents are living in two houses then it happens automatically she says and there is nothing you can do to stop it, everyone knows that. Only little kids think their parents will make it up and live happily ever after.

My mum has not said anything about a divorce and nor has my dad, but I 'spect they are not saying because they think I am just a kid and too little to know anything. Parents are always doing that and it is just silly. But I think that they ought to try living in one house again. Mum always says if you can't do something you should try, try again but they are not trying at all. For a start, it is cheaper because if you live in two places you have to get two loaves of bread and two jars of strawberry jam and two fridges and two cookers and two of everything. And if you only need one of something you'd have more money so you can get proper Nikes instead of lookalike ones from the market and your mum and dad can get you a mobile phone.

Another reason is, why my dad should come back and live with us is that we have four chairs in the kitchen and at mealtimes Mum used to sit on one, me on one, Nat sort of on one and Dad on one. And when Dad finished eating, he used to pick up his plate and pretend he was going to throw it right across the room like a frisbee but then he went over and put it in the dishwasher like Mum taught us to. And now there is an empty chair and Mum moved it away from the table and put it by the wall but it does not look right.

Gail

Nat makes sure he's not at home when Scott calls for Rosie. Once or twice he has been in, but it must have made it that much harder for him—seeing her go skipping down the stairs off for treats with his dad. Usually he disappears to Steve's for the day. God knows what they get up to; Nat says they do homework or go swimming and just "hang out"—whatever that means.

When he was little, Nat used to act as if Scott was exclusively his dad, and they were best of friends. I'd watch the pair of them chasing round the garden, rolling on the ground and yelling. And it wasn't just Scott trying to humour Nat either—he was loving every minute of it himself. Then I'd call out, "Tea's ready!" and tell them both to wash their hands, as if Scott was just another child.

"See this?" Scott would say, holding up a bit of cauliflower on the end of his fork. "It's a meteor fragment. Gives you supernatural powers if you eat it."

Nat would sit there with his mouth open, eyes huge and serious, trying to decide if it could really be true. And then he'd eat it. But if I tried to get vegetables down him, he'd cross his arms and shake his head. I'd coax him or bribe him with the promise of something nice for sweet, but he'd sit there shaking his head at me until I gave up.

Scott's own childhood was—well, short on fun, shall we say? I can't imagine he ever played like that with *his* father. Not a man who's over-fond of children, I'd say, 'specially not his own. Scott doesn't like to talk about it much, says the past's the past and it's best forgotten. But his face gets this thoughtful look—just like Nat's when he was little and wondering whether a cauliflower floret could really have come off a meteor—as if he's imagining an entirely different universe.

With Scott and Nat being so close, Nat never showed much sign of being jealous of Rosie. He's always teased her, of course, but there was a gentleness to it; if anything, he was protective of her. One time, some older girl at school had had a go at Rosie. I was all for rushing straight down to the school and speaking to the teacher, but Scott wouldn't let me—"You've got to let kids sort this stuff out on their own. She's got to stand up for herself. You're not going to be riding to the rescue when she's twenty-five, are you? Or when she's forty?" I suppose he was right, but I thought he was being callous at the time. Then, the next morning at breakfast, Nat said Rosie wouldn't be needing a lift because he'd be walking her in. Rosie just smiled, swinging her legs to and fro, and chewing her toast. And he did. He walked her in and met her at the end of the day three days in a row. And we never heard another peep about this other girl.

But now, since Rosie's been going off with Scott on their own, Nat's changed. He's always trying to get a rise out of her, saying she's just a baby or that she's being a goody-goody. So I end up defending her, of course, and telling him off—and that makes it seem like I'm always against him, and never on his side. With Scott gone, it must feel as though no-one's on his side. I wish I was better at this, or that at least I could be more laid back about it.

Scott always had a way with Nat. If Nat was in a strop or had done something naughty, Scott would make it all right somehow. He'd go up to Nat's room and the two of them would fool about on the computer for a while or they'd suddenly both appear in the hall and sit squashed side by side on the stairs, putting on their skates and saying they were going "for a blade round the block." They'd be bumping each other's arms, their heads bent, racing to see who could lace up their skates first. Then they'd sail off down the front path, leaving the door wide open, Scott taller of course, but looking like a young lad himself, racing Nat to the corner, the two of them, arms swinging, calling to each other. And then they'd come swooping back, banging on the front door and ringing the bell because neither of them had thought to take their keys with them. They'd skate into the hall and come right on into the kitchen till I told them to take their skates off. And they'd be laughing about something they'd seen or some neighbour they'd frightened the life of, whizzing past at 90 miles an hour, and to look at Nat you'd never know he'd even been in a strop.

And when Nat used to come back from swimming practice, Scott would cup his hand like this, as if he was holding up a stopwatch. He'd just look at Nat and Nat would say his fastest time that day and they'd do that high-five thing. Scott was always dead chuffed, bursting with pride. I am too, of course, but I never know what to ask. If I say, "So, how's the diving going?" it's the week he's concentrating on his arm action or if I say, "Fast time today?" they're doing stamina training and time's not important. Scott just seemed to *know* somehow.

It's not that I wish Scott was back. It's not that. It's just that he could handle Nat, you see. And I have to face it, I can't. I don't seem to be able even to have a two-minute chat with him without it escalating into a row. I don't know how to talk to my own son.

Thank heavens for Rosie. If it wasn't for her, I'd have to throw in the towel and resign from being a mother. It's odd, if anything, I'd have thought Nat would be the more robust one of the two of them, but I think maybe we've underestimated our Rosie quite a bit. She gets this wistful look on her face sometimes, but otherwise she seems to be doing OK. Most of the time, she just seems to get on with it, whatever it is. Like with Sundays and seeing her dad. It must have been so strange for her at first, but now, after just a few weeks, it's as if she'd never had her Sundays any other way. She has her bag sorted, she's eaten her breakfast, cleared away her plate and cup, and is all ready and waiting for the second Scott comes walking up the path. I bet we could all learn a thing or two from Rosie.

Scott

Yesterday, I phoned Gail at work. No, I wasn't looking for a repeat of our last civilized discussion, but I was sick of washing out the same four pairs of underpants in Jeff's basin.

I reckon they have some kind of unwritten code of honour in GPs' surgeries, like all the receptionists agree to never answer the phone before thirty-two rings, a sort of Customer's Charter in reverse. Anyway, she answers the phone in her special singsong surgery voice: "Huntsham-Surgery-Good-Morning," her voice going up at the end as if expecting you to applaud.

"Hi," I say. "It's me."

"Yes? Why are you ringing me here?" Her voice dropping with each word, sounding less and less singsongy and more and more drop-dead-you-bastardy. "Don't ring me at work."

"Oh, take a chill pill for God's sake. I just want to come and fetch a couple of shirts and things."

"Good. I've nearly finished sorting out your rubbish. Come tomorrow morning, at 9.30, after the kids have gone to school."

"But I—"

"So that's 9.30 a.m. then, for your appointment." Singsong again now. And she hangs up on me.

You won't believe this. I get home about twenty past nine this morning, but I think well, hang on a sec here, let's hold fire till half past and not give Gail another excuse to have an epi. So I'm sitting in the car around the corner so's not to look like a complete prat in case one of the neighbours sees me waiting ten yards from my own house. It gets to nearly half past, so I lock up and stroll towards home. Now, get this, as I'm fiddling with the sodding latch on the gate—I always meant to fix that—I see that there's a note on the front door, like for the milkman or whoever. Then I see that it says SCOTT on it. I mean, is she trying to make me look small deliberately or what? Well, clearly she is. What if someone saw it? So I open it and it says: S—*Stuff round the back.*—G.

Right. That's it. Fifteen years of marriage and that's the best she can manage. So I'm starting to get a bit cross by now, and thinking I've had it with being all Mr Calm and Reasonable and bending over backwards and waiting until the exact second just so's not to annoy her.

So I go round the back and there on our patio is our big green suitcase, two bulging black bin bags and two cardboard boxes. Taped to the suitcase is another note. This one says: *You can have any other stuff I find once I've had time to sort it out. Don't* [underlined three times, the pen lines gouged deep into the paper] *call me at work*.

PS The dentist phoned to say you'd missed your appointment on Friday.

Shit. I'd forgotten the sodding dentist. Hardly surprising, given my whole life's gone down the tubes. My teeth aren't exactly top of my worries.

I take a look into the boxes, peeling back the carrier bags that Gail had taped on top like lids. I don't get it. She can barely manage to say hello to me on a Sunday but she goes to the trouble of taping Safeway bags over my stuff so it won't get wet if it rains. Maybe it means she still cares. Hoo-sodding-ray, she cares. In one of them there's my waterproof radio, with the hook to hang it from the shower rail, and a weird mixture of stuff: my alarm clock with Superman on it that Nat got me for my birthday one year, two pairs of old trainers that I never wear any more, my mug that says "Shouldn't you have left for work by now?" on it.

. . . And there's my beach towel on top of the other one. I grab one end of it and go to flick it out, thinking huh, surprised Miss Prim and Tidy didn't fold it properly, realizing the same second that it's like that 'cause she's bundled it round something, something quite light but maybe a bit fragile and as I'm thinking that, the something, *somethings* it turns out, hit the sodding patio.

They're face down, but I know what they are, know it straight away, like I'd know Rosie from the back anywhere, with her funny walk, doing a sort of skip every few steps, and her white socks all pulled up so neat and those funny things girls wear in their hair—like plastic ladybirds or bees or butterflies—bugs basically but in pink or, in Rosie's case, mauve of course. And Natty, shuffling and scuffling along like he's got astronaut boots on, and it takes too much energy to lift his feet properly, kicking at the paving stones, swaggering from side to side trying to look tough, his hair all over the shop, a stranger to the hairbrush, that's what Gail says. Yup, I love that, a stranger to the hairbrush. Anyways, they were their school photos, the latest ones, only taken a couple of months ago. I know, I know—we're sad suckers, aren't we, we always say we won't buy them, they're overpriced, we'll take our own, they'll be much better, all that. Then Rosie brings back her envelope and Natty brings back his and they're saying, "Don't get them, Dad, Mum—they're rubbish."—Actually, Nat says "They're crap" but you get my drift. "Don't waste your money," they say, but Gail and me sitting there, looking at them as if they're photos of the only two children on the entire planet and how could we possibly not buy them?

They'd fallen one half on top of the other. I felt—I don't know—half scared even to pick them up. Even though I can see what they are, I don't want to see them really, truly 'cause I'll know what it means, what Gail means by giving them to me: This is it. This is all you, Scott, are getting. I have the real thing. You can have the photographs.

The most recent ones, too, so I'll be reminded every time I look at them that this is when I lost them, this is when they stopped being my kids, like they'd died or something.

I pick up the top one and turn it over. It's the one of Rosie, unbroken thank God, looking back at me with a small shy smile, her hair in whatsits, bunches, sticking out either side of her head like handles, but all smooth and soft like Gail's. She's wearing a mauve top, her best top, specially for the photo. I remember Gail ironing it at the time.

"But Mu-um, I've *got* to have it. It's the photos today."

"Well, honestly, Rosie, why on earth didn't you tell me before? It's not even dry. You'll catch pneumonia if you wear it."

"But I *have* to. It's my best one."

"You're a little nuisance sometimes, you really are. I've got better things to do than stand here all morning trying to iron this dry. Right—I'm putting it in a bag, Rosie, and you can change into it for your photo. It's too damp to wear all day. No arguments, please."

And Nat joining in: "Hey, Rozza. Act like you're a model—Excuse me, Miss, I have to change now for my photographs. Is the make-up lady here yet?"

"Don't put ideas in her head, Nat, and HURRY UP—you'll be late."

*   *   *

The memory makes me smile. Then I pick up the other photo. Nat. There is a horrible noise as I pick it up. The sound of edges of broken glass grinding against each other. And there is Nat, my Natty, staring coolly back at me, his familiar half-smile covered by a crack, his face fractured by splintered glass. I sink to my knees then, there on the patio, holding this broken picture of my son, thinking what have I done, what have I done? I turn it over, scrabbling at the back, undoing the frame to pull out the picture, rescue him from the sharp shards of glass.

I shake out the pieces from the frame—leaving a sort of semicircle of fragments around me, like when I eat a bread roll in a restaurant, a fan of tell-tale crumbs—Scott was here. That's it, I thought, that's what it'll be like—splinters wherever I go—work, home, in the street, me walking along, leaving a trail of shattered glass behind me, shattered people, lives, a swathe of destruction in my wake. What have I done? What have I done?

I kneel there on the patio, holding the photo in both hands, for what feels like an age but perhaps it's only a few minutes. Then I get up and cast around for something to sweep up the glass, try to shove it to one side with the edge of my shoe. Ten seconds with a dustpan and brush would do it. What happens next, I don't think about it, not really, what I'm doing. It just seems the obvious thing to do. I wrap the beach towel round my fist and I smash one of the small windows of the glass lean-to—conservatory, Gail calls it, but it's not exactly all palms and tea tables, more of a back porch with ideas above its station—and reach down to open the catch on a big window. I clamber in and find the key to the back door Gail stuck under a plant pot after the time Rosie got locked out the back and was calling for ages and we couldn't hear her over the TV. Too easy, far too easy. We really should have locks on all these windows, I think, as I come into the kitchen. Hunt about for the dustpan, where does she keep the sodding thing? Not in the broom cupboard. Under the sink. What's she keep it there for? Let myself out the back door, sweep up and come back in. Then realize there's now even more glass, on the floor of the lean-to and in the plant pots. I clear up as well as I can, picking out bits from the leaves and the soil and going at the floor with a cloth. There's a whacking great size 10 footprint on the tiled floor near where I'd jumped down. I nearly left it there, like a message to Gail—don't think you can keep me out.

I check the time. Gail usually finishes work at two and she often trots off to the shops instead of dragging back here and going out again to pick up Rosie from school. So that means that at most I'd have till about ten to four and at least until twenty past two if she comes straight back. Loads of time to get back to work, pick up a new pane of glass, come pack, putty it in, clean up and wah-boom, no sign of Scott on the premises. I begin to feel a bit pleased with myself. I picture myself doing it every week if I felt like it—come in, help myself to a coffee, biscuits, apple from the fruit bowl, have a poke round, see what everyone's up to. After all, it's my house. Still, I thought, better not get carried away now, as I'm pushed for time. As it is, the putty won't dry in time and it'll pong a bit, but she's got no reason to be poking about out here this time of year so she's not likely to notice. Besides, I've got no choice. I'll have to risk it. Either that, or leave it broken and next thing I know I'll have the police rolling up at work.

Then I catch sight of my house keys, in an ashtray— nice touch, Gail—they still have my key fob on, with the photo of Gail in it, the one I took when we went on holiday to Cyprus. Her hair was longer then and it spilled over her shoulders and she looked tanned and happy and sexy. I pick up the keys and put them in my pocket, then I take them out again. The ashtray's on the sideboard in the lounge so I reckon she'd twig right away if they were suddenly gone. Another time check. I'd have to take them to the key place on the way back to work, have a new set cut while I pick up the glass for the window, come back, replace my old keys in the ashtray, do the glass, clean up, then skedaddle. And time's ticking on. Jeez, I hope she goes shopping.

See, told you. It was a piece of piss. Well, almost. I dropped off the keys, then zoomed back to work. Martin was out on a job and Gary was bleating about some bloke who'd told him to get a move on when he was cutting. Denise said where had I been, there were umpteen messages for me in the book, and had I remembered to look in on that job in Hawes Crescent, no. 14, they wanted a quote. Yes, I said, I was going there now, right now, and could she tear out my messages and hand them over, I'd do them on the move, no, I couldn't stop now, something had come up, and Gary while you're standing there with your mouth open, cut us a piece of glass, mate, here's the measurements, and make it snappy. Cheers.

Afterwards, I went back to work and sorted out the thousand and one problems they'd managed to create while I was out, told Lee it was his turn to tidy up, then sat down with Harry and allocated the jobs for the next day. My heart was still racing but I didn't mind. I kind of liked it, matter of fact. It made me feel alive. I dug my hand down into my left-hand pocket every now and then, just to feel the newly cut keys, pressing my fingertip along the metal zigzag of the latch key, the chunky prongs of the Chubb. They made me feel excited, somehow, hopeful, like they were more than just the keys to my house, that they were the keys that would give me back my life.

Nat

It's not fair. Mum keeps picking on me while Rosie's little Miss Perfect the whole time. Makes me sick. Mum said she was talking to some doctor at the surgery and he said how it was normal for boys of my age "to be clumsy and knock things over a lot." He said there was some research done a couple of years ago that showed it was all to do with growing too quick so we can't tell how far away things are like if we're putting a mug on the table and we think the table's nearer than it is. Mum said this all casual like she's saying what's for eats tonight, so I said,

"So? What's your point?" kicking at the other kitchen chair while I'm sitting there.

"My *point*, Nathan—don't kick the chair—is that there's no need for you to worry about being a bit, well, awkward, at this age. It's just a normal part of growing-up for lots of boys. I'm sorry if I get at you about knocking things over. I'll try to be a bit more understanding now I know you can't help it."

I rocked my chair back onto its back legs, pushing against the table leg and started counting off on my fingers, making my points: "Number one, I do not 'knock things over a lot.' Number two, where do you get off talking to some stupid arse—"

"Nathan!"

"—doctor bloke about me? Three, that's just crap, that is—how can getting tall make you not know where the stupid table is? He must be bonkers. And four—"

She looked at her watch, then back at me. God, that really gets to me. Every time.

"Is this going on much longer, Nathan? Only I've got to get off to church to confess to being a bad mother. They let you off with only three Hail Marys if you get there before ten."

"Oh ha, ha. Excuse me while I pick myself up off the floor, I'm laughing so hard. And *four*—you're always saying it's rude to interrupt—"

"Is that number four . . . ?"

"You did it again! You did it again! I don't believe this."

"You've forgotten what number four is, haven't you, Nathan?"

"No, I haven't. I haven't. It's just you interrupting me all the time. It's a miracle I can speak at all having grown up with you lot and Rosie squealing all the time and you being all smart-arsy and Dad being—well—"

I saw her blink when I mentioned Dad. Good. Serves her right for being so mean and talking about me to a doctor as if I'm some kind of loony or something.

"Anyway, I didn't forget. Number *four* is, I am *not*

awkward and don't go round telling everyone I'm some kind of dribbling retard who drops things all the time." My foot slipped on the table leg then so my chair suddenly rocked forward again with a thunk. Mum rolled her eyes in that "Kids, eh!" way she does, so I kicked the table leg and got up and shoved the chair in until it hit the table. Then I walked out and nearly knocked myself out on the stupid doorframe. So I kicked that as well and went up to my room, digging my toes in to make semicircles on the stair carpet just to annoy her.

She came and knocked on my door when tea was ready but I said I didn't want any. What's the point? If I'm not there, she and Rosie can eat on their own and be all giggly and girlie. I'm not listening to all that. So I waited till they'd done, then I went down and put mine in the microwave and had it in front of the TV. I'd rather eat on my own anyhow.

Scott

Harry's taken to asking me if I'm all right practically every half an hour. He's not clueless, he knows something's up. If Gail had been sensible and taken me back by now, I'd never have had to tell him. It's weird though, aside from my kids, Harry's the last person in the world I'd want to know how badly I've loused up— but at the same time, it'd be a real load off my mind to tell him. I don't like hiding stuff from him. He's always been straight with me. Maybe it won't be so bad. I just don't want to feel like I've let him down, you know? Harry wouldn't cheat on Maureen in a thousand years. It's not that he's blind to other women, he's got an eye for a short skirt same as any man, but he'd never act on it, never. Harry couldn't tell a lie to save his life.

I feel worse about telling him than my parents. I'll get round to notifying them at some point, but it's not like they're ringing up morning, noon and night enquiring after my welfare, you know? They're quite fond of Rosie, I guess, in their own way, but I once heard my dad say to Nat, "You're just like your father was at your age," and, no, it wasn't meant as a compliment. Luckily, Nat thought it was—he looked up to me then—and he went round with a big smile on his face. I've never forgotten it. I looked at my dad and I didn't say a word, but inside I was thinking, "See, you miserable git, not everyone thinks I'm a waste of space. My son loves me—and that's all that matters." Dad looked away and poured himself some more beer without offering me any.

The only reason I'll have to tell them at all, the parents, I mean—yeah, that's how I think of them, *the* parents, like *the* Browns or *the* Smiths, like someone else's family. We happen to be related but I figure it was just down to a glitch in the universe or a mix-up at the hospital. If it wasn't for the fact I look practically like a replica of Himself when he was younger, I'd swear for sure I'd been adopted. Though why anyone who doesn't like kids would take the trouble to adopt them I've no idea. Oh yeah, I'll have to let them know—and suffer the barrage of I-told-you-so and marriage-is-for-life and but-it's-no-surprise-to-us stuff and other tokens of parental love and support—I'll have to tell them I'm not at home just now in case one of them croaks, 'cause they'll need someone to pay the undertaker.

Anyway. Telling Harry.

Friday. It's ten to eight in the morning and I'm sitting in the office. One good thing about staying with Jeff is I'm getting in to work earlier and earlier every day to spend as little time as possible in his house. I hear Harry come in. The lads aren't here yet, but I've not got long so I know I'd better get on with it.

"Harry?"

"Yup." He sits down and looks at me over the tops of his glasses. This is hard. I want to tell him, but I don't know what to say. Maybe I'll do it later.

"Coffee?" Just tell him for God's sake, just say it.

"Oh, go on then." He nods and stretches up for the green invoice file. "And Scott?"

I'm on my feet, heading for the kettle.

"Fill me in some time about what's up with you, will you? The suspense is doing me in."

I stand behind him, so I can't see his face. "You've not got a terminal whatsit, illness, or anything?" he says.

Weirdly, the thought makes me laugh. Life would be a whole lot better, a whole lot simpler if I was dying. I'd be so brave, struggling to speak as Gail lovingly tips a glass of water to my lips, tears pouring down her cheeks as she whispers how much she loves me, how she can't imagine life without me. Sheila would rush down from Scotland to be by my bedside. Russ might even fly over from Canada, you never know. And the kids—ah, no. No. At least I'm not dying. Things could be worse. (If you're listening, God, that's not a request, that last statement; this is plenty bad enough, thanks.)

"No, no." I pat him on the shoulder. "I might look as though I'm at death's door. And, yeah, I feel like it too, but physically I am A-OK and—"

We both jump as the bell dings—someone's come in the main door.

"Aww-right?" Lee's face appears round the edge of the doorway. He comes barging right in and starts telling us how smashed he got last night, then the phone starts going, Gary arrives, blinking and bleary-eyed, and Denise comes in and starts fussing round my desk.

Finally, I get off the phone and Harry looks across at me.

"We've not been fishing for ages," he says. "Fancy going down the coast one night?"

I nod. Fishing. Fresh air. Sound of the sea. Clear my head a bit.

"Yeah, good one. When?"

"I'm easy. Tonight?"

"Why not? You check the tides, I'll get the bait."

Even though I've got the keys to home now, I'm not going to chance zipping in and whipping away my fishing gear. I reckon Gail would be bound to notice. We could just take Harry's tilley lamp and windbreak, but I still need my rods and stool. I'll have to call Gail. Oh joy, oh joy.

"Hi, it's me, but you can keep your hair on, I'm not ringing to get up your nose. I just want to pick up my fishing stuff."

"Good. I've been meaning to clear out that cupboard for ages."

"Well, there you are then. This'll give you a head start."

I go over at three, before Gail has to go fetch Rosie from school.

She doesn't say a word when she opens the door, just gestures to the cupboard.

"I don't need to take it all now . . ." I start selecting the stuff I need just for tonight.

"I'd rather you didn't leave anything."

It takes me three trips, backwards and forwards to the car.

"Well, that's that then." I stand on the front step. "Gail, I—"

She's not looking at me, but she shakes her head, her mouth pinched tight shut.

"Sorry," she says, "I can't—it's—I have to go. Rosie . . ."

"Course." I want to hold her, I want to stroke her hair and hold her close as I can, tell her I can make everything all right again. I try to gulp down the lump in my throat. The door starts to close.

"Tell her I'll see her Sunday!"

We pull up by the promenade just after 9.30 p.m. Harry gets out and looks up at the sky. It's a clear night, cold but not raining at least, and the stars are sharp and bright as pins. There's already a line of blokes dotted along the shore. Fathers and sons mostly, I reckon, but maybe some are just mates like me and Harry. We lug all the stuff down onto the beach and set up.

And now we're done fiddling with the rods and the bait and the tripods and the shelter and the lamp. There's just me and Harry and the sound of the sea sucking at the shingle and the sky dark and huge above us.

"Um . . ." I start promisingly. Why is this so hard? "Might even land a bit of cod tonight."

"Only if we go down the chip shop." Harry laughs and lights up one of those funny slim cigars. God, I'd love a smoke. I haven't touched one for nearly seven years, but I could murder a fag right now. I mustn't. I promised Nat I wouldn't. "So, what's occurring then?"

"Thing is . . ." I get up and start fiddling with my reel. ". . . I'm not exactly living at home right now . . ." Firm in the tripod a bit more with the edge of my foot ". . . See, Gail and me—well, she sort of threw me out and she doesn't seem in a tearing hurry to have me back."

Harry doesn't laugh. He doesn't make any crass jokes. He nods and passes me a Kit-Kat.

"Hm-mm. Another woman, was it?"

"Well, yes—and no. Yes, there was, but it was very brief and it really didn't count, and no, there isn't now and it didn't mean anything anyway. But Gail won't believe me or, even if she does, she's using it as an excuse to get shot of me. She looks at me like I'm a bit of dogshit on her shoe."

Harry laughs at that, but not in a snide way, and he turns to face me.

179

"So, where've you been staying?"

"At my mate Jeff's. He lives like a student, only without the books or the brains. He's forty-two but still believes in the washing-up fairy—just thinks it keeps missing his house by accident. I spend every night clearing up. I've never done so much cleaning. Still, stops me thinking. About everything."

"Stay with us." It's somewhere between an invitation and a command and his tone takes me by surprise. I wonder if he's just saying it because he feels sorry for me.

"It's decent of you, mate, but I—"

"I mean it. We've got a spare room. We'd love to have you, give Maureen someone to fuss over again."

"No, Harry." I poke another finger of Kit-Kat into my mouth for something to do but it feels thick and sticky on my tongue. "I wouldn't want to put you out." I look down at my feet.

Harry picks up the Thermos and pours us both some coffee.

"You wouldn't be, you daft bugger. Not at all. It'd mean a lot to us, in fact. You know, since Chris went away . . ." That's his son, who went off for a trip Down Under years ago, met this Aussie woman and settled down, never came back, 'cept about once every three or four years "You've been—well. You know what I mean." He gets out his hankie and vigorously wipes his nose with it. It's a white cotton one, the sort no-one has any more, 'cept old guys like Harry. "You're more than welcome's all I'm saying."

"It should only be for a couple of nights," I assure Maureen as I stand on her front step the next evening, having told Jeff I couldn't impose on his generous hospitality a moment longer (if I stayed another night there, I'd be tempted to do away with myself—eat the contents of his fridge for a guaranteed death by salmonella). Maureen flutters round me, trying to take off my jacket while I'm still holding my bag plus some chocolates I picked up for her on the way. "I'm sure Gail and I can straighten things out." My voice sounds confident, the voice of a man barely disturbed by a minor temporary setback. I have resolved to be positive. She can't really mean it's all over, can she? She's just having me on, trying to put the wind up me.

"You stay as long as you like." Harry claps me on the shoulder and takes my bag.

"It's nice for us to have a bit of comp'ny." Maureen toddles off into the kitchen. "Nice cup of tea, Scott?"

I fancy a nice beer actually. Or a nice several beers. Or a double Scotch and soda.

"Tea would be lovely, Maureen. Thank you." See, I do have manners when I need to. Gail says I'm beyond help, but then everything I do or say is wrong to her, so what can you expect?

The spare room is bright and cheerful enough and the bed feels comfy when I sit on it.

"This was Chris's room." Maureen says it with reverence, as if he'd died or something, but I resist the urge to bow my head. "You've not much with you." She nods at my bag.

"No." The back of my car is chock-a-block with my stuff in bags and boxes covered over with that old check blanket, and Harry's stowed my fishing things in his shed. "There's a bit more in the car."

"Fine!" Harry opens the wardrobe doors wide. "Plenty of space in here. Plenty of space!"

I feel like a kid who's been allowed to go and stay with his favourite aunt. Not that I ever did, 'cept for one time when Mum was ill with some "trouble in the downstairs department," as she put it. I don't know what was wrong with her because everyone stopped speaking any time us kids came in. She had to go into hospital for a few days, though, and because there were three of us—Russ and Sheil and me—and obviously my dad couldn't take care of a hamster for half an hour, never mind three children, we were palmed off to three different houses. I went and stayed with Jessie, Mum's younger sister. I don't know why we never saw her the rest of the time, I think maybe there'd been a bit of a falling-out. Well, for me, it was like being treated like royalty. When I got there with my pyjamas and that in a carrier bag, I didn't have anything so grand as a suitcase, Aunt Jessie gave me a hug and a kiss then told me to sit by the fire while she made the tea. Then she called me through to the kitchen and I had lamb chops (two!) with crinkle-cut chips and there were peas and tomatoes and mush-rooms. And fizzy limeade to drink. It was bright green. Then I had a big deep bath, deep enough to practise hold-ing my breath underwater, and they let me stay up and watch a film on telly with them. Then Aunt Jessie said, "Off to bed with you now, Dennis." I know, it's before I decided to call myself Scott. "You pop up and I'll come and tuck you in in five minutes. Don't forget to brush your teeth."

And she did! She came up and tucked me in! Like in a storybook. She sat on the edge of the bed and told me not to worry about my mum (I wasn't), and she'd be bet-ter soon and I said, "If she doesn't get better, can I come and live here?"

She laughed and said I was a little angel, but that I wasn't to upset myself, of course Mum would get better.

Then she bent over and kissed me—right here on my forehead. She tiptoed to the door.

"Shall I leave the landing light on, or do you not mind the dark now you're a big boy?"

At home, we barely had the lights on at all—"I'm not burning money leaving lights on day and night."

And then I did something I've never done since, something we used to have to do at school, something I'd stopped bothering with once I'd realized it didn't work.

I prayed.

I prayed that I could live there for ever with Aunt Jessie and Uncle Mikey, I prayed that they'd like me so much that they wouldn't let Mum and Dad have me back. Worse, I prayed that Mum wouldn't get better so they'd have to keep me. Then I prayed that, if I couldn't stay, then would God at least let me die in the night so that the last thing I'd know was the smell of chops coming up the stairs, the murmur of my aunt and uncle talking in the front room, the sheets and blankets tucked so tight around me I could barely move and the spot on my forehead where I'd been kissed good night.

Rosie

Dad has gone to stay at Harry and Maureen's. He says it is only going to be for a few days most probably but that's what he said when he went to his friend Jeff's and he was there for weeks. I said is it like being on a sleep-over like if I go round Kira's or she comes to stay and we talk in the dark till her mum or my mum comes in and tells us to shut up and go to sleep. Dad said it wasn't quite the same because he sleeps in a different room, so he has nobody to talk to when they turn the light off. I wanted to know if him and Mum talked in the dark when he was still at home, but I thought maybe it would make him go all sad again so I never asked. I think mostly grown-ups don't talk much when they have a sleepover because that means they are doing IT. Nat says grown-ups are always shagging and even when they're not they're thinking about it or wanting to do it. He says he thinks about it the whole time, but I bet he doesn't because he won't even be fourteen for ages and ages, not till next year, and he's never done more than have a snog. Anyway, I think he's lying about them doing it all the time because when you listen to grown-ups they're always going on about how tired they are and what wouldn't they give to have more sleep. Dad says when you're a kid you spend your whole life wanting to stay up late but then when you're grown-up and can stay up as late as you like, all you want is to go to bed early. But when I'm a grown-up I will stay up till 3 or 4 o'clock in the morning most nights probably and I won't get tired at all. And I'll eat sweets in bed, I'm going to have this great big jar of them, pear drops and cola cubes and Fruitellas and sherbert lemons all mixed up together, right by the bed so I won't even have to get up and I'll never brush my teeth.

My dad phones me every other day at the same time and I sit on the stairs to be ready for 7 o'clock. Nat shouts at me to hurry up.

He goes, "What can you have to talk to him about? Any *normal* person would be dead bored of him by now after having to put up with him all day every Sunday."

"I don't *have* to. I like Sundays. You're just jealous because you keep missing everything and we do lots of things, and make up games and quizzes, and we have a completely brilliant time the whole day, much, much better than we would if you were there because you always spoil everything."

And anyhow, it's true. When Dad was at home, he was always talking to Nat and if I tried to say anything, Nat used to talk all over the top of me really loudly and Dad wouldn't listen to me any more. Nat said he didn't spoil things, that I was a little liar and he was going to get me. So I ran downstairs to Mum in the kitchen and she said, "What are you two tearing about like mad things for?" and Nat went back upstairs again and made a rude sign at me over the banister.

He is very cross with Dad and when I said I was seeing him on Sunday the first time he wouldn't even speak to me. He did after a bit, but only 'cause he forgot that he'd said he wasn't going to speak to me any more. I told Dad that Nat couldn't be cross with him for long, because even when he promises to hate you for ever and never talk to you ever, ever again, he always forgets after a while and then he is just Nat again and it is all right. And Dad said, yeah, he guessed so, then he patted me on the head as if I was only little, but I never said anything.

Gail

It was suppertime, so I knocked on Nat's door.

"Hey—www-dot-Nathan, it's mother-dot-com here. Any chance of seeing your adorable little face some time this century? I'm beginning to forget what you look like."

"Mn."

"Chicken stir-fry with noodles."

"Mn."

"Now, please. While it's hot."

It's so nice, I feel, that now my son is starting to grow up we can really communicate with each other. I'm thinking of buying another computer so at least I can e-mail him. It's the only language these people understand.

Only the other day I asked Rosie to call Nat down for their tea but when I came out to the hall, she was on the phone. She was phoning him on his mobile—in his bedroom, rather than go upstairs and call him.

"But you said you don't like us shouting in the house," she said, when I asked her what on earth she thought she was doing. As if this was a satisfactory explanation.

"And have you lost the use of your little legs?"

"This way is faster."

"No, it isn't, Rosie. It's lazy and it's a waste of money. Please don't do it again."

Eventually, Nat came shambling down the stairs, half folded over the stair-rail for some reason. It would be great if just once he could walk normally. He always seems to be moving in a peculiar way, like some action toy you'd test out to see how many poses you could put it in.

"Ah. You look kind of familiar," I said, ushering him to the table. "Nat, isn't it?"

He jerked his head up. Never try to be humorous with your children; it only gives them another reason to regard you with contempt.

"Anyone ever told you you'd make a great comedian? Really, I'm like totally laughing my socks off here."

I sighed, an all-too-familiar sigh which seems to have become a part of me. I am a woman who sighs. Most worrying. I never used to sigh. It's probably an age thing, which is even more worrying. I doled out the food—wrestling the noodles into three portions and roughly tipping the chicken and vegetables on top. It felt like I was filling a cattle trough, just providing fodder for hungry mouths, with no thought for pleasure or presentation. But cows probably have better table manners than Nat. Sorry, that was mean of me, he's not that bad. Actually, he is that bad. You should see how he eats spaghetti. I just make sure I'm not sitting directly opposite him so I don't have to have a full frontal view. I've given up trying to get him to eat normally. Maybe he'll grow into it in time.

"It's just I think it's important for us to sit down and eat together as a family . . ." There was a pause. I think I could have phrased that better. "It's good to eat together and talk, swap news and so on, hmm? I s'pose if it was up to you, Nat, no-one would ever have a real live conversation face-to-face; we'd sit in three different rooms and only communicate using a chat room on the Net, hmm?"

No response.

"You like us all eating together, don't you, Rosie?" Come on, can't I have someone on my side? Call for back-up, as Nat would say.

Rosie swung her legs and took a sip of her lemon squash.

"It's OK."

Massive enthusiasm all round, then.

"We're not becoming one of those families who eat on trays in front of the TV every night."

Nat stabbed at a piece of chicken as if he were trying to kill it. I fought a strong urge to rest my head gently on the pillow of noodles in front of me.

"Why ask then?" Nat picked up a single strand of noodle and lowered it from a height into his mouth. "You make out you're asking us what we think, but it's just some act so you can pretend you care. If me and Rosie wanted to eat nothing but chips and stay in our rooms the whole time, you wouldn't let us. You go on and on and on about having family meals, but we're not a family anyhow, so what difference does it make?"

Then he scraped his chair back from the table and walked out.

Well done, Gail, I thought. You handled that really well. I'd best give him a while to cool off. Still, it's more than he's said in days.

"Is this free-range?" Rosie said, poking at the chicken with her fork as if it had some disease.

"Yes," I lied, crossing my fingers under the table, the way I did when I was little. "Eat up now."

"'m not really hungry. Besides, I think I'm vegetarian again."

"Oh, *Rosie*. Well, just try and eat a little bit then, OK?"

"Can't I have a choc ice instead?"

I give up. I haven't got the energy for all this. It's not fair that I have to do everything on my own. I vote for somebody else to be the grown-up for a while so I can lie down in a darkened room. Preferably for about ten years. Maybe when I wake up, Rosie and Nat will be delightful, civilized adults bringing me cups of tea in bed and—who knows?—even putting their own clothes in the washing-machine. True, it's not that Scott was ever much help either, but at least I could kid myself that there was another adult at the helm. Don't tell anyone I said this but: Roll on Sunday. Rosie's out with Scott, Nat goes to Steve's. I make myself some breakfast and have it on a tray and it's back to bed for a couple of hours with a good book or the Sunday papers. Bliss. Sheer bliss.

Scott

I had a couple of jobs to do within spitting distance from home, and they took less time than I thought, so I figured I might as well pop in. Ever since I had those extra keys cut, they've been burning a hole in my pocket. So I parked round the corner, dodged from tree to tree up the road to give the net-twitchers something to worry about, then let myself in.

It was pretty weird, being in my own house yet feeling like a thief. The thought made me tempted to nick something, you know? So I'm looking round the living-room—the TV? Video? I think they *might* just notice that. Whip a couple of CDs instead. OK, so I've got nothing to play them on. It's the principle that counts, right? The gesture, I mean.

Then I pad upstairs, having taken off my shoes so there's no tell-tale size 10 impressions in the squashy landing carpet. Pleased with myself that I thought of it—I reckon I'm quite good at this. I probably could have been a private detective. You don't have to go to college or anything for that, do you? Meanwhile, moving back to reality for a sec. Actually, Nat's feet can't be far off size 10s—must be all those hormones or whatever they say there is in meat. Number of burgers Nat eats, I can't understand why there's supposed to be a crisis for British farmers. They should stick him on the cover of the paper:

LOCAL LAD SAVES BEEF INDUSTRY SINGLE-HANDED

Go for a piss. Leave the seat up, thinking nyah-ner to you, Gail, Goddess of Nag, go out, then back in again to put it back down, reckoning she'd throw a wobbly at Nat. Into Gail's room—sod it—*our* room. Perch on the edge of the bed for a minute as if sitting next to someone sick. Then I flop back and just lay there staring at the ceiling, looking at the lampshade and thinking how I didn't like it all that much—it's pretty horrible really, but I'd never thought about it before even though I must have looked at it—at least twice a day, say last thing at night and first thing when I wake up. We've been in the house bit over eight years, so what's that make? Over 5,000 times? A lot anyway. Actually, no, it's less than that because we redecorated in here only two years ago and got a new shade, so—oh, bollocks, who cares? The point is. I don't know. Yes—the point is that I'm a bloody good husband—and the lampshade is proof. See, I've put up with this vile lampshade for over two years and never complained once. That ought to count for something. None of the things that ought to count ever do, do they? Why is it always up to the women to decide what matters? Like having one brief shag with someone else is everything—OK, two brief shags, whatever—but being nice day in, day out and putting up with the Lampshade from Hell means bugger all? Whoever said we've got a male-dominated society wants his head looking at. *Her* head probably.

I pull back the bedspread then and curl up under it, lay my head on Gail's pillow, but she must have just changed the bed because there's only a clean laundry kind of smell and not a Gail-smell at all. I slip my hand under the pillow and pull out a nightie of Gail's, made of some slithery, shiny stuff. I press it to my face and there's a trace of her on it. A definite whiff of Gail, that perfume she wears and some other smell that's just her, her skin, her hair, whatever. I feel a bit choked up suddenly, tell myself I'm a daft bugger, rubbing the cloth against my cheek. It's all soft and silky. I wonder if . . . ? Sod it, why not? It's not like I've got anything left to lose. I attempt to stuff the nightie inside my jacket but it just slides out again, so—I know this sounds a bit pervy but I can't think what the hell else to do with it— I wind it round my waist, tucked into my trousers all the way round, then tuck my shirt back in over it. With my jacket on, you couldn't see a thing. Then I carefully smooth the pillow and put the bedspread back so it's all neat and peer at it from every angle.

I poke my head round Rosie's door. She is *so* tidy. Funny kid. Take a quid out of my pocket and hide it in one of her shoes at the bottom of the wardrobe. I'm just leaving then when something catches my eye. A new poster. Before she used to have this poster of dolphins on the wall. But now I see it's been bumped—demoted to the far end next to the window. Pride of place, where she'd see it when she woke up each morning is a pop poster, one of those bands where they all look about twelve and they're all singers—well, allegedly anyway—and you can hear music but no-one seems to be playing any kind of instrument, you know? But she's way too young to be into bands and stuff. Actually, maybe last Sunday she did say something about a band. But she's only a little kid for chrissakes. Next thing she'll be dolling herself up to the nines and rolling in at two o'clock in the morning off her head on E. I'll ask her Sunday, about bands I mean, what she likes and that.

Still, the thought made me feel a bit weird, to be honest, like she was growing up without me—you know that playground game they used to play way back when I was alive—Grandma's Footsteps, was it? You turn your back and the others try and slowly sneak up on you, but you turn round suddenly and try to catch them moving. Like that.

I come back home once or twice a week now, whenever I can fit it in. I come in the day of course, usually mid-morning, just to—I don't know—have a look, I suppose. See what's occurring. It's not against the law or anything, is it? Couldn't be—it's my house after all, right? Our house. Besides, it's not as if I'm breaking in or anything. I'm using a key—'cept for that first time and there were extenuating circumstances, i.e. I was very pissed off, so I really had no other option. Now, it's no different than if I was a totally normal husband doing shift work, say, and coming home when the rest of the family were out. Completely normal and ordinary. The only difference is that I'm not on shift work, of course. Oh yeah—and the family have no idea that I'm even here. But it's not as if they'd really mind. Aside from Gail, obviously.

Still. It's good to be here. I don't think I ever really appreciated having a nice home before. You don't till you suddenly find yourself living out of a bin bag. Oh, you know what I mean, in someone else's back bedroom then. Being at Harry's is all right, and I'm not ungrateful, but it's not the same as having your own place where you can just drop yourself onto the settee and put your feet up or wander round in your underpants. This is no palace, I grant you, we've not got gold taps or silk wallpaper, but it's warm and comfy and got everything we need. Everything I need. Telly, video, music centre, all the gear. Decent power shower all tiled round by yours truly. Dishwasher. Wife. Children. Shame you can't replace them out of a catalogue: "I seem to have lost my wife and kids, but I see you've a nice set there on page 72. Have you got them in stock, but with a less stroppy looking wife? Fine, I'll take them. Deliver them on Tuesday. Thank you."

It's so quiet here now. Looking back, I think I was

hardly ever in the house on my own, so you could always hear, well, just typical family noise really: the TV, Nat thundering up and down the stairs, music— Gail listening to the radio in the kitchen while she made the tea, Nat playing his CDs, the dishwasher humming away or the clothes washer or the ping of the microwave or the kettle coming to the boil. And Rosie, asking questions, the way she does: "Da-a-a-d, you know Mount Everest? Well, why do people keep climbing up it?" It's a mystery to me, love, I can barely manage life down here. Mind you, Everest sounds kind of tempting after the last few weeks I've just had.

Just have a quick scout round, I've not got long today. Harry'd never say a word, bless him, but he must be wondering why my calls keep taking me so long. I go in the front room and stretch out on the settee to watch a bit of telly. God, it's crap, daytime TV, isn't it? No wonder people want to go out to work. I channel-hop every six seconds or so then give up on it. Tidy the cushions and shake them to plump them up again. See, I am a good husband. Admittedly, I never used to bother doing that, but I'm a changed man, really I am.

A nose round upstairs. No sign of male occupation, thank God, other than Nat's spot cream in the bathroom. I wonder if Gail'll start seeing someone. A boyfriend, I mean—you know, just to get back at me. It's way too soon, of course, but she might as a sort of retaliation, revenge thing. Nah. She wouldn't. She wants me back, I'm sure of it, it's just she's painted herself into a corner with all this playing the Outraged Innocent Victim crap and she doesn't know how to get out of it.

Rosie's room is shipshape as usual, but with hundreds of little bits and bobs everywhere—I don't know, girlie stuff, her snow shakers, of course, and tiny glass animals and boxes with shells stuck on them and small soft toys with googly eyes and dishes filled with elastic thingies for her hair and grips or clips or whatever they are, and flowers carved out of wood and boxes with secret catches so you can't open them and funny plastic rings with outsize jewels on them that she's saved from Christmas crackers.

Inside the wardrobe, her clothes are all put away properly. Not like me, King of the Plastic Sacks. The dresses and skirts are neat and straight on hangers, the tops and trousers folded on the shelves. I walk my fingers along the line of hangers to find her favourite dress. It's this one, see, with the light blue spots all over it? She loves this one, though it must be too small for her now. She wore it last summer when we went on her friend's birthday picnic. There were three families in all and we just lazed around most of the day, having too much beer and stuffing our faces with chicken and cold meat loaf, snoozing in the sun while the kids played some game that seemed to involve lots of running and pushing and shouts of "You cheat!" I remember this one moment—I must have just woken up from a bit of a doze—and I half sat up. And there was Rosie in her spotty dress—running, picking her feet up high because of the long grass and literally shrieking with delight. She looked like a picture. The dots on her dress were exactly the same colour as the sky behind her—bang on they were, you couldn't have got a better match if you'd been sat there all day with a paintbox.

I felt ridiculously proud. I know, she wasn't doing anything especially clever or amazing, but she was my daughter and she looked so pretty and happy, running like the wind, and just bursting with life that I was dead chuffed. And then, just as suddenly, I came over all sad. How much longer would she be like this, I thought, leaping through the grass and without a worry in the world. All too soon she'll be a teenager and she'll be skulking in her room and throwing a strop every two minutes and slamming doors and wanting to be pierced all over the place. And then she'll be like the rest of us, struggling to earn a living, pay the mortgage, find someone to settle down with, raise a family, trying to put a bit by for a holiday or a new kitchen or a new car, worrying about her tax or the latest food scare or whether her husband's shagging someone else. Ahem. Whatever. And there'll be no more running through the grass, shrieking with joy, outrunning the wind.

I guess I felt sad for myself, too, sad that I've become a pathetic old git, wasting my life worrying and moaning and going nowhere when I should be out there rushing through the long grass, whooping at the sky. No, not necessarily literally. You know what I mean.

I plucked out the dress and swung it round, the way I

used to swing Rosie when she was little, remembering her laughing and bossing me, telling me to put her down, put her down right now, but knowing from her laughter and her eyes that she's loving it. I held the little dress close for a minute till I thought, "Hang on a tick, you're losing it, mate. You'll start blubbing like a baby in a minute if you don't pull yourself together."

I didn't think I could face Nat's room after that. Not the untidiness, 'cause I never gave a toss about that, not like Gail. Just—well, you know. I patted his door as I passed then went downstairs. Checked my watch. Gail's not due back for hours. Easy-peasy. Shoes back on and I'm out the door and off back to my car with no-one any the wiser.

Nat

His rods are gone. Everything. The whole lot. The lamp. And the tent. And the big green umbrella. Now there's just my rod in the cupboard, all on its own. I guess he's really not coming back. See, I said he wasn't, didn't I? I always said it.

Tonight, the phone rang and I picked it up without thinking. It went all slow motion like an action replay, watching my hand lift the phone and suddenly knowing it was him but too late to let go. I didn't say anything.

"Hi," Dad said, "Gail? Who's that? Rosie, is that you?"

I said nothing, holding the phone away as if it had germs. He phones Rosie like every day practically. She sits on the bottom step, twirling the ends of her hair round and round her finger and telling him what she's done at school. I say, "That your boyfriend? C'mon, get off the phone—you've been on for hours." It really winds her up.

"Nat? Nat. Come on, Natty, don't be like this. It's me—Dad."

Uh-duh. Yeah, like who else would I refuse to speak to? He can be really thick sometimes. I wanted to speak, wanted to say, "Dad who?" in a snotty voice, "Not the dad who fucked up everything and is nothing to do with me any more? That dad?"

"Natty?" he said again. "Hey." He didn't say anything for what felt like ages. Well, two can play at that game. I could stand there all day. "Well. Get Rosie for me will you then?"

Rosie was out at a friend's, but why should I tell him? I put the phone on its side with a loud clunk and shouted up to Mum.

"Mu-um. Ph-o-o-o-ne."

"Who is it?" She came running down the stairs.

I shrugged.

She gave me one of her looks. Like really scary—not. I went into the kitchen so I could still hear and opened the fridge. Stood in the cold eating a hunk of cheese, nibbling it like a rat, making ratty squeaks, ratty-Natty, and swigging some juice from the carton.

". . . he doesn't *want* to, Scott. I can't make him."

"I'll do what I can, but frankly you should have thought—hang on a sec—"

I saw her arm reach across to close the kitchen door. I snuck closer, just in time to hear her bang the phone down. The door opened immediately. She's so suspicious all the time.

"What?" I said, sidling back towards the fridge.

"Nathan!" she was practically bellowing.

"I can hear, you know. I'm not deaf."

"Nathan," she said again, all quiet and scary—but really this time. "Don't eavesdrop on other people's conversations all the time."

"I wasn't—I'm just here having a small piece of cheese. I suppose you'd rather I starved to death?"

"Don't interrupt when I'm cross, Nathan, or I'll get a lot crosser. And don't be melodramatic. I won't have you snooping—it's very rude for a start, and no-one ever heard good of themselves that way, so I—oh, for goodness' sake—" Mum came towards me and I suddenly thought she was going to hit me. OK, I know she never has, well not for years, 'cept about twice maybe—one time after I ran out in the road and nearly got run over and the other time I made a V-sign at an old lady but it wasn't fair I got a smack—I only did it 'cause she swore at me for no reason, shouted at me right in the street. She was a total loony. And she was smelly.

I dropped the cheese and Mum went even more ballistic.

"Whatever's wrong with you, Nathan? Pick that up right now and cut off the bit where it's touched the floor. Come out of there, you're practically in the fridge. I must have told you a thousand times, don't stand there with the fridge door open. It makes it over-rev. You're as bad as—well. Please, please, Nat, just close the fridge door, OK?"

*   *   *

As bad as your dad, she was going to say. Just like your father. That's what everyone says. You take after your dad. You're so like your dad. Aaah, they say, Aren't you just like your dad?

I'm not, I'm not, I'm NOT, I wanted to shout—I'm not like him. I wouldn't run off and leave us all in this mess and abandon a little kid who's practically a baby and expect my son to sort everything out and grow up overnight and be the man in the family just because I was stupid and selfish and mean. I'm not like him. I'm not.

Scott

I have to admit things aren't looking so promising on the Gail-begging-me-to-come-back front. You'd think she'd be missing me a bit at least. She's probably hiding it. That'll be it. But if I'm not moving back in the next couple of weeks, I'm going to have to bite the bullet and notify the parents. No, I know it's not like they give a toss about my marriage or my happiness and well-being or anything, but just in case they do ring, I'd rather they didn't hear it from Gail. My mother has been known to phone from time to time and ask me to come round, say if a tap needs a new washer or they've a shelf wants putting up, you know, the kind of job that only a precious and much loved son who can't say no could do. Why should they call for a handyman and waste their hard-hoarded money when Idiot Boy keeps coming to the rescue?

I reckon it's best if I just drop in on the off-chance. There's no point phoning in advance, 'cause it's not like they're going to be cracking open the Champagne in my honour, is it? No, I'm being unfair. Give her credit, my mother always makes me a cup of tea when I go round there. And she always says, "And how's life treating you, dear?"

That's how she sees the world—like you're a discarded plastic bag in the street and life may pick you up and fly you about in the wind or leave you laying in the gutter and you've got no say in it whatsoever. Actually, I feel like that at the moment, but it's no way to carry on, is it?

If I'm moronic enough to say "Not too bad, thanks," then they usually start dropping heavy hints about things that need doing round the house and they were thinking of getting some lamb in for the freezer but they're a bit strapped for cash just now—and the pension's not much, is it?—of course they've never been extravagant—not like some people they could name—specially her along at number 6, all fur coat and no knickers—*they've* always been careful, of course—waste not, want not—but it's nice to have a bit extra, isn't it?—you never know when you might need it—oh, am I sure—can I really spare it?—well, it's appreciated—they'll tuck it away safely—oh, not the bank, no—somewhere safe—it's been nice having a visit—and p'raps I'd remember to bring some sweets next time—it's fruit jellies, she likes, she can't eat toffees now, with her teeth—and your dad'll take some tobacco—you know the kind he has—he likes a smoke, does your dad—all he's got now is a smoke and a flutter on the dogs.

My father's retired now, of course. Used to work on the railways. And the house isn't far from the tracks, you can hear the trains. He likes that, my dad, the noise of the trains, the sound as it crosses the points. There's not many things he likes, but that's one of them. Mum used to take whatever work was going, seasonal jobs on the farms, fruit-picking when she was younger, then piece-work from home, stuffing envelopes and making up crackers for some company ahead of Christmas, bright red crépe paper and shiny gold stickers spread out on the table in the middle of July. We used to try to get the jokes, to read them out, but she told us not to touch them, case our filthy hands made marks on them and the customers complained.

I've got to drive down Westbury Road, so I pull over and nip into the bakery there for some cream cakes. My mum's like a junkie when it comes to cakes. You see her eyes light up and her pupils go all glinty as she fusses in the cupboard, looking for the little tea plates, not the best ones, of course, they've not been used once, since they got them for a wedding present nearly fifty years ago. She gets out the cake forks, though, as she would if they ever had company round—which they never have, not being over-fond of people in general—having company's an expense, isn't it?—people expecting scones and fancy cakes and all sorts—thinking you're made of money—it's not necessary, is it?—they've not got the time or the patience to be putting on airs with that sort of thing.

*　*　*

Miracle of miracles, my father's out when I arrive, so my mother—apron apparently glued to her front as always—is in what passes for a good mood in this household.

"Ooh! Dennis!" This is not an expression of maternal delight at seeing her youngest return to the family fold, you understand. No—she has spied the promising white cardboard cake box, tied with ribbon. Still, I bestow a rare kiss on her cheek in a sudden fit of something-or-other and she waddles through to the front room to fetch the cake forks.

"Where is he then?"

"Gone for his tobacco." My father smokes the thinnest roll-ups you've ever seen. No, thinner than the thinnest ones you've ever seen. Each one contains about three and a half strands of tobacco, which he carefully arranges and straightens and rearranges on the cigarette paper balanced on the arm of his chair. He then licks along one edge with trembling tongue and rolls it up unbelievably slowly. The whole process takes so long, you have to fight the urge to grab it from him and say, "Here—I'll do it!" He then pokes this sad apology for a cigarette in his mouth and leaves it hanging there, stuck to his wet bottom lip for another few minutes, while he stomps around looking for a light and blaming whoever crosses his path for hiding the matches.

I should tell her now, quickly, before he gets back. Then she can pass on the joyous news after I've left.

"And how's life treating you, dear?" She says the words, but her attention is focused solely on the three plump cream cakes as she opens the lid of the box to reveal their glory. There is no question but that she'll have first pick. Her hand hovers, then settles on the chocolate éclair. One fat finger darts back into the box to recapture a tiny blob of cream that has brushed off the éclair onto the side of the box.

I grab the meringue, leaving my father with the vanilla slice—the one we all like least. Ah, you're thinking, why didn't he just buy another éclair instead then? Or another meringue? Or something else altogether? Why bother with the vanilla slice at all? But of course, that would be missing the point. In our family, at least half the pleasure *depends* on knowing that you're eating the cake that someone else would have wanted. My parents only ever really enjoy themselves if they're certain that someone else is thoroughly miserable. I will just say, I'm not like that the rest of the time—it's just when I'm around them, I find myself acting the way they do.

"Life," I say, ignoring the dolly-sized cake fork and lifting the entire meringue up to my mouth, "has given me a ruddy great kick in the teeth." She's not listening anyway, concentrating on her cake, so I might as well carry on. "Fact is, Gail and I had a bit of a barney and things got a bit out of hand . . ."

"You never give her a slap, did you, Dennis?"

"No! Of course not!" My mother, of all people, should know I'd never hit anyone. Specially not a

209

woman or a kid. How could she think for even a second I'd be like—that I'd do that?

She looks round with a guilty face then lifts the cake's paper case to her mouth to lick the traces of cream and chocolate left on it. "No. But we're—we're having a kind of a trial separation."

That sounds good. I must use that again. Trial separation. Sounds very adult—you've had a ruck, you're thinking things over, you're both having a bit of space, sort yourselves out. Sounds a lot, lot better than she chucked me out on the street and won't let me come back.

It is at this moment that the old man returns.

"Dennis is here!" my mother calls out, though her tone sounds more like a warning than an exclamation of joy.

"Oh. Is he?" His voice comes from the kitchen, where he's entered round the back. I hear him shedding his coat, the same old brown one he's had for ever, smelling of tobacco and musty rooms and that haircream that only old guys seem to use; I think you have to show your pension book before they let you buy it.

"What's 'e want then?" he calls out. The tap goes on in the kitchen, water splashing onto the metal sink. There's a bar of soap at the side that sits on one of those funny little pink mats covered in rubber suckers like the underside of an octopus. The soap is the old, hard, green sort that lasts for ever. I don't think you can even buy it any more. My mother no doubt bought a box of 100 bars thirty years ago and they're still slowly working their way through it, pacing themselves so it lasts them till they die.

"There's a cake on the side there for you, dear." My mother, trying to please.

"No éclair then?"

I wink at my mother, briefly conspirators.

"They were all out," I call back.

Finally, he enters the room, gives me a nod and settles into his chair. His chair. It smells like his coat and has the same brown, worn feel—its whole life has been spent moulded to his body. There's a darker patch where his head rests. One time, my mother got one of those white things, you know, like a serviette you put on the back of your chair, but he said he couldn't be fiddle-faddling with that like some old woman. That was way back, when we walked around holding our breath, never knowing what might set him off. He tugs at his waistband then undoes his trouser button. Sets the cake, still in the box, on his lap.

"Shall I fetch you a plate?" My mother, pathetically trying to preserve the niceties.

"Do I look like I'm wanting a plate?"

You'll have gathered that charm is not one of my father's outstanding qualities.

"So, what's up with him then?" He's not looking at either of us, but he's talking to her, to my mother.

Her teacup rattles, suddenly loud, in its saucer.

"Dennis was just saying . . ." She looks at me and her voice falters.

I am forty years old, for God's sake. I don't have to be afraid of him any longer. Still—I stand up—to feel taller, bigger, more grown-up. I lean against the mantelpiece, a man at ease.

"Gail and I are having a trial separation." There. Not a waver in my voice.

"What's that when it's at home? Chucked you out, did she? Always thought she was too good for us, that one." He laughs and looks round for a cup of tea. My mother heaves herself up with as much speed as she can manage and goes through to the kitchen.

"No. It's a mutual thing. We agreed—"

"A what? Speak normal, can't you?"

"We're just working things out." It sounds lame, pathetic, untrue.

"Marriage is till you go to your grave." Funny how he makes it sound like a life sentence rather than a source of happiness. "I've stuck by your mother all these years."

The other way round, more like. Who else would put up with him? He starts looking around him, feeling down the side of the seat cushion, already losing interest.

I shouldn't have come. I don't know why I did. Why, after all these years, am I still stupid enough to hope it'll be any different? No, I'm not saying I want them to hire a brass band to welcome me home. It's just—it'd be nice if just once they'd say, "How are you, son? It's good to see you." That's all.

"Where's them bloody matches gone?" he says.

Gail

"Hey, babe, how's it going?" Cassie phoned me at work. She and Derek had been away for a fortnight's holiday in New York and I hadn't realized how much I'd come to rely on her daily calls, checking that I was still bearing up.

"Oh, you know. So-so."

"So-so—not bad? Or so-so—fucking awful?"

I laughed. I can't remember the last time I laughed.

"The second one." I was about to ask her about her holiday when I sensed someone behind me. They're not keen on personal calls at the surgery because the lines are so busy as it is. "Yes, Mrs Dickson, if it's just a repeat prescription, there's no need for you to see the doctor."

"Big Brother's watching, I take it. Can I come over later and bore you with my holiday piccies? Eightish?"

"Yes indeed. Goodbye now."

Dr Wojczek leant a little closer.

"Sorry to interrupt you, Gail, do you have a minute for me?"

"Of course!" I called over to Tess to cover the desk then followed Dr Wojczek to his room. I stood with my back against the door, clutching my notepad in front of me.

"Please ..." he gestured to the other chair, the patient's chair.

I perched awkwardly right on the very edge of the seat. He has a way of looking at you that is incredibly intense, so you imagine he knows every single thing you're thinking. His eyes are really deep, dark brown, and also he rarely blinks so I can't look at him for more than a split second without feeling peculiar. One night a few months ago, I had a dream with him in it and, well, to be honest it was, you know, a—a naughty dream. Then the next day, when he said good morning and looked at me, I was so embarrassed. I was convinced he was going to say, "You disgusting slut! How dare you have such obscene thoughts about me?" He didn't, of course, but I still say he *knew* and ever since then I find it even harder to meet his gaze.

"Is this about my work?" I sounded flustered and defensive. Of course, I've been distracted, but I don't think I've made any serious slip-ups.

"I don't know. Should it be?"

"Look, I know I haven't been as focused as I normally am—but it's just a temporary problem—it really is—and I'm sorry—but—" I plunged on, getting faster and more pointless as I went on. God knows if he could make head or tail of it. I'm not making fun of his English, no; he's been here for years, and, if anything, he speaks better than most English people, more precise. Only his voice tends to rise at the end of his sentences, so it sounds as if he's asking a question, even when he isn't.

He nodded calmly.

"There is nothing wrong with your work. As always, you are efficient, capable, good with the patients?"

"Then that's not why you wanted to talk to me?" I felt such a fool. He shook his head.

"I notice, of course, that you are not happy . . . ?" Then he looked right into my eyes and it was all I could do not to burst into tears and sob hysterically in front of him. I could feel myself welling up so I looked down at my notepad and started drawing a series of loops across the page, the way Rosie would. ". . . and I am here any time you want—or perhaps you would prefer Dr Kerr?" Jane Kerr, my own doctor. "But, no. It is not for me to intrude in your personal life? If you are unhappy with something here at the surgery, you must tell me, yes?"

"Yes. No. There's nothing. I love it here."

"Good. Perhaps you will think about becoming full-time then?" he smiled. They'd asked me twice before, but I've always put my family first. It would mean Rosie going to after-school club or round to Kira's. Still, we could do with the extra money.

"I'll think about it." I got up and made to leave.

"And you will remember that I am here?"

"Yes. I will. Thank you."

Cassie. Thank heavens for Cassie. She brought Rosie a snow shaker for her collection with the Statue of Lib-

215

erty in it, and a baseball cap for Nat that he said was "Ace. Like majorly cool with a capital C"—which I think meant he liked it. Once the kids had gone upstairs, Cassie whisked out a pair of pink pants for me from Bloomingdale's—with "Bloomies" across the bum.

"They're great—shame no-one else will get the good of them."

"Your choice, babe. I bet there's no shortage of blokes who'd like a closer look at your lingerie."

We started looking through her photos.

"You thought any more about having Scott back?"

"Of course. There's nothing else I can think about. I'm so sick of myself, listening to the same old thoughts going round and round my head, it's driving me crazy. At least work keeps me sane, being so busy means there's no time to think."

"So what's the verdict?"

I shrugged.

"I don't know. I really don't. I suppose it sounds awful but sometimes I think if I had never found out, maybe that would have been OK. I'd never have known and I wouldn't have had to do anything, d'you see?"

"Mm. Ignorance is bliss, yeah?"

"Sort of. But I can't go back. I do know and I can't un-know it now. And anyway . . ." I held a photo up close. "God, don't tell me you let Derek out in that hat?"

"Don't change the subject. And anyway, what?"

"Can I ask you something first? If Derek left, what would you miss most about him?"

"Seeing his artificial leg propped against the chair first thing when I wake up."

"No, stop kidding. Really."

"I'm not kidding. Every time I see it, standing there on its own, still with its shoe and sock on, I feel this great rush of tenderness towards Derek. He's such a strong person, and he's always been there for me 100 per cent, when I got made redundant, when I had that horrible cyst thing, remember? And—most of all, about not having any kids. He's a rock. He never moans. Then I see his leg, or I watch him hop across the room, and I go all mushy inside and I just want to cover him in great big sloppy kisses.

"Anyway, never mind me," Cassie gathered up the photos and packed them away briskly. "What do you miss most about Scott? Let me guess. Not the way he helped so much around the house, presumably?"

"No."

"Not his love of serious intellectual conversation?"

"Right again."

"Still, he is a laugh, you have to give him that. It is that, right?"

I shook my head.

You know, if anyone had asked me, back when we were still together, if anyone had said, "What would you miss most?" I'd have guessed it would be that. That's what it used to be, you see. In the beginning, in the very beginning, he made me laugh. He was always clowning around. But someone clowning around when they're twenty-four and you're out with a whole bunch of you going for pizza or to a disco, it's great. But when he's forty and you've got a family and you're trying to juggle the bills and worrying about your kids and planning and organizing, well, it just doesn't seem so funny any more.

"What then?"

"I miss having him deal with it when there's a spider in the bath and I miss having someone to put my cold feet on in bed."

"Seriously?" she said, scanning my face, then seeing the answer there. "Holy shit."

"I know."

"But then that means . . . ?"

"Yes," I said. "It does."

Afterwards, I felt strange inside, all churned up, and I couldn't think straight. Saying it out loud, admitting it to Cassie, wasn't the same as just knowing it in my head. As long as it was just in my mind, I could try to hush it up, ignore it, hum a tune to drown it out.

I made some coffee, even though it was after eleven by the time she left, then I went upstairs and ran a bath. I kept thinking of Cassie's face, that look of near-horror because she realized exactly what it meant.

I dropped my clothes on the floor. Deliberately. Sounds silly, but it felt like a treat, telling myself I didn't care, that I could be like a child tossing my things in a heap instead of folding them on the chair, that I could be irresponsible and—well, and spontaneous, that I could be like Scott, I suppose. Except, of course, even as I dropped them, I was thinking all this and knowing that when I got out of the bath I would pick them up and that I would hang up my towel properly and leave everything tidy, so it wasn't all that spontaneous.

I sank back into the bath, and let my mind wander, thinking about friends and couples I'd known over the years where one of them had had an affair and what had happened. Sometimes they'd split up but sometimes they hadn't. And, suddenly, now I knew why, what the difference was. It was so simple. The ones who'd stayed together had stuck it out—because they *wanted* to. It wasn't that they were stronger than us or that the wife didn't care so much that her husband had cheated on her or even that she believed that he'd really change. It wasn't any of that. The simple fact was that they wanted to be together *whatever it took* and they would go through all the pain and hurt and anger they felt in trying to work things out because at the end they would still be with the person they wanted to spend their life with.

And now I was left with this cold, sad fact that I knew I didn't want to be with Scott for the rest of my life but, much worse than that, in some part of me I must have known it for quite a while. Which meant that the moment I found out about Scott's pathetic little fling wasn't the beginning at all. The beginning was much, much earlier. Years ago even. And I hadn't really noticed. Or, if I had, I'd decided to ignore it. I'd concentrated on the children, fussing round them and bustling round the house being busy, nagging Scott because it was easier than facing up to the fact that we had nothing to talk about, that we just happened to be sharing a house for convenience's sake. And it meant that I'd been doing exactly what I'd always accused Scott of. I'd blamed him and blamed him and blamed him, making out—and really, truly believing it in my own mind— that it was 100 per cent his fault and that it was all just to do with him and his stupid wandering willy.

But now, this—this was much harder because it means that I'm responsible too. I knew how serious our problems were but I pretended nothing was wrong, even to myself. And now Scott's hurting and I'm hurting and far, far worse than anything else, Nat and Rosie must be hurting and I can't bear it. As long as it was all Scott's fault, I could be angry and self-righteous and kid myself that at least I was still a good mother. And now I can't and I don't know if I can bear it, I don't know how to bear it. I don't know how.

Nat

Last Sunday, Steve had to go away with his family to visit his grandparents. Normally, I go round there and we play games on his new PlayStation and do a bit of homework and have a big Sunday dinner. His mum says she likes having me and it's no more trouble to cook for six than it is for five anyway. Steve says going to his grandparents' is a real drag and that they're like majorly sad crumblies, but he really likes his gran, he just won't admit it. I like my nan and grandad, that's Mum's parents, not the other lot. We never see my dad's mum and dad much, 'cause Mum hates them. I mean, even *before*—y'know. It's OK by me, because I don't like them either. We call them Granny Scott and Grandad Scott, but the nice ones are just Nana and Grandad. Grandad Scott stinks of tobacco and he's always got this titchy roll-up stuck to his lip like it's just landed there by accident, and his hair looks all greasy and he scratches himself. And he makes snide remarks the whole time, specially to my dad. And Dad goes all funny around him—he won't sit down hardly, tapping his foot like he's about to make a run for it, and he never laughs when he's there, not ever.

Whatever. Anyway, I told Mum I couldn't go round Steve's on Sunday and she said why didn't I stay home and hang out with her. That's what she said: "You could *hang out* with me if you like." It sounded funny when she said it, like she was putting it on, trying to sound like me. But she's all right, I guess. For a parent. Steve thinks my mum's really cool and he starts talking all polite if he comes round and smarming up to her, but I told him he wouldn't like her so much if he had to live in the same house as her the whole time and be nagged to death about hanging up the towels and putting your shoes away and doing your homework and stacking your plate and stuff in the dishwasher and phoning if you're going to be late. Steve says they all do that, it's what parents are for. But, I mean, *get a life*. You'd think if you were grown-up you'd be out having fun and doing whatever you like, not worrying about whether your son's left his trainers halfway up the stairs.

But Jason said I could go out with him and his dad on Sunday. He says his mum and stepdad dump him on his dad on Sundays so they can stay in bed all day, doing it.

"Nah!" I go. "They're too old. They must be past it by now."

"They're always at it," he goes. "One time I found a pair of my mum's pants by the breadbin."

"Euch! That's gross! What's she leave 'em there for?"

"'cause they were shagging in the kitchen, stupid."

I give him a shove.

"Don't call me stupid. Why'd they do it in the kitchen then, smart-arse?"

He shrugged.

"Dunno. 's what people do, innit?"

"Maybe in your family, dipstick. D'you cook your tea in the bedroom then? Wash your dishes in the bath? Sound like a bunch of loony-tunes to me. You wanna watch it or they'll send you up the hill."

That's what we say if someone's a bit psycho—"up the hill"—'cause that's where the loony bin is, on that hill on the edge of town. If you get taken there, they give you injections with a whacking great needle as thick as your finger practically. My dad said they stuff you full of tablets, whatsits—tranquillizers and that—dope you to the gills, he says, so you'll be nice and quiet and not give the staff any trouble. He said it's disgusting and they should close the place down. Then my mum told him off and said to stop exaggerating, you're scaring the children, and that she's sure it's not like that any more, it wouldn't be allowed, blah, blah. I bet it is.

Mum said I could go with Jason on Sunday as long as I did some homework on Saturday and would promise to finish it Sunday evening and she'd want to see it to make sure. Yeah, yeah, drone, drone.

So Sunday, him and his dad come and pick me up.

They couldn't come till eleven o'clock, so I had to hide out in my room when you-know-who came to collect Miss Goody-Goody. I looked down from my window, hiding behind the curtain. I'd make a great spy. See him come bounding up the front path, looking like really heartbroken—NOT—that he's about to spend yet another Sunday without his only son. His hair's going thin on top. I wanted to tell him to wind him up, ask him if he was planning on being a monk. We like to wind each— Used to like. Whatever. He's getting old. Becoming a crumbly. He'll be forty-one soon. Rosie keeps on about this idea she's had for his present. Yawn. I don't see why I should get him anything. I haven't got any money anyway. I can't even use my mobile now 'cause I've run out of talk credits and Mum said she wouldn't get me any unless I started helping out around the house more and we all have to watch the money a bit more now. I don't see why me and Rosie have to suffer.

We went bowling. Like we did on my birthday. But Jason's dad's not the same. For a start, he's like always got to be the best, yeah? I mean, course he's bigger than us and that. And stronger. He's bound to be better, but when we went before, with my dad, he still made sure everyone was having a good time. I mean, he's like an ace bowler, my dad, but he still helps anyone else who wants him to, and he offers you a lead if you want one, and if you do a good bowl he cheers for you. But when I nearly got a strike this time, I knocked down eight pins, right? And Jason's dad just goes,

"Not bad, son. Not bad." And winks at me.

"I'm not your son, creep," I went—only quiet, so he wouldn't hear me.

And he kept on telling knock-knock jokes like as if we were only Rosie's age or something and we had to pretend to laugh. It was so embarrassing.

When he brought me back, I remembered to say, "Thanks for taking me out, Mr Hall. I had a really good day." Without Mum having to nudge me or anything. But it wasn't a really good day. I only said it 'cause you're supposed to.

"Hey, pardner!" he goes, bellowing from the car like so loud my eardrums start trying to climb out my ears to escape. Like he thinks he's in a Western or something. "You can call me Rob next time!"

Like he's doing me a favour. Can I really? Gee, the excitement's like getting too much, you know? I'll call you Creep instead if you don't mind, how's that?

At least my dad's not a creep.

Scott

I can't stay any longer at Harry's, it would put a strain on everybody. Maureen's a nice woman, don't get me wrong, but she will not stop fussing. I don't know if she thinks I'm completely clueless or what, but she treats me like I'm an invalid. If I go to put sugar in my tea, she rushes across to do it for me. She even cleaned my shoes the other day; I left them by the front door and when I came down in the morning they'd been polished. Well, it was either her or the pixies. It's kind of her, of course, but it just makes me embarrassed. A couple of days ago, I was padding about the house in my socks and one of them had a hole in it. I know, I know—bit sad, but I can't find anything in these great sacks full of stuff that Gail so lovingly packed for me. Maureen's making her thousandth cup of tea of the day—it's a wonder she's ever off the toilet long enough to drink it, I don't know why she doesn't just tip whole teapots of the stuff straight down the drain, cut out the middle man—and she says, "Ooh, look, you've a hole there wants darning, Scott. Just pop that sock off and I'll see to it."

I'm thinking of putting her up to go on the telly—

now, in captivity, the last woman on planet Earth who still darns socks. It's like, sorry, but have you not got enough to do with your time or what?

Anyway, so I lift my jaw up from the floor and say no thanks, not to worry and I go up to my room and tip one of the sacks out on the bed to hunt for some more. There's a bit of a shortage of ones that actually match, far as I can see—it's like playing Snap! only I'm having no luck finding a pair, unless you count one grey one black as being close enough. And then I start thinking, which is never a good idea if (a) your entire life's gone down the plughole and (b) you happen to be me.

What the fuck do you think you're doing? I ask myself. You're forty years old. Nearly forty-one in fact. You've screwed up your marriage. Your only son won't even speak to you. Your nine-year-old daughter's got more sense in one of her pigtails than you've got in your whole body. You've got no home, no family, no life and no future, and you're sitting on some other bloke's single bed in someone else's house just 'cause they took pity on you and if you're not careful you'll still be here in ten years' time. The three of you'll be toddling round together in nylon zip-up jackets and brown crêpe-soled shoes, going out for cream teas or a nice little drive of a Sunday or, if you're lucky, the occasional pub lunch with one pint of beer. You'll be one of those boys who never left home but still goes everywhere with their parents. Only they're not even your own sodding parents, you've had to nick someone else's—how sad is that?

And you'll go to Bournemouth or Margate for a week packed full of thrills every summer or off-season because it's very reasonable then and you can always put on another sweater, can't you, and a little drop of rain never hurt anyone. And you'll be fifty years old but you'll be the youngest person on the whole promenade and no woman will ever look at you 'cept it won't matter a toss because your cock will have long since fallen off from disuse and you will be without question the saddest bastard on the entire planet.

So I reckoned it really was time to move on.

The next morning, I checked the tourist office's website and printed out their list of Bed and Breakfast places. I'd rather be in a proper flat or house of my own of course, somewhere I can bring the kids, so they can stay over. If they want to. But what's the point? Gail will probably be on the phone any day now, asking me to come back. At least with a B&B I can clear out any time I get the word.

It was an out-and-about day for me anyway, mostly doing quotes—in town and a couple in outlying villages. I figured I could look at a few possibles on my route.

The first one is down a back street near the station. The window in what the landlady immediately—and unbelievably optimistically, as it turns out—refers to as "*your* room" has curtains the thickness of tracing paper, only less attractive. You can kind of see that they must once have had some sort of pattern, but they've been so faded by the sun and dust and age that they can't be bothered to be patterned any more. They've just shrugged their shoulders and given up. God knows how they've got faded by the sun because this is not a sunny room we're talking about here. We are talking welcome to the Land of Gloom. She switches on the overhead light, but the bulb must be about 3 watts because it makes absolutely sod all difference. The wallpaper is some colour that can't be arsed to work out whether it's grey or green with a knobbly design on it that makes me want to pick bits off with my fingernail. The bed is low and would be perfect for a kid of about ten. I doubt Rosie could even fit in it. There's a rug the size and sumptuousness of a pocket handkerchief set mysteriously at an angle in one corner—presumably to cover up the bloodstain of the last tenant who must surely have shot himself out of depression.

Hideous is not the word. It is through hideous and out the other side. It is so awful that I can barely speak. Instead, I nod vigorously and pat the bed pointlessly to make it look as if I'm considering it all seriously. She tells me that it is very spacious, which might work if I was a blind person, but given that I've still got the use of my sight I can clearly see that it is not only not spacious, but that it is in fact only a nice size if you were planning on using it as a spare closet. I nod anyway, heading for the door, saying thank you so much, I'll certainly give it some serious thought, yes indeed, I've got your number, thank you.

*　*　*

At least the next one can't be as bad. I comfort myself with this thought as I pull up outside an OK looking terraced house in a quiet street on the north edge of town.

For once, I'm right. It's not "as bad." It is worse, much much worse. There is the distinctive odour of reheated cabbage, always a favourite with me, and it almost—but not quite—manages to cover up a sort of undercurrent whiff of piss. The room has been decorated by someone who thinks orange and brown is the way to go when it comes to colours—except for the bed, which has a quilted velvet pink headboard with—oh, joy!—a yellowish head-shaped stain in the centre. The bed is bigger than the last one at least but when I bounce gently on the edge of it, it feels and sounds as if the mattress has been stuffed with old newspapers. The wardrobe is a child-size one in genuine wood-effect melamine with Disney cartoon stickers on the insides of the doors. There is a dark green old person's type chair with one of those doily things on the back and, in the corner—I kid you not—a tubular framed commode that looks like it's been nicked from a hospital and it's half-covered with an old army blanket. I tell her it's terrific, really, but I think I need something a bit nearer the junction for the M20. In fact, I'd rather sleep on the junction for the M20, with my head sticking out from the slip road.

By the time I get to the third one, I'm ready for anything. But the room's all right actually. It's bright and you can even turn round without accidentally rearranging the furniture with your elbows. The woman seems nice enough but on the side of nosy. Where am I from? What do I do? I'd already decided to be a bit economical with the truth and say I was a rep for a pharmaceuticals company because I figured that'd make people's eyes glaze over and they wouldn't know what else to ask. That's what my mate Roger does and it is boring beyond belief, even he says so. I say I'm seeing new customers in the area so I'm not sure how long I'll be staying, maybe just a couple of nights or maybe a few weeks, it's hard to say. But this one wants to know am I married, have I got children, what do I like for breakfast, do I prefer tea or coffee and I'm finding it all a bit much when I hear a loud banging on the wall. She flushes then and scurries out, closing the door behind her.

I hear her raised voice through the wall:

"That's enough now! Enough! There'll be no dinner for you if you carry on like that!"

I'm thinking "Poor little mutt"—but I'm not sure I want to stay somewhere with a dog, could be barking its head off at all hours. Funny how I never heard it bark though and I'm wondering how it made that banging noise when she comes back in.

"All sorted!" Her voice is bright and chirpy and she claps her hands like a nursery teacher calling the children to attention. She sees my face and realizes she better say something. "It's just Raymond. He's fine really. No trouble 99.9 per cent of the time. It's just we had a teensy problem this morning getting him to take his medication. Now, don't you worry—he stays in his room most of the time. You won't hear a thing. Good, thick walls, these."

At this, there is a low moan from the other room, followed by more rhythmic banging. She smiles even more brightly and I hotfoot it out to the hallway, saying thanks so much, I'll have a think, be in touch, cheers now. Bye!

I get some quotes sorted out and measure up for some french windows a few miles south of town, then go and have a dekko at this barn conversion down on the marshes. Some total prat has put in cheapo council-house type windows and they've been badly done anyway and the whole thing's a right old pig's breakfast. Fortunately, the woman agrees with me and she wants decent casements put in instead and she's thinking of having some doors done while we're at it so Harry'll be pleased. Anyway, I trot round to do a bit of measuring and calculating and she brings me a cup of tea and we're nattering away and she tells me the reason they've got so much space is they're planning to do B&B but they can't start advertising for guests because it's not finished yet but they've got a bank loan as big as India's national debt so they better get on with it.

I ask to have a nose round one of the bedrooms and it's all right. Better than all right, but it's not been decorated yet and the old wallpaper's peeling off in places. So I say how would you like your first proper customer and you do me a good deal and I'll wallpaper the room for you and give you a good price on the windows. And we barter a bit and then we shake on it and she says come back tonight and the bed'll be made up and she'll even throw in some supper seeing as how I'm their first real guest.

Now all I have to do is tell Harry I'm moving out.

Rosie

Yesterday, Nat said I was just being nice to Dad 'cause he buys me chips and toys and stuff. He was leaning against my wardrobe and I ran at him and hit him as hard as I could until he held my wrists and threatened to give me a Chinese burn. When I charged him, it shoved him hard against the wardrobe and it made a bang against the wall, so Mum came running upstairs saying what was the matter, what were we up to and Nat said it was nothing, he had just dropped something and why did she have to fuss over everything all the time, no wonder Dad had left.

Mum went all quiet then. I thought she was going to say something, but then she made her mouth go all tight and squished like it was just sewn on like Alfie-Bear's. She looked at me, then she looked back at Nat.

"Is that what you think?" she said.

Nat jerked his chin up, the way he did when that big boy down the road said he was going to sort him out and he put his hands in his pockets and twisted his trainer into the carpet as if he was squishing a bug. He shrugged and made one of his noises that isn't a real word.

"Mn."

Then Mum told me to go downstairs or to my own room and I said why should I, it wasn't my fault, Nat started it, it wasn't fair, just because I'm little I always have to miss out on everything, then Mum told me not to answer back but to go downstairs right this minute and play quietly or look at my book. I kept my mouth closed but I stuck my tongue out at her inside my cheek so she couldn't see. When I got to the stairs, I heard her say, "Rosie?"

"Mn," I copied Nat's noise.

"Have a chocolate cup cake if you like. In the red tin."

I had meant to go only halfway down the stairs so I could hear what she said. I bet she was going to give Nat a good telling off. You can always tell 'cause she starts calling him "Nathan" and her face goes all serious like this and she folds her arms like a teacher. Serves him right, horrible pig. I meant to listen, but by the time I was halfway down I was thinking about how many stairs I could jump to the bottom and how I bet I could do four instead of three, but how I would wait till later in case I made too much noise and Nat might get let off. And how I would eat my chocolate cup cake.

It's best if you peel the icing off slowly first, all in one go. It's all smooth and shiny and round, like a brown ice rink. So, you carefully peel it off and put it to the side 'cause it's the best bit. Then you pull back the silver paper from the spongy bit and eat the sponge. Then you eat the icing, really slowly, letting each bit melt in your mouth. Then at the end you go round the silver paper case where all the chocolate icing has got stuck in the grooves and you scrape it off with your bottom teeth.

When my dad eats a cup cake, he eats it all at once in three bites—gulp, gulp, gulp. But he lets me have the silver paper.

Nat is disgusting when he eats his. He licks at the icing until it is all sticky, then he folds the icing bit over like a sandwich and eats that. Then he puts the sponge in his mouth, the whole thing in one go and it makes his cheeks go all fat and he tries to talk and crumbs come out of his mouth and Mum tells him not to talk with his mouth full and can he please just try and eat something normally for once, he's not a baby any more, for goodness' sake, can he just make an effort.

Mum does not eat chocolate cup cakes.

Scott

I am lying in bed with the quilt half over my face, telling myself that it's not rain I can hear pattering against the window. It is definitely *not* raining—because, if it *is* raining then Scott's Master Plan of taking Rosie for a long, leisurely bike ride along the coast will have to bite the dust. So much for Plan A. And, because I barely possess two brain cells to rub together, I haven't given much thought to a Plan B. That's not much thought as in no thought at all, not of any kind. We've done McDonald's to death. We've seen every film out that's suitable for kids.

It's probably just a little light drizzle. We can wear our waterproofs and she's got a helmet anyway. Barely more than the odd spot of rain. A passing shower. Check the clock: it's already after nine. Bugger—it's already cutting it fine if I want a cooked breakfast. My sole treat of the week in this black hole that I laughingly call my life is tucking in to a decent brekkie on a Sunday. After all, what's the point of staying in a B&B if you're only getting B but no B?

Drag myself to the window and open the curtains.

Just an inch. No point in overdoing these things.

It is *pissing* down outside. An entire crew of effects people must be up there chucking down bucketloads of water from a great height. This isn't rain, this is a monsoon. I need webbed feet to go out in this. And where are my wellies and my walking boots? In the garage at home. Of course. Much though Queen of Tidiness likes chucking out my stuff, I notice she never gets round to offloading anything that I might actually need. Still, maybe as the weather's so foul she'll let me come back in the house and spend some time with Rosie indoors. I mean, she's not going to want Rosie to get pneumonia, is she? I could see Natty as well. He can hardly ignore me if I'm right there in the house, right? Yeah, and maybe Gail'll put down a nice big plate of steak and chips in front of me, give me a big squelchy kiss and say, "Welcome home, darling!" Dream on, Scotty, dream on.

What the hell do people *do* with their children all day? The dads, I mean. Is there some secret place they all hang out that I haven't been let in on yet? It's probably a club, like Freemasons. The Sunday Fathers. Once you've been through all the initiation rites—your wife telling you to drop dead, your son pretending you don't exist, your nine-year-old daughter feeling sorry for you, sponging off your friends like a sodding charity case, living like a student in a bedsit—then maybe you get your club badge and they tell you how it's done. They teach you the special Sunday Father look, the cheery wave to your kid as you get back in your car feeling like someone's just ripped your guts out and it's another week before you'll see her little face again.

They always say museums and art galleries, don't they, but what would I know about stuff like that? What would I do in a museum? That's for smart-arse proper dads, ones who can tell their kids all clever stuff and show off how much they know. What if you don't know anything? I'm not going to show myself up in a museum. I'll feel like a right prat, watching the other dads point out all the different bones in a Tyrannosaurus or explaining the principles of aerodynamics. I never know things like that. Jeez, I barely know what day of the week it is half the time.

When I come down, Fiona asks have I time for a proper breakfast, it's filthy weather out there, have I seen? I put on the toast while she cracks some eggs into a pan.

She's a woman. She might know what to do. I clear my throat and she half turns towards me.

"Say you had a nine-year-old girl to entertain on a rainy day, where would you take her, d'you think?"

"Would this be your daughter by any chance?"

"Mmn."

Fiona reaches into a cupboard for a plate, talking to me over her shoulder.

"Well, what sort of things does she like doing?"

I shrug. "Dunno, really."

* * *

I say it casually, without thinking, but suddenly it makes me realize that I really don't know. What does Rosie like doing? My own daughter who I've known her whole life and I'm here asking a virtual stranger who's never even met her what the hell I should do with her.

I turn away and concentrate on buttering the toast, fiddling with the jars on the counter as if I can't make up my mind whether to have marmalade or jam or Marmite. Fiona flips the eggs out onto the plate, carefully slides two halves of grilled tomato alongside.

"How about taking her swimming? Can she swim?"

Swimming. Swimming without Nat? Unthinkable. It was Nat who taught Rosie to swim when she was only five or six. Nat's a star swimmer, swims for his school. Beats me every time and it's one of the few things I'm not bad at. Whenever I walk past a swimming baths and get a whiff of chlorine, I think of Nat. No. No swimming.

I shake my head.

"Yeah, she can, but I don't fancy it myself." It sounds lame, selfish. I gesture at the rain outside the window. "Feel I'd never get dry again, you know?"

The pan hisses as Fiona plunges it into the sink.

"Oh, OK. Cinema perhaps? There's a paper there with the listings in if you want. Or ice-skating? I'm not sure where the nearest rink is though . . ."

It's about 30 miles away. Sixty miles round trip. Sounds a bit far, but it's easier when we're in the car. Facing front, playing games with the cars and the registrations.

Racking up points every time you spot a car with the latest reg. or shouting out a word that uses all the letters on the number plate. Rosie's good at that. Better than me half the time.

". . . or a museum?" Fiona tops up my coffee and leans against the counter. I don't know what my face looks like, but it must be a picture, 'cause she says, "Oh, come on—they're much better now, not like they were in our day." She makes it sound as though I'm hundreds of years old rather than a man still (virtually) at his peak. "There are plenty of things for the kids to do and try out. None of those dusty exhibits mouldering in glass cases with faded labels on any more. Everything's interactive now. You might even enjoy it yourself."

My memories of museum visits are not so hot, as you'll have gathered by now. A few depressing school trips (my parents are not exactly the museum-going type), with teacher making all us "difficult" boys hold hands with the "good" girls as an attempt to keep us under control. The girls are outraged by being lumped with us and we're not exactly chuffed either even though we take pleasure in pinching them and giving them Chinese burns, flirting with them by being obnoxious, the only way we know how at the age of ten. As soon as teacher's eye is off us, we shake off the girls' hands and are up to whatever mischief we can think of. It all sounds pathetically mild now, what with the papers full of children sniffing glue and smoking crack on every street corner.

We just ran around like wild things, touching anything that said do not touch and capering about, whooping and pretending to be chimpanzees. No, I've no idea why. It seemed like fun at the time.

And that awful, awful moment on a day trip when everyone gets out their packed lunch and you sit with the boy who lives next door 'cause at least you know he won't have any posh cake or cans of orangeade or fruit either, just a single round of cheese or sardine sandwiches, a couple of plain biscuits—and a flask of tea as if you were a grown-up navvy on a building site and not a kid out for the day wishing he was someone else. And you make out you're not all that hungry, you had a massive breakfast you say, with bacon and eggs and that, and you make fun of your mum, she must be going scatty, she's forgotten to put your crisps and your drink in, shame 'cause they were salt and vinegar and there was a can of 7-Up, you know 'cause you saw them right there on the counter, still you're not fussed, you'll have them later while you're waiting for your tea. And you drink the contents of your flask because you're thirsty, but all you can think of is how much you'd give to be normal and to hear the sharp hiss as you open your can of Coke or 7-Up or Fanta, still cold from the fridge, sweet and fizzy glugging down your throat, bubbles giggling up your nose, gulping it down fast so you can do burps deliberately—see who can do the biggest burp—me now—no, me. It doesn't work with tea.

Gail

How did my life get to be like this? I didn't ask for this. When I was a little girl, I used to dress up and play weddings with my sisters. Mari used to make some poor boy down the road be the groom (which was a non-speaking part as far as we were concerned, aside from saying "I do") and the two of us would take it in turns to be the bride and the vicar. Lynn was always the bridesmaid, of course, because she was the youngest, but we let her wear this sparkly headband as a tiara and catch the bouquet so she put up with it. I thought that when you grew up, you got married, got your washing-machine and your fitted kitchen, your three-piece suite and your drinks cabinet, and then you lived happily after. I mean, I literally thought that that's what happened—just because you were grown up.

And then, even when I was a teenager and supposedly had enough sense to know better, each time I started going out with someone new, I'd have this flutter of excitement in my insides, thinking, "What if this is *it*?" And I'd start picturing it in my head, our wedding I mean. And this is after I've been out with the guy once.

I'd be thinking about my dress and what sort of sleeves it would have and how low cut it should be at the front and whether it should be pure white or maybe ivory would be better, and wondering if it would be best to go the whole hog and have the big fairytale number with the enormous skirt like an outsize meringue or should I be a bit more sophisticated and have something draped and elegant with a little beaded bolero jacket. I'm serious. I'd go on and on like this in my head.

Then, of course, I'd go for the second date, and we'd see a film or something, and he'd try to grope me in the back row or we'd go for a meal and he'd eat with his mouth open and all my dreams—the dress, the flowers, the speeches, my dad looking pleased as punch—the whole lot would go out the window and I'd be looking over this guy's shoulder in the restaurant trying to see if anyone better had come in the door.

Then I met Scott. Right away, I liked him. The other guys I saw, they were all smooth, trying to impress and thinking they were slick. But him, he couldn't get his words out. I knew he liked me from the way he would hardly look at me and the way he spilled his tea when I smiled at him. I thought he was sweet, just like a big kid really.

And, guess what? Scott *is* just like a big kid. He doesn't plan for the future most of the time, he doesn't remember anything important, only silly stuff that you'd never need to remember, stuff about sports and bands and strange things he's picked up from quiz shows. "How many sides in an icosahedron?" he'll suddenly say while we're driving along. "I've no idea, Scott. Just tell me and get it out of your system." He calls me a spoilsport, wants me to guess. Once, taking the mickey, I said why don't we play I Spy (Rosie wasn't even in the car). "Righto," said Scotty, taking me seriously, "I spy with my little eye something beginning with S—B—." Know what it was? No? Neither did I. It was Squashed Bug, on the windscreen. What can you do with a man like that?

Our Big Day turned out to be nothing like all my childish daydreams, of course. By then I was a bit more hard-headed and we were saving up to buy our first house. My parents said they'd be happy to splash out on a fancy wedding for me, or I could have the money for a deposit on a house. Scott said it had better be my choice as the money was coming from my family (I think his parents' sole contribution was an extremely ugly fake crystal bowl that I gave to the Oxfam shop at the first opportunity) and he knew what girls were like about weddings. So we put the money down on a house and had a small wedding at a registry office, with me in a pale pink suit. See, here's our wedding photo, God knows why it's still out. I'm wearing this ridiculous flower thing in my hair and Scott's in a grey suit with sleeves that were just too long so he looks like a boy out in his first grown-up jacket.

Then we had family and friends back to my parents'

home for a buffet and my father made a proud speech, telling everyone about what I was like when I was little, how neat and organized I was, standing in the lounge playing teacher, my dolls all sitting in a row, me telling them to behave themselves or they'd be sent to the headmaster. Thank God Scott's father didn't try to make a speech. I don't remember him saying anything much, I mean not congratulations or anything. Scott's mother stationed herself by the buffet table, as far as I can recall, refilling her plate every few minutes and looking round nervously as if she thought someone would come up and stop her at any moment. Still, it was a good day, and we were both very happy.

But, after all my dreams, now look at me. It was awful telling my family about Scott moving out, I felt so ashamed, like I'd let them down somehow. Mum was beside herself, twittering round the kitchen and making cups of tea every two minutes. Mari lost no time in saying how she'd always known it would come to this, if only I'd listened to her in the first place, she'd always said, hadn't she, that Dennis was no good, wouldn't ever amount to anything, coming from council house stock (yes, she actually says that) and trying to drag himself up by marrying me—as if we're royalty or something. She's a terrible snob, Marian, she thinks having a four-bedroom detached and a double garage with remote-control doors makes her a bloody Duchess. "That Dennis," she calls Scott when she's stuck in her you-could-have-made-something-of-yourself-if-you-hadn't-married-a-loser groove—"that Dennis has done nothing but hold you back." I've always claimed that I don't feel held back, which isn't exactly 100 per cent true, but I wouldn't give her the satisfaction.

To be fair, I don't think she meant to be unkind. It's just she's got one failed marriage behind her already and I don't think everything's exactly a bed of roses with Robert either. He's Husband No. 2, but he might as well be the Invisible Man, I can't think when we last saw him. He's one of those men who's all hearty handshakes and rather crass jokes, trying to seem jolly the whole time, but when you actually talk to him, he sounds depressed. He wears those trousers with the permanent perfect creases down the front, and it always looks as if they're holding him up somehow, rather than the other way round.

Dad was lovely, though: "All marriages have their ups and downs," he said, making sure Mum was out of earshot first. "Maybe you'll find a way to work things out. Scott's a good man at heart, you could go a long way and find worse." Then he stood there, holding me, the way he used to when I was just a girl and had got in a stew about something or other.

I shook my head slowly.

"I think it's too late for us to work things out."

"Well, if not, not. So long as our Gaily's happy though, eh? That's all that matters to us."

"I'm OK, Dad. I'll be OK."

Scott

You know, I look back and think about why I ended up in bed with Angela and I know, whatever I say, it's going to sound like I'm trying to shift the blame and I'm not. I'm really not. All I'm saying is, if the restaurant's always closed you can't blame a bloke for trying the café, can you? After all, it's not as if I'd gone off Gail or anything. I still fancied her. She's got this gorgeous smile—well, used to have, can't say I've seen so much of it the last couple of years come to think of it—and really nice straight teeth. That sounds a bit like she's a horse that I'm judging or something but I don't mean it like that. She's sort of clean and pretty looking but her smile is really sexy, like she's all wholesome on the surface but dead horny underneath. And she's got knockout legs 'cept you'd have to have X-ray vision to see them because she almost always wears trousers these days because they're more practical and she's not messing about tarting herself up to please someone else thank you very much. But she used to—wear skirts, that is.

First time I saw her she was wearing this dress. It was white with little red dots all over it. It wasn't especially short or anything but it swirled around her legs when she moved so that you noticed them and wished it were shorter and her hair was all shiny and I wanted to touch it. It was in that old caff that used to be in the middle of town—the Mocha Bar it was called; still had its fittings from the Fifties, chrome and padded banquette seats and jazzy-patterned lino. So, I was there with a mate and she's there with her mate and then she goes up to the counter for something and I'm up there faster than a whippet out of a trap, then looking all casual. She's standing, waiting for Sylvie behind the counter to brew the tea. And Sylvie's got it well sussed already and giving me this "So are you going to chat her up or not?" look and swirling the teapot round and round slowly, giving me time.

"Yeah, tea for me as well then, please Sylvie." My opening remark. Stunning. Who could resist me? And if you thought that was cool, how about my dazzling follow-up? "Got any doughnuts left?"

Anyway, this dream creature in the dotty dress, instead of giving me the pitying look I deserved, actually turns and smiles at me. So I'm a goner then. There's no hope for me. I'm practically dribbling. And this is when I lead up to the Big Move. I nod at her.

"All right?" I say. Can you believe it? And, remember, I wasn't fifteen when I met her. I'm too embarrassed to say. Oh, sod it, I was twenty-four—and no problems with the girls normally, I'd been around. But this one reduces me to a bumbling idiot. No patter. No clever compliments. No nifty innuendoes. Bloody hopeless.

"Yes, thank you," she says, smiling at me as if I've said something quite intelligent or amusing. "You?" she adds.

"Yup," I say, then, thinking it sounds too curt and abrupt, instead of keeping my big mouth shut like any sensible person I carry on: "Yes, indeedy, I'm all right. Certainly. All right, all righty. No worries." By now I'm swearing at myself inside, digging my fingernails into my palms to jab some sense into me, ready to stick my head in the urn and end it all. Out of the corner of my eye, I see Sylvie slowly shake her head to herself and start to pour the tea.

Then she says she hasn't seen me in there before and I say I do come in there, often actually, meaning to encourage her to come there again so I can accidentally on purpose bump into her but it comes out a bit rushed and a bit strange and it sounds like I'm being defensive, offering an alibi or accusing her of being dumb or a liar or both.

And so I realize that it's all hopeless and I might as well have two doughnuts and bugger the spots, so I turn to Sylvie for my tea.

"Well, maybe see you around then?" says the dream creature. "I'm Gail, by the way."

The cup rattles in its saucer as I lift it, slopping some over the side. I stare at it, trying not to spill any more at the same time as trying to look casual as if it doesn't really take 99 per cent of my concentration to transport a cup of tea all of ten feet to my table.

"Yes. Definitely. Yes." I risk a quick glance away from the cup to look at her. What a smile. "I'm De— Scott." This was round about the time I'd decided to skip the Dennis altogether and use my surname instead.

"DeScott?"

"Scott." I square my shoulders and try to look smooth. "Just Scott." I nod coolly. "See you around then."

As I clunk my tea down on the table, more of it slops into the saucer, which now looks like a ruddy soup bowl. I won't turn round, I tell myself. I won't turn round. I won't.

I turn round. She is laughing with her mate, probably giggling about what a fathead I am and about how I can't manage to hold a cup of tea properly.

"I wouldn't mind either," says Roger, my mate. "You jammy bugger."

He was right. That was it, with Gail. On good days, I always feel—felt—I was a bit of a jammy bugger. And what the hell does that make me now?

Nat

Mum said, "Well, of course, I won't make you go. Don't see how I *could* make you. But . . ."

I sat there, yawning, wishing she'd hurry up and get the lecture over so I could go round Steve's. Mum was watching my foot as I jiggled it up and down and you could tell any second now she was going to say, "Nathan, please stop fidgeting, I'm trying to talk to you," but she bit her lip. I stopped anyway for a second to watch her face, then started again, trying to speed her up a bit.

"Nat, you know your dad loves you very much . . ."

I snorted. Yeah, right. Funny way of showing it. That's why he couldn't stand to live in the same house as me any more. Mum does come out with some crap sometimes.

"He does, Nat. I know it's hard for you to see while you're still so angry with him. You and Rosie mean everything to him."

I raised my left eyebrow at her to show I knew it was total crud what she was saying. It looks really cool.

"It's just your dad and I—well—you know, sometimes grown-ups find they can't live together any more and they decide it will be better for everyone if they live apart for a while."

Give me a break, puh-leese. Why's it up to the parents to decide? What bright spark came up with that idea? They should have left it up to me or Rosie. I yawned again. I think she's been reading all those sad self-help books. How To Tell Your Kids You're Getting a Divorce, that stuff. Should be How To Tell Your Kids You've Fucked Up Big Time.

"Scuse me? You talking to me?" I leant back in my chair. "I'm not Rosie, you know, you can't pull that 'sometimes grown-ups need to be apart for a while' stuff with me. Why don't you cut the crap and just tell me when you're getting a divorce?"

She sighed and slumped down onto my bed and started trying to straighten the duvet out which was a non-starter because she was sitting on it.

"Oh, Nathan. I don't mean to talk to you as if you're a baby, but you've no idea how hard this is."

"Shouldn't have got married in the first place then, should you?"

She looked up at me.

"How can you say that? You and Rosie are the best thing that's ever happened to me and your dad . . ."

"Yeah, yeah . . . and the divorce?"

"We're not at that stage yet, Nathan. Your dad and I—"

"Can I go yet? I said I'd go round Steve's."

"Well, I think this is pretty important, don't you?"

I shrugged.

"It's no big deal. People get divorced the whole time. Celebs never stay married more than two years. It's to keep themselves in the papers—big battle slugging it out in the courts then fairytale wedding to the next one."

"That's hardly the same thing, is it? This *is* a big deal, Nat, because this is *us*. Anyway, I just can't bear the thought that you or Rosie would ever think—even for a second—that your dad and I having this time apart means we don't love you."

I put my feet up on my desk to loosen my laces, thinking when I got round to Steve's I would check out this new game he got sent from his aunt over in LA. She sounds pretty cool. How come he gets an aunt who knows all the best games and sends him brilliant new ones like months before they're even out here and I get the kind of aunts who knit me crap sweaters barely big enough for a four-year-old and who ruffle my hair and ask me how I'm enjoying school. 'Cept Sheila, that's Dad's big sister. She's cool, but she lives all the way up in Scotland.

I looked back at Mum. She had that look, like she was waiting for something, so I figured maybe she'd asked me a question.

"Mmn," I said and sort of smiled a bit.

"Good." She got up and put her arms round me and tried to give me a hug.

"Mu-uum." I pulled away.

"Oh, you. You're not too old to give your mum an occasional cuddle, are you?"

"Mn."

"Anyway." She stood behind me with her hands on my shoulders. "I'm glad we've had a chat. And you will think about it, eh?"

"Right." Think about what? I got up, shrugging her off. "I'm off to Steve's." I stopped in the hall as I grabbed my jacket and shouted back up the stairs. "What's for tea tonight?"

"Not sure. Pasta with some devastatingly delicious and unusual sauce probably."

"Pasta *again*. Can't we go down the chippie?"

"We'll see. No promises. And Nathan?"

"What?"

"Back by quarter to seven at the latest if you want to eat, please. If you get held up, *phone*. No excuses."

"Yeah, yeah, blah, blah. Why don't you just get me an electronic tag so you know where I am the whole time?" Unbelievable.

Rosie

When I come back from seeing my dad, Mum is ironing or getting the tea ready. She kisses me and says, "Had a good day, darling? Do something nice?"

Now I know what to say and what's best not to tell. One time, I came home and told Mum that I had chips and a Coke and a chocolate nut sundae and then we had cake in a little café. She said I must be sure and make Daddy give me a proper meal, not just chips and then I heard her on the phone to Dad and she was very cross and said he was like a bloody kid himself, didn't he know anything, what was he thinking of and that he would never change, he was always irry-something and he must jolly well get a proper hot meal inside me with vegetables and not be pouring rubbish down my throat all day long and spoiling me for normal food.

Natty doesn't ask me about what I do with Dad, but I know he wants to know, so when I come in I creep up to his room. I lie on his bed while he watches his TV or plays on his computer. He says he is not playing but "doing stuff" but it is mostly games or e-mailing his friends or surfing the Net or talking to people in chat rooms until Mum notices and gets cross about the phone bill and that she can't use the phone. Nat says she's mean and how come we're the last people on the planet with only one phone line, then Mum says he's becoming a right little spoilt brat and that lots of people don't even have enough to eat and he should be grateful. Then he makes that face he does when he's in a funny mood. He doesn't say anything, but he tilts his head like this so his hair falls forward over his eyes and there's no point saying anything to him then because he won't answer.

Nat has old toys under his bed which he says he doesn't play with any more but when Mum said we should pass them all on to the children's ward at the hospital, he said he had to sort them out first and then he didn't do it. Also he has magazines with pictures of motorbikes in and one time I found a rude one with naked ladies in it and I said I was going to tell Mum but Nat said he would give me a Chinese burn if I did and I better not. I wouldn't have told anyway. Nat said it wasn't his, but that Steve must have left it to get him in trouble, and the next time I looked it wasn't there.

I look through whatever's lying around on his floor or under the bed and say where we went and what we did and what I ate and what we bought and what we saw. Nat never asks anything but when he wants to know more about something, his hand goes still on his mouse and he leans back in his chair and kicks his feet forwards until they touch the wall. Mum will tell him off because he's always kicking things and he leaves big black marks everywhere from his shoes. He leans back and I tell him things like, "So then we went to the beach and we saw a funny man with a hat on and he was talking to himself and I said he must be a loony and Dad said no, he might be a spy or a detective working undercover and was just pretending to be a loony so that no-one would suspect anything and that we should just act natural and then run and hide behind the break-water. So we did and we crouched on the pebbles and Dad looked over the top and then I looked over the top to see if the man was still there. But he wasn't." Then Nat said the man was probably hiding behind another breakwater because he thought we must be the loonies because we were acting so daft and suspicious and if we weren't careful someone would call in the men from the loony bin. But Nat was only saying it to try to scare me. He didn't mean it. I could ask Dad. Mostly he does-n't know the answers to things when you ask him, but he doesn't mind. Before, when he was at home, if I asked him questions, he'd say, "Ask Mum" or "Ask your teacher" only now he says, "Mmm, let's see now, where would we find that out?"

Scott

Hello, yes, it's me. Here I am, back home again, playing silly buggers, acting like a prowler round my own house. Well, I had an hour or two to kill before my next call and I couldn't be arsed to go back to work. I wander through to the kitchen. Looks tidy. Pick up an apple from the bowl on the counter and bite into it. Ha! I guess it's a bit of a pathetic victory but I feel as if I've just pulled off a major bank job. At least it's a crunchy one. Have a stretch out on the settee for a few minutes. I mean, it's still half mine, right? Do you think you can get, what's it called?—you know, access rights or whatever, to a settee? It's dead comfy, this one, and big enough so your legs aren't hanging off the end.

Then I trudge upstairs—yes, shoes off first. You're proud of me, aren't you? I can tell. Quick look at Rosie's room, everything all neat and in its place, even the postcards and photos on her pinboard are all pinned on dead straight. Go into Nat's room and snort with laughter at the contrast with Rosie's. You'd never guess they were related. Don't even see how I can get in without treading on everything. Not that he'd notice. You could let a

Tyrannosaurus rampage around in there and the place'd probably look a whole lot tidier than it does now.

I sit at his desk for a minute and lean the chair back on its rear legs the way Natty does, pushing my feet against the wall. The monitor and hard drive lights are on on his computer, so I just sort of nudge the mouse a tad to clear the screensaver. He's supposed to turn it all off if he's out for hours but he's always forgetting. Can't think who he gets that from, must be Gail's side of the family. Well, I reckoned he might have left it mid-game and I could just play for a couple of minutes. Sure as hell wasn't likely to be his homework on the screen. Anyhow, I was just looking, OK? Not snooping. All right, maybe a bit of snooping, but I didn't think it was going to be anything, nothing private.

It's a word document, with his address at the top, on the right, like you do for a business letter, as if he's applying for a job or something. And then there's the date but three days ago. And then underneath that, it says,

Dear Dad

And that's it. The rest of the page is blank.

I sit there for what feels like forever, a lump in my throat. I keep trying to swallow. Then those two words go kind of blurry and my chest feels tight and I can't move. I feel like I might stay like that for the rest of my entire life, picture them finding me, a skeleton in Nat's chair, my bony fingers still clinging to the mouse, my jaw gaping.

I'd probably still be there now if something hadn't jolted me out of it, something that's the one thing I absolutely don't want to hear, can't believe I'm hearing: the slam of a car door right outside and Gail's voice from the front step.

"Can you manage that, Rosie? Leave it if it's too heavy."

Oh, shit. Shit, shit, shit. I'm up on my toes and out to the landing in a second. Peering over the stair-rail to see Gail's outline through the frosted glass of the front door—skid into the bathroom—no, you idiot, not in here—into Rosie's room—everything way too small to hide in or under—back into Nat's room—try to crawl under the bed but there's too much crap—back into our room—open the window—Christ, I'll break my sodding neck jumping from up here—yank open the wardrobe— Jeez, why do women have so many sodding clothes? How's a man supposed to hide in the wardrobe when it's full to bursting with 400 sodding outfits you've never seen her wear even once? Footsteps running up the stairs. Quick—under the bed. Bathroom door closing. So glad I didn't hide in there. Right, that gives me at least a minute if she's having a wee, as long as Rosie's not in the hall. Back out from under the bed—onto the land-ing—coast's clear. Flush of the toilet. Bloody hell, that was fast. She's never that fast when we're at the pictures or having a meal out and I'm sat there like a lemon for hours. Down the stairs, heading for the front door. Oh, dear God, shoes—where the hell did I put them? I know, I know—in the front room. Can hear Rosie in the kitchen—whizz past the half-open door—dash in—grab the shoes—heading back to the door when I hear Gail again, coming downstairs. Jesus H. Christ, can't the woman spend a minute tidying her hair or something? Why's she in such a hurry all of a sudden? Leap back into the front room and crouch down behind one of the armchairs. Marvellous. This is comfortable—I can't stay like this for long, I'll get cramp. I'm not designed to be folded. Round and round in my head, I'm saying, "Keep calm, keep calm," telling myself it's OK, that I'll look back and laugh about all this at some point. Big mistake. Soon as I think that, I realize it *is* kind of funny and I nearly laugh out loud. Bite the inside of my cheek hard, too hard, nearly take a whacking great chunk out of it. Then I take a sneaky look over the top of the armchair. I reckon I only need about 30 seconds clear to scoot to the front door, open it quietly and sprint down the front path and round the corner. As they've only just come in, I don't even have to shut the front door because they'll think they've left it open by accident. I creep to the door and listen.

"Peanut butter sandwich, Rosie?"

Excellent. She'll have her back to the door for at least a minute. I tiptoe to the front door, still clutching my shoes, turn the latch slowly, out and pull the door to behind me and I'm down that path faster than Linford Christie being chased by a velociraptor. The front gate clangs behind me but I don't look back. Don't stop till I'm at the car. Then I shove my feet into my shoes, get in and lean my head on the steering wheel.

Then a nasty thought comes to me. I don't believe this. Oh shit. Where the hell did I leave the sodding apple core?

Nat

At school, we did like how to write a proper letter like if you're applying for a job or something. Useful, huh? Kind of thing you need to do the whole time when you're thirteen. Miss Farnham showed us how you lay it out with the address and the date and all that, then she asked us like when would you use it and Toby who's a total nerd said,

"Please, Miss, if you were reserving a hotel room in advance." He is such a suck-up.

There were a couple of other "Please, Miss" type ideas, writing to your bank manager and stuff. It was such a thrill, I could barely sit still, you know? We were all supposed to be taking notes. Then Miss says, "Nathan, how about you? Do you have a suggestion? When might you want to write a formal letter?"

"I wouldn't, Miss, I'd send an e-mail."

"Yes, Nathan, but that wouldn't always be the most appropriate method of communication, would it? And, even if you were to send it by the e-mail, you might still want to phrase your letter in a formal fashion." She is the Teacher that Time Forgot, no doubt about it.

I thought a sec, doodling in my rough book, then I said, "Yeah, right, like if you wanted to complain about something . . ."

"Good, yes, that's right. What kind of complaint would merit a formal letter, do you suppose?" Can you believe it? That's how she talks the whole time. I'm glad she's not my mum—*What do you think would merit being selected as an edible item for the breakfast table, Nathan? Jeez.*

"Dunno. Well, yeah, like if you wanted to complain in a shop say if you bought some Nikes and they were loads of money then they fell apart after you'd worn them like only one time and the shop never give you your money back, you could write to the chairman . . ."

"Yes . . ."

"—Or if you thought someone was *incredibly boring*, you could write to complain and tell them to be like *less* boring . . ."

There were a few laughs round the class but Miss went all red and said, yes, fine, let's not get carried away and that it was best to confine your letters of complaint to issues that were specific such as faulty goods or booking hotel rooms rather than just your subjective views on other people which were really only a matter of opinion and not what we were concentrating on just now.

Then Joanne Carter stuck up her hand.

"But Miss? Miss, in the papers, people are always writing in to complain about everything. And that's only opinions, isn't it? My dad reads them out at breakfast."

"Yeah, that's right, Miss," I said to back up Joanne. She looked back over her shoulder at me and smiled. She's dead pretty. She's got really nice hair. I might ask her out. Dunno. Have to see.

For our homework, we were supposed to write a formal letter. You put your own address at the top, then you put the other person's address or the company you're writing to or whatever. And you do the date and then you start off Dear Sir or Dear Mr Snotface. Miss said I should have a go at doing a complaint letter seeing as how I seemed to have so many ideas on the subject. I think she was trying to get back at me, but in that special smarmy way teachers have like they're much cleverer than you and there's no way they're going to let you forget it. So I thought about going one better and writing to her.

Dear Miss Farnham
Further to my recent comments in your class this morning, I am writing to complain *formally* about the tremendous, mind-blowing, stratospheric tediosity of your lessons. Might I enquire as to whether you have any plans to make any of your lessons even slightly interesting? If not, I should like to inform you that I will be unable to attend for the rest of the term. I have consulted my doctor and he thinks I am well in danger of dying of boredom and that it is better for me not to risk it.

Also, as well as being very BORING, you had a
ladder in your tights which my Mum always says is
something that looks dead trashy.
    Yours sincerely
    Nathan Scott

I was getting quite into it by the end so I thought I'd
have a crack at writing a letter to my dad as well, but it
was a whole lot harder. I put my address and then the
date and then I put,

    Dear Dad

Then I just sat there. I thought of everything I wanted to
say:

    Dear Dad
    I hate you so much. You have left us in a right
    mess. Mum keeps crying in the bathroom with the
    door locked and turning up the radio so we can't
    hear, but we're not stupid. Rosie has started suck-
    ing her thumb again and Mum says she must stop
    because she can't afford to be getting her braces for
    her teeth. Every time I ask Mum for money, she
    does that frowny face and says we have to be more
    careful now. Plus another thing is I think Rosie
    misses you, like when you used to go in and kiss
    her good night and make up stories about space-
    ships and bionic rabbits and girls with magical

powers. I never seem to have any money and I haven't been bowling for ages. I am fine. How are you?

I read it back and then I deleted it, all except for the Dear Dad bit, and I tried again.

Dear Dad
I am writing to complain about what you have done to our family. It doesn't bother me any, but you have got Rosie to think about because she's only little and she needs two parents not just one. Also since you went Mum gets in a big state every time anything goes wrong like the car or the washing machine. She says it's not that you used to fix them or anything but at least she could moan at you or you'd call the garage so we wouldn't get ripped off, like she would because she's a woman.

Nah. Another go:

Dear Dad
Is it true that you were unfaithful to Mum and slept with another woman? Was it going on for ages or more of a one-off sort of thing? You are always saying to me that I should think ahead and not rush into things that might get me into trouble, so I guess you should have thought of that before and then you would still be at home and it would be OK still.

It's hard, this letter thing, isn't it?

Dear Dad
Come back. Please. I wish you hadn't messed up
but you did and it's too late. You and Mum said
there's no problems in the whole world that can't
be fixed by people sitting down and talking about
it, but all you have done is gone off and all Mum's
done is cry and get cross and drop plates.

Sod it. Delete, delete, delete, delete . . . I went back letter by letter, don't know why, watching the words dis-
appear one by one until it just said "Dear Dad." Maybe
I'll have another crack later. Dunno. S'pose it was a stupid idea, writing to him. And I still had to turn in something for homework. I looked round at the walls of my
room, and my posters, then wrote my formal letter to
the chairman of Ferrari.

Dear Sir
I am writing to complain about the acceleration in
your latest F40 model. At that price, I was expecting it to reach Mach 3 in under 10 seconds and para-
chute-assisted brakes as standard. However . . . etc.
etc.

Miss was well impressed.

Rosie

It's not fair. Nat said I was in his room but I wasn't. He told Mum that I'd touched his computer and she said maybe I was doing my homework on it and it was only fair for him to let me use it when I need to. And she said if he couldn't be sensible about it, we'd have to move the computer downstairs and that would be the end of it. Nat said I'd left my apple core on his desk and Mum said why didn't he just put it in the bin and stop going on about it because she wasn't going to spend the rest of her life keeping the peace between us two and we could sort it out between ourselves. Then she said that, seeing as how Nat's the oldest, she didn't think it was too much to ask for him to be a bit more grown-up about this sort of thing and it was only an apple core and could we all just move on and forget about it.

Then Nat came in my room and said I'm not to use his computer without asking first and he shouted at me and said I'm not to eat or drink near the keyboard. He said I was just a baby and I might have broken it or made it all sticky. I told him it wasn't me and I never used it and I wasn't even in his stupid old room, but he said, well, who else could it have been then? Mum never uses it and there isn't anyone else. But it wasn't me.

I told Dad on Sunday about the apple core and about Nat being so horrible, and he was really nice and got me some new mauve sandals for summer and said I could have some nail varnish too. It's got all silver glitter bits in it. But then when I went home and showed Mum, she said I was too young to wear nail varnish. I told her that loads of girls in my class wear it and she said she didn't care and she wasn't having me look like a—well she wasn't having it anyway. Then she said maybe I could wear it for family parties and things like that, but not for school. So I said OK, but can I put it on my toes 'cause no-one would see it then, but I can still show it to Kira and Josie at breaktime, and she said I could.

It is my dad's birthday on Friday. He is forty now, which is already fairly old. He says that it isn't and that you are only as old as you feel on the inside, and that's what matters. He said that last year, on his birthday, and Mum said if that was true then she must be about 120 because she is tired all the time. Nat said he feels like about eighteen or nineteen so everyone should treat him like a grown-up, and Dad said if he wanted to be treated like an adult, he'd have to start acting like one. And Nat said, huh, he could talk. So Dad made like he was going to punch him, but he was only playing, and Nat did it back. That was when they were still friends. That was before. And Dad said he thought I was about twenty-eight on the inside because I'm always so sensible. I said I'd like to hurry and grow up, but Mum said you shouldn't wish away your childhood because it's the best time in your life. And Nat said yeah, right, how could it be the best time in your life when all it meant was that you got bossed round by everyone else and couldn't do what you wanted?

I am nearly 10. But not yet. I will be 10 in four months, one week and three days. In the evening. I was born at 10.28 p.m. It says so on this little pink card they gave my mum at the hospital. And it says Sex: F. That stands for Female. It doesn't say my name: Rosalie Anne Scott, because they didn't know yet that I was me.

I have got my dad a present but I'm not going to tell you what it is because it's meant to be a surprise. I made it myself. Well, I did part of it anyway. Mum said I could give it to him when I see him on Sunday but it's got to be on the actual day, or it's not the same. Nat hasn't got him anything and he says he's not going to. I think he's really mean. I asked Mum if we could deliver my present for Dad on Friday after school and she said it all depends, we'll have to see, but that's usually what she says when she means no.

Nat

I went in the sweet shop on the way home from school.
I got some crisps and a Mars Bar then when I go to come
out, I see Joanne looking at the birthday cards. You
know, *that* Joanne. So I go over and stand like I'm
choosing a card too and I'm trying to think of something cool to say. Only I can't think of anything.

"Hello, Nathan." She's smiling.

"Hello." I have to do better than this. How crap am I?

"Who are you getting a card for?"

Who am I getting a card for? I'm about to say, "No-
one. How d'you mean?" but I manage to stop myself
just in time. I'm stood here staring at the cards, right, so
I must be getting a card.

"Er, my dad. It's his birthday."

"How old is he then?"

She tucks her hair behind her ears and starts fiddling
with that little silver star she always wears round her
neck. I can feel myself going red.

"Er, really old. Forty-one."

She laughs and turns back to the cards. There are
loads for fortieth birthdays, lots of cartoon ones with

blokes looking in the mirror and jokes about being old and past it. I can't see any for forty-one.

"That's not all that old," she says, "*My* dad's forty-six. Anyway . . ." She takes out a card from the Grandmother section of the rack and looks at it, staring down at this picture of flowers in a vase. "Jason said your dad's left."

I look at the cards and grab one with a red Ferrari on it.

"Yeah. So?"

She shrugs.

"Sorry. I wasn't being funny. I just—well, I'd miss him if it was my dad, that's all."

"Yeah. Whatever."

I open up the card to read the inside, but the lettering's kind of blurry. I can feel Joanne right next to me. Her arm's touching my arm. She's reading the message on the inside.

"Oh," she says, then leans across me to reach out another one from the rack. "How about this one? This one's for dads."

She holds it out to me and looks at me. Then she opens it out and reads the inside.

"See," she says, reading the verse out singsong. It's one of those crap poems you get in birthday cards. Dead corny, you know?

I shrug and dig into my pocket for a tissue. My nose is running and I'm fighting the urge to wipe it with the back of my hand. No tissue. Just half a packet of chewing gum and some change.

"'s all right, I guess. Bit over the top." I offer her some gum and she takes a stick and slowly unwraps it.

"Yeah, but I bet he'd like it. Last year, I made up a poem for my dad's card and he said it was the best poem he'd ever read."

"If I did that for my dad, it'd be the *only* poem he'd ever read."

She laughs then taps the card for her gran against her nose so all I can see are her eyes over the top of it, like she's looking over a wall. You can tell she's still smiling even though you can't see her mouth any more.

"Well, s'pose I better go and pay for this then." She's still standing there. What's she waiting for?

Then I get it. She's waiting for you, you dipstick. I hit my forehead. I try to make it look like I'm just pushing my hair out my eyes.

"Walk you back if you like?" Casual as you please. Not bothered one way or the other.

"OK. You getting the card?"

I look down at the two I'm holding, one in each hand.

"Might as well." I hold up the one she picked out. I don't have to send it if I don't want to, but it'd look rude if I shove it back in the rack after she chose it.

Then I open the Ferrari one again, just to read it before I put it back.

It's not for dads at all. Inside it says: Happy Birthday Dearest Son.

Scott

How did I get to be so old? Tomorrow I'll be forty-one. Practically as good as dead. I know—I should have got over the whole forties hideousness, mid-life crisis thing last year. I thought I had. Actually, no—being thirty-nine was the worst. Because at thirty-nine, there's no getting round it, you're nearly forty—and the only way to not turn forty would be to top yourself, and that's not getting you ahead of the game either, is it? Last year, the nearer it got to my birthday, the worse I felt. I'd look in the mirror while I was shaving and be thinking "You're nearly forty. You're not a young man any more." But, inside, I still felt like I was about seventeen—and that was on a mature day. In my early twenties, I was still a bit of a lad, you know, fancying myself as having the gift of the gab with the girls; then I met Gail and we fell in love and all that, got engaged, got married. But even doing grown-up stuff, like buying our first home, getting a mortgage and what have you, it always felt a bit like I was playing at it, and that any second someone would come along and ask me what the hell I thought I was up to. Then the kids came along and I was working all hours to pay for everything and I was too knackered to notice that I'd stopped being a lad. You see—*inside*, I still was. But on the outside, I must have looked like a normal adult going to work and taking care of my family and falling asleep in front of the TV. The whole of my thirties just zipped by. One minute, I had a new baby; the next, two kids both at school and wanting new trainers every week.

And because I'd built the whole thing about turning forty into this enormous great deal, and was so grouchy about it and thinking I'd have a crap birthday, of course it ended up being brilliant. Gail threw me a surprise party with all our friends and a great spread and I drank beer and wine till it was coming out my ears and kept telling Gail how much I loved her. Yeah. Anyway, I enjoyed myself. So really, being forty-one should be easier. I've jumped the major hurdle so this should be a piece of piss. But now I feel like I've got off on the wrong foot for doing my forties. They say life begins at forty, in which case I've managed to screw up right at the start. Say I manage to struggle on till I'm eighty or so—that means I've another forty years to spend trying to sort out the mess I've made of the first forty. You'd think I'd be due some kind of good luck by now, wouldn't you? A few years sipping rum punch on a Caribbean beach having various portions of my anatomy licked by skimpily clad totty?

I figure I must've got some other sad git's life by mistake. I didn't ask to have a dead-end job and a semi-detached in a crap provincial town with the worst ring road in the history of mankind, you know. That's not the box I ticked when I filled out the application form. I ticked Big Mansion with Swimming Pool, Slick Car and Hefty Wodges of Cash, far as I remember. There must have been a mix-up. I'm only in this life as a result of an administrative error. I want a refund. And somewhere there's some toerag swimming up and down my pool who can't believe his luck.

This year, what are the odds on Gail organizing me a birthday surprise? I've got more chance of being struck by lightning. Actually, with my luck, I've got a lot more chance of being struck by lightning. If you're listening, God, that's not meant as a reminder. I wasn't volunteering—just pointing out it's my birthday tomorrow so feel free to have a day off if you're getting tired of pulling out all the stops to make my life a complete misery. Sod it, I'm not even going to tell anyone. I'll just forget the whole thing and reschedule it for a couple of months' time once Gail's calmed down and we're all sorted out again.

I am forty-one today. I am a forty-one-year-old man living in a bed and breakfast and hoping that I'll wake up any second now and discover it was all just a lousy dream. At least I should get cards from the kids though. I mean, Natty would send me a card, right? Gail's got the address. I have my shower and shave, telling myself in the mirror that I could easily pass for a man in his early thirties. I go on down to breakfast and ask Fiona if there's been any post.

"Don't think so. Why—you expecting something?"

"Yeah, well, no—not really. It doesn't matter."

"It's not your birthday, is it?"

"It is actually."

"Ooh, happy birthday! Sorry, I'd have got you a card. Is it a big one? Let me guess, it's not your fortieth, is it?"

So much for thinking I can pass for thirty-two in a dim light.

"No. Forty-one."

"Well, that's all right then. You're past the worst."

Is that the best that can be said of my life, that I'm past the worst? Cheers.

I sit down and scan the paper, trying to cheer myself up by reading about the misfortunes of others. Never works that, does it? Think of the starving children in Africa, the teachers used to say at school when you didn't want to choke back the pigswill we got dished up as dinners. Send it to them, then—that's what we thought, what we always thought. Sure, I feel grateful I happen to have been born in a country where I'm not likely to actually starve to death, where I've got some sort of roof over my head, but I don't say it makes me actively happy. Besides, it's not like I've never been hungry, coming in from school and being doled out a thick slice of bread and marge sprinkled with sugar and trying to eat it slowly 'cause you don't know if you'll get anything else later and you can't ask case you get a clip round the ear. I'd never go back to that. I'd do anything to keep my kids from living like that. Anything. I mean it. I'd rob a bank if I had to. Once you've lived like that, you feel like it's still out there, waiting to drag you back—and you have to keep away from it or it'll get you, and all you'll be able to think about will be money and food, food and money the whole time and you won't be lucky enough to escape a second time, you know it, so you better make damn sure you stay away from it in the first place.

Fiona puts down half a grapefruit in front of me. There is a glacé cherry in the middle, an unexpected birthday treat, and a single small candle with a flickering flame. It is so pathetic I want to cry.

"Come on then, birthday boy. Make a wish and blow it out."

I puff out my cheeks as if I am blowing out a flaming bank of forty-one candles and not just one standing alone. One blow and it's out.

I wish I was someone else.

At work, things go from bad to worse. None of the lads have remembered. No surprises there, but Harry, who might remember, is a no-show. Maureen phones to say he's feeling off-colour so he's not coming in and nor is she because she wants to keep an eye on him. Lee and Martin keep messing about and between them manage to crack a double glazing unit that we'd just finished. Gary has just been chucked by his girlfriend and is mooning about with a face as long as a wet weekend. It is Denise's day off. No-one even offers to make a cup of tea.

At five to twelve, I hear the toot-toot of the sandwich van and I go out, thinking well, at least I can stuff my face and bollocks to everybody else. Thingybob, the sandwich girl—woman—whatever, smiles at me which I notice, partly because it feels like the first proper smile I've had all day, and partly because I've always had a bit of a soft spot for her. No, I don't mean I want to jump her bones, just she's got a nice face and a nice smile and well, you know. OK, I would jump her bones given the chance, but I don't want you thinking I'm just a shallow bastard who's always up for a shag.

I order Spanish omelette in a bap which might sound odd but I can assure you is the dog's bollocks when it comes to filling you up and making the world seem a better place. I tell her not to bother wrapping it and I take an enormous bite straight away, asking her for two chocolate muffins at the same time.

"No chocolate ones left. Sorry."

Could today get any more crap?

"Oh, come on! It's not even twelve o'clock. How can you have run out already?"

She looks a bit taken aback and she flushes.

"I said sorry. It's been really busy today. I can't antici-pate it when half my customers are in need of a chocolate fix, can I?" She looks at me and then her face sort of soft-ens. "Having a bad day?"

"You could say that, yeah. Sorry." I dig down into my pocket feeling my eyes prick, and make heavy weather of hunting for change so I don't have to look up. I am def-initely losing it today. Get a grip, man. Get a grip. "It's my birthday actually and so far it's been a non-stop jam-boree of laughs, treats and extravagant gifts, you know?"

This is her cue to make some smart comment about my age—when's my Zimmer frame arriving and can she offer to drop me off at the post office to collect my pension. Any second now.

"I'm sorry," she says, treating me to another one of those smiles. It feels like a gift. It's a smile that deserves a bit of rustly paper and fancy ribbon round it. "Happy birthday." She ducks down beneath the counter. "Would you settle for a piece of lemon cake instead? Or cherry and almond? It's home-made."

"Go on then. I'll take the cherry."

I offer the money but she raises her hand firmly like a cop stopping traffic.

"Hold it right there. It's on the house."

"Really?" I wonder whether I should chance my arm and ask for a birthday kiss, too, seeing as how she's in a good mood, but she might just give me a slap round the chops instead. Also, standing there in her van, it makes her higher up than me, and she seems impossibly out of reach. With my luck today, it's probably best not to push it.

I realize I'm standing there with my mouth open, just looking up at her, without saying anything. She must think I'm not quite the full quid.

"Well, cheers then," I wish I could think of something clever to say. I wish I could at least remember her name so I could drop it in casually. I wish . . . I wish. "Thanks again. See you." Stunning. You'd think a man of forty-one would be better at this by now.

"Hope your day picks up," she calls after me.

Of course it'll pick up. At least once you hit bottom, the only way is up, right?

Wrong. Gail always said I was too optimistic.

In the afternoon, I hear on the grapevine that one of our regular clients has just gone out of business. I check the invoices and, yes, they still owe us money. Not a lot, but not so little we won't notice it. I make myself a cup of tea to go with cherry and almond cake, but the milk—which admittedly had been a bit of borderline case in the morning—has given up the ghost and gone blobby and disgusting in my mug. We've no more fresh, so I have to make do with black coffee.

I ask the lads if they fancy going down the pub after work for a birthday booze-up but Lee's got a date with some hot-to-trot babe who lives miles away and he's got to go home first to change. Martin's going bowling with his wife and another couple. Couples, couples everywhere. And Gary doesn't feel like it, thank you, and to be frank, he looks in a worse state than I do. So then I call up Colin and Jeff and Roger and say, hey, lads' night out, come on—let's get slaughtered, thinking I should have sorted this weeks ago but I didn't because I've been concentrating on surviving from one day to the next and my birthday didn't seem like top of my list of priorities. But Colin says he's not allowed out (What is he? Twelve?) because he got pissed one night two weeks ago and Yvonne still hasn't forgiven him for falling over the hall table at two in the morning and making her think they were being burgled. I get Roger on his mobile, but he says no can do, he's over 200 miles away at a sales conference. Jeff—who of course has even less of a life than I do, but not by much—says yeah, all right then, with his usual level of enthusiasm; he doesn't mind tagging along, but he's a bit skint and I say that's OK, I'm paying, my treat, you daft bugger. But if you were looking for someone to cheer you up, Jeff wouldn't exactly be Number One on your list, you know?

So we go to the pub and for the next three hours and over the course of several pints and one or two shorts, or possibly three or four, we take it in turns to moan about how crap our lives are. We get into a rhythm with it after a while, him then me, then him, then me, and I'm thinking what we really need's one of those timers so we get fair shares, you know—like you have in the kitchen to time your eggs or remind you to take the pizza out the oven. We've got one—Gail's got one at home which looks like a miniature kettle and you sort of wind it up to set it, then it goes off with an incredibly loud ring which makes you jump out your boots. It's bloody loud. God, I don't even have that any more. No life, no wife, no sodding kitchen timer.

Then we go for a curry up the High Street and stuff our faces with poppadoms and chicken balti and lagers, and by now I'm way too drunk to drive home and I've left my car in the pub car park anyway, but I can't face staying at Jeff's in the Land where Everything is Brown so we lean against each other at the taxi rank and he says he really, really loves me, I'm his old mate and I've never let him down, not ever and I say something stupid along the same lines and we give each other a big hug and I fall into a taxi and he weaves his way back up the High Street.

To start with, I give the driver my address. My home address. And it's only when he pulls up outside and asks for the fare that I remember that I don't live there any more and can he carry on and take me to where I should be. He's overjoyed, of course, and says am I just messing him about, do I realize he's got a living to earn, he can't be driving all round town on the off-chance I might remember where I live, and I've clearly had far too much to drink and I better not be making a mess in the back of his cab or there'll be trouble. And I say no, no trouble, I don't want any trouble, thank you, I'm not messing, I just need to go to my good old B&B, it's just round the ring road a ways—and then out a bit.

When we finally get there, I unfold myself from the back seat, give him too big a tip, and concentrate on slotting my key into the lock, trying to do it silently which of course means I make fourteen times as much noise as normal.

Miraculously, some flowers have appeared in my room, with a card propped up against the vase, signed from Fiona and Dave. On the bed are another two cards and a package, plus a note from Fiona saying they were dropped off earlier in the day.

Three birthday cards. See, not everyone in the world hates me.

The first envelope says *Dad* in childish writing. I knew Rosie wouldn't forget.

The card says "Happy Birthday Daddy! You are 41! [thanks] Lots of love from Rosie. XXX" The writing is in blue, with mauve kisses. She's made it herself. On the front is a purple butterfly, made of cut-out bits of felt, with silver glitter on its wings. The package is also from Rosie. I tear off the paper, which is patterned with yellow teddy bears, and find a box. Inside is something heavy, wrapped in pink tissue.

It is a mug. White and hand-painted. On one side there is a man with dark hair and a blue shirt, I guess meant to be me, holding hands with a girl—Rosie—wearing a mauve dress. On the other side, it says, in shaky lettering, I LOVE MY DADDY.

The other card—amazingly, unbelievably—is from

286

Nat. As I open it, I realize I've spent the whole day trying to tell myself there'll be no card from him, preparing myself for the fact that my son wants nothing to do with me. But here, right here on this bed, is a card. Inside, Nat's written "To Dad." Then there's one of those verses:

I hope this birthday is the best
That you have ever had
Because to me you are the tops,
The greatest living Dad.

I'll spare you what happens next, but let's just say I get a bit choked up and—well, it's a pitiful sight and I'm just dead glad—for once—that I'm in that room all on my own. I'm a forty-one-year-old man sitting on a single bed in a rented room with no life and no future sobbing his guts out. So why is it that, suddenly, I feel like this is the best birthday I've ever had?

Lesson Three

Scott

I'm still in Limbo Land at the moment, a kind of elephants' graveyard where the rootless ghosts of what used to be real men with wives, homes and families go to drift about until they get themselves Sorted. "Things'll improve as soon as I'm Sorted," we say. "It'll be easier when I'm Sorted." "Once I'm Sorted, I'll have a proper place with a Jacuzzi and a snooker table and one of those Yank fridges as big as a Cadillac with that ice dispenser gadget on the front and I'll leave empty lager cans all over the lounge floor if I want." I'm beginning to suspect that Being Sorted isn't something that automatically happens: you serve your misery and living-out-of-a-suitcase time and then you get your Sorted badge. I have a nasty feeling that it might involve having to Do Something. Even the thought makes me want to go and lie down (with a magazine under my shoes—I've had my feet lifted that many times to have a bloody *Family Circle* slid underneath it's become a habit, even though it used to make me feel like a dish of peanuts being plonked down on a coaster).

I must, must, MUST get my own place soon. No two

ways about it. A flat probably, just to rent. There's no point buying somewhere—even if I could afford it—because Gail might still have me back. I've not given up on us yet. And maybe, if she sees that I'm behaving myself, got a flat, and I'm keeping it nice and clean and everything, well, she'll see that I am responsible after all, that I'm not such a bad bloke. Plus then Rosie could come and stay on the weekend. And—. Well. Maybe in a while. See how we go. One thing at a time. Still, I could go and see a couple of letting agents. Rosie can come too. She likes helping her dad.

Then I'll have somewhere proper to bring her when it rains. Couple of weeks ago it pissed down and we'd seen every kids' movie going, so I ended up bringing her back to show her my room at the B&B. It's all right, but it's not the same as a real home, is it? I've put up the new wallpaper now, but it's all a bit heavy on the rosebuds and frilly curtains for a bloke. There's this kidney-shaped dressing-table with a glass top over some sort of pink cloth and a pink padded stool that's so low it feels like you're sitting on a potty. I've a kettle at least and a couple of cups, but the kettle lead's so short I have to kneel down on the floor or balance on the potty-stool to make the tea—it's like one of those effing pens in the bank on three inches of bloody chain, as if your whole life's ambition is to nick a snidy plastic biro with some naff logo on the side and a nib that's all gunged up with ink. Yeah, that'd be worth whipping out your lapel pocket with a flourish, impress your mates. Rosie was a total star about the room, of course, said it was lovely and she sat at the dressing-table and pretended to powder her nose and all that. And she's promised to paint me a picture to put up on the wall. She's good as gold, don't know where she gets it from. And what was it she said last week? Oh, yeah, that's it. I said I'd take her to this place that does these brilliant ice-cream sundaes. And like a berk I didn't bother to check first and we get there and it's shut—'cause it's a Sunday, see. It'd have been better if she'd had a bit of a moan or demanded loads of sweets instead. But she didn't. She just said, "Never mind, Daddy, we'll get lollies from the sweet shop"—like that, as if she were consoling me. I felt gutted. I'm going daft in my old age.

Don't get me wrong. Fiona and Dave's place—the B&B—it's OK, and I've enjoyed the decorating. I've been giving them a hand with the other rooms in lieu of rent. Gail would never believe it if she could see me now. I'm a changed man, honestly I am. At home it was always nag, nag, nag—when are you going to finish doing the bathroom?—you said you'd put up that shelf—what're the chances of getting that door fixed before the next millennium? It felt like she was on my case the whole time, you know? Thing is, I actually *like* doing this stuff. I'm not bad at DIY and all that and, call me sad, but I get a bit of a kick when I've finished a project and you can see you've made a good job of it. But when you're being nagged to do it, you somehow go off the whole idea. You feel like you're right back at school and teacher's giving you a flea in your ear about the home-work you never handed in (again).

Come to think of it, a lot of the time I felt like I was a bit of a disappointment to Gail, like I was a snotty kid who was always coming in from playing with dirty knees and ruined shoes. Or a bad dog who kept getting under her feet and she'd have been a whole lot happier if I could have stayed in my basket and stopped bothering her. Well, I guess she's got what she wanted now.

Maybe I could do some decorating jobs on the side to earn a bit more. Fiona and Dave said I was way better than some other guy they'd used. He was pricey, too, that's why they started trying to do it all themselves and why it's taking them for ever. I could have a business card done and everything, make it all pukka.

Reminds me, I said I'd go back to Harry's and do their downstairs cloakroom as a thank-you. I owe them both big time. Maureen's taking an age to decide on the colour. She's keen on those not-quite-white shades, you know? Can't see the point of them myself. I mean, have a colour or don't have a colour, make your mind up. I can't be fannying about with this white with a hint of pink bollocks. Harry's been saying he'd do it for ages, but he's not got round to it. Says when he gets home, he just flops into his armchair and falls asleep in front of the telly. Poor old stick, he's looking his age. I keep telling him to cut down on his days, but you know what Harry's like. Even when he's on holiday, he phones in every day. I reckon he thinks of First Glass like it's his baby or something. Must be nice to feel like that.

OK, OK, I knew you'd notice. I admit it, I was avoiding the subject deliberately because I don't—I can't. Well. What is there to say?

Nat. You're wondering about Nat, aren't you? Bet you're thinking, has the man lost the plot completely? What happened with his son after the birthday card? I was kind of hoping you wouldn't ask. It's not that I'd forgotten about him. I'd sooner forget how to breathe. I think about him the whole time—when I'm at work or out on a job, driving along listening to the radio, having a quiet pint in the pub. I'm not being sentimental or any of that, it's just that so many things remind me of him, see? Like, when I go into the paper shop in the morning and I see his favourite crisps and I think of how he used to make himself a crisp sandwich for a snack, standing there, leaning against the kitchen counter and seeing how big a burp he could do. I don't know where he gets his manners from. Gail's lot most probably. Or we'll get some total goofball customer in and I'll be thinking, "Can't wait to tell Natty. Natty will crack up when I tell him that."

But I can't tell him. It's well over a month since my birthday, and we've had Easter since, but I've not seen him once. I thought the card meant that things were OK, that we were cool again. The next morning, I was like a kid on Christmas Eve. I kept thinking of how it would be, all the stuff we could do together again—swimming, roller-blading, fishing off the beach, or just hanging out, computer games, surfing the Net, whatever. So I rang to say thanks for the card, left a message on the machine and said, "See you all Sunday?" Then when I turn up that Sunday, Gail says she's sorry but he's gone over to his new girlfriend's house. I didn't even know her name or anything and I didn't want to ask Gail. Next thing you know he'll be twenty years old and getting married and I won't know a dicky bird about it until I see the announcement in the paper.

So much for thinking that I'd been taken off the blacklist. Serves me right for daring to believe I might be starting to have some kind of a life. I thought maybe he'd started to grow up a bit. Gail would say that's rich, coming from me. I guess she's right. Who am I to talk?

In the beginning, I was convinced Gail had somehow poisoned his mind against me. I told myself she must have done it to get back at me because she'd gone off the deep end about Angela. But even all the time I was trying to convince myself of it, I knew it wasn't true. Whatever else you may say about Gail, she'd never use the kids that way. She just wouldn't. I won't say there haven't been surprises and I still think she over-reacted ridiculously over one tiddly mistake. But she's been pretty straight about the kids and, on the whole, she doesn't do me down in front of Rosie. But I couldn't figure out why Nat wouldn't speak to me. OK, I slept with someone else—so that makes me a bad husband. Fair enough. I guess it makes me a cheat, a liar and a louse (feel free to disagree at any point). But I don't see that it makes me a bad dad, does it? I mean, it was a bloody stupid thing to do, but it's just between me and Gail, right? It's nothing to do with Nat and Rosie. So how come I'm the Big Bad Wolf? It's not like I walked out the door without a backwards glance and shot off to Mexico never to be seen again, is it? I mean, I'm here. I'm doing my best. What more can I do?

Nat

At Easter, I went on a school trip and we did rock climbing and abseiling and canoeing, loads of things. It was pretty cool and Rosie was dead jealous because she couldn't come. Mum said I should send a postcard to my dad to thank him for paying for the trip, and she gave me some spending money and some stamps and wrote out his address, but I never had time and it's not like he'd notice anyhow.

Steve wasn't on the trip 'cause his family has this ginormous big get-together thing at Easter, when they all go and camp in the fields on his uncle's fruit farm. Steve says it's brilliant and they have pillow fights and you get to drink cider and they do barbecues. But it was only his family, so I couldn't go. I didn't mind, it was pretty wet most of Easter. Jason came on the trip and he was OK, but when we snuck outside one night with Neil and Kieran 'cause Neil had brought some fags with him, Jason had a massive great coughing fit when he inhaled so we nearly ended up getting caught.

Me and Joanne started going out. We see each other on

the weekend and most days I walk home from school with her and sometimes I go round her house and we hang out there or she comes to mine, and we e-mail each other like the whole time practically. She's pretty cool. :-) Turn it on its side, stupid. And she sends me this winking one ;-)

Rosie keeps saying, "Do you snog? I *know* you do. What's snogging like? Tell me, Natty. Tell me, *ple-e-e-e-e-ase.*" Then she goes, "Do you use your tongues and everything? Kira said snogging's when you move your tongue all around in the other person's mouth and that's why they look like they're chewing when you see them on TV. But I said then your spit would get all mixed up and that's disgusting. I'm never going to snog, if I have a boyfriend and he says he wants to snog me I'm keeping my mouth closed the whole time."

I'm not saying a word.

I'd been going to ask Joanne out for ages, but first she was seeing this other boy from school and then I found out that she'd chucked him, but I didn't know if she liked me or not. I would have talked to Dad about it, but how are you supposed to ask someone something if they're not even there? Then one night we were having our tea and Rosie goes, "Natty's in lo-o-o-o-ve, Natty's in love!"

"No, I'm not. Stupid."

"Yes you are and I know who she is and she begins with J."

"Just shut up, all right?"

Then Mum joins in, "C'mon, Rosie love, behave. Don't wind up your brother."

Then when Rosie went up to her room, Mum goes, "I don't want to be nosy, Nat, but I'm really pleased for you if you've met someone nice."

"She's OK."

"And . . . have you asked her out?"

"Mn."

"Do you know if she likes you?"

"Mn."

She tops up my Coke then and puts some more ice in it just the way I like it. "You know," she goes, "women, girls, always like to be asked out . . ."

"Yeah, but what if she says no, then I'll feel like a right dipstick, won't I?"

Mum wrinkles up her nose like this, then she goes,

"There's worse things in life than feeling like a dipstick from time to time, Nat. Sometimes you have to take a risk, otherwise you might as well live your whole life in a box."

I dunno. Was funny hearing Mum say dipstick, she never used to say things like that, it was more like the way my dad talks. I wonder what it would be like to live in a box. S'pose it depends how big it is and if it had windows and that. You'd have to have holes at least, for air, and maybe your food would be piped in through a tube or poked through the holes so you could only eat things

that would fit—chips one at a time and hot dogs without even the bun. Spaghetti. Fish fingers. No pizza. Life
without pizza. Nah, I couldn't do that.

Sometimes I go round Joanne's house for tea or on a Sunday and they all sit and eat together and it's all proper and
her mum cooks the tea only they call it supper and her
dad's there and her kid sister and they all talk all at the
same time, while they're eating and everything. Joanne's
dad asked me loads of questions about what I want to do
when I grow up and about what I like and that. Then he
goes, "And will you be able to keep our daughter in the
style to which she's become accustomed?"

Only his face is dead serious, right? Then Joanne
nudges me and says, "Da-a-a-d, stop it!" and her mum's
laughing and she says, "Pay no attention, Nat. My husband has a peculiar sense of humour."

"Yeah, he does." I never meant to say it out loud. It
just kind of slipped out.

And then they all started laughing again. But it was
OK. It was kind of funny really.

Joanne says maybe I should go with Rosie and my dad
one time. Like on a Sunday, yeah? Just to see what it's
like. And Jason says it's not so bad, you get used to it
pretty soon and then it seems like only normal and then
after a while he says you can't even remember what it
was like before. But I don't want that to be normal. I like
it the way it was before. Otherwise, it'd just be like

going to visit your aunty or something, and you've got to be on your best behaviour and say thank you for having me and all the time you're counting the minutes till it's time to go back home. I reckon it's probably best if I leave it for now. In any case, it's not as if he's missing me or anything. Rosie says they have an excellent time without me, so there's no point me tagging along and being in the way.

Gail

This morning I stood in the shower and, as I started shampooing my hair, I suddenly noticed that I wasn't crying, and, what's more, I didn't feel like crying. And it wasn't the first time either. I don't think I've cried for over a fortnight. I can't believe I didn't notice before. Maybe my body's run out of tears. You know I'm not one to witter on about my feelings, but after I faced the fact that I didn't love Scott any more and, worse, that I'd managed to hide it from myself for so long, I felt just appalling. Sick with shame. Every morning, I'd get out of bed and feel like a newborn foal, facing the shock of being alive on unsteady legs. Then I'd stand in the shower and cry. Like clockwork. Turn on shower, wait for it to get hot, step in, reach for soap, start crying. It felt allowed somehow because I was already wet, if that makes any sense, as if my tears were only so much water, washed down the drain as if they had never been. It felt safe in the bathroom, with the radio turned up and the shower on so the kids wouldn't hear me. And I could tell myself that it was OK, that I was just getting it out of my system so I could be strong and calm for the day ahead. I had to hold myself together for Rosie and Nat. Nervous breakdowns are all very well if you've got the time and no-one else depending on you, but if you're a mum, then it's really not an option, is it? Besides, it's not as if I was bottling it all up. Our phone bill will be through the roof this quarter. Cassie deserves a medal. But I'm OK. I survived. I'm still here.

Rosie said Scott had her looking in estate agents' windows on Sunday. I said, "Is he planning to buy a house then?"

She shook her head.

"Dad says it's too much money. He's going to rent a flat. Then I can go and stay. I'm going to have my own room and Dad's going to paint it whatever colour I like and I'm going to have a huge big pinboard to put up all my drawings and photos."

It made me feel a bit strange. I don't know why. It's good that he's starting to move on, of course, getting himself a bit more organized, with a proper home. The kids'll be able to stay over some weekends then. That'll be nice for them and a bit of a break for me which God knows I could do with. Well, Rosie's obviously keen to go. Nat might be another matter. It just feels a bit odd. Like it means that he's really not coming back. I know, I know, Cassie would say I'm being a dog in the manger, not wanting him back but not wanting him to be able to get on and make a new life without me either. That's not true. It's just it feels so final somehow.

The first few weeks after he left, Scott looked a bit rough, to be honest. Sort of crumpled; his trousers hadn't been ironed and he was wearing trainers. But after a while he smartened up and now he always looks neat and tidy when he comes to pick up Rosie. It's nice to know he's learned how to use an iron after all these years. Makes me wonder why I got stuck with doing it the whole time when clearly he's more capable than I thought.

I can't imagine Rosie staying away from home. She goes to stay the night at friends' houses sometimes, of course, but this would be different. She'd have her own room permanently, a room that I would never see probably, a whole part of her life that would be nothing to do with me. When Mari split up from Gerry, her first husband, she wanted to stop him seeing the kids because— well, because he was a complete waste of space and had been sleeping with one of Mari's friends for years. Don't ever let me get like that. I hope I'd never sink so low as to use the kids against him. Not for his sake, but for theirs. I think they've got enough on their plates without us two using them as a battleground, though Rosie seems to be taking things in her stride.

I see her now, the way she is on a Sunday, bounding out the front door to meet Scott coming up the path. She's just so different around him—compared with the way she used to be. I suppose it's because she gets him all to herself on a Sunday, and she never had that before. Rosie was always shy when she was little. If I bumped into a neighbour in the street and stopped to chat, she'd hide behind my legs and had to be coaxed even to say hello—and she even seemed shy with Scott, as if she didn't have a right to make any demands on him. Sometimes she'd stand near his chair, watching him, waiting for him to pay her attention, but she'd never just climb up onto his lap the way Nat did when he was little.

I remember once years ago, Rosie was about three, I think, and she and I were meeting Scott and Nat in a café. It was at the seaside and they'd gone to look at the fishing boats or something and Rosie was tired and it was really a bit far for her to walk. So we were in this sweet tearoom place, then suddenly she looked up and said,

"There's Nat and Nat's daddy!"

She'd spotted them through the window. It was a funny thing to say, but sort of awful at the same time.

"He's *your* daddy too, Rosie," I said.

"No." Her voice all serious, speaking to me as if I was silly and had made a mistake. "That's *Nat's* daddy."

But she was right in a way. That's how it seemed. It wasn't that Scott didn't love Rosie. He did. It's just he really didn't know how to be with her, how to talk to her, listen to her. Whereas with Nat—sorry, but, well, Scott is *such* a kid, you have to admit—it was just as if they were best friends, boys of the same age playing together.

It's taken him nearly ten years to realize he's got this wonderful daughter. And now he's lost his son. I feel sorry for him, really I do. You'd have to know Scott, really know him, to understand how it must be killing him, eating him up inside. He hides it as well as he can, I know what he's like, but I don't know how much longer he can stand it.

Rosie

I want to tell, I want to tell, and my dad says I can tell first. He's got a new flat and I'm to have my own room. He said he would decorate mine first, before the kitchen or the living-room or anything, but I said he should paint his room first because I've got my room at home as well but he hasn't got anywhere else at all, and then his face went all sad and I wished I never said it.

Mum is giving Dad some things for the flat from home—sheets and pillows and knives and forks and the plates we don't use any more and a tablecloth that Mum says is too small and those chairs that she doesn't like. Dad is really pleased and says it's going to be the best flat ever. Uncle Harry came round with the big van from work to help Dad pick up the things. He's not really our uncle at all, we just call him that and it's good because we've only got one uncle and he lives millions of miles away in Canada so we never see him. When they came with the van, Nat stayed in his room and wouldn't come down even though he likes Uncle Harry, but I looked up when I was outside and Nat was looking out the window from behind the curtain. Nat says that now that Dad's got a flat that means he's definitely never coming back, but Nat is only saying that because he is in a bad mood because I told him that there's only two bedrooms and there's nowhere for him to stay. He said he didn't care and he bet it was a totally crappy old flat and he didn't want to go anyhow, but he is just jealous. Dad told me that the very next thing he was going to buy was a sofa-bed so Nat could come and stay too if he liked, but I never told Nat because he was being a pig. And anyway, it's not the same as having your own room.

When Dad first went away, Mum said it was because they were getting on badly and needed to have some time away from each other. But Nat said he left because he went off with another woman. I asked Nat if that meant Dad was going to have a baby with her and Nat said I was stupid and that people are always doing it, not just when they want a baby, didn't I know anything? I did know. I was just asking, that's all. Miss Collins says we should never be afraid to ask if we want to know something. But in any case, when I went to the flat with Dad, there wasn't anyone else there and I think if Dad had a girlfriend he wouldn't need a flat in any case because he could sleep over at her house and also he would be better at doing the shopping and I would not have to tell him what to get and which is the right sort of spaghetti and the best tomato ketchup, so I think Nat is wrong, but when I try to tell him, he won't listen and says I'm just a baby and no wonder I don't know anything. But I do.

Dad said that when he's done my room, I can have my friends round. I'm going to have a sleepover with Kira and Josie and maybe Florence and Nicola as well, and we can have a midnight feast with popcorn and chocolate raisins and Hula Hoops. You put them on your fingers like rings, then eat them off one at a time.

Now when Dad comes to pick me up on Sunday, Mum is nice to him and sometimes she smiles and says thank you when he gives her the envelope. Nat says it is money and he told Mum she ought not to take it but should throw it back in Dad's face. Mum said we couldn't possibly live on what she earns and Nat was being a silly, ignorant little boy. Then she said she was really sorry and asked him to sit down so she could explain it properly to him, but he said he had to go to swimming practice or he'd be late. Nat has started asking if he can wash the neighbours' cars for money because he says he is saving up and also he wants to buy talk time for his mobile because it's hardly ever worked since he had it because he never has any money and Mum says she can't be paying out for anything that isn't essential. Nat says that it is essential and that if you haven't got a mobile then you're nobody, and I said: "But I haven't got one" and he said: "Exactly. See what I mean?"

He's a pig. Maybe I will get one for my birthday. I asked Mum and she said the whole thing is just getting completely out of hand and what was the world coming to when children thought they couldn't survive without having a mobile phone and I said they'd been banned at school and if teacher sees you with one, she'll confiscate it till the end of the day and Mum said I'm not surprised, good for her. I asked Dad if I could have one for my birthday and he said we'd have to see, and also I told him that my pocket money has to go up because I'll be double figures. I'll be 10. Josie's 10 already, but Kira won't be 10 for ages and she is very cross that we'll both be double figures and she won't.

Scott

Dah-dah—sound of trumpets, please. One good thing
has happened. Yes, to me, Scott, Magnet for All Things
Crap. I found a flat, somewhere not too far from home so
it'd be easy for the kids to come visit. Renting turned
out to be bloody pricey, especially via an agent, they're
total leeches these people, they really are. Fortunately,
Harry said he knew somebody who knew somebody
who had a cousin etc., etc., and this guy was up for letting me have it dirt cheap for six months on condition
that I decorate it and he'd stump up for the paint and
wallpaper. And, given that I couldn't afford anything
else anyway, I said yes.

It's a two-bedroomed one, so I can do up a room for
Rosie, however she wants, maybe with a stencil of
ponies cantering all the way round, and a purple quilt.
That's her favourite colour, purple. Sorry, mauve. Have
to watch the money though. If Gail would pull her finger out and earn a bit more, everything'd be easier. She's
got some front, come to think of it, calling me irresponsible. Look who's worked his arse off all these years to
support us. Don't suppose there's any danger of her

going full-time at the doctor's surgery, that'd help out. I hope she's nicer to the patients than she is to me. Just imagine some crumbly comes limping in and Madam says "You're two minutes late. Dr Whatsit will feel ever so let down." For now, we agreed that I'd give her X quid a week—and no, I'm not saying how much but it's a buggery sight more than that Child Support Agency would have made me fork out so don't go trying to hang that one over my head. Not that I begrudge it. I'd never see Nat and Rosie go short. Nor would Gail, to be fair.

Once, when Rosie was just a tot, Gail wasn't working then and my paypacket wasn't much to write home about, we'd seen this toy trike. A little yellow seat it had, and blue wheels. Well-made, too. So we started saving so's we could get it for her for Christmas and then my car went and died on me and that had to come first and bang went most of our Christmas money. Then, it's the week before Christmas and Gail tells me to shut my eyes and she drags me into our garden shed. And I'm thinking "Oh, hello, is this my lucky day?" and I'm starting to feel a bit frisky and reaching out my hands to give her a fondle when she tells me to open my eyes and I do and there it is, the trike. And I'm thrilled to bits—as much as if I'm still a kid myself and it's for me. It made me feel all funny inside, like a pain almost and I couldn't even say anything for a bit.

Gail just squeezed my arm and we stood there, as proud as if we'd just delivered a new baby. Turned out she'd taken on doing some bloke up the road's washing and ironing. That's what she said. Later I found out she'd sold her gold bracelet, too—the one she wore all the time—to her sister Mari who'd been trying to get it off her for years. Soft as a steamed puddin' that woman is, when she wants to be. Yeah.

I was sorry to leave Dave and Fiona's, though. They made me a farewell dinner and booked me to come back and decorate the last two rooms. For real, live money. But now I'll really be all on my own. I feel like I've left home. Course, when I first left home, when I was seventeen, it was different. Couldn't get out of there fast enough. I lived in this total dive with my mate Roger and his girlfriend of the time. Now it sounds like I was a bit of a spare prick at a wedding, but it was OK. I'd done casual work before then, but this was when I got my first regular paypacket, so I had money in my pocket and I was away from home, away from *him*—and that was all that mattered.

The flat's no palace, I'll grant you, so don't go thinking I'm having an easy time of it here. It's definitely on the wrong side of grotty, but it should scrub up well enough, and it's not as if I'm short of evenings with not a lot to do, you know. At least it's got a cooker and a fridge. I can't afford much in the way of furniture yet. Rosie and me looked at futons because they're cheap and could double up as a settee, but I'm sorry—could they make them a bit more uncomfortable, do you think? What are they made of—granite? I reckon you'd get more kip clinging to the window ledge. I feel like I'm missing something when it comes to futons, like there's a big futon conspiracy that no-one's let me in on. I know they're cheap but what else have they got going for them? They're all scuttling about down on the floor so you fall over them or stub your toe on the base. And they look like some great wodge of raw pastry when they're lugged back into a sofa-bed.

So I thought, no I can't be doing with this, sleeping like a student at my age, and I went mad and bought myself a proper bed. Call me a stupid optimist if you will. Why, oh why, did I do that, you ask, given that I've not got women lining up round the block demanding access to my body twenty-four hours a day? What am I wanting a double bed for? Because buying a single bed when you're forty—all right, all right, keep calm, forty-one, just checking you're still awake—is too sad for words and if I truly thought I'd never have sex ever again in my whole life, I'd end it all right now this very minute.

Not that I'm being overwhelmed with offers at the moment. Frankly, if anyone under sixty looked even halfway keen, I'd probably take them up on it. "You'd need a paper bag, mate!" That's what Lee says if he's talking about a woman who's a bit rough looking, so you wouldn't have to look at her face. If she's really ugly, he says she's a double-bagger. He's a bit of a tosser, Lee.

I'm not like him, but I must confess, being a man and not yet six feet below the daisies, I do think about doing

315

it with most women I meet. Like the sandwich van lady. You should see her muffins. Really. And I used to have the odd fantasy with Fiona in it sometimes, at the B&B. Fortunately, I do have some self-restraint. Not much, I'll grant you, but I was in no rush to get chucked out on my ear twice in one year. Besides, her husband Dave's become a bit of a mate as well; we've started to go for the occasional drink, have a chat. He's got a good sense of humour and he doesn't think the world revolves around football either. And at least he's not as depressed as Jeff.

But I could definitely do with a woman. I'm not cut out for all this sleeping on my own lark. It doesn't suit me. Actually, it's not even the sex I miss most; it's not like I've lost the use of my hands, y'know, but it's not the same. And you can't give yourself a cuddle, can you? You can't snuggle up to yourself or do spoons or stroke your own hair and whisper yourself "Night-night, sweetheart, sleep tight."

Mind you, the last—what two, three years?—maybe more even—I can't say Gail smothered me with affection either. It was more a case of quick peck vaguely in the direction of my face, "Night then," turn over and we're both snoring our heads off by the time we hit the pillows. 'Cept Gail would say she doesn't snore.

It's not just we hardly had sex any more, though I still say we hadn't done it for at least two months when I was tempted from the straight and narrow by Angela. Gail and I were still doing it—making love, I mean—

only it felt like it was once in a blue moon. I wish we'd marked it on the kitchen calendar, 'cause she claims it was practically every week and I say it was more like once or twice a month. And it was still nice and everything but a bit, well, the same. Not surprising, really. I mean—me, I'm up for anything (within reason, and not including anything involving gerbils or other wildlife), but if you want to tie me to your bed with your black stockings and have your wicked way with me, you just carry on. I'll give it a go. But Gail, well, she knows what works for her and that's what we do. Did.

Anyway, I digress. My new bed's a double, that's the point, so I'm ready and waiting if you know any drop-dead gorgeous babes you want to send round. Gail even said she'd look me out some bedlinen and spare pillows and that, and I went to pick up some other bits and pieces from the house—a chest of drawers, a couple of chairs, that old table we kept in the garage, the telly from our bedroom, so I reckon I'll be all right. Harry lent me one of the vans from First Glass and he gave me a hand too which was good of him. I'm not sure he should still be hefting things about at his age, but he wouldn't take no for an answer, daft old bugger. Rosie was in charge of the move and we had to put different coloured stickers on the things to go in different rooms and she wrote out a list to make sure I did it all properly. Yes, Ma'am! She's becoming a right little bossy-boots—no, I'm only kidding, it's nice to see her getting so confident after she's been so shy most of her life. Yeah. It really is.

Nat

Now he's gone and got a flat. See, I said he wasn't coming back. I don't care anyhow because I hate him. No I don't. Not any more, not like I did before. I just don't care. If he wants to be stupid and pathetic and keep showing himself up, it's nothing to me.

Mum's being really embarrassing. Like at first, when he left, she just let him go and she didn't try to stop him or anything, and I bet she never even thought about us. But now when Dad comes to pick up Rosie, Mum's got on all this lipstick and she wears these clingy tops like for girls. I told her she was much too old for them and it just looks stupid, and she said,

"The day I start taking fashion advice from a teenage boy, and one who can't even manage to tuck his shirt in at that, it will be a sad day indeed."

I mean, it's *supposed* to be like that. Doesn't she know anything?

I know he did it with another woman. Like a mistress or whatever. I bet it was someone younger. I thought when he left that he went to live with this woman, but Rosie said he was in a B&B. She keeps acting like she knows everything, but she doesn't because she didn't even know about the other woman until I told her. She didn't even know hardly anything about sex till I told her last year. She thought it was all eggs and tadpoles, she didn't know any of the good bits. He was probably just waiting till he could get a flat and his girlfriend'll probably move in then, that's what'll happen. That's how it always happens, and pretty soon they have a whole other family, then they forget about you and all you get is a card and maybe a CD once a year on your birthday and that's it. I don't care anyhow.

Rosie's being such a suck-up. She keeps going on about Dad's new flat and how he's going to do up a room specially for her and he said she can have anything she likes, she can have it all in mauve if she wants 'cause it's her favourite colour. I said it sounded like it would look really dumb to have it all the same and she wouldn't be able to find the bed if it was the same colour as the walls, would she, then she said well, it wasn't up to me, was it, and she was going to choose what she wanted and I was just jealous because there wasn't a room for me and even if there was, she bet Dad wouldn't decorate it specially because I hadn't spoken to him for months and it jolly well served me right.

I hate Rosie too. I hate all of them. I might move in with Steve, his mum says she likes having me round there, though his dad makes all these pathetic remarks that are supposed to be funny, looking at me and going to

Steve's mum, "You know, I was sure we only had the three children. Did you adopt another one while I popped out for fags?"

"Never mind him, Nathan love," his mum says. "You're always welcome here, you know that. Here, have some more potatoes."

Steve said his mum was only being nice to me 'cause she felt sorry for me 'cause my dad left, so I wrestled him to the floor and made him take it back.

"You're just dead jealous 'cause your mum likes me more than you."

"So?" He was trying to hit me, but no chance. I'm a better fighter than he is. "Mums are always nice to other people's kids. It's what they do. It doesn't mean anything anyhow. She's just being polite. They're only a pain in the neck with their own kids. Everyone knows that."

That's not true, is it? Mind you, my mum is always nice to Steve and I don't reckon she likes him all that much. And she's nice to Jason, even though he's always picking his nose.

I dunno. Maybe I'll go and live in London on my own. They'll put it on the news and say I've disappeared and Mum and Dad will have to go on TV, crying and begging me to come home. I might go to America. Kieran's family took him to New York and he said it was brill, just like being in a TV cop show, the police had guns just like they do on TV and there were yellow taxis and ginormous great skyscrapers everywhere. We never go anywhere. We went to some stupid Greek island a couple of years ago and Mum and Dad both got sunburned and could hardly move. I did too. Rosie only didn't because Mum put sun gloop on her about every 10 seconds and made her wear a hat and long sleeves even though Rosie went all whiny and said she wanted to go brown.

Last year we went to one of them dome things that's always warm inside. Dad said it was spooky and he felt like we were in this vast playpen being observed by scientists and he kept ducking out of sight behind the plants so they couldn't watch us. Mum said she didn't care who was watching so long as it was warm and she didn't have to cook. She liked it 'cause there was loads of stuff for me and Rosie to do so she didn't have to look after us. Well, Rosie. I don't need looking after. It was OK when we got there with a whacking great water chute and a wave machine and everything, but you couldn't swim properly because there were too many people, and anyway we should have gone to New York. I've started saving up for a flight. Jason's supposed to be saving, so he can come too, but he keeps spending his money. He is clueless sometimes. I don't want him holding me back if I decide to take off suddenly. I'll have to see. It's OK. I'll probably just go on my own.

Gail

"No," I said. "Absolutely not."

Cassie stuck her tongue out at me.

"Come on. Why not? What have you got to lose?"

"I don't have to give a reason. I just don't want to. I'm too old for all that." Cassie was trying to fix me up with a date. A blind date if you please. With a work contact of her husband's, some man called Michael. Divorced.

"Oh, right then. You've booked your plot already then, I take it?"

"What? What plot?"

"Your cemetery plot. Why not move in now? You sound like you're ready to. If you don't want to get the good out of life any more, shove over and make room for someone else."

She took my arm and propelled me over to the mirror.

"Look. What do you see?"

"A very pushy, pain-in-the-bum best friend?"

"Ho-ho. And . . . ?"

"Me. I see me, of course. Should I be expecting someone else? What's your point? That I'm getting on a bit so should hurry up and lasso a man before yet another wrinkle takes up permanent residence?"

Cassie stood, hand on hip, scrunching up her nose at me.

"Finished? All I'm saying is you talk as if you're 103 but—"

"I might as well be. Women of forty aren't in huge demand, you know. How many forty-year-olds do you see on the cover of *Cosmopolitan*?"

"Thirty-nine. Why are you rushing into being forty? It'll get here soon enough. But no. You're right. Sign up for the geriatric day care centre. You're no use to the world now."

"Aaaarrggh! Cassie, I may have to hit you in a minute. The fact is I'm very nearly forty and I feel like I look every single day of it. But even if I looked twenty-two and had the body of a supermodel and the face of an angel, I'd still not want to go on a blind date."

"Babe, if you looked like that, you wouldn't have to."

"Oh, charming!"

She plonked me down on the couch.

"Hey, relax, will you? I'm joking. You know you're attractive so let's just cut out this poor-little-plain-me bollocks, OK? Look, all I'm saying is if you really don't want to get back with Scott, then why not start having a bit of fun? I don't think a convent would take you in now anyway, so you might as well be getting your end away."

I shrugged. Still, I bet Scott's not been going without. We all know what he's like.

"It's not that I don't miss making love. I do. And cuddles and male company, all that, but I don't think I could handle a date. It's just not me."

"What? You can't handle going out to dinner and the cinema? Those are the best bits. Are you completely barking?"

"No, not that. I mean having to laugh at a whole new bunch of terrible jokes and getting used to a *different* set of disgusting habits, and putting up with their macho driving and listening to them moan about their ex-wife. Everyone's got so much baggage by the time they're our age."

"Better that than some spurting virgin still living at home with his mum at forty-five."

"True."

"So you'll meet him?"

I wrinkled my nose.

"You swear he's definitely not a psycho?"

"I dunno—I believe he may have mentioned something about his collection of axes—oh, for heaven's sake, Gail, he's just a bloke."

"And he's not bald?"

"Thinning, but only at the front."

"Height?"

"For God's sake, I don't know. Not a gnome anyway. Anything else? Quantity of nostril hair? Willy length and diameter? Name of shop where he buys his underpants? Meet him and if he's hideous, then just smile politely and don't give him your phone number."

I thought about it for another minute.

"OK, then, I'll do it. But I'm not promising to enjoy it."

"Heaven forbid."

To be fair, although Michael was certainly no James Bond, he wasn't bad looking. He was smart and tidy at least and what was left of his hair had seen a comb in the recent past. There was a little light sprinkling of dandruff across his shoulders but then we're none of us perfect, are we? He held my chair out for me at the restaurant, which threw me completely having spent most of my adult life with someone who just plonks himself down and is already wondering what he'll have for dessert without noticing I'm still wrestling with some huge great chair that seems to be made of lead. Scott thinks if he even remembers to say thank you once a day then he's doing well.

Cassie had told me that Michael was "forty-something," by which she apparently meant about fifty-five. The plus side of this was that it made me feel incredibly young and I had to stop myself from skipping across to the bar and kicking my legs up in a can-can.

"So hello there, Gail!" he said, darting forward to kiss me on the cheek when he introduced himself. Not a good start. What on earth makes a man think you want to be kissed by someone you've never even met?

"Well, here we are!" he laid a hand on my arm. "And what's your tipple, Gail? No, let me guess! Campari and lemonade, am I right? Or are you dying for a gin and tonic? I know what you girls are like." He leant towards me then, as if he was telling me a very important and intriguing secret.

This particular *girl* is just *dying* to pelt you with ice cubes, I thought, edging away subtly so he'd stop grabbing my arm every three seconds.

"Just a white wine please."

He grinned and gave me this sort of knowing nod, like he'd guessed all along that I was really a white wine girl.

"Medium?"

"Dry."

Actually, I do prefer medium, but I can't bear people who act like they know you and come over all chummy immediately.

I couldn't figure out exactly what was odd about him at first, but then it hit me. For all his breezy manner and apparent confidence, he was actually seriously depressed. No, not a little bit down in the dumps. Not having a bad day. Depressed. Underneath the jolly exterior, you could sense this great, awful black hole of sadness. I looked away, embarrassed, as if I'd accidentally seen him naked. And the jolliness only made it worse, more desperate somehow. He looked like depression was his natural vocation and now that he'd found it he had no plans to look around for something else to occupy him. His skin had the dull, almost grey look of someone who's spent too many hours writing letters of complaint to the council and not nearly enough time playing beach-ball.

Near the end of the evening, Michael leant right in close to me: "It's been great to meet you," he confided, "I really feel I've moved on from the pain of my marriage now."

I smiled sympathetically and made one of Nat's vague "mn" sort of murmurs.

"You know," he said, smiling as if he was about to tell me a joke, "my wife and I had stopped having sex. We hadn't made love for over five years."

"Hm-mm." I nodded, trying to look caring in a detached, don't-you-dare-touch-my-arm-again sort of way, as I reached behind me for my jacket. Why are you telling me this? I thought. I don't want to know. Maybe he imagined I might whisk off all my clothes out of pity and say, "You mustn't go without sex for even one more minute. Take me now!"

"Well," I said, looking at my watch. It was quarter past ten. "I really must be making a move. The babysitter, you know . . ."

Cassie found the whole thing hilarious, of course.

"Bet it makes you appreciate Scott now, eh?"

"Is *that* why you set me up with Michael?"

"Hey, no. No, I didn't. I'm sorry. He really sounded like a nice guy from what Derek said."

"He was OK. I'm not blaming you. But, he was just so sad. Everything about him, even—look, he had these really well-polished shoes, OK?"

"Well how the hell is that sad? Shows he takes care of himself. You were always pissed off with Scott and saying he should smarten himself up."

"Shut up for two seconds and I'll tell you. It was sad *because* somehow you could just tell that he'd really taken his time doing them, that he hadn't just given them a quick buff up while he was running out the door like the rest of us. I bet he'd sat down with a proper shoe-cleaning kit and spun it out because he didn't have enough else going on in his life."

"You could still have whisked him home and tried to shag some life into him. Then he'd have taken his shoes off and you wouldn't have had to look at them."

"Thank you, Cassie, Queen of the Agony Aunts. Do you ever dispense advice other than: go out and get laid?" She looked at me, head tilted to one side in that way she has. "I know, I know, you think I'm a horrible person. I should have been more sympathetic, but I felt if I'd spent even ten more minutes in his company then his sadness would have, I don't know, engulfed me like a great clammy grey cloud. All I wanted was to get the hell out of there as fast as possible."

"Ah, well. It's all practice. And now you've got the first one out of the way, you won't be so nervous when you meet someone else."

"You're right. I'm sorry to whinge, I know you meant well. Anyway, it did have its plus side . . ."

"He paid for dinner?"

"No, we went Dutch. But after, when I came home, I sat up a while in the kitchen and gradually this great wave of, well, *relief*, swept over me. I know it sounds mean, but I was just *so* glad that I was me and not Michael, that I've got my two gorgeous, precious kids, my sisters, my parents, you—people who love me, I suppose, people I really love. I don't ever want to be that lonely. I'd rather be back with Scott again than be like that."

Nat

Our Aunty Mari came over last night—to babysit Rosie. I don't need anyone looking after me. Mum said she was going out with a friend, but I reckon it was more like a date. For a start, she took like about fifteen hours getting ready. Normally, when she used to go out, which was practically never anyhow, it was more like fifteen minutes. Mum came downstairs in this blue dress that she never wears any more. It comes all the way down to here at the back so she can't wear a bra with it. She came in the kitchen and I gave her a look, then she went straight back upstairs again and came down in a black skirt with a red top and a jacket over it.

She got back quite late, after half-ten. I stayed up, waiting for her to come home, and I looked out the window to check out the guy when I heard a car pull up outside, but it was just Mum getting out of a taxi.

Then this morning I'm eating some Sugar Puffs straight from the box when Mum comes in.

"Good time last night?" I did that thing with my eyebrows, making them go up and down really fast. "You were late enough."

And then she laughed, which was kind of weird, and she rolled her eyes the way Dad does. Used to.

"Not really, but thank you for asking." Then she came over and tried to hug me.

"Mu-u-um! Gerroff!"

"Oh, Nathan. You're *so* precious, you've no idea."

I think she's lost the plot. What's brought on all this luvvy-duvvy stuff?

"What's up with you then?"

"Nothing's *up* with me. Actually, yes it is. I suddenly feel rather lucky and pleased to be me for once. It's a nice feeling."

Oh no, I thought, that's all we need. Don't tell me she's gone all flaky for this guy. Flake City, here we come.

"You seeing him again then?"

"What? Who?"

I shrugged and chucked a Sugar Puff high in the air and caught it in my mouth.

"This guy. Your *date*."

"Ha! You little detective, you." She gave me another squeeze and kissed the top of my head. "Nope. Definitely not, in fact."

"Mn."

"You think that's why I'm so cheerful?"

"Mn."

She leant against the counter and fished into the

cereal box. She never does stuff like that. Normally, it'd be: Get yourself a bowl, Nathan. Sit down and eat properly, Nathan. For goodness' sake, Nathan, can't you eat like a normal person?

"No, it's not that. Hey, these aren't so bad without milk, are they? It's just—well, you know I'll be forty next week."

"Yeah. You've gone on and on about it so it's not like I've been allowed to forget."

"Have I really? Sorry. Well, maybe I have. I've felt pretty lousy about it to be honest, as if my whole life is over. Especially with the problems between your dad and me, you know?"

"Mn."

"It sounds strange maybe, but suddenly I feel like I've woken up. So I'll be forty—so what? Big bloody deal. I'm still healthy, still attractive—don't you *dare* give me that look, Nat, you cheeky so-and-so—and I'm not giving up on myself. Or not yet at any rate."

I still say she's becoming a bit of a loony tune since Dad left, but at least she was in a good mood and wasn't telling me off, so I guess maybe it's OK.

"Oh. Right. Mum?"

"Yup?"

"Can you lend us some money so's I can get some talk time for my mobile?"

She laid her head down on the counter like she was about to go to sleep.

"I give up." Then she chucked a Sugar Puff at me. Parents aren't supposed to do stuff like that, are they? I mean, Dad always did, but he wasn't like a real parent anyway, he only ever said parent stuff about doing your homework and not watching too much TV when Mum told him to. And now she's getting just as bad. I don't know. Parents. I mean, what are they like?

Scott

We've got into something of a routine, me and Rosie. I pull up outside at bang on 10 a.m. on a Sunday. I cheat actually—I get there a few minutes early and park round the corner so I can arrive on the dot. Well, it means Gail's got no excuse to have a dig at me and Rosie seems to like it. She stands by the window in the front room with her nose pressed to the glass so she can watch out for me. I don't even need to ring the bell.

Rosie flings open the door, jumps up to give me a hug, then kisses her mum goodbye and settles herself in the car while Gail and I see to the business end of things, i.e. the handing over of vast sums of money from me to her. She tells me when there's anything extra the kids need but, give her credit, she never asks for extra for herself. She's decided to start working longer hours at the surgery now, so that'll ease things a bit all round. True, the money's nothing to write home about, but then she says what else could she do? I've always thought Gail was pretty brainy actually, a lot brainier than me that's for sure, but she's never pushed herself. Yeah, I know, like who am I to talk?

On Sunday morning, we go out for a bike ride, then we find somewhere we can have a lunch—a roast or shepherd's pie—proper food, not just chips as Gail says; I *am* trying here. In the afternoon we rent ourselves a video and sit on my settee with our feet up like an old married couple, then at the end we rewind to see all the bits we liked best again. Or we have a look round the shops and Rosie helps me get bits and pieces for the flat. She picked me out a vase and some cushions, she says you have to have things like that or it's not a proper home at all.

A few times, we've gone up to London for the day. We even went to the Science Museum. I know, I know, I said you'd never get me in a museum till I'm long dead and they want my bones for a display case: Late 20th century/early 21st century male. Origin: South-east England. Note how the skull and skeleton show signs of excessive stress consistent with having suffered a crap life. Actually, we went because of some project she was doing at school to do with methods of transport, and they've got models of aeroplane wings and that sort of stuff which all move and it showed you how a plane goes up in the air and stays there. It's all to do with the shape of the wing and the speed of the air over it and under it. I think. Funny, I always thought planes stayed up because you're all on there with your fingers and toes crossed and praying like buggery that it's not time for your number to come up. The museum wasn't half bad actually. It's more like playing now, with things to do and funny demonstrations and computers and everything. She said I was embarrassing because I kept having a go at all the things, but they never had them when I was a kid so I don't see why I should miss out now. Still, I wish Nat had been there. He'd say he was too old for it, but I reckon he'd have got a kick out of it. If we go again, I'll tell Gail, see if he fancies coming along.

Gail says I should write him a letter as he won't speak to me if he answers the phone, just goes and gets Rosie. It made me think of that time, when I saw what was on his computer screen. Just "Dear Dad." Maybe he didn't want to say anything else, or didn't know how. Must run in the family because I had a go at writing to him, I really did, only I'm not much of a one for letter writing and I couldn't get it to come out right. And in the end the only bit that seemed to make any sense was "Dear Nat" and "love from Dad"—and I didn't think that would make much of a letter so I never sent it.

On Sunday, Rosie asked me about Christmas.

"Da-a-a-a-dd-ee-ee?" she says. So I know she wants something. Mostly she just calls me Dad.

"Ye-e-e-e-s, Ro-o-o-o-s-ee-ee?"

"Silly!" She hits me on the arm. Children are so violent these days, what's the world coming to?

"Go and pick on someone your own size, you bully!" I rub my arm, hamming it up like mad and screwing my face up in pretend pain. "What do you want, Piglet?

336

More pocket money? The latest Nikes? Fame and fortune? Whatever it is, the answer's probably no, so go ahead, ask away!" I pat my pockets. "Your old dad's a bit short of the readies this week."

"*No*, Daddy." She takes out her purse. It is pink with tiny beads stitched on all over it but there are gaps from where Rosie has pulled off some of the beads with her teeth, one at a time. She says it stops her biting her nails, but her nails are so short now there's nothing left to bite anyway. She unzips the purse and shows me her little stash of money. "See?"

"You little hoarder—can I have some?"

She chews her lip for a moment and pokes through the contents with two fingers.

"OK. How much do you want?" Dead serious.

"Oh, Rosie, sweetheart!" I pick her up and whirl her round in the air the way I used to when she was just a tot. "I don't want your money. I was just kidding."

"You can if you want." Aged nine (sorry, nearly ten), going on thirty-five. She tucks her hair back behind her ears.

"I'm fine." I take her hand and we swing arms as we walk along, heading for the harbour to see the boats before we go for fish and chips. She does a funny half-skipping step to keep up with me. "I'm chuffed to bits you offered me your money, but hey—"

"What?"

"I don't want you worrying about money, love, OK? Just 'cause things are a tad tight at the moment doesn't mean we're on the breadline. Your mum and I would never see you or Nat go without."

"What's on the breadline?"

Questions, questions.

"You'd make a great quizmaster when you grow up. Or you could host *Newsnight*, have the politicians quaking in their shoes. On the breadline means being poor—like only having enough to eat bread, I suppose. Actually, now I think of it, I'm not sure it is that. I think it comes from being so poor that you were given free bread but you had to queue up for it. Surviving and no more."

"Only bread. No chips?"

"Uh-huh, no chips."

"No . . . roast chicken with peas and gravy?"

"Definitely not. No. And absolutely no Barbies or DVDs or PlayStations or any of that."

"Oh."

I don't want to turn into a boring old fart (too late, too late, I know) who's always droning on about the past and how it was in my day, but kids today, sorry, but they haven't got a clue, have they? I mean, thank God they haven't and all that 'cause I've always sworn Rosie and Nat would have everything I never had. But they think being poor means living in a house with only one telly or having to borrow the latest computer game from a friend. I've never told my kids much about what it was like when I was growing up. This is only thirty years ago we're talking about here—but it feels like a whole other universe, a different millennium. Actually, it was a different millennium, but you know what I mean.

We lived in this row of council houses—my parents are still in the same house, all these years later. Thing is, none of our neighbours were flush either, so at least we were all in the same boat. If anyone had called us deprived, we wouldn't have had a clue what they were on about. We thought everyone went round with a hollow feeling in their stomach the whole time. I used to have fantasies about food—steaks and chicken and plates piled high with chips and ham and tomatoes. I swore that when I was grown up, I'd have a fridge that was always full—and I do. We used to get pickings from the allotments, too, with one of us on lookout—raspberries nicked from under tents of green netting, corn on the cob roasted over a fire we'd make down by the back of the gravel heaps, carrots sometimes—we'd lay on our stomachs on the river bank to wash off the soil. I even ate raw rhubarb once. Never again. Gave me a tummyache so bad I thought I was dying.

One winter it was so cold, my dad got me and Russ to knock down the garden fence. He wouldn't do it himself, of course, lazy sod. Bit by bit it all went on the fire, the whole lot. Then half the neighbours sussed what we'd done and did the same. Next time the man from the council came round, we said we didn't know what happened, honest we didn't, some blooming thief must have come and nicked them in the night. He never believed us, of course, but they still came and put up new fences in the spring. So we all did it again the next year.

Anyway.

"You know Christmas?" Rosie says, walking backwards on her heels as I steer her round obstacles like litter bins and lamp-posts.

"Thing in December. Coloured lights and presents and stuff, right? Leaving every parent in the land bankrupt? That thing?"

"Da-a-a-d! Stop it!" She gives me a shove.

"Yes, my little angel. Do I know Christmas? Yes, I do. It's not for ages and ages yet. It's barely summer. What about it?" But I already know what about it. Oh, shit, I'm thinking. What the hell are we going to do about the C-word. I kind of hoped, well, assumed, that I'd long since be back at home by then, and I'd be enjoying the festive spirit in the bosom of my family with carol-singing round the tree and that, you know? Oh, OK, arguing over the telly and nursing a hangover and feeling fat and saying, "No, *you* said *you* were getting the batteries"—still, you get my drift.

"Well," says the little voice at my side. "Nat says now you've got a flat of your own that means you're never coming back, not ever, and you won't be home for Christmas."

Someone has wrenched apart my ribs and ripped out my heart. I can't swallow, can't barely breathe. I can't look at her, see her sweet little serious face looking up at mine. Can't bear to see her trying to hide her disappointment, pretending she doesn't mind.

We've reached the harbour now. I could distract her, point to one of the boats and say, "Oh, look!" The air is thick and tangy with salt, the smell of decaying fish. Gulls cry above our heads, endlessly wheeling round looking for food.

"Thing is . . ." I squat down, lean my back against a bollard ". . . I'd love to be home with you for Christmas, but I—it's a long way off and . . ."

How do you tell your nine-year-old daughter her mother won't have you back because you had sex with another woman? I mean, where do you even start?

"—but I don't know if it's going to be possible, love."

"You *could* if you really *tried*. You're always telling me not to give up."

I take her hands and squeeze them in my own. Such small hands she's got. How is a small person with such small hands supposed to grasp this sodding great unwieldy mess?

"You're right, love, you're right. Grown-ups are great when it comes to dishing out advice and lousy at following it themselves. How can I—you see, sometimes grown-ups don't get along—and—no, that's not it—see, I made a, well, a mistake, see—but like a *big* mistake—and it upset your mum a whole lot—and that's why it's best if we live apart for a bit or—maybe even a long time. But you know you'll always be my best girl and I'll definitely see you at Christmas and bring you presents. You just try and stop me!"

Her mouth smiles at me, but her eyes aren't joining in the fun.

"Look—remember that time that other girl stole your best pen?"

"Alice. Yes. My mauve one."

"Yes, the mauve one. And do you remember how you were really, really cross with her, but then she gave it back and you were all friends again?"

"No. Teacher made her give it back, then I pinched her in the playground and we don't sit together any more."

"Oh," I'm regretting I ever got started down this road. I'm not much cop at this stuff. "Maybe that's not such a good example. The point is—your dad did something bad—for which he's very, very sorry—but, for now, we're . . . well, we're not sitting together, your mum and me, OK?"

"I'm not four, Dad. You don't have to talk to me as if I'm a baby."

"Sorry. I was just trying to make it all clear."

She twists a strand of hair round and round one of her fingers and looks down at the water in the harbour.

"Nat said that you shagged another lady and she's your mistress."

I can't do this. It's too hard. Just when I think I've taken a small step forward, that I'm handling things, something happens and I'm right back to square one with my guts yanked out of me and gasping for breath like a mackerel on a sand dune. If I could only turn back the clock. If I could only. If.

"Oi—language! Don't say shagged, it's not nice. And don't believe everything your brother tells you. I do *not* have a mistress and I never did. That's totally wrong. That would be a very bad thing and I certainly don't, not at all. Now, come along and let's have a look at these boats—see that big one at the end there. What would you call it if you owned that one, eh?"

Gail

On Thursday, Scott asked if he could come round to pick up his walking boots. Nat was out at swimming, of course, and Rosie was up in her room, so I said he could come into the kitchen. I had some spare kitchen things that I thought he could do with for his flat, just a couple of saucepans and utensils and so on. Then halfway through, guess what happened? Nat arrived back and came crashing into the kitchen like a rhinoceros, practically taking the door off its hinges. Impeccable timing as always, thank you, Nat.

It was pretty awful. Scott just stood and stared at him. His face went white. Literally. I thought of what people say—"he was white as a sheet" and he really did look like that, as if all the colour had suddenly been bleached right out of his face. I sat at the table, sort of clutching myself, willing it to be all right. But Nat wouldn't even look at him, just stood staring at the floor then started messing about in the fridge and spilling Coke everywhere and creating havoc as usual.

I felt so tired, just being in the room with both of them. The air seemed to be thick with all these things

NOT being said. Scott didn't tell Nat he was sorry, didn't tell Nat that he loved him. Nat didn't say how much he was missing his dad. And I couldn't help. I sat there, cradling my head in my hands, just waiting for it—the situation, the tension, all the not saying—to go away. Maybe I should have left, given them time to sort it out on their own. Then Nat walked out and Scott looked absolutely stricken. Like he might even cry. Scott absolutely never cries. I've seen him come pretty close sometimes but he never—oh yes, except when Nat was born. I can still picture him standing there, holding this miraculous precious bundle in his arms, his face bent close over Nat's, and all these tears spilling down over his cheeks.

I reached out and laid a hand on his arm, but he flinched and said he was fine and better be making a move, he had to get back. I handed him the bag of kitchen things, but he wouldn't even meet my eyes, just said thanks and he'd see me Sunday. I watched him walk back down the path and his shoulders were hunched as if he was trying to keep warm against the blast of an icy wind. I wanted to call after him then, run after him, just hold him for one minute, tell him it would be all right. But I stayed where I was, watching until he reached his car, and then he was gone.

I asked him about it once, about not crying I mean—way back when we still occasionally had what could pass for a real conversation. We'd been watching some film on television. And it was such a weepy, I cried buckets, mascara all streaked down my face. You could see Scott was moved, his eyes go all shining but his face looks sort of clouded, like you can't see what he's thinking and his body goes stiff. His stomach muscles were tight and rigid, as if he was held together by bands of steel. At first, he pretended not to know what I meant.

"You're having me on, aren't you? Blokes can't be crying every time they watch some soppy drivel on telly."

"Come on, you can't say it didn't affect you."

But he didn't want to talk about it, just said he'd taught himself not to cry when he was a kid once he realized it couldn't help, not ever. Crying never got you anywhere, all it ever did was make things worse and let the other person think they'd won. But if you could just hold out, they'd never know they'd got to you, there'd be some part of you they couldn't touch, that was just you and you had to keep that bit as strong as you could and not let anyone else mess with it, not ever. And I said "It's just a film, Scotty, there is no-one else winning now, not now." He didn't look at me, just sat there shaking his head very slightly from side to side, his eyes glassy and far away. No, he said, it was better that way and now it was just the way he was.

It was because of his father. Scott doesn't talk about it, but you've only to see them in the same room together to work it out for yourself. That man is the best argument for euthanasia I've ever come across. People like that shouldn't be allowed to have children, as far as I'm concerned. And his mother's not exactly the doting type either. I don't know why Scott ever sees them at all. God knows, it's not as if he owes them anything, they only acknowledge his existence at all when they want something. They're vile people, the pair of them and that's one duty I'm not sorry to have given up. When I think about it, it's amazing that Scott's really not a bad dad. It's not like he had much of an example to follow.

Nat

I come back from swimming and *he* was there. I come in the front door, dump my bag and go in the kitchen to get a drink. The door's shut, which it never is, but it turns out it's 'cause he's in there with Mum. They're sat at the table, opposite each other like he's interviewing her or she's interviewing him. As I open the door, they both look up.

"Natty!" He leaps to his feet like he's heard the starter's pistol and he'll be off round the track, heading for the tape. He knocks his chair over behind him but he doesn't even pick it up straight away. If I did that, Mum would say, "Nathan!" in her snotty schoolteacher voice. He takes a step round the table, but Mum puts her hand on his arm.

"Nathan." Mum's voice is quiet. "Could you give us a minute alone please."

"I just came in for a drink." Dad's staring at me I know, but I can't look at him. I look down at my trainers and bump the toe of my right trainer against the top of my left one. Bump, bump. Eyes glued to my shoes.

"Get it and take it upstairs then please." Don't know

why she's saying please all of a sudden. Normally, it's just "Nathan, do this!" or "Nathan, do that!" like I'm a slave or something.

I go to the fridge. He's watching me. I feel like someone on one of those video diaries, with the camera filming everything I do. I open the fridge. Mum must have been shopping. There's some of that cheese I like. I take it out.

"Just get your drink for now, Nathan. There's juice in the door there."

"Any Coke?"

"In the larder. Don't turn this into an epic event please."

"Yeah, all right. Keep your hair on. I can't help it if I'm thirsty, can I?" So I've got the Coke out on the counter and the fridge open because I want some ice and the cupboard open to look for a glass. I hear Mum sigh. She's always doing that. Then he says: "Nat." That's it. That's all he says. But he says it real quiet, not like how he normally does. Normally—like—before, I mean—he goes, "Hey—Nat!" or "Natty—how's it going?" But this was different, like he was just seeing how it sounded or something.

I've got my back to them anyway, reaching into the cupboard, looking for a beer glass, one of those dimpled ones, with the handle, like you get in a pub. Coke always tastes best from a beer glass.

He coughs, then he says it again, only like this: "Nat?"

I pour the Coke, but it's one of those ginormous great

bottles and I spill some of it on the counter. I don't have to answer him. Ice. I need ice.

Then I hear someone say "What?" It's me. I didn't mean to, but my mouth said it. I put the top back on the Coke and whack the ice tray hard on the counter to loosen the ice. Then I turn it upside-down and knock out eight cubes into the glass.

"*Please* shut the fridge door." Mum's always on about closing the fridge. I turn round then, see Dad rolling his eyes at me, doing his she's-off-again face. I start to smile and do it back, but then I remember.

Mum's sort of slumped over the table, with her head half resting on her arms like she's about to go to sleep or something.

"If you want to come with me and Rosie next Sunday you can, you know."

Next Sunday. He's definitely not coming back. I *knew* he wasn't. All that stuff Mum came out with—"We're just having a little time apart." Parents are full of crap. I poke my fingers into my glass to pick out an ice cube to crunch.

"'m busy."

"We could go bowling if you like. Or roller-blading? Fishing off the beach."

I shrug.

He's not coming back. I'll be like Jason, going backwards and forwards between Mum and Dad like a ping-pong ball. Jason spends all weekend listening to his dad being snide about his mum, saying she's sucking him dry of every penny he earns and why should he be paying anyway when she's got Mr Wonderful with his suits and his fancy ties keeping her in the lap of luxury. Mr Wonderful's Jason's stepdad. Well, sort of, he hasn't married Jason's mum because she's not divorced yet. Jason says Mr Wonderful isn't wonderful but he's not as bad as his dad says he is. But when Jason goes back to his mum's on Sunday night, she goes, "I don't suppose he's fed you properly" and "Did he remember to give you your pocket money this time?" Jason says they never stop moaning and he just wants to put his fingers in his ears sometimes and go la-la-la, I'm not listening—the way you do when you're just a kid.

We used to go fishing, me and Dad. I've told you about my rod, yeah? The reel is excellent. Ex-cell-ent. I haven't been for ages.

I crunch another ice cube and Mum does her sighing thing again.

"Or whatever you like." Dad gives this little kind of weird laugh. "I could get my secretary to call your secretary, see when you're free."

That's what he used to say, ever since I was just a little kid. He started it—I dunno—as long ago as I can remember. I think it's 'cause like this one time he goes,

"Are you ready for your tea now, Natty?" And I'm playing on the floor with my cars and I shout, "No!"

And so he goes, "Oh, right. Shall I get my secretary to

call your secretary to arrange a more convenient time?"

You have to hear the way he says it, really posh, like he's the big boss in a suit and all that. As I got older, I'd do different replies like, "You can't—she's off today."

Or I go: "She says I'm booked solid till Christmas."

Or: "I could fit it in now—before I have to fly to New York."

I finished crunching my ice cube. It sounded really loud in my head, like it was a real rock or something.

"Nah, 'm busy. Gotta go."

Then I went out.

"Nathan! Shut the door! For the *hundredth* time!" Nag, nag, nag. I went back and gave it a really big tug so it'd bang shut. Then I leant my head against the door, see if he'd say anything. But he didn't.

Then there was Mum's voice, just loud enough for me to hear.

"I'm sorry," she said.

I don't know why she's saying sorry. I thought it was all supposed to be his fault. He's the one who's run off and left us. That's why Mum kept crying in the bathroom with the radio turned up loud. She makes out she's fine with the whole thing, but she's not.

I go upstairs then, taking them two at a time, and into Rosie's room.

"How come you never knock on my door but I have to knock on yours?"

"'Cause you're only a kid, Rozza." I go in and dive full-length onto her bed.

"Natty! You'll break it."

"Nag, nag. You're getting as bad as Mum."

"Natty?"

"Yes-ee?"

"Did you hear what Mum and Dad were saying?"

I turn onto my back and stretch my legs back over my head to try to kick the wall.

"Boring stuff mostly. You know, grown-up stuff."

"Daddy's not going to come back ever, is he?"

Rosie's sitting on her chair, swinging her legs, bouncing that old bear up and down on her lap.

"Nah." I swing round and drop my head over the side of the bed and rest it on the floor. "Anyway, we're better off without him, Rozza. If he wants to go off with his stupid mistress, that's his loss. We'll be OK."

"He hasn't got a mistress, he said so."

I do a kind of wonky somersault and crash onto the floor, just missing my Coke glass by about a quarter of a millimetre. I reach out to grab Rosie's bear and make him do acrobatics on my stomach and my legs. She likes it when I do that.

"Well, he's a liar if he told you that. You should know better than to believe anything *he* says."

"Can I have some of your Coke?"

I hand it over.

"OK. One sip. No gulping. And don't take any ice."

"Will you come with us next time?"

"When?"

"On Sunday. With Dad."

I turn the bear upside-down and bounce him up and down on his head.

"Dunno. Doubt it." I reach for my glass. "You've had your sip. Give it back." Then, right there, I see it, a bump in the side of her cheek. Ice.

"Oi! Rozza!"

She looks up at me.

"Mmm?"

I can still see it, but for some reason I shrug and let her off.

"Never mind." Then I head out the door. "Got to do my homework. See ya, kiddo."

She likes it when I call her kiddo.

Gail

Cassie said we should go for it, but I had my doubts. Mega-doubts as Nat would say. What if it doesn't turn out right? I kept saying. What'll I do then? What then?

"You're only young once," said Cassie. "Well, only middle-aged once at any rate, and I'm in no hurry to be a cauliflower-head. Are you? Why be old before your time?" That's what she calls old ladies, cauliflower-heads, because of that hair they all have.

"But I *am*. That's just it. I *am* old before my time. I'll be forty in two days and I'm not ready. It feels as if it's all downhill from now on."

"Get away!" Cassie aimed a fake blow at my head. "Believe me, I'll be first in line to tell you if I see you capering up the High Street with a ring through your navel and a belt masquerading as a skirt. But just 'cause you're forty doesn't mean you've got to wear effing navy slacks the rest of your life, does it?"

Cassie's forty-four and still has a heavy hand with the mascara wand, it must be said.

"S'pose not."

"Right then. Are we doing this or not?"

* * *

I knew if I thought about it too long, I'd never do it. Let's face it, if I thought about it at all, I wouldn't do it. But this is the new me. I refuse to be the woman who has no life. I suppose sometimes you have to stop thinking and planning and just get on with it. God, if Scotty could hear me say that, me who's always saying to him, used to say, "Scott, you have to think things through first. Everything has consequences." He used to tease me because I always like to plan ahead, used to joke: "Gail loves to be spontaneous—yup, every Wednesday at two o'clock. She puts it down in her diary, don't you? 'Be spontaneous.' And every other Saturday: 11 p.m.—'Get carried away.'"

"I can't look. I can't look."

"Oh, behave," said Cassie. "One sec. Right. Now look."

I peeked through my fingers, like at a horror film, expecting to see, I don't know, "The Amityville Hair-style," "Hair-Care on Elm Street."

I opened my fingers a bit more.

"It certainly *is* red, isn't it?" I took my hands down. My mascara had run, of course, from having my hair washed, so I had panda-eyes, but aside from that . . .

"Well?" Cassie stood, hands on hips, watching me in the mirror. "Should have done it before your hot date with Michael. You'd have had him dribbling down his front."

356

"I think he does that anyway, it's all those tranquillizers. Next time, see if you can fix me up with someone who's not been on medication for ten years." I turned from side to side. The redhead opposite me turned too. "Is that really me?"

Cassie nodded, smiling smugly back at me.

"007," she said holding out the hairdryer at arm's length in front of her. "Deadliest woman with a Braun 2000 this side of Dover."

"Actually, it's not bad, is it?" I tweaked at the front, pushing a strand off my face.

"Not bad? Not bad!" Cassie laughed and knocked back the last of her Bacardi. "You're beyond help—you look fucking gorgeous!"

There was a beeping as the second alarm clock went off.

"Ah-hah!" I tugged at Cassie's towel turban. "Time! ladies, please! Your turn now. Get your head over that bath, Blondie, and let's have a look at you."

Scott

"Happy Birthday," I say, as the door opens. "Holy shit."

Gail looks a total knockout. Her head is all red. Her hair I mean. Gorgeous deep red and shiny. She's got on these big dangly earrings instead of small studs like she normally wears, and she's wearing a new dress, well new to me anyhow. It sort of slithers and slinks all the way down nearly to the floor and it's kind of silvery. It looks soft and silky like it's begging me to touch it and it's all I can do to stop myself reaching out and sliding my hands all down her front. Even her feet look nice, in silver sandals with nail polish on her toes—a coppery colour like her hair. And, get this, she isn't wearing a bra, which is so unlike her it's untrue. I come this close to saying, "Wey-hey, putting on a show for passers-by? Where can I get a ticket?" Fortunately, I manage not to and that's why I'm still alive to tell the tale. She's not got much up top (which she's dead touchy about, but I never minded), but what she does have is all jostling about under there and her nipples are sticking out, little bumps under the silky material.

"Oh," she says. "It's you. Hi, Scott, what do you want?"

"Nice to see you too, Gail. Great dress, by the way. You never used to dress up to do the hoovering."

"I'm just trying it on for later. Is it—well, do you think it's . . . all right?" Is she serious? What's wrong with women? Why can't they ever tell when they look 100 per cent shaggable? Still, I remember not to stand there with my tongue hanging out and instead opt for a small but friendly smile and a modest compliment.

"It's very nice. Really suits you. But don't be wearing it around anyone under-age, OK?" She smiles and folds her arms across her chest. No, no, *no*—let the world get the good of those nipples. "Anyway, I was just passing and thought I'd pop by to wish you a happy birthday—" I flourish the flowers from behind my back like a conjuror "—and give you these."

"Oh. Well. Thank you, Scott. I wasn't expecting anything. That's sweet of you."

"Well, it *is* your fortieth. I could hardly—"

"Gosh, so it is. Thanks for reminding me. I'd better stick a note on the fridge door in case I forget."

I sigh and roll my eyes at her.

"Come on, Gaily—I didn't mean—well, sorry anyhow. And have a great birthday. You look ace. Terrific. You really do. Not a day over thirty-nine. No, just kidding. I'm *kidding* for chrissakes. You look about eighteen." I look at my watch. "Does your mum know you're still up?"

She shakes her head at me, then clucks her tongue softly, the way she does when she's trying to make her mind up about something.

"I'm having a party. You can come if you want. About eight." She leans against the doorframe, stretching her dress more tightly over her tits. Down boy, I tell myself, don't screw up now, you're doing well. "Thanks again." She holds the bouquet up like an Olympic torch. "For the flowers." She looks down at her dress then and tweaks at the material against her thigh, sliding it between finger and thumb. Need a hand with that at all? If so, look no further. I'm your man.

See, she's dead horny looking when she can be bothered. I wish she'd bothered to dress up for me a bit more often. You know, I never planned to do the dirty on Gail. All right, I confess, I came pretty close a couple of times before Angela, but it's not like I've been sat through day after day of married life thinking, "Now, how can I sleep with someone else?"

But if I had been going to sleep with someone, planning it I mean, I wouldn't have picked Angela anyway. For one thing, she's not really my type. Not that I exactly have a type—I mean, if it's wearing a skirt and a smile, it's my type—but if I did have a type, she wouldn't be it. Not that she's been begging me for a repeat visit either. I phoned her a while back, just to see how she was and that, but she was cold as a sodding ice-pop, said she'd rather I didn't contact her again. Yes, Ma'am!

No, if I'd been on the lookout for a bit of extra-curricular attention, I'd have gone for thingybob, who brings the rolls. Whatsername. The tasty woman in the van, who comes round with sandwiches and stuff, drives round town to the offices and workshops like ours. I've never even seen her outside her van so I've no idea what she looks like from the waist down. Might have fat ankles like Denise. Or an artificial leg like Cassie's husband. Two artificial legs. No legs. I wonder what it'd be like doing it with someone with no legs. Do you think they take them off when they have sex? Or leave them on? I was thinking about this actually because I was reading an old paper in the pub the other night. In the magazine bit there were these two women—one had no legs and the other had one leg and they were drop-dead gorgeous, both of them, and I thought, well, I wouldn't mind if they were up for it, either of them. Or both.

But I digress. Oh, yeah. Thingybob. What I do know is there's not many women who look good in an apron but she's one of them, and she's got really nice arms. She's always pushing her sleeves up and when she reaches out to give you your change, you can see the soft hairs on her arms and you have to stop yourself giving them a bit of a stroke. Her hair's dark brown, nearly black, and she wears it back in a ponytail or sort of piled up in a heap on top of her head. Pale skin. Eyes—dunno. Yes, she has got eyes. Blue maybe. Might be green. Or hazel. It's hard to tell 'cause she's higher up, you see, what with standing in the van looking down at us poor hungry mortals. See, we don't really get many women on the estate aside from Denise who I don't count and a couple of old birds here and there, but not anyone who'd be a front-runner if you were in need of a leg-over. Even Thingybob's not an obvious choice. No make-up, or not much. The lads flirt with her, of course, and so do I, but it's only like keeping your hand in, it's not for serious. She looks sort of . . . sensible. The kind of girl whose hand you had to hold at school when you walked to the library once a fortnight—you know, the bad boys with the goody-goody girls to keep them in line. What *is* her name?

Rosie

My Mum is forty, which is old but she's not as old as my dad yet. He's forty-one. Mum says you can't ever catch up. I saved up and got her this little box to put your rings and things in. It's made of china and Mum said she really liked it and she's put it on her dressing-table. I got it last Sunday when I was out with my dad and he said p'raps we better get her a pair of earrings too, to go in the box, so I picked some out, but he had to give me the money 'cause I didn't have any left. Mum's hair is really, really red. When I first saw it I said I liked it but she didn't look like my mum any more, but actually I do like it now. Cassie did hers too only hers is blond. She says it is called Blonde Bombshell and Mum's is called Red Alert. I said can we do mine as well so my hair can have a name too and Cassie said you don't need any help at your age, you're beautiful just as you are but we can call you English Rose or Little Princess, how about that?

My mum is having a party at home and I'm helping. Cassie is coming round to help too. We are going to do pizzas (yum!) and garlic bread (yuck!) and dips and different kinds of salads and trifle and cheesecake and I'm allowed to stay up ever so late as it's the weekend tomorrow and it's a special occasion.

The doorbell went while Mum was trying on her dress and Cassie and me were making a pukey rice salad with lots of bits in it. Then Mum came in the kitchen holding this big bunch of flowers and Cassie said, ooh, have you got a secret admirer then? And Mum said, actually they're from Scott and then she put them on the side and went back upstairs to change again.

Cassie asked me to find a vase and arrange the flowers. Then she said, well, that's nice of your dad, isn't it, and I said yes. He always used to get Mum flowers on her birthday but I thought maybe he wouldn't this year because she never got him anything on his. But maybe he forgot that.

Mum came back in wearing her jeans and clapped her hands and said she'd better get a move on with the cheesecake and she should have made it yesterday. Cassie gave her a funny look and Mum mouthed "Tell you later" at her, then Cassie said was it too early to open some wine and Mum said yes, it was, but what the hell, let's live dangerously and she got some out of the fridge. Then Cassie let me have a sip from her glass, but it was horrid and made my mouth feel funny. I don't know why grown-ups want to drink it the whole time when it tastes nasty and it only makes them go all silly in any case.

Scott

Stop me if I'm imagining things, but I do believe my wife is flirting with me. That dress is doing dangerous things to me. Not the kind of thing she normally wears. It leaves very little to the imagination, though that creepy doctor bloke looks like he's imagining all sorts of things. If he puts his hand on her arm one more time, I'm going to go over there and—and what? Sort him out? Take him outside? Start a fight in the middle of Gail's birthday party? That'll win her over for sure. OK, but I can't be held responsible if I have to accidentally tip my beer over his trousers.

Look, look! I don't believe this. Now he's fiddling with one of her earrings, peering at it so he can get closer. He's practically standing on her foot. Do you mind, that's my wife. Oh please, come on—you're going to have to do better than that, matey, pretending to admire her jewellery so you can get right up close and touch her. We've all been there, done that. But Gail's no fool. She's not going to fall for whatever old flannel you're giving her.

But she's smiling at him! Oi! You'd think she'd move

away a bit. Her nipples are practically poking him in the chest. Well, bollocks to that, I'm not letting him have a clear field. Specially not in this jacket. I've been told I look dead good in this jacket. I cross to the buffet table and pick at the food, edging closer to Gail.

"All right there?" I feel Gail's hand rest for a moment on my back. Hello. I'd say she's a tad tiddly. More than a tad. Time to seize my advantage.

"Mmm. Great nosh." I bring my arm up and rest it ever so lightly round her waist. I resist the temptation to slide my hand down across her bum, though with that dress, this uses up almost all my powers of concentration. Man of Steel, that's me. See, I can restrain myself when I try. "Did you do it all?" I ask, trying to keep her talking, but all I can think of is sliding those little thin straps down off her shoulders and watching that dress slither to the floor.

"God, no. Cassie helped me. Rosie too—she's been brilliant. And we cheated on the pizzas, of course."

On cue. Rosie comes across and nestles under my other arm. I try not to look too smug, but inside I'm crowing—see, you can have all this in one handy package: husband who still fancies you rotten, adorable daughter, and—I look round for Nat, who catches my eye then immediately, obviously turns away and mooches out of the room.

I have a good feeling about tonight—if I can just handle it right. Time for another beer. I head for the kitchen.

Nat is there, picking at the bits on a piece of pizza. He looks up when I come in but doesn't speak. He sneaks a glance at the back door.

"Natty."

I see his jaw clench.

"I just want to talk to you."

He shakes his head no.

"Please, Nat. Give me a chance, I need . . ." The words dry up in my throat. Why can't I do this? I want to go over to him and hold him, tell him I love him, tell him how it really is. Is that so very hard? I don't know how to do this stuff. I've never been good at it. Whenever I open my mouth, all I ever seem to do is put my foot in it.

The door swings open then and Cassie breezes in with a stack of dirty plates.

"Hi, boys! Having fun?" Her voice is bright, but her face looks guarded. We used to get on great, Cassie and me, but I reckon I'm no longer Flavour of the Month. I suspect she's as puzzled by my presence here as everyone else is.

"Mn," says Nat.

"Just popped in for another beer." I open the fridge and clink about inside, taking my time.

Cassie puts the plates down on the counter.

"Your mum said, have you taken the quiche out?"

"Yeah." Nat grabs an oven glove. "Just doing it."

Then the two of them start fussing around the stove and poking at the quiche and looking for knives and another plate and what can I contribute to all this activity? Nothing. I slide back into the hall. There's no-one else there, so I quickly slip upstairs. I can always say I'm just using the toilet, that the downstairs one had someone in it. So strange being back here again—officially, I mean, not like when I come for my, well, extra visits. It feels worse somehow this time. Before, when I've let myself in with the keys I'd had made it felt like I was playing at it a bit, having fun, knowing she didn't know I was there. But this is different. I go into the bedroom. Our room. I want to lie down on the bed the way I do when I come here on my own. I want to climb under the covers and stretch out my arms and legs, clinging on like a starfish at the bottom of the ocean, clutching onto the mattress so that no-one can drag me away.

I don't lie down. If I do, I'll never be able to get up again. I back out the door, watching the bed as if it might suddenly make a grab for me.

Back downstairs, I re-enter the fray. In the front room, Dr Whatsit is singing some kind of stupid Polish folk song. Is he for real? I look across at Nat and, for a split second, we share a how-bonkers-is-he? look, then Nat remembers that it's me who's Public Enemy Number 1 and he turns his half-smile into a yawn and looks away.

At least I don't make an arse of myself in public. OK, let me correct that—at least I don't make an arse of myself by singing folk songs in public. That should count for something, right? But, no, he comes to the end and people are actually clapping and smiling. Must just be being polite. I am not singing to seduce Gail, no way. But this calls for desperate measures. A full-on offensive. I go right up behind her and blow very gently on the back of her neck. She starts slightly and gives a little gasp, so quiet you'd have to be standing right up close to hear it, so close you can feel the warmth of her body and smell the lingering scent of shampoo on her hair. Then she leans back, until she's just touching me. I squeeze her shoulders very softly and she doesn't push my hands away. A cheap trick, breathing on the neck. But it works and all's fair in love and war, right?

Nat

"What's *he* doing here?" I nudged Rosie.

"Why shouldn't *Dad* be here?" Rosie said through a mouthful of pizza. She can be such a goody-goody.

"Don't talk with your mouth full."

"*You* do. Natty, don't spoil the party. Please, please. You're not to. Mum'll kill you if you do. She asked him. And it is *her* birthday." Rosie was holding onto my arm, tugging at my sleeve. "I'll never speak to you ever, ever again if you spoil it. Not ever."

"Leave off, Rozza. You'll pull it out of shape. Look at him, sucking up." *He* was leaning over Mum, filling her glass, standing really close to her, the sleeve of his jacket touching her arm. Yes. Exactly. He was wearing a jacket outside work. Told you he was sucking up. And *she* was smiling at him, touching his arm and doing all that stuff. And have you seen her *hair*? 'Nuff said.

He tried to come over, to talk to me, but I just grabbed this old dear's plate and said I was on clearing duty, whizzed out to the kitchen. Well, she'd nearly finished.

Saw Rosie standing next to him, leaning against him, putting on her sweet face. And Dad patting her on the head like she's a dog, bending down, pretending to be interested in some stupid kid thing she was saying, and Rosie running to the table to fetch him a cherry tomato 'cause they're his favourite but like she really was a puppy fetching his slippers. I'm going to start calling her Rover. Here, girl! Here, Rover! Daddy's here! Sit up and beg! Do a new trick for Daddy. Bet she's only sucking up 'cause she wants a new bike. Makes me sick.

Then I saw Mum flirting like really obviously with Dr Whatsit, from the surgery. The Polish guy with the funny name no-one can say. He was laughing then he crept in close like a cheetah going in for the kill, and he held one of her earrings between his fingers, touching it in a spooky way and he kept nodding as if it was like the most amazing thing he'd ever seen, yeah right. Like a doctor's really interested in jewellery and stuff! And Mum was lapping it up, throwing her head back and giggling like the stupid girls you get in Our Price looking at the CDs. It made Dad cross though. His hand went all tight round his bottle of beer and his other hand was in his pocket jangling his keys.

Mum went into the kitchen for more pizza, so I followed her in.

"Hey!" she said, "Having a good time, Natty?" She danced across to the stove, trying to be cool or something. So embarrassing. "Come to give us a hand with the pizza? Chuck that oven glove over, will you?"

"Mum!"

"Why are you shouting, for heaven's sake? What's up?"

"Don't you think you should just, you know . . ."

"Don't you think I should just, you know, what, Nat?"

I hate it when she does that.

"Well. You're knocking back the wine, Mum. We'll be down the offie every two minutes the rate you're going."

"Nathan, I'm *not* drunk. I've had a couple of glasses of wine—*not* that it's any of your business. What on earth makes you imagine you can suddenly dictate how I behave?" She was cutting the pizza into wedges, but really hacking into it like she was chopping up a body or something, the knife going thunk-thunk into the board. "But—" she said, hack, hack, "—if I *do* want to get drunk on my fortieth birthday, I certainly can't think of any good reason why I shouldn't, can you?"

"Fine. If you don't mind embarrassing yourself . . ."

"Meaning?" She stood with one hand on her hip, holding the pizza knife.

I shrugged.

"Nathan?"

"Flirting with Dad after he left us. And that doctor. You're just showing yourself up."

She put down the knife.

"I'm putting the knife down so I don't end up in prison for infanticide, Nathan. You really don't know when you've crossed the line, do you? When I want advice on social behaviour from a thirteen-year-old boy not exactly famous for his poise and good sense, I'll know where to come, all right? In the meantime, if you're going to be a rotten little party-pooper, I think you'd better take yourself off to bed, don't you?" She looked across at the kitchen clock. "Yes, it's after eleven. Go to bed."

"You're having me on, right? Rosie's still up and she's practically a baby."

"Yes, Nathan, but unlike you she isn't behaving like one. Night-night. Say good night to your aunties and Nan and Grandad and Cassie before you go up, please, and no you can't take pizza up to your room so don't ask."

"I don't believe this."

"Get out of my sight, Nathan, *now*—before I bite you."

I didn't care. Who'd want to stay at a daft party like that anyhow, with crumblies everywhere spilling their drinks and little kids running round and creepy doctors and Mum making a twat of herself and *him* everywhere you looked.

Rosie

I wore my blue velvet dress with my glitter hairband for the party and Mum said I could put on my nail varnish only Cassie had to do it for me 'cause when I did it it didn't look like how it's supposed to and we had to take it all off again. Then Cassie asked if she could borrow some too so we'd both be matching.

You'll never guess what—my dad came to the party. He said Mum invited him and he bought her a present as well as the flowers. She opened it and it was a silver bracelet to go with her dress and it was really pretty. Mum liked it a lot, you could tell, but she tried to give it back to him and said she really couldn't accept it, it wouldn't be right. But Dad wouldn't take it back, he said he'd lost the receipt and she just might as well hang onto it because he had no use for it and couldn't she just accept it as a gift, no strings attached. I think maybe he meant ribbon. Anyway, she liked it because she put it on straight away and normally when she says she likes something but she doesn't really, she puts it back in the box and lays it on the side and then she hides it in the back of the cupboard.

Dr Whatsit from the surgery was at the party and he sang a song and clapped his hands and stamped his feet and made everyone else clap as well. It was a nice tune and I clapped, but it wasn't in English, so I don't know what any of it meant. I think he likes my mum because he kept looking at her all the time and my dad didn't like it one bit.

Nat was really cross about Dad being there and he kept trying to spoil it, so Mum sent him to bed and I got to stay up later than him for the first time ever. It was brilliant.

Scott

7:42. Red numbers on the clock. The clock on my side of the bed. *Our* clock. *Our* bed. I think about last night, my hands slip-sliding over Gail's dress, her front, the feel of her through the slippery material. Stroking her neck, fingers hooking under the straps of her dress, nudging them off her shoulders, the dress catching for a second on her breasts, her hips, then falling to the floor in a silvery pool. Gail standing there just in her knickers and sandals, suddenly embarrassed, awkward, laughing—and me edging her closer to the bed, kissing her, stroking her warm back, squeezing her bum, the two of us flopping onto the bed—"Wait, wait," she says, sitting up again, fumbling with the straps on her sandals then kicking them off. I reach for her, pulling her closer, my hand in the dip of her waist, cupping her breasts, her tummy, tracing the scar of her Caesarean, her rosy scar, we call it though it was only pink at the beginning, Rosie scar— my fingers moving down, along the edge of her knickers, teasing her, walking over the soft cotton, a path over her thigh, rubbing her through the cotton now, feeling her press against me, hard, unexpectedly urgent, her hand pushing against the swell in my trousers—tugging at my belt, trying to undo the sodding buckle, both of us clumsy in our haste—me saying, "Christ, oh Christ," yanking off my trousers, pulling off my shirt—one instant, hovering on the brink—Gail beneath me, her legs parted, open to me, her face tilted to mine looking up at me—and then—God, the relief of it—sliding into her—sinking—being enveloped, lost, nothing else. Moving now, familiar yet strange after all this time, mouth on mouth, hips colliding—her skin sticking to mine— God, that's good—getting faster—o-o-o-o-h yes, yes indeedy, here we go, o-o-o-o-o-o-hhhh—and Gail's saying "Don't stop, don't stop," and I reach down with my hand, feeling her juices and mine all over me, and I rub her gently, then faster, working her up, watching her face, until I feel her shudder beneth me, her soft grunt, eyes closed. She murmurs into my shoulder, I kiss her hair and we slip into a hot and tangled sleep.

This morning, now, waking up, I catch sight of the clock, then turn to see Gail, her head on the pillow next to mine where it should be. The last few months feel like no more than a horrible nightmare. Perhaps I did dream it. We can pick up exactly where we left off. A family again. Cover over the cracks so you'd never even know they'd been there.

I lie on my back looking up at the ceiling and start telling myself how it's going to be. I'll fix the front gate for a start. Get window locks on that conservatory window at the back—I'm not having every sodding Tom, Dick and Harry come hopping in here any time they feel like it. We'll go out as a couple more—snazzy restaurants, dancing, shows. And as a family. On the bikes. To the coast. Holidays. Cornwall. Greece. Swimming in clear seas. Windsurfing maybe. I've always fancied a go at that.

All I need now is a cup of tea and a bacon sandwich and I'd be in Heaven. Nope. Now that I plan to be a grade A husband, I will get the tea. I carefully slide out of bed so as not to wake Gail, put on my pants and tiptoe downstairs, quiet as a thief. Whistle chirpily as I wait for the kettle to boil. This is going to be so great. I sashay about the kitchen, singing to myself, and sliding the drawers out and bumping them shut with my bum. I even remember to wipe the tea rings off the worktop with a cloth. I've turned over a new leaf. Everything's going to be fine. Everything's hunky-dory.

Gail

I hear sounds of activity downstairs. The unfamiliar sounds of someone else up before me, the splashing of water in the sink, the banging of the fridge door, the clang of the breadbin lid. Maybe Nat's sorry for being so foul last night, maybe he's been transformed butterfly-like into a wonderful adult human being? Maybe Rosie's got up to get herself a glass of milk. I turn to look at the clock—7:51 a.m. I close my eyes again and tell myself I have had a peculiar dream. I drank too much last night, way too much, and that has given me strange dreams. Strange, *rude* dreams. There is an unmistakable stickiness between my thighs. Maybe I got lucky and seduced Dr Wojczek? Dear God, please tell me it was Dr Wojczek, I think, knowing it wasn't, remembering him sweetly kissing my cheek as he left last night, squeezing my hand. I turn onto my side. There is a definite dent in the pillow next to mine. A Scott-shaped dent. Oh shit.

Nat

I come down this morning to get myself some juice and I'm halfway down the stairs when I hear singing coming from the kitchen. A *man* singing. And not just some man. My *dad*. He can't sing to save his life, so there's no way it could be anyone else. So I creep down the last few stairs and take a sneaky look round the doorway. It *is* him. What on earth's he doing here? Oh no. I don't believe this. I do not believe it. One minute Mum's chucking all his stuff into bin bags and won't even say his name, the next she's letting him back and—you know. I'm not staying if he's moving back in. How can she after what he did to us and everything?

He's dancing round the kitchen in his pants, making tea and singing. He should hush up. Rosie might hear. Actually, he looks kind of funny, he keeps opening the drawers then knocking them shut with his bum. I'd like a go.

But he's not supposed to be here. When he walked out on us, it was a bit crap at the beginning, OK? It was hard. Look, he'd been around my whole life then suddenly I wake up one morning and he's gone. Then Mum starts giving us all this "Your dad and I need some time apart" stuff. Don't know why she was covering up for him when he was the one who walked out. He could have told us first. He could have come and said what was going on. I'd have listened. I'm not too young. But he didn't even try. He just went, then left it to Mum to make something up.

But now—now we've got sort of used to it, him not being here. And we're doing just fine without him. We don't need him any more. Only now he reckons he can just come strolling back in like he only went out for some milk and it took him a bit longer than he expected.

No way, José. Sorry, but no dice. I'm not just going to sit back while those two arse about going backwards and forwards, and him moving in and out whenever they feel like it. If Mum wants to make a complete prat of herself, that's her lookout. That's parents for you. And Rosie will be jumping up and down with excitement—"Daddy's home! Daddy's home!" 'Scuse me while I take a puke.

I'm going to count up my savings, see how much I've got now, how far I can go. Then maybe I'll go round Steve's, see if he's up for going away. Joanne wouldn't come. I know what she'd say—"Talk to your mum about it." It's all right for her, she's got normal parents, not loony tunes like mine. Or I could talk to Jason. He's had all this parents being crap and driving him up the wall. He might know what to do.

Gail

Scott thinks that the fact that we—well, that we ended up in bed together, means that everything is OK between us again. It was a stupid, stupid thing to do. I can't believe I was so stupid. What on earth did I think I was up to? I can't blame Scott, much though I'd like to, because we all know that he has no self-control. I admit that it was actually very nice. Nicer than normal—I mean than what used to be normal, for us. I haven't been so turned on for ages. But it was a mistake. A huge mistake. I'd had too much to drink, certainly that was partly to blame. And I was feeling . . . what? Sort of frisky, I suppose. Yes, frisky and flirty and—old. Oh God, please don't tell me I did it because I was grateful that someone could still find me attractive at forty? That is just too pathetic for words. No, I don't think it was just that. Maybe I wanted to try and salvage— what? I don't know. Just *something*, something good from what we had, what we once had. This morning was awful, Scott was strutting about like a randy cock- erel; I only managed to get rid of him by saying I didn't want the kids to get a shock and that my parents had said they'd pop round and I wasn't sure when they'd get here. I promised to phone him later. He tried to kiss me on the doorstep, but I just gave him a quick peck and told him to get a move on.

I'm too embarrassed to call Mari or Lynn, specially after letting them both go on about how they were sure I'd done the right thing in separating from Scott. Mari's never been a huge fan of his, but then she is a bit of a snob, though Lynn used to like Scott but she's become something of a men-basher the last couple of years. Scott used to say it was because she was in need of a good shagging, but that's the kind of thing you'd expect Scott to come out with and I told him it was a dreadful, sexist, awful thing to say and he shouldn't say things like that. It was true though.

So I call Cassie and confess all to her.

"I thought you two were looking a bit flirty-smiley at the party. It's nice to know you're not without your old-slapper moments like the rest of us."

"Well, technically, we *are* still married of course."

"Oh, lighten up. It's good for you to let your halo slip a bit once in a while."

"What the hell's that supposed to mean? You make me sound like such a prig."

"I'm only joking. Anyway, tell all. Was it good? Was it worth it? Is the old magic still there? Has he lost his touch?"

"Nosy! Actually, it was good, better than I remembered. Maybe it's just because I've been going without."

"True. Nothing like ravenous hunger to make you appreciate a crust of stale bread."

"Oi! Do you mind? I said he was good."

"A-ha! You leapt to his defence. So, you've still got feelings for him then?"

Well, of course I've still got *some* feelings. Mostly, they're irritation and frustration. I can't imagine ever feeling completely neutral about Scott. I'm not sure you ever can once you've been married to someone.

I sighed.

"No, Cassie. Not those kind of feelings. Really I haven't. It's all over. I don't know what I was up to, sleeping with him. I didn't mean to, it was just a crazy mistake. But I think Scott's got it into his head that we're heading for a second honeymoon. I keep expecting him to turn up any second with all his belongings in tow."

"Oh, Gail. What are you going to do?"

"Er, hello? What do you think I'm ringing you for? Best friend—that's your job. Start doling out the sensible advice."

"Okey-doke. Right, you ready?"

"Pen poised. Fire away."

"Do it quickly and do it now."

"What? Is that it? Do what?"

"Tell him, you fool. If you really are 100 per cent sure you don't want to give it another go, then you mustn't string him along. Get on with it and deliver the good news before he starts packing."

"Maybe I could send him a note?"

"No. Do it in person. I'll come and take the kids out if you want. I'm free all afternoon. Then I can call in later to see how it went."

"To check up on me, you mean."

"As you like. Hop to it, girlie."

Oh, please don't make me do this. Please can someone else do it. I don't feel well. I need to go and lie down. OK, I'm calm. I'm taking deep breaths and I'm very, very calm. I will call Scott and say I need to see him and have a talk. My voice will be calm and civil but not too warm. I will say I've made a mistake, that I'm very sorry if I've misled him and that certainly wasn't my intention. I'll say thank you, thank you for having me like I tell Rosie to say after she's stayed at a friend's house. No, I won't say that. I'll say I had a nice time, thank you, but that it hasn't changed anything. It'll be fine. It won't be as bad as it is in my head, it's never as bad as you imagine, like going to the dentist's. Oh God, I wish I could make it yesterday and I wouldn't touch a drop of wine, I wouldn't even have asked him to the party. Or I wish it was tomorrow and I'd already told him. Maybe he'll be fine with it. He's probably regretting it, too. Regretting it and wondering how to tell me. This is going to be fine.

Scott

"Scott," Gail says, calling me on my mobile. "Sorry to disturb you, but I think we need to have a chat. A talk, I mean."

She is being very polite. Serious and polite. This is not a good sign.

She doesn't say: "Darling! Last night was wonderful!" She doesn't say: "It's made me realize just how much I've missed you." She doesn't say: "Move back in tonight. I've cleared half the wardrobe for you."

She says she wants to see me for a talk. But, I have to say, so far talking doesn't seem to have done me a whole lot of good, you know? Every time I open my mouth I only end up making things worse. So when Gail says she wants to talk, you'll understand if I don't immediately start leaping up and down for joy. No. What I do, weirdly, is I remain calm, which is a bit of a novelty in itself. Actually, I really do feel calm and I can't understand it, it's not like me to be so calm.

"Yes," I say to Gail. "A talk. Good idea. Shall I pop round tonight?"

"It's probably better when the kids aren't around. Cassie's taking them swimming this afternoon. How about twoish? Half-two?"

I'm still at work but we only do a half-day on Saturdays, so I'll be clear by then and it's quiet as the grave today in any case. Harry is out the back checking we've got all the pieces he needs for someone's conservatory he's starting on Monday. Lee and Martin aren't in and Gary is supposed to be tidying up the workroom, but doing it like he does everything, like he's on the moon and moving v-e-r-y s-l-o-o-o-w-l-y. I take Harry out a mug of tea and a packet of bourbons.

"Cheers, Scotty mate." He ducks his head to blow on his tea. "What you got planned for tomorrow then? How's my little angel?" Harry's dead fond of Rosie. And Nat. Always asks after them. He and Maureen think of them as their grandkids really, not surprising as their own are umpteen thousand miles away.

"She's a star. A little star. She's helping me get the flat sorted. You know what she's like. She should be running the country by the time she's twenty."

"And ... ?" He pauses, takes a slurp of his tea, not looking at me. "Any change?"

I shake my head.

"Nah. Still out of favour." I squat down and tap the edge of one of the panes as if checking it. "I miss him, y'know. Can't help it."

Harry's hand on my shoulder.

"I know," he says. "You just hang on in there."

"Hi!" Gail tucks her hair behind her ears, which makes her suddenly look very young. She looks like she could be Rosie's big sister. "You better come in."

I lean towards her and she turns her face slightly, with an awkward smile, so I kiss her cheek.

I sit at the kitchen table while she flutters around, making a pot of coffee and digging around in the depths of the dishwasher for clean mugs and generally making heavy weather of it.

"Biscuit?"

I have the distinct feeling she's putting off saying whatever it is she's prepared herself to say. And I can't say I'm in all that big a hurry myself. I eat my biscuit slowly, looking down at it between bites with interest as if it's some rare and ancient Roman coin I've just unearthed rather than a chocolate chip 'n' hazelnut cookie.

"Well," says Gail.

"Well," I say.

She laughs.

"Last night . . ." She tucks her hands under her legs so she's sitting on them, like a little girl.

"It was lovely," I say, smiling at her. "Really great."

She flushes and starts fiddling with the chain round her neck.

"Yes, it was certainly very nice, wasn't it?" She sounds as if she's describing an afternoon tea, with cakes and scones. "Um. Yes. Well . . ."

I know what she's going to say, of course. How clueless do you think I am? If I haven't learned anything these last few months, then there really would be no hope for me. I may not be Mr Sensitive, but I'm not a complete dipstick either. I'm just letting her stew a bit, that's all. I don't want to make it too easy for her.

"Hmm?" I reach for another biscuit.

She gets up then and crosses over to the coffee maker and makes a show of fiddling with it.

"This doesn't seem to be very easy." She keeps her back to me. Her head bends forward as if she's peering into the top of the coffee thing, then suddenly I see her shoulders shaking and I realize she's crying. She's not making a single sound, but she is definitely crying.

I get up then and go and stand behind her. Lay a hand on her shoulder.

"No-o-o-o—" Her voice wails and her words come out in tight gasps, "You—don't—understand—it's—not—I—can't—I—don't—you—"

I put my arms round her softly and feel her lean against me. I've wanted to hold her for so long and now I am but it's not the way I thought it would be. It's not the way I thought it would be, but it's the way it is. She's sobbing now, her body shuddering against me as she tries to speak, to choke the words out.

"It's all right," I say, holding her like a child, the way I used to with Nat when he had a bad dream. "Sssh now, ssh. I know. It's all right. I know. I know."

And I do.

It's too late for me and Gail. It's been too late for a long time. I think Gail knew—maybe even before she shut the door on me that night. It just took me a long time to see it. Just because we had sex, I kidded myself that it meant everything was all right with us again, that we could just wipe the slate clean and things would go back to the way they were before. But, if I'm honest, I know that it could never have been as simple as that. I liked the idea of "us," you know? Of belonging—to a family, to a couple. I liked being part of something that wasn't just me by myself. But I don't even know that there was much of an "us" any more. The best thing we had going for us was the kids—and we've still got them, so maybe we haven't done too badly after all. I'm not sure why Gail slept with me again—maybe she'd simply had a bit too much to drink, I've given up flattering myself and trying to believe she couldn't resist me; maybe she just wanted a cuddle and then got carried away; maybe she didn't feel so hot about turning forty and wanted to feel young and gorgeous and sexy. Can't blame her for that, God knows. Maybe, like me, she wanted to make things all right—even for only one night, to pretend we were young again with no kids, no pressures, no responsibilities, and life was easy.

I keep wondering if there was a moment when it disappeared, what we had, like if it slipped out the back door one night at ten to twelve? I guess that's not the way it goes. I suppose it happened slowly, gradually crumbling away from under us like a dodgy cliff while we were too busy getting through from day to day. It started not that long after Rosie was born; there never seemed to be any time for us any more. We were just parents. Sure, I would have a night out with the lads, or Gail would go out with a girlfriend or one of her sisters once a week, but if it was just us on our own, we'd end up watching the telly or renting a video.

And it wasn't even just that. I still remember something my brother-in-law said when he married my sister, Sheila. Doug's a real laugh, you know, and you'd think he'd make a really joky speech. But he didn't. He just said all these things about how great Sheila was and how much he loved her and—I'll never forget it—he said, "Being with her helps me to be the best that I can be. I feel like I'm a better person when I'm with her." I felt a bit choked up, only I didn't click why at the time. You see, that's not how it was with Gail and me—not for me and I reckon not for her either. We didn't bring out the best in each other and, if you do that for too long, I reckon that after a while you forget that there's any best left to bring out.

Looking back now, I feel such a fool for trying to kid

myself for so long that it would be OK between us. It's like a child of six could have seen that Gail didn't want me back, but I kept ignoring all the incredibly obvious signs, telling myself everything would be back to normal and that I could just slip back into my old life like a pair of well-worn jeans and it'd be a perfect fit. I suppose it was easier. As long as I told myself she'd have me back, I didn't really have to do anything. I could just drift along, never making any plans, because everything would be fine as soon as I was back home. But it wouldn't have been. Gail would still have been Gail, and I would still have been me. We'd have been back sharing a bed, a roof—pretending we were fine and telling ourselves it was better for the kids at least. And it's better to be miserable in company than miserable on your own, right? So what if you've been out of love so long, you don't even have the memory of the memory of what it felt like to be so full of life any more, to feel your heart thumping, the blood humming through your veins? At least that other person, they're familiar, right? At least there's someone sitting opposite you at the breakfast table, even if you find yourself re-reading the back of the same cereal box every morning so you won't have to look into their eyes and know that there's nothing left to say.

Nat

How she could have let it happen? Let him walk out on us a second time? She should never have let him in past the front door, never mind inviting him to the party and going all fluttery-eyed over him and letting him, you know. And now he's gone off again. At least Rosie didn't know about it.

Cassie comes round a lot and she and Mum sit up late drinking wine and eating all the ice-cream in the freezer so there's none left for us, and Mum's always on the phone to her or to my Aunty Mari or Aunty Lynn. When I come past, her voice goes quieter and she stops saying anything interesting, then she goes "Mm . . . mm" or "Hang on a sec" and waits for me to move away.

She should have given him a whacking great punch. That's what I would have done. There was this boy in my class once who was being bullied, right? Simon. And when it came out there was this whole big thing at school and we all had to sit round in a circle and say what we felt about it and go through the school's anti-bullying policy all over again. It was bloody stupid. We've got it on posters all over the school in any case and a load of other ones as well about how you're supposed to behave and about being polite and not chewing gum in class and respecting the school premises and all that and no-one takes a blind bit of notice of any of it. Anyway, they wrote to all the parents and Mum insisted on "having a talk." I told her no-one bullies me, but she said we should discuss it—especially 'cause Rosie had that problem one time. But that was ages ago and she's never had anything since then. Mum said it was important that I understood that if ever anyone tried to bully me, I should come straight to her or Dad and tell my teacher and blah blah blah blah blah. Dad just nodded and said, "Your mother's right" but later on when we went roller-blading, Dad said, "If anyone ever picks on you, Natty, if there's a group of them, you suss out who's the leader then get him on his own and hit him once as hard as you can and you'll get no more bother." Mum says there's never an excuse for violence and you can always resolve things by talking, but she and Dad tried it and now look at the mess we're all in. Dad says people who tell you there's never a need to use violence are usually people who've never been on the wrong end of it themselves and that if some toerag is trying to punch your lights out, then saying, "I really think we should discuss this in a civilized way" isn't going to cut much ice. I mean, who cares about being civilized when you're the one laying in the gutter with your head kicked in?

*　*　*

I boil the kettle for a Pot Noodle. Mum comes in.

"All right there?" she says.

I nod at the kettle. "'s just boiled." I shrug. "You want—coffee? Instant, I mean. I'm not messing about with that other stuff."

The look on her face is something else. Jeez, it's only a coffee.

"Uh, yes. Yes, thank you. Thank you very much, Nathan. That's really thoughtful of you."

"Yeah, all right. Don't go overboard. 's no big deal."

"It is to me."

She sits down at the table and I pass her over the coffee, only spilling a little bit.

"Care to join me?"

It's better to stand. It makes you grow taller. I stay leaning against the counter.

"Mn."

"Nathan." She's looking down into the coffee and keeps touching the mug as if it's a gold bar or something and she can't believe it's really sitting there on the table in front of her.

"Mn." Not another lecture, please. Give me a break.

"Nat. I realize these last few months must have been pretty strange and confusing for you."

"Whatever." I stab at my noodles and mush them around with my fork.

"Don't worry, I'm not planning to lecture you. Just hear me out a minute."

"OK. Shoot."

"I've made a bit of a hash of things . . ."

"Mn."

"Quite. Well, I have. There's no getting round it. I think it's been easier for Rosie in a way because she's younger and she's carried on seeing your dad. But you—I worry about you, Nat."

"'m fine." I shovel a forkload of noodles into my mouth, but they're still too hot.

"I really don't want you to see your dad as the villain in all this."

I roll my eyes. Puh-leese. The guy walked out the door without a second thought—what would you call him?

"No, really, Nat. You know, I think in grown-up relationships, when they don't work out and everything seems like a big old mess—well, there's usually no heroes and no villains, hmm? Just people trying to do their best—"

"Yeah, right."

"—*trying* to do their best—even though it may not look like it from the outside."

I dig down into my noodles and give them another sloosh round. If you don't do that, it's never mixed properly at the bottom.

"You know," she blahs on. "Like when you're swimming—and you're going as fast as you can and you're trying *so* hard, you really are, but . . . well, sometimes you just don't win. Because that's just the way things *are*."

"I usually do though. 'Cept in backstroke and butterfly."

"True. But have a little compassion for the rest of us who trail a couple of lengths behind, eh?"

She gets up then and starts pulling things out the fridge and the cupboards to get ready for our tea.

"All I'm saying is, please try not to blame your dad too much, OK? And if you could see your way to giving him another chance, go out with him one Sunday, it'd mean a lot to him, it really would."

"Should have thought of that before he walked out on us then, shouldn't he?"

"*Walked out?* What do you mean? He *didn't*, Nat. I thought I explained it all to you. I thought you understood—we were having a lot of problems and we needed some time apart."

Excuse me? Like, uh-duh, do I look like I'm Rosie? I'm not buying it. How clueless does she think I am?

"Mn."

"Quite the contrary, in fact. I threw—well, I *asked* your dad to leave."

I stop twirling my noodles. They look like worms, have you noticed that? Like slithery, slimy worms. Dead worms.

It can't be true. I reckon she's making it up to cover for him. Grown-ups are always saying it's wrong to lie but then they lie the whole time. You can't trust anything they say. Not any of them.

Scott

This is the last time. Absolutely, definitely the last time. I won't come back to my house again. Well, not uninvited, not like this any more, sneaking around. I'm not even sure why I'm here now—except it feels like I'm saying goodbye. I go round each room, touching the furniture, patting the settee as if it's a dog, sliding my hand along the sideboard, walking my fingers over the top of the TV, then I make myself a coffee and go up to our old bedroom. Gail's room now. I open the wardrobe and run my hand along the clothes, feeling them, remembering when she wore them. OK, mostly not remembering—Gail always says I never notice what she wears, but that's only half-true. See, this dress here, this blue one, she wore that when we had that Greek holiday. And these black trousers, she wears these practically all the time. And this white top, she looks really nice in that when she's got a bit of a tan. I go over to the dressing-table and lift up the lids of the glass pots—cotton-wool in one, earrings in another, a necklace with big mauve shiny beads on it that Rosie made her. Tucked into the mirror frame are her birthday cards from the kids. The one from Nat is a shop-bought card, a cartoon one. There's a woman in curlers on the front peering at herself in a mirror and it says CONGRATULATIONS ... then inside it says, ". . . Only another 20 years to go and you can start collecting your pension." The one from Rosie is hand-made, of course. It has 40 on the front in enormous multicoloured numbers and a flower on a long stem that sort of snakes its way all round the edge as a kind of border. Inside it says HAPPY BIRTHDAY MUMMY. YOU ARE 40 TODAY. LOTS OF LOVE FROM ROSIE XXX.

Then I go into the kids' rooms. Rosie's room is dead cute, you should see it. I've finished painting her room at the flat now and laid some carpet down and got her a bed so she can stay over every other Saturday night, but she needs a desk and a chair and a lamp to make it all proper. It's going to be a great room. Eventually. I bought a sofa-bed, just in case Nat—. Well, see how we go, eh? Nat's room is a mess, of course. Nothing new there then. I'd like to leave him a bit of pocket money 'cause he always seems to spend his in about five minutes. Where can I leave it so's he'll find it but won't realize I've been here? His sports bag is on the floor. There's a damp towel in it and an old pair of trainers and two empty crisp packets, a small carton of juice, some computer game I've never even heard of and various other items such as odd socks and shower gel. Right at the bottom, I find four postage stamps and a torn piece of paper with my old address on it in Gail's writing. Hmm.

What's all that about then? I crumple up a tenner then flatten it out again and tuck it half under the rigid bit at the bottom of the bag.

His roller-blades are hanging up on the back of the door. You should see him skate, he's the biz. The main man. Actually, I'm not bad myself. For a crumbly.

Gail will be back soon. I better get a move on. The dishwasher's empty, so I wash up my coffee mug like a good boy, dry it and put it back exactly as it was in the cupboard. Then I take one last dekko round the kitchen, the front room, looking at everything as if I'm trying to memorize it for a quiz, close the doors behind me the way Gail leaves them till it's just me, standing alone in the hall, and then there's nothing left to do but step out onto the front path, lock the door behind me, and I'm gone.

There's a toot-toot and Harry sticks his head round the office door.

"Want anything from the sandwich van?" he says.

"Not sure what I fancy." Getting to my feet slowly. "I'll come and have a look." All casual. No rush. Strolling out.

Three in line in front of me, Lee never missing an opportunity to chat up any available totty as usual. I get there and I'm pausing as if I can't make up my mind, waiting a tick for the others to drift back inside.

Thingybob nods and smiles.

"Not seen you for a while. I thought maybe you'd defected to a rival sandwich-maker."

I wrinkle my nose in what I hope is a suave and sexy way.

"Would I do that? Besides, there aren't any."

"You're full of cheer today, aren't you? What's up? I like to think I can count on you to give my day a little lift."

Is she having me on? At least she's smiling.

"Sorry, it's just life's been a bit hectic of late, you know? Too much work, too much dashing around all over the shop. Domestic hoo-hahs, that kind of thing."

"Oh?" She looks into my eyes for a second. Green. Her eyes are green. I have to stop myself from saying it out loud, or she'll think I'm a moron. "I'm sorry," she says. "Sounds tough."

"Yeah. Well." I cough attractively. For chrissakes, lighten up, boy. "Nothing a chicken baguette can't fix."

"Oops. Sorry. I'm all out. I don't know what's with everyone today. They've all got the munchies. I've only got sandwiches or ordinary rolls. And I've no fresh chicken left either. But . . . hang on. How about mozzarella and tomato on ciabatta bread? I can do that if you don't mind waiting?"

"Sure. Sounds swish. Are you branching out?"

She shrugs, talking over her shoulder as she reaches up to a high cupboard.

"I always have it. I just don't normally offer it to you lot. Didn't think it was your cup of tea. I take them to

401

those units out by the river, you know? There's a design place and a recording studio. They love all that—ciabatta, focaccia, smoked salmon bagels."

"And we're not sophisticated enough? I can't imagine what makes you think that." I pretend to wipe my nose on my sleeve.

She laughs, looking down at the bread as she cuts it.

"Basil?"

"No, Scott. And you?"

"The herb, silly. Do you want some in your sandwich?"

"Go on, then. Sod the expense. You didn't answer my question." She's still looking down, sprinkling the torn leaves over the tomatoes and reaching for a sheet of greaseproof paper with her other hand.

"Which was?"

"Your name. I don't know if you ever told me it. If you did, I seem to have forgotten. What?" She's looking at me like I'm brain dead.

"You're kidding, right?"

"Don't tell me. We used to go to school together or we were married once and I really ought to know it?"

She shakes her head and laughs again.

"Take a step back."

"Why? Are you going to hit me?"

"Don't tempt me. Go on. Step back. What do you see?"

And there it is, in ginormous great red letters under the hatch:

Fresh rolls and sandwiches. Home-made cakes.
Delivered to your door or desk.

"So. Ella. That's your name then."

"No, it's really Tatiana, but this was on the side of
the van when I bought it and I couldn't afford a respray,
so I changed my name instead."

I look up at her. Not a flicker of a smile.

"What, really?"

She sighs.

"You're slow this morning."

I bang my forehead against the side of her van and
moan softly to myself. "Jeez. I am being so thick today.
Make that every day. Take me to the vet and put me out
of my misery."

"Oi! Leave off the van. Half of it still belongs to Bar-
clays."

"Sorry." I look up at her again looking down at me,
like Juliet on the balcony. She smiles and hands me a
piece of coffee fudge cake.

"On the house. Here." She hands me a business card.
"Case you ever want to order extra rolls," she shrugs,
"—or anything. Or to reserve a mozzarella and tomato
special."

"With basil?"

She nods.

"Except on Wednesdays," she says. "That's his day
off."

Gail

Yesterday, I got home from work earlier than usual. I'm full time at the surgery now, but I came straight back because Rosie was going to Kira's after school. I came in, dumped my bag on the kitchen table and went straight over to fill the kettle, make myself a good strong cup of tea. And you know what? The kettle was warm. I noticed it but didn't register at once that it was odd, that of course it shouldn't have been. Then suddenly it clicked. Still warm after eight hours, when I left this morning? Also, it was nearly full. For one second, I had the horrible thought that we might have had a burglar. But the kitchen looked exactly as I'd left it. I crept into the sitting-room. No sign of any disturbance there either. Anyway, what kind of burglar would break in and make himself a cup of tea but not steal anything?

Ah—only one kind of burglar. The Scott kind. It has to be him. How the hell did he get keys? Where did I put his old keys? They were in that awful old ashtray in the lounge. I know, I moved them so I didn't have to keep looking at them, and so the kids wouldn't have to see them. Understairs cupboard, on a hook on the back of the door. So I checked and they were still there, still with the key fob with that horrible old photo of me. God, I looked so young. Nasty dress though, and those flicks in my hair. Thank God I've got better taste these days. He can't have broken in, he wouldn't have the nerve. Anyway, I'd have noticed. He must have sneakily taken the keys when they were still in the lounge one Sunday when he came to pick up Rosie, and then had them copied and put them back.

I wonder how many times he's been here. I moved the keys weeks and weeks ago, so it must be more than once. It's strange, now that I think back, there were a couple of times when I had the feeling that someone had been in the house. But it seemed crazy, particularly when nothing had been stolen and there were no signs of a break-in. Like that time when my nightie went missing. I was sure I'd put it under my pillow, but it just vanished. First, I thought Rosie had borrowed it for dressing-up, and when she swore she hadn't, I wondered if perhaps she'd ripped it or something and was scared I'd tell her off, and it was only an old one anyway. Then I thought maybe I was losing my marbles—practically every day I seemed to be forgetting what I was supposed to be doing and mislaying things and leaving things in odd places, so it just seemed yet another proof that I was falling apart.

I'm not sure what to do about it. I can't let it carry on,

of course. He's got some nerve, I'll say that. I can't understand it though, especially after—after he was here last, when I told him—tried to tell him—that I couldn't, didn't want him back. I was so anxious about it and then, in the end, he made it so easy. I didn't even have to explain, but he seemed to understand.

Sunday. I told Rosie to go back upstairs for a few minutes and sort out her games kit so I could wash it today while she's out with her dad. Then I asked Scott into the kitchen.

"Fancy a quick coffee?" He looked surprised and a bit on edge, like he'd be ready to run for it if I were to pounce.

"Oh, cheers then, Gail. What's brought this on then?"

"What's brought what on?"

"Well." He shrugged. "Inviting me in. Giving me coffee. The red carpet treatment."

I walked across to the kettle and patted the side of it. Watched his face.

"Gosh!" I said, my voice upbeat like one of those permanently cheery TV presenters. "The kettle's still warm from earlier. It's amazing how long it stays hot, isn't it?"

He got it straight away, I could tell from his face. He looked ashamed. Guilty. And very, very embarrassed.

"I didn't think there was much point in keeping you out on the doorstep if you're only going to sneak in when you feel like it anyway."

"Wasn't sneaking." He avoided my eyes. "And anyway, it was the last time, I swear it. I wasn't ever going
to do it again."

"You can skip the pouting and the it wasn't me, Miss,
schoolboy act, Scott. What on earth did you think you
were doing? I could have you arrested. Were you spying
on me? Like a stalker? It's so creepy. I thought we were
going to be straight with each other now—you know,
after last time. I thought we were both beginning to
move on."

"We *are*. I *am*. Honestly."

"Tell me then, Scott. Why? How long have you been
doing it?"

His body sagged in the chair, like an old dog that's too
tired to do tricks any more. He shook his head and, for a
moment, I thought he was still trying to deny it. But
that wasn't it. I think he was just sorry and ashamed and
didn't even understand it quite himself.

"At first, it was just because I could, you see? I had
the keys copied and I felt like I was being clever, getting
one over on you—thinking you couldn't keep me out
even though you thought you had—and then, I don't
know—I—I—just wanted—still—to be with you—with
all of you—and I'd go into Rosie's room and look at her
bits and bobs and her posters—and Nat's room with all
his mess everywhere and his roller-blades hanging up on
the back of the door—and it—and you—and you—and
it—smelt like home, you see—and—I—I didn't harm
anything. I promise. I was very careful—I—tried—I—"

His voice caught in his throat and then he started to cry. Yes, Scott—crying. His face just sort of crumpled up like an old hankie, tears spilling down his cheeks. It was so shocking, like seeing rocks crumble into dust before my eyes. I could hardly bear to watch his face. I went and stood behind him then and laid my hand on his shoulder. I wondered if I should hold him, put my arms around him the way he had with me, but it would have felt so strange and I wasn't sure how much comfort I could offer him.

"I'm sorry," I said, squeezing his shoulder.

He nodded, wiped his face on his sleeve. I tore him off some kitchen roll. "Mops up all household spills," I said.

He laughed and blew his nose.

"Wash your face here if you like." I gestured at the sink. Neither of us wanted Rosie to see he'd been crying. I passed him a hand towel.

"Sorry," he said. "Don't know what came over me."

"It's all right. You don't have to be strong every minute of the day, you know. Makes me feel better about things somehow."

"Mmn. Me too, I guess." Then he fished out a key ring with two keys on it and dropped them into my palm. "It really was to have been the last time. Honestly, I mean it." He smoothed his hair. "Now, how do I look? Passable?"

"Good. You look fine. Like how a dad should look."

"Oh, go on." He shoved his hands deep down into his pockets, the way Nat does, then he smiled at me. "Do I really?"

Scott

OK, as far as I can see, here are my options. I can (a) spend the rest of my life mooning around, wishing I'd done it all differently, (b) go and hole up in a cave in Morocco or somewhere and get into religion or smoking opium or something or (c) get my act together and start having something that might remotely resemble a life.

But the simple fact is I'm forty-one years old. I can't be going out on the pull in bars and clubs or trying to snog some girl in the back of the cinema, can I? I'd feel ridiculous. I know what I want though. I can see it in my mind. I'm laying stretched out on a couch, a nice long one where I don't have to scrunch up my legs. And my head is resting in this woman's lap. She's stroking my hair, her fingers sort of kneading my scalp, and it feels so good and relaxing, I feel like I'm floating. She smells nice, too, it's like a fresh smell, like really, really clean air, like you smell when you're walking in a wood and you've stayed out too long and it's dusk, not like perfume at all. Then, when I open my eyes to look at her, she smiles but her face goes all misty in front of me and the whole picture starts to dissolve. It's really frustrating.

That's it. That's my entire fantasy. I know, it's deeply sad. What happened to all my old favourites, you know, the ones you have in the shower—the taking-her-up-against-a-wall one and the doing-it-in-a-lift-stuck-between-two-floors one and the diving-between-her-thighs-beneath-a-long-tablecloth-in-a-restaurant one. Yes, of course I still have those. I'm not dead yet. I'm just saying, I think I'm going soppy in my old age, that's all.

I suppose I should give Jeff a call. Or Roger. Ask them if they fancy a lads' night out. To be honest, I'm not feeling keen as mustard on the idea myself. I'm not sure I want to get totally smashed out my head and wake up not knowing how the hell I made it home to bed. I should have asked out that Ella, the sandwich girl. Woman, sorry. I like her. But it's after five now. Where does she go the rest of the day, I wonder? I mean, if she does sandwiches for offices and stuff, she must be free after lunchtime. I could give her a ring, say I wanted to order an extra muffin or something. I'm sure she gave me her card. I had it here somewhere. I could have asked her this morning if I'd been at work. That's the trouble, she'll forget my face soon. If I'd spent less time being a dipstick and creeping about my old house, I could have been chatting her up. I go through my pockets. You never know. No luck.

It's gone five now and I can hear the lads getting ready to go. Denise finishes tapping away at the keyboard and shuts down the computer.

"I'm off home then."

"Not out tonight?"

"No." She blushes like a schoolgirl. "Ray's coming over. I'm cooking him a dinner."

"Good. Hope it goes well. I'm pleased for you, Denise." I don't know why I'm talking like that, as if I'm her father or something, but I am pleased for her. Denise deserves a life. But so do I. I can't spend every single evening painting the flat and making it perfect. I am good at decorating and all that, and—even worse—I enjoy it, but I still need a social life. Suddenly all my friends depress me. None of them ever do anything new. I'd love it if just once Colin or Jeff or Roger would ring me up and say, "I've jacked in my job and I'm going to the airport tomorrow and see what's available. Wanna come?" Colin's hated his job for at least the last ten years, far as I know, but does he leave? No. Course not. Because it's steady. It pays the mortgage. And what else could he do? And look at me, who am I to talk, still here after sixteen years? It's not the same though—I don't hate my job for a start.

Right. I am now going to go back to the flat and cook myself a proper meal like a real grown-up. I'm not going to phone for a pizza or stop off to pick up fish and chips on the way home. I shall go via Tesco's and get something to cook. A chicken maybe. And some potatoes and some of those green things you're supposed to have. Vegetables. Then I'm going to go through every pair of trousers I own with a fine-tooth comb until I find that card with whatserface's number on it. Ella. What if she doesn't remember who I am and I have to attempt to describe myself? What if she lives with someone and he answers the phone? I can't really say I'm ringing to order an extra muffin. Maybe I could order a whole platter of sandwiches, say I'm having a party or something. Yes, terrific idea, Scott, you're a genius. That's all you need to make your life complete—thirty-two rounds of assorted ham, cheese, salad, beef, salmon and what have you and a small forest of cress. All just to ask her out for a drink. Give me a break, I haven't been on a date for over fifteen years, you can't blame me if I'm a bit out of practice.

By the time I'd been round the supermarket, got back to the flat and unloaded the shopping, I'd forgotten about looking for Ella's number. I couldn't believe how much stuff I'd bought when I was shopping. I only went in for a chicken and some potatoes and stuff. I got a trolley because it's easier and I didn't want to look like a sad, lonely bastard with a basket—I always feel sorry for people who are shopping for one. You can see in their basket and they've got like a ready meal that says Cottage Pie for One in enormous letters. Then they've got maybe one onion, a small tin of sweetcorn, and a couple of bananas, plus a tin of cat food if they're really sad—oh yeah, and a packet of those mini chocolate swiss rolls. And you can just see their whole life there. That they've worked out exactly what they're going to have for their evening meal and then they think, "Ooh, I'll be naughty and have a treat" and they get this packet of cakes, mini-rolls or whatever. I mean, it's all right if you're a student or whatever, but you don't want to be letting other people see you with a Cottage Pie for One when you're my age. But the problem with having a trolley is it looks so empty and pathetic if you've only got a few things, and I thought I could do with some extra bits and pieces anyway, for when Rosie comes round. So I got some ice-pops to freeze and some biscuits with marshmallow in them. Then I thought about Gail saying I'm not to feed her rubbish the whole time, and I went back to the bit where the fruit and veg are and I got some apples and a big net of oranges.

It soon mounts up though, doesn't it? It cost a lot more than I thought. Still, at least it looked like I was a proper person buying for a whole family. I should've waited till Sunday and brought Rosie with me. She always knows what are the best buys and she's always putting things back and saying, "No, Dad, not that one, you should get this one." She cracks me up, she really does.

Anyway, I put all the things away back at the flat,

then get the chicken and potatoes and vegetables out again so I could cook them. I tell you, that kitchen's got practically nothing in it. All I could find's this one enormous roasting tin, big enough to take a huge turkey. I put my chicken in there and it looks a poor little thing, sort of marooned and tiny and in need of its mother. So I shove some onions and potatoes around it to make it look less pathetic and whack it in the oven before it starts making me feel sad.

While it's cooking, I give the hall another coat of paint. It's all coming along now, this flat, beginning to feel like a proper place of my own. I'd like to make Rosie's room a bit special though, not just somewhere for her to doss down. It's a bit boring at the moment.

After supper, I wash up, then lay on the settee to watch the news. Must've fallen asleep because suddenly it's after midnight. And that's when I remember that I'd meant to phone Whatserface. Ella. I'm about to start going through all my trouser pockets when I realize I couldn't really phone her after twelve in any case. It's taken me weeks to get round to it, but now that I have it in my mind, I'm impatient to get on with it. I could chat to her tomorrow, when she comes round to the estate. No, I can't because tomorrow is Saturday and she doesn't do Saturdays. I wonder why not—we don't stop wanting sandwiches just 'cause it's the weekend. I suppose most of her customers don't work Saturdays either, so it's hardly worth getting her van out if it's just a couple of glaziers. Monday it is then. That's if I survive Sunday. I suggested to Rosie we go roller-blading and I've not done it for ages. I used to go with Nat a lot and he's ace at it. Anyway, Rosie's fed up of him always being better than her at that kind of stuff so I said we'd have a practice somewhere quiet.

OK, I also thought that maybe if he heard that's what we were doing, he might want to come too. It's not so bad now, not as bad as it was at the beginning. Then, every time I went to pick up Rosie and walked back down the front path again without him, I felt this pain. A physical pain, like someone had sewn a rock into my chest. I kept thinking the front door would suddenly open again and I'd hear him call, "Dad! Wait for me!" his footsteps running to catch up. Then, after a while, the weeks go by, and you tell yourself it's not so bad, you can handle it. You tell yourself that because you haven't got a choice, your son doesn't want to see you and you've only yourself to blame—so what else can you do but handle it? Roller-blading on Sunday. Maybe he'll come.

Sunday. Rosie carries her roller-blades in a clear bag so everyone can see them. Hers are girlie ones—pink, and they only just still fit her. If she has fun today, we'll have to see about getting her some in a bigger size.

"Don't suppose Nat wants to come?" I make my voice casual, with a shrug in it. "We're blading down at the old airstrip."

Gail raises her eyebrows and says she'll ask him, he's

here for once, why don't I come in a minute, she'll just pop upstairs.

Rosie and I stand in the hall, whispering for some reason like we're in a library, and making silly faces at each other. Rosie says we must talk in alien language, so the earthlings can't understand us.

"Spreditski-nurdle?" I say.

"Wuddok. Krattle-boff-tik," she says.

"Zeshkrit fagen-sprodnik!"

"Scott?" Hm? Sounds too familiar. Gail, coming downstairs. "Rosie, love, get a couple of drinks from the fridge for later. There aren't any shops down there, are there?"

As soon as Rosie goes into the kitchen, Gail drops her voice.

"I think he really wants to come, but he doesn't want to lose face and look like he's caved in, you know what he's like."

I nod, but I've not talked to him for so long, I'm not sure I do know any more.

"He says he'll consider coming, but there are conditions . . ."

"What is this—hostage negotiations?"

Gail tilts her head on one side, waiting to carry on, being patient with me.

"He says you're not to try to talk to him and he won't come for the whole day and he doesn't have to speak to you."

"Should be a fun day."

"Scott, come on. What do you think? He has to be round at Steve's by one in any case. They're expecting him for lunch."

It'll be tough, I know that. Still, it's Natty. Natty, who I've barely seen for months, no more than glimpses through doorways or the sight of his back as he skates away from me on a Sunday morning, speeding down the street to some other lucky house.

"OK. It's a deal. Tell him." I'll bring him back, then take Rosie for lunch.

"At least I'm getting fit," says Gail, running up the stairs again.

Nat's roller-blades are black with red markings on the sides and silver-grey wheels. They are the only footwear Nat owns that ever get to see a lick of polish. Nat skates like he swims—free, easy, like he was born to move this way. Funny when he looks almost awkward when he's just walking along.

He comes crashing down the stairs like a one-boy rhinoceros stampede, jumping the last four steps and totally avoiding my eyes.

"Take your jacket, Nat," Gail says.

"Don't need one."

"Take one anyway."

He unhooks his black one from the coat pegs and swings it over his shoulder, his skates tucked under his arm, heads out to the car.

Gail and I attend to business, the handover of funds

for the week, and she says, can I remember to bring back Rosie's swimming towel next time, it could probably do with a wash, and I say, no need, it's sorted, I've already washed it. I can tell she's surprised, and I feel ridiculously pleased with myself.

In the car, Nat is in the front passenger seat and Rosie is whining.

"Dad, I always sit in the front. Tell Nat it's my seat." She kicks the back of his chair with some force. "Nat, you can't just grab it the first time you come with us. It's not fair."

"Hey, Rozza, no kicking! But if you've had it every week up till now, it must be my go, right?"

"Da-ad?"

"Come on, Rosie. You have it on the way back, eh? Or we'll never get going."

A small pause, while she considers how much mileage she can get out of this.

"Can I have a lolly then?"

What is it with kids? You spend your whole life trying to bribe them or barter with them or threaten them every step of the way. Before you have kids of your own, you're so smug and superior, aren't you? You tell yourself you're not going to spoil them the way you see other parents doing, you'll know just how to handle it if they throw a wobbly in the supermarket. And then you have them and next thing you know they're wailing fit to bust in the biscuit aisle and you're shoving a chocolate bar in their face fast as you can and begging them to behave themselves. And you may be six feet tall and they only come up to your knees—but look who's won?

"Yes, you can have a lolly, but only after your lunch." This is so both of us can maintain the pretence that I'm still the one in charge. Fortunately, Rosie understands this, so she accepts that I have to be allowed to get my own way sometimes.

The airstrip is the biz for blading, I must say. It's smooth as a rink but with great tufts of grass that have busted their way through the asphalt, which you can use as small jumps or to slalom round. There are two other people further down, also roller-blading and, beyond that, a man and a boy with a remote-controlled toy aeroplane, buzzing above the strip like an outsize bug. The strip is perfect for Rosie but too easy for Nat. He needs proper jumps and ramps really. I watch him whiz by at speed, a dark shape against the clear sky like some great black crow. I skate along more slowly, so Rosie can keep up, then Nat says he'll show her how to do flashy turns and I have a sit-down in the grass and weeds by the side and watch them both for a while. Nat takes both her hands and skates backwards, towing her in front of him. Rosie squeals, "Too fast! Slow down!" but she's loving it, you can see. Even backwards, he glides—glancing behind him now and then to watch for the tufts of grass. Then he looks across at me and, just for a moment, I think I see him smile. But I'm not sure because the sun is in my eyes. I tell myself it's a smile, of course it is. But it's only a moment and when I raise my hand to shield my eyes, he's looking at Rosie again and the smile, if it was ever there, is gone.

Lesson Four

Rosie

I am

IO

Gail

Somehow we all survived the school summer holidays, though I must confess I spent the last two weeks praying for the start of the new term so I could have my precious little bundles off my hands again and return to sanity. Scott pitched in more than he ever used to at least, though it wasn't that much help with Nat who's still taking things slowly as far as his dad's concerned. Nat went out on a few trips with Scott and Rosie, but only if it was swimming or seeing a film, still I suppose it's a start. We'll all just have to be patient. Scott even took Rosie up to Scotland to stay with his sister while Nat was away in Cornwall with Jason, and they had a great time. Rosie loves Sheila and they all made a fuss of her and she came back with what feels like hundreds of tartan knick-knacks for her room including some horrible furry little gonk *thing* clutching miniature bagpipes.

Also, it was Rosie's birthday—10 at last! It feels like she's been looking forward to it for ever. Anyway, we had a party at home for her and Scott and I agreed that Rosie would love it if he came as well. He managed to behave himself fairly well (for him) and had the kids playing silly games and shrieking with laughter and they all got very excited and thought he was wonderful and he was grinning from ear to ear like a big kid himself. Then we turned up the music and we adults had drinks in the kitchen while the kids held a mini-disco in the lounge—have you seen the way they dance these days? All wriggling their hips and sticking out their flat chests, desperate to be sexy—except they're only ten years old. It's truly hideous. Then they practised the dance routines they've seen on the telly being done by those awful bands they all go mad for, and I spent most of the next day trying to scrape up bits of ground-in cake from the carpet. Scott wanted to join in the dancing, but I thought it would embarrass Rosie (have you seen Scott dance?) and talked him out of it.

What else? Oh yes. Now don't laugh but I did go on another date. Well, more than one actually. I've been seeing Dr Wojczek. Greg, I mean. It's short for Gregor. He doesn't really look like a Greg, but I can't quite bring myself to say Gregor because it sounds silly. I knew he had been married but I'd assumed he was divorced or separated, but actually he's a widower. His wife died two years ago of cancer—just before he joined the practice. Poor man. It must have been awful.

Anyway, we went out for dinner to that rather posh restaurant in Wye and I felt very nervous, which was silly because of course I've known him for nearly two years. It was strange though, being out with someone else. For the first hour or so, I was thinking, "I don't know how to do this. Should I be laughing more? Should I be talking less? What if he finds me boring?" Then after a while and a couple of glasses of wine, I forgot to think about how I was and what impression I was making and I started to enjoy myself. And there were candles and we had wine and I ate far too much and it was all such a treat, I can't tell you. When you're cooking for a family day in and day out, desperately trying to think of something new that you can defrost or whip up in half an hour and that your children won't push round their plates saying, "It tastes *funny*," it is so wonderful to be taken out to dinner. Except all through the evening I couldn't stop wondering what it would feel like to kiss a man with a beard—because I never have, not in my whole life. I was sitting there opposite him and I kept imagining it. I had to stop myself lunging across the table at him to have a quick stroke. I thought it might be really prickly.

Course, Cassie was on the phone at crack of dawn the next day, when we were all in our usual chaos, tearing round trying to eat breakfast and find our games kits (you know what I mean). She said,

"Sorry, I couldn't wait. How was it? Did you *do* it?"

"It was only *dinner*! Of course not!"

Honestly, what does she think I am?

* * *

We didn't do it till our fourth date. And, by the way, it's not prickly. But it does *tickle*.

Nat

It was Rozza's birthday. She had all her little friends round for a party and a disco, but it wasn't a proper one, just dancing around to CDs in the front room. We pushed all the furniture against the walls and Mum changed the light bulbs in the lamps so there was a red one and a blue one and a green one. It was quite funky actually. Well, it was OK for little kids. And we had piles of fried chicken and jacket potatoes with different fillings and Mum did Coke floats with ice-cream. My dad came and goofed around for a while. Rosie liked it.

In the holidays, I went with Jason and his family to Cornwall and we did windsurfing. You fall off a lot at the beginning, but it was still pretty cool. Jason's stepdad tried to do it but he's a bit of a noodle and he couldn't balance right. I guess he's too old. Bet my dad could do better than him. Yeah, well. Still, the stepdad—Mr Wonderful, that's what they call him, only not to his face—he's not so bad, he's better than Jason's real dad if you ask me. He got us loads of ice-creams and he doesn't keep asking you stupid questions the whole time, he just lets you alone.

Yeah, I went out with Rosie and my dad a couple of times, so what? It was only swimming and blading and that. It's not like I had to talk to him much or anything, only to say what I wanted when we got something to eat. Big bloody deal. I wasn't going to go, but Joanne said I must be a loony tune letting Rosie have all the treats by herself and she'd never let her little sister get away with it.

Mum's going out with someone, and Rosie and me wind her up about having a *boyfriend*. He's like way too old to be a boyfriend, of course, he is majorly decrepit. Mum says he's "only forty-five." Yeah, like I said, a total crumbly. And he's got a *beard*. Creepy. It's that Dr Whatsit only we're supposed to call him Greg as if he's a mate or something, so mostly I don't call him anything, 'cept I call him Weirdy Beardy to Rosie. When he came to pick up Mum the first time, he shook my hand and said, "Hello, Nathan. How do you do. Or you prefer Nat, yes?"

"Mn."

"Your mother tells me you are quite the hotshot with computers."

"I do OK."

"I really envy you. Gail is trying to teach me how to use mine properly at the surgery."

"*Mum's* teaching you?!"

He must be seriously crap.

"Oh, yes." Then he looks at her with this soppy face. Vomit time.

Rosie says she bets they snog a lot, but I reckon they are getting a bit old for it. Anyway, he hasn't stayed over yet—not unless he sneaks out at six o'clock in the morning. Next time he comes round, I'm not going to go to bed till I know he's left. I asked Mum if he was moving in and she said,

"No, course not! Do you really think I'd install some man without talking to you and Rosie first? Besides, I'm in no rush."

She can't get married again yet anyhow, until she gets a divorce from Dad, and that'll take ages and ages.

We're back at school this week. Thrillsville.

Scott

I guess you want to know if I ever had enough guts to phone up Ella, you know, the sandwich lady. Well, no I didn't, but only because I didn't need to in the end. I had to bide my time till after the weekend 'cause I couldn't track down her card and I didn't know her surname so I couldn't look her up. I'm no good on the phone anyhow. I'm better when I can see what I'm doing.

But, come Monday morning, I'm ready to make my move.

I hang back till after the small queue's subsided and there's only a couple of blokes lounging nearby, eating their rolls outside in the sun.

"Hey there. So what treats have you got in store for me today?"

She smiles.

"Oh, mostly leftovers and a few stale crusts. Still, you just name what you want, then I can tell you I'm all out."

"Now that's what I like—a woman who can satisfy my every need."

I was right. Definitely no wedding ring. But maybe she takes it off so it doesn't get all covered in crumbs.

"I've got that chicken in herby mayonnaise thing you like." Ah-ha. See, she notices these things. "Or Spanish omelette? Roast beef? What do you fancy?"

Don't ask.

I go for the chicken and while she's doing it, I pounce, smooth and slick as a panther.

"Um . . ." I say.

"Ye-es?" She's smiling at least. Come on, mate, get a move on. She'll be off in a minute. Don't you just hate working under pressure?

"You do a great job, feeding us lot day in and day out."

"Thank you. It's nice to feel appreciated. It makes getting up at six every morning to begin the day's buttering while I'm barely conscious seem almost worthwhile."

"Maybe I could do the same for you some time?"

She pauses, her knife poised mid-spread.

"You're volunteering to help me butter my rolls? Or you want to make me a sandwich?" Her face is straight, her voice deadpan.

"Er, neither actually. Just wondered if you fancied going for a bite to eat some time." Casual. Keep it casual, case she says no. "Or just a drink. Or a coffee."

"Oh. OK."

"That's OK as in yes, right?"

"I guess it is." She bags up my chicken baguette and gives the bag a neat twirl, then she looks straight at me and gives me a grade A, full on, green light, bell-ringing, neck-tingling humdinger of a smile. "What took you so long?" she says.

Anyways, we fix up a where and a when and we meet outside that nice old pub on the river and I get there early. And when this woman appears and smiles at me, I'm thinking, "Hmm, she's a bit of all right" before I click that it's her, the sandwich lady, Ella I mean. Only she's wearing a dress and there's not an apron in sight and her hair's loose, falling around her shoulders and, yes, my God, the woman's even got legs. Two of them. And not bad legs at that. For some reason, I seem to have forgotten how to breathe and I feel myself blushing like a sodding schoolboy and, dear God, does none of this ever get any easier? Then she waves and comes over and she says hi and I say hi and after a little bit of awkwardness we're up and running and talking like there's no tomorrow and no, I'm not telling you it all now, you'll just have to wait.

Gail's seeing that doctor from the surgery. Dr Whatsit. Only Gail says it like this: Dr Vocheck. Yes, the one whose idea of being the life and soul of the party is to treat everyone to a rousing folk song in a foreign language. I'd rather listen to Rosie speaking in alien. Sprid-ski zekroddok? Actually, sometimes it feels like we really know what we're saying. I'd probably do better talking like that the whole time.

Gail told me after she'd been out with him a couple of times. I can't say I was overjoyed at the thought. I don't know if she's had sex with him yet and, frankly, I'd rather not think about it and if that makes me a miserable toerag with double standards then so be it. Anyhow, we had to work out how we're going to handle the whole going out with other people thing. I'm not having someone moving straight into my house and putting their feet up on my settee and sleeping in my bed and living at my expense. Not a chance. I told Gail that and she said,

"What sort of man would have so little pride that he'd sponge off another man like that? Don't be ridiculous. Credit me with having some taste and sense at least, won't you?"

Anyway, so we agreed: what we get up to is our own business but no flaunting it in front of the kids. That means no overnight "guests" when Nat and Rosie are around until the person's been introduced slowly and they get on OK with them. No snogging on the stairs, no strangers wandering round the house naked. I told Gail she can't be trailing a whole string of different men through the house.

"Yes, that does sound like me, doesn't it? You can talk. And excuse me, I notice none of this will hold you back much."

We still have a bit of a ding-dong now and then, but we can't keep it up any more, we've lost the heart for the battle.

Rosie stays with me every other Saturday night now and sometimes one night mid-week if we can get ourselves organized and remember what she needs for the next day, but Nat still hasn't set foot in my flat. He barely says a word to me, even if he comes out with me and Rosie, which he's done all of four times I think. Not that I'm counting or anything. I don't know what I have to do to square things with him. I hope he decides to make up with me before I'm on my deathbed. There's probably a way to deal with this, but I'm buggered if I know what it is. I wish I knew how to talk to him. In the past, like before, him and me always got along, but it was just him being him and me being me, we never had to think about it, certainly never had to talk about it. But now—well—I'd like that back again and I don't know how to get from where we are now to where I want us to be and I reckon Nat doesn't know either. Or, worse, maybe he likes it this way, maybe he really doesn't want me in his life any more. Shit. I know I have to find a way to talk to him, I do know that—but please won't somebody tell me what the hell I'm supposed to say?

Gail

Scott's seeing someone else. At first, I thought it must be *her*, that woman he slept with, and I wondered if he really had carried on seeing her all along. But he insists it isn't and, for once, I believe him; he's got no real reason to lie any more.

Rosie tries not to talk about her, Ella, in front of me, which is sweet of her, but sometimes she can't help it and she babbles away about what they've got up to together.

"Ella and me made fairy cakes and she let me weigh all the sultanas and everything and put out the paper cases. We had to do forty-eight because she's got lots of customers and they all like cakes and she's going to show me how to make brownies."

And this domestic whiz turns out to have an artistic streak too. Rosie says she's doing a painting on her bedroom wall. I'm pleased for Rosie, of course I am, it's just I'm beginning to feel I'm just the boring old mummy who can't compete with this creative *girl* who seems to know what bands are in and what colour nail polish is fashionable. OK, she's not really a girl, Scott says she's nearly thirty-seven so she's no spring chicken either, but she *sounds* young. At least she's not some eighteen-year-old bimbo, that would be much worse. But I think Rosie's getting fond of her and it's not that I'm jealous or anything, but I can't say I'm overjoyed about it.

Nat won't even meet Ella. Since he found out Scott had a girlfriend, he's retreated more into himself and he refuses to see him on even the occasional Sunday, so it feels like one step forward, two steps back at the moment. Scott says,

"Of course I don't have to see Ella on a Sunday if Nat's not ready to meet her. Rosie and I always have part of the day on our own anyway. Just tell him, can't you? I want him to see the flat."

"I'll try."

Nat's desperate to see Scott's flat, too. I know he is. He'd die rather than admit it to anyone though, so I'll have to make it sound like he's doing Scott a favour. It would be nice not to have to go through all this, to play it straight, but Nat's got so much pride and now I think he's been angry for so long that he can't see any way out of it without losing face. I wish I could make it easier for him.

Nat asked me if I was going to let Greg move in. He said it almost as if he thought it was inevitable—as if I'd really just let someone waltz in here with his suitcases without even discussing it with my children. Anyway,

I'm in no rush to become a one-woman support service for another man just yet. I enjoy Greg's company and yes, thank you, things are very nice in the bed department too, but I'm happy with things as they are. He's a lot more serious than Scott, which takes a little getting used to, and he's much more thoughtful and sensitive too, which I like. Also, he *listens* when I'm talking. Cassie says we should have him cloned. It's odd, but now I find myself being rather silly at times, and encouraging Greg to loosen up and live a little. The other Sunday, I had him dancing along the beach. He showed me how to do the polka. That'll come in handy for all the balls I get invited to, won't it? No, really, it was fun. Before, with Scott, I seemed to turn into this awful uptight Victorian-style governess, endlessly trying to keep him in line. It's just terrific to have some time off from being the sensible one.

Scott

"It feels kind of strange to be looking down at you for once." We're standing outside Ella's house, after that first date, and I'm wondering whether she'll ask me in for coffee or if we can skip the coffee and cut straight to ripping each other's clothes off. "I'm so used to gazing adoringly up at you in your van."

"As it should be, of course. Shall I stand on a box so you feel more at ease?"

"Nah. Don't do that." I move a bit closer, leaning in towards her.

"Why's that then?" Her face is only a few inches from mine, her lips soft and smiling.

"Because I don't want to get neck-ache when I kiss you . . ."

After a couple of minutes, or possibly a couple of weeks, she pulls away and starts burrowing in her bag for her keys.

"Um . . ." she says.

"Hey—that's one of my best lines. Go get your own script."

God, that smile. I'd go without food to be on the receiving end of that smile—and you know what a one I am for my nosh.

I pull her close again.

"If you're planning to drag me indoors and have your evil way with me, I want you to know that my resistance is really low at this time of year, so I can't guarantee to put up much of a fight."

"Ah, that wasn't it actually. Look, no big deal or anything but I have to tell you something—"

I do not like the start of that sentence. It's not got a lot of promise, has it? It's the kind of sentence that finishes up with "I'm married and my husband's about to come out with his shotgun." I like sentences that begin more along the lines of, "This is the way to my bedroom" or "This bra's uncomfortable, do you mind if I take it off . . . ?"

"It's just, well, I don't want to start liking you and then you find out and—*whoosht!*" She goes like this with her hand, like an object zipping by at speed.

"*Whoosht?*" My hand does a repeat performance.

"Yes, you know, out the door and I won't see you for dust."

"I'm not that fit, believe me. There's men of ninety run faster than me. So, what's the big secret? Only if you want to warn me about your husband and he's going to bust out the door any second, I'd better be getting a head start on him."

"Hardly. No. I've got a child, that's all. A boy. He's two and a half."

"Does he have a name, this small person?"

"Jamie."

"Hang on—let me check my list . . ." I hold out my hand like a clipboard. "Alfred, Ben, Charlie—dum-dee-dah, here we go—Jamie. Yes, on my list of approved names. Shouldn't present any problems. Why's it a secret? Is he the result of a drunken fling with a politician?"

She wrinkles her nose up at the thought. It's a pretty nose, a nose I would like to kiss at this moment, so I do.

"That's nice. Believe me, a lot of men run a mile soon as they know you've got a kid."

"I told you about mine."

"Not the same. They don't live with you full-time."

Too true, too true.

She stretches up to kiss me.

"You really OK with it?"

"Sure. So long as he doesn't insist on sleeping in the middle . . ."

Cut to three weeks later if you will. It's a Saturday afternoon. Jamie's playing round at Cora's house, that's Ella's sister, with his cousins. It's raining, and not just a few light droplets either. This is rain that's not going to give up and go home until you are seriously soaked, this is rain with *attitude*. We were planning on going for a bike ride along the old towpath by the canal, but as we're not a couple of ducks it's not looking like such a hot idea.

"Might as well stay in really." I nuzzle at her neck.

"I could carry on with the mural in Rosie's room." It's a castle and hills she's painted on the wall. She's a bit of an artist, is Ella. She likes to do some every week so there's something new each time Rosie comes to stay. "I was thinking of adding a lake and some swans." She tips her head back and half leans against me.

"Swans, yes. Could do that . . ." I very gently start licking her earlobe.

"Or I could go back home and bake some cakes for the van next week."

"Cakes, yes. You could . . ." Tucking her hair back so I can kiss the skin behind her ear.

"Or we could do a jigsaw puzzle?" Her breathing's faster, more ragged now.

"Jigsaw. Hmm-mm . . ." My hand slips down, sliding between her jeaned thighs and she half crumples against me.

"Or you could take me to bed . . ." Her mouth open to mine, her hands roaming up under my T-shirt, stroking my skin.

"Um, jigsaw puzzle's probably the best bet." My words slur out between hot kisses. I try to sneak my hand down the front of her jeans but they're a good, snug fit. Struggling with the button now, the zip, leading her to the bedroom. She opens her eyes.

"Let's take it slowly," she says.

"OK, we'll start with the edges."

* * *

Take it slowly! Take it slowly? Is she kidding? I've waited months for this. Well, all right, three weeks then, but I've fancied her for ages so it counts as longer.

But slowly it is.

First, she draws my T-shirt up and over my head. Starts kissing me all over my chest, spacing the kisses out like a row of seeds. Her fingers lightly skim my skin, driving me crazy. Actually, if this is taking it slowly, I reckon I could stand a little more of it. I've never had anyone pay me so much attention.

She helps me off with my trousers. Yeah, I know, I'm forty-one, I've been managing to undress on my own for years, but she offered so what can you do? It'd be rude to say no, right? My pants virtually have to be peeled off me by this point, though if she leaves them on a minute longer they'd probably burst right off me or spontaneously combust.

Oh, hello, this looks promising. Ay-ay-ay . . . my eyes are rolling into the back of my head. God, I've missed this. Gail was never all that keen, to be honest, so it became a bit of a twice-a-year, birthday and Christmas treat, and it's one thing you can't do for yourself. Ella's mouth is strutting some majorly funky stuff here and her hands aren't just loafing either. I have died and gone to Heaven, there's no other explanation. You can put "At least he died happy" on my headstone.

She leans me back on the bed, then quickly strips down to her bra and pants and climbs astride me. Bends to kiss me, her tongue flicking over my lips, gently drawing my bottom lip between her teeth. God, that's good.

"I want to be inside you." It's what I mean, but it sounds feeble. It doesn't sound like enough. "I want to be inside you, around you, through you, over you, under you, filling every inch of you . . ."

"You'll have to be pretty supple."

"I'll be down that gym first thing in the morning." I reach round her to unhook her bra. Circle her left nipple with the tip of my tongue then open my mouth wider to suck. She shivers above me.

"Cold?"

"No," she smiles, drowsy-eyed. "Just shivery."

"Here. Come under the covers."

She snuggles up close to me.

"Any chance of removing these knickers in the next—oh—two seconds or so?"

"I was planning to keep them on. Good old-fashioned form of contraception—the barrier method."

"You think I can't sneak my way round these? Dream on." I start stroking her thighs, teasing her, tracing a path over and around with my finger, hearing her breath catch in her throat as I stray from the path. I press harder, feeling her through the damp lace.

"Funny. Seems to be some kind of moisture down here. Perhaps I should investigate?"

"Must be environmental humidity—but you'd better check."

"Ah, yes, that'll be it." I start to burrow down under the quilt. "Seems to be at pretty high levels in this part of the country."

Her legs shudder and widen for me.

"Oh, it is," she says, "It is."

I'd tell you the rest but Ella says it's private and also too rude for general consumption. Sorry.

Nat

There's this knocking at my bedroom door. I carry on with the game. Then Mum's voice, sounding all concerned.

"Nat?"

"Mn."

"Can I come in?"

"What? Can't you reach the handle or something?"

Excellent. This teacher at school, Mr Perkins, does this thing, right. When someone says, "Sir, sir—can I go toilet?" Perky goes, "I don't know. Does Granny have to take you?" First time he says it, none of us got what he meant. Whoosh, straight over our heads. Then he tells us it's like *can* isn't the same as *may*. *Can*'s what you say when you mean something's possible, like you can manage to do it and *may*'s when you're asking if you're allowed, wanting permission or whatever. Anyway, I remember it 'cause Andrew nearly wet himself while Perky was telling us. He won't let you go unless you say, "Please, sir, may I go to the lavatory?" He says it's common to say toilet, but everyone else on the entire planet says it 'cept for him, so what does he know? And even when you remember to ask how he

wants he says you should have gone at breaktime and
can't you wait till lunch.

It's wasted on Mum. She opens the door.

"Nat? What are you on about? Can't you—" She stops
then and crosses her arms. "Good game?" Ah, the try-
ing-to-be-nice strategy. She's been doing a lot of that
lately. Actually, she's not so bad. Just don't tell her I
said that, OK?

"S'all right."

"Natty?" She only calls me that when she's trying to
get round me or treat me like a baby. "I thought you
might be doing your homework?"

"Mn."

"Could you switch off the game please."

I turn away from the screen for a nanosecond. Fatal
error. Terminated by an android. Thanks, Mum.

"Now look what you made me do."

"Oh, for goodness' sake, Nathan, is that how you plan
to spend the rest of your life? How's that going to help
you get your GCSEs? You could be anything you
wanted to be—a doctor, a lawyer, a—"

"Yeah, right. Don't you watch the news? There's no
jobs anyway."

"So we might as well all give up now, is that right?"

"I'm just saying, what's the point?"

She plonks herself down on the bed. There's a bit of a
rustle 'cause I still had a mag under my duvet from last
night, but she doesn't seem to twig. She starts looking

round at the floor, like she's about to tell me to tidy it up, but she gives it a miss for some reason.

"But Nathan, look at your dad, for example . . ."

I give her a look. Oh, puh-leese. Since when has he ever been an example of anything?

"I know you're still angry at him, and—well, I hope you'll come to see he's not as bad as you think. But my point is—your dad never got the chance to do much with his life, you know? He's bright, but he left school as soon as he could at sixteen, with no qualifications to speak of, and that was it. He had to take the first job that came along. And he's gone on that way. He works hard, but he could have done so much more."

"Yeah, like Dad could have been a doctor or a judge?"

"Well, maybe not a doctor." She does this spooky kind of smile. Jeez, I bet she's thinking of Weirdy Beardy, then she goes, "He's not much of a one for studying. And definitely not a judge, no. But he could have done *something*. Something that really interested him, I mean, something that made him look forward to each day. He could do his job in his sleep. It's a waste, Nat. Don't make the same mistake."

Another rustle as she stands up. I hold my breath. She comes over and rests her chin on my head, the way she does with Dad sometimes. Used to do. Actually, it was kind of OK.

"But you're not a doctor either and I bet you did all your homework. I bet you were a right goody-goody—like Rosie."

She gives me a shove.

"Was *not*." She rests her chin back on my head again and puts her arms round me. "There's nothing wrong about being like Rosie and you know it. But no, you're right, Nat, who am I to talk? I've wasted a lot of time, too, because I didn't have a clue about what I wanted."

"Yeah, but I don't know either."

"That's OK. The thing is, you don't need to know exactly what you want in your whole life when you're only thirteen. But don't leave it as late as me, hmm? Learn from my mistakes. Start noticing what you really enjoy so you know what you're aiming for in life. But you also have to be prepared to work hard to get it."

"There you go then." I reached for the mouse and selected "New Game" from the menu.

"There I go what?"

"I want to work in computers, so this counts as work, right?"

She laughs and kisses me on the top of my head, then she ruffles my hair like I'm a little kid or something. I shake her off but she keeps laughing.

"You're beyond help. Tell you what, Nat?"

"Mn?"

"You work a bit harder at school and I'll start thinking about getting myself some kind of training too. That's a promise."

"Sure."

She stops outside on the landing and I hear her voice from the other side of the door.

"Supper's in twenty minutes. Macaroni cheese. And Nat?"

Another android exploded to bits on the screen. 140 points. 160. 200.

"What?"

"Do your homework."

Rosie

My dad's got a girlfriend. She's called Ella and she's got freckles on her nose and she's got a little boy whose name's Jamie and he's two and a half. On Sundays, when I go out with my dad, sometimes they come with us or they meet us in the afternoon so I still get Dad all on my own in the morning. If we have lunch with all of us, I try to get Jamie to eat up his vegetables because he says he doesn't like them except for peas and he drops a lot of them. I told him that his carrots were really sweeties just made to look like carrots, so he ate some of them. One time, Dad said we should all go for a picnic on the beach and take a pack lunch. He turned to Ella and he said,

"How about whipping up a few rounds of sandwiches then? You'd like that, wouldn't you?" He was laughing. And she put her hands round his neck as if she was going to strangle him, but she was only playing.

Dad likes her, you can tell, because he holds her hand when we're walking along. I told Nat Dad's got a girl-friend, but he said, "So? Tell me something I don't know. I knew that. I told you in the first place."

I tried to tell him that I don't think it's the same one but he wouldn't listen.

Ella is painting a picture right on the wall in my bedroom at Dad's. She said she is very rusty at painting but she is miles better than me. Dad is good at walls but he can't do pictures. What she's painting is a castle on a hill and there's birds and clouds in the sky and it'll be the only painting like it in the whole wide world. Dad said she went to art school and did painting when she was younger and then she made jewellery and used to sell it on a stall in a market but she had to give it up because she couldn't make enough money. Ella doesn't get any money in an envelope because Jamie hasn't got a daddy, so she has to work really hard all by herself. I tried to tell Nat but he put his fingers in his ears and told me to shut up and stop talking about smelly Ella the whole time. But she is not smelly except for sometimes she has perfume on and she let me squirt it on my neck and my wrists like a lady and Dad said I smelt very nice and posh and now he'll have to take us both out to a fancy restaurant and put on his best suit so as not to let the side down.

Scott

Hey—it's not bad this talking lark, is it? I stay at Ella's a couple of nights a week now and we do lots of it—talking, I mean. She can't come to mine, 'cept at the weekends of course, because she doesn't want to unsettle Jamie plus she has to get things ready for the van. She's up at the crack of dawn, buttering away against the clock, then she loads up, with all the spare fillings in plastic tubs, and the paper bags and everything. She's a one-woman whirlwind. Sometimes I try to help her, but I can't keep up so I just do the lifting things into the van bit. She gets Jamie up and breakfasted too, though he's a self-reliant little fellow.

I'm teaching him to dress himself, but it's a tricky business when you come to think of it and, frankly, at that time in the morning, I'm not all that hot at it myself. Jamie reminds me of Nat at that age, wanting to do everything himself and going mad with frustration when something's just a bit beyond him. The first few times I stayed there, Ella bundled me out the house as soon as she got up. Then one time, I just could not lever myself upright from the bed until it was seven so I bumped into Jamie and he pointed at me very accusingly and shouted: "You were in *my* mummy's bed!"

"She said I could because my bed's broken."

"*I'm* not allowed any more!"

He likes to shout does Jamie, but he's a sweet kid. Anyway, when I'm there, me and him have a bit of a chat about manly matters over our cornflakes, then Ella's sister Cora drops in, scoops up Jamie and whisks him off to nursery school which luckily is next to the junior school where her own twin girls go. In the afternoons, Ella sorts out the van and restocks, then she has the twins for an hour or two after school to give Cora a break. They've got it down to a fine art, so they tell me, and it mostly goes without a hitch, but they're both completely knackered the whole time. Cora's husband works a night shift in the mortuary at the hospital, and so far as I can see his sole contribution during the day seems to be nothing but a lot of snoring.

Anyhow, because of this hectic frenzy Ella calls a life, she has to be in bed by ten most nights, but if I'm there on a sleepover, as Rosie would say, we stay awake and talk for an hour. In the dark. Ella says she and Cora used to talk with the lights out when they were kids, they'd whisper to each other and make up stories. We never did that. We wouldn't have had the nerve. The old man would have murdered us in our beds if he'd heard a peep out of us once we were supposed to be asleep.

"He sounds like a barrel of laughs, your dad."

"Oh, he *is*. It's like a non-stop pantomime, being in his company." Her arm slides across me, her skin cool against my stomach.

"You seem amazingly un-bitter about it though. I mean, I know you joke about it, but it must be painful surely? Aren't you angry?"

"What? Angry that he's a foul, mean-minded, violent arsehole who wishes I'd never been born, you mean?"

"I'm sure he's not *that* bad, but—well, yes."

"Not really. I've given up thinking about it. I mean, yeah, it was crap at the time, but none of us knew any different, and—well—we all survived."

"Yes." Her hand strokes my cheek. "But much more than that, you've made something of yourself and you're a great father to boot. Still, you must have missed having a dad you could look up to?"

"You don't miss what you never had, do you? I'm OK."

"It's good that you've got Harry in your life," she says. "Thank God for being a grown-up—at least you get to adopt some new relatives if you like. No reason why you should stay stuck with the ones you're born with. He means a lot to you, Harry, doesn't he?"

"Mmm, I guess so. He's all right, is Harry."

It's nice, this, talking in the dark. You can say things you couldn't say in the daytime. Ella's body curves close into mine, our legs bent at the same angle. Sometimes I barely know which parts are her and which are me.

"My turn," she says, as we turn together, facing the other way. "Your go to spoon me." And she wriggles back onto my lap, sighs and settles into sleep.

While we're on the subject of my wondrous family, did I ever mention that I was a mistake? I may have let it slip somewhere along the line. The Gruesome Twosome had decided to call it a day after they'd had Sheila and Russell. I guess they felt there was only so much happiness they could stand, you know? Yeah, right. More like they decided the carpet couldn't take the extra wear and tear. Anyway, it wasn't so much a decision, I think, as that they'd more or less stopped "having relations" as my mother puts it—which, to me, sounds like what you'd say if you asked your aunty and uncle over to tea. But my mother doesn't like people speaking about the "S" word in front of her. It makes her wrinkle her nose up as though she's just got wind of a nasty whiff.

Anyway, a brief lapse occurred. Either that or a lone brave sperm made a slither for it across the vast desert of the marital bed and managed to struggle on under the flannel marquee my mother favours as a nightie, elbowing its way bravely like a commando in hostile territory. That's a horrible thought, I wish I'd never got started on this. Yeuch. However it happened by some happy accident—ha!—I came into the world. It's no wonder half the time I feel unsettled, like I'm not really supposed to be here at all and any minute now they'll discover my visa's expired and boot me off the planet altogether. Still, it's not my fault, is it? I didn't ask to be here either. But now that I am here, you'd think the parents could at least put a brave face on it and act like they're happy. To be fair to them, I can't accuse them of favouritism, 'cause they didn't exactly smother Sheil or Russ with love either. They like them better now, but only because they live so far away and communication's been reduced to Christmas and birthday cards. My mum's especially proud of the fact that Russell lives in Canada—bit like the way Harry and Maureen are about their son Chris in Australia, now I come to think of it. My mum's always saying, "My son Russell, who lives in Canada," as if it's her achievement, like it reflects well on her. Which it doesn't. I mean, why's she think he moved over there in the first place? Wasn't for the beaches and the non-stop sunshine, was it? And Sheil up in Scotland. OK, it's only 400 miles, but she knows they're too mean to stump up the train or air fare to be dropping in on her every other weekend, and that's the way she likes it. So how come I'm the only daft sod who still lives within spitting distance of the old dears? No, not literally—they're a half-hour drive away. It's not like my mum or dad have ever begged me to stay in the neighbourhood; my mother doesn't turn to me with a twinkle in her aged eye and say, "Scott, dear, it's such a comfort having you live close by"; my father's not on the phone every morning, asking me if I fancy going for a round of golf.

Still, I've never really had the urge to move away. I did when I was a kid, I wanted to live on an island and spend my days shinnying up palm trees and swimming with dolphins. I imagined making a dugout canoe for myself and living off the fish I caught in the sea. I don't know how I thought all this was going to happen, why I'd be chosen to live in some paradise but everyone else at school would end up working in the dog food factory or behind a till at Tesco's. And then, the longer you're in a place, the harder it gets to see yourself somewhere else, you know? Your mates are nearby, you've got your work, your house, then pretty soon, you've got a wife and kids, and the idea of living on an island seems like a stupid fantasy, a daft childhood dream so crazy you tell yourself you never even wanted it in the first place, it was just something you used to think about as a game, playing make-believe, no more than a silly kid's game.

And it's not so bad here, after all. I've got my kids, well—Rosie likes to see me. And I've got Ella. And even when everything went belly-up on me, at least I had my work to keep me together. So it might not look like much to you, but I've done worse. I know it can't compete with being an astronaut, say, or an overpaid footballer—how many little kids say they want to be a glazier when they grow up?—but being a glazier was the first job I ever really liked. Once I started learning the trade, I found I was good at it, and then there was the managing side of things, bringing in new business and that, and I seemed to be all right at that, too. See, all my life I was told I'd never amount to anything and I know it's not much, but I've got my own bit of turf now, you know? And it counts for something. It counts to me.

Gail

It was parents' evening at Rosie's school. Before, Scott used to try to wriggle out of going to that kind of thing. Not that he didn't care about the children's education or how they were doing, to be fair, but Scott has a *big* thing about school. He wasn't exactly a star pupil himself, as you can imagine—he spent most of his school years messing about and getting in trouble with the teachers, and left as soon as he could. His mum was always keeping one or other of them off school so they could help out at home. He'd be kept off for just about any reason—to chop firewood, dig the garden, even go fruit-picking in season to bring in extra money. Scott said the Truant Officer was round at their house practically as often as the milkman. But his mum just lied, of course, said he'd been poorly or had a bit of a cough or a tummy-ache. I know, you'd think that kind of thing stopped centuries ago.

Scott and I are almost the same age, only a year and a bit apart, but you'd think we were born on different planets so far as our childhoods are concerned. He thinks it's hilarious that people are always on about how much better it is to raise children in the country-side. He says it's just as well they got plenty of fresh air because that's *all* they had most of the time. Mind you, I'm not sure that his parents were quite as short of money as they made out. I think they're just bloody mean. And it's not just the money. They don't even speak much, almost as if they're too stingy to let any words out. His mum'll offer you a cup of tea, but she'll put the sugar in so she can control how much you have. She stands like this, all hunched over, clutching the sugar bowl in case you were going to make a grab for it. They don't even open the curtains all the way, as if they're scared the sunlight will come streaming in and steal away some of their hard-hoarded misery.

Oops, I'm getting like Scott, wandering off the point. Anyway, I rang him about the parents' evening, and told him I'd be happy to go on my own and report back afterwards. But he said he wanted to come too and perhaps we could call a truce for the evening and go together.

"*I'm* not at war with you, Scott. I haven't got the energy. I can manage to behave like a civilized adult—because I *am* one. But can *you*?"

Inside my head, even while I was speaking to him, I was thinking, "Oh, for goodness' sakes, Gail, what do you sound like? You're not a prefect now. Don't be so fucking smug."

"Probably not," said Scott, laughing. "Still, what say I

have a crack at it for half an hour and if I feel myself slipping, I can just nip out to the playground and have a run round, OK?"

Well, we saw Rosie's form teacher and she said everything a parent could want to hear, so you'll excuse me if I have a brief boast—she said that Rosie's bright and keen and always tries her best and that she's got a lively, enquiring mind and is a pleasure to teach. Scott and I were beaming away, hoping the other parents would overhear. She also said that sometimes Rosie seems rather quiet and thoughtful, but that was only to be expected under the circumstances. I gave her a rather thin smile at that point and I could see Scott champing at the bit, wanting to tell her to mind her own business, but I kicked him under the table and he managed to restrain himself for once.

Rosie

Mum and Dad came to the parents' evening at school. When dad was still living at home, he never used to come. And now he's in his flat, he said he really wanted to come and wouldn't miss it for the whole wide world. He picked Mum and me up and we all went together in his car, then he brought us home afterwards and we got chips on the way back. Dad bought some for Nat, too, and he put extra vinegar on them the way Nat likes, and got him a pickled onion, and he gave them to me to look after and told me to be sure to give them to Nat. I think Nat is still being stupid about Dad, but he can't hate him all that much because he ate the chips and then he went and breathed all horrible pickled onion on me and did a big burp and Mum said he was disgusting, but she was laughing when she said it.

My room at my dad's is nearly finished now. I've got a carpet and there's a rug by my bed which has got fishes on it and we went and chose a special duvet cover for my bed when we were in the market. It's all blue and it's got a unicorn in the middle of it and all these clouds like the ones Ella painted on my wall. The unicorn is like a white horse with a twirly-whirly horn coming out of its head which looks like a long, pointy shell or a really tall ice-cream like the ones you get from the van in summer. Mrs Lewis said it's supposed to be magic. I asked my dad if he believed in magic and he said he wasn't sure but he could do with some if I knew of any that was going about. Mum says she doesn't believe in magic, but she still makes out there's a tooth fairy who puts the money under your pillow when you lose a tooth but everyone knows it's your mum who puts it there really. Mum's friend Cassie says there is magic, and she says she keeps it in her make-up bag and every morning it works a miracle for her.

Mum bought me a lamp to go in my room at Dad's place and Dad put up a pinboard for me on my bedroom wall, so I could put up some postcards and pictures like I have at home. I've got a photo of Mum on my board and a photo of Nat but he's covering half his face with his hands and sticking out his tongue so it doesn't look all that much like him. I have a photo of my dad too, but I keep that one in my bedroom at home because when I'm at the flat he is there too so I don't need a photo of him, I can just look up and there he is.

Scott

I had the mobile off half of yesterday because I was round at Ella's doing something very important which couldn't possibly be interrupted, and I didn't get a chance to pick up my voicemail messages until lunchtime. And yes, it was very nice, thank you for asking. No, not the messages. What on earth's the point of us all being slaves to mobile phones now? Far as I can see, it's just to give you the illusion that you've got a buzzing, happening kind of life, the kind of life where people need to be able to reach you twenty-four hours a day when, as we all know, 99 per cent of the population uses them to say things that you wouldn't waste your breath on if you were standing face to face. And for someone like me, all it means is you're more stressed because customers and suppliers and every Tom, Dick and Harry can hassle you whenever they feel like it, so you end up switching the phone off, then telling people you were working in a basement and had no signal. Then half the time you forget to charge the sodding thing or you're in some kind of dead zone and are stood there in the middle of a street like a total prat saying,

"Hello? Hello? Are you there?" looking like you've just been let out for the day and your carer'll be back for you any second now to wheel you away to the happy home.

Anyway, the posh voice comes on saying, "You have . . . six messages. To listen to the messages, press . . ." blah, blah. A couple are just boring things to do with work then there's this one from Maureen, you know, Harry's wife from First Glass, with a big pause first like she's not sure whether to leave a message.

"Scott, dear. It's Maureen. Sorry to ring you so late, but—well—it's Harry, you see. Perhaps you could call—oh, but I won't be there. Or you could—no—I don't think—well—perhaps I'll try you again later. Goodbye, dear."

What do you do with people who leave messages like that? Still, it was timed at half-twelve at night, long past Maureen's cocoa and bed time. Shit, I hoped like hell Harry was OK. It didn't sound good. I'd better give him a call at home. The next message was Maureen again.

"We're in the Roughton Hospital, Scott, but I'm not sure what—" her voice dropped as she obviously turned away to speak to someone and I pressed the phone right into my ear to try to hear her: "Oh—I'm not sure they'll let you in—you see it's family only—you better come—I'll ask the—I'm sure they'll—yes—Goodbye, dear."

By now, I'm practically yelling at the phone.

"What? For chrissakes, what? What's happened, you silly cow? Tell me what the fuck's happened!" But as it was just her recorded message it didn't have much effect.

Then there was one from Gail.

"Scott, now don't panic but it seems Harry's been taken into the Roughton. Maureen left a garbled message on the answerphone but she wasn't very clear and I couldn't really make head nor tail of what she was saying. I don't want to worry you, but it sounds as though Harry may have had a heart attack. I don't know anything else, I'm sorry. I hope he's OK. Give him my best won't you, when you see him? Take care. Let me know what's happening if you get a moment."

And a last message from Maureen.

"If you could just come and see him, Scott. He was asking for you, see. He's in the . . ." It sounds as though she's speaking through a gobful of cornflakes. Can't hear a frigging word.

At the hospital, I finally make it to reception to ask for Harry's whereabouts, having had to accost about fifteen strangers in the car park for change for parking. It can't be right, can it, charging in a hospital car park. What if you're in to see your dying mother or something? "Tell Ma to hang on just a few more minutes—I've got no pound coins." Colin got clamped in there one time so I didn't dare risk it. Risk it and go as a biscuit, that's what Rosie says. God knows where she got that from. Anyway, they track him down on the computer for me and I spend another half-hour waiting for the lift and wandering round dead-end corridors that must have been laid out by the bloke who designed Hampton Court maze.

I'm sure I pass the same sign saying "Mortuary" at least three times. I wonder if Ella's brother-in-law's in, I could pop in and say hello. No, he works nights. Anyway, it gives me a shiver just to think about it, what a creepy place to work. Behind that door are actual dead bodies, you know, people who were once—well—people. I mean proper, real live people who had jobs and drove cars and had sex and traipsed round Safeway of a Saturday morning and taught their kids how to ride a bike and who drank too many lagers once a week and liked prawn won tons—or didn't like prawn won tons but at least had an opinion one way or the other, you know? Only now all they are is cold dead *things*, with no more feelings or thoughts or opinions than if they were just outsize leftover won tons themselves. God, it's depressing.

Eventually, with the aid of a compass and directions from a passing nurse, I find the ward and ask at the desk for Harry Wilcox.

"Oh, are you his son?"

I hesitate. Maybe Maureen's told them that in case it's family visiting only. There's a lump in my throat and I'm finding it hard to swallow. "Are you his son?" I want to say yes. He's been more of a dad to me than my own's ever been, that's for sure. God knows I wouldn't be feeling this crap if it was my own dad. Yeah, I know that's a horrible thing to say, but it's true. Then suddenly that makes me think about Nat—all this tumbling through my head in a couple of seconds—hoping that one day he won't be standing in a hospital ward wishing it was me lying there and not some other bloke he'd come to think of as his dad.

Maybe Harry had said it. He must be OK—awake and thinking of me as his son. I bite my lip and clear my throat, which sounds really loud like I'm standing next to a microphone.

The nurse smiles sympathetically. They must be used to grown men making complete fools of themselves in public.

"It's all right," she says. "Your dad's out of intensive care. He's doing really well. Next bay along on the right." She turns away then back again. "You got here very fast. I thought Mrs Wilcox said you lived in Australia. Did you charter a Concorde then?"

The light dawns.

"Oh, no. That's Chris." Chris. Harry's son. Harry's real flesh-and-blood son. He lives in Melbourne, has a good job and a big house in the suburbs. Harry and Maureen have been over there twice, think the world of him, though I know Harry's hurt that Chris ever went there in the first place, hurt his only kid has never showed the slightest interest in taking over the family business. Harry used to talk about retiring over there one day, said Chris was always asking him to come, but I knew it was just talk. I didn't think he'd get a residency permit for a start and anyhow, Harry's as English as they come. He might go on about loafing on the beach and watching the girls in their bikinis, but it's just what blokes say, isn't it? Harry couldn't survive more than a week without his HP Sauce and his pint at the George and Dragon. He needs to be around lousy weather and customers changing their minds every three minutes—or what would he have to worry about? What else would keep him going?

So I walk to the next bay and there's a bed with a mound in it that I guess must be Harry because next to the mound is Maureen sat in a chair and knitting away at top speed like she's going against the clock at the Olympics. I say hello and bend down to kiss Maureen on the cheek.

"How is he?" I whisper. His skin's got that greyish, waxy look people often have in hospitals—it's all that crap food and fluorescent lighting, I suppose.

"Having a nap, love," she whispers back. People always whisper in hospitals, don't they? Like in a library. It's creepy really, like what you'd do if someone was already dead. Though I can't see the point of whispering round a corpse—what you gonna do, wake them up?

I cast around for another chair but Maureen gets up.

"Sit here a minute. I'm desperate anyway." She stuffs

her knitting into her bag and scuttles off in search of the toilet.

Harry's eyes flicker open and he turns his head towards me. His voice is so quiet, I can barely hear him, so perhaps it's only my imagination that I hear him say:

"Son?"

"I'm here, mate."

"Glad you came."

I pat his hand awkwardly and lean in closer to hear him.

"Been overdoing it on the squash court again, then?" Harry hasn't done any kind of sport since 1972 as far as I know. He always says his only exercise is chasing late payments and, to be honest, he's not much cop at that, I usually end up doing it. "Or were you having it away with a young floozie and she wore you out?"

A smile crosses his face.

"I should be so lucky." He looks round vaguely. "Where is she?"

"Who—Maureen or your floozie?"

"Behave. Herself. Maureen."

"Toilet. Why? Do you need something? I can get it, unless you want me to hold your bedpan."

He shakes his head.

"Good just having you here . . . thought I was a goner for a while there."

"No chance, mate. You're tough as old boots—when's the last time you even had a cut, for chrissakes?"

Harry's hands are like leather. "We'll have to slip something nasty in your tea when we want rid of you. Anyway, never mind the chit-chat, what happened? Don't skip any of the gory bits."

So he tells me—as much as he remembers anyway. He'd been sitting in his armchair at home having coffee and a biscuit and watching the telly. It was one of those docu-soap programmes about—get this—a sodding hospital, and it was kind of funny but dead depressing at the same time because there was no money and half the staff were walking zombies who got about five minutes' kip a day and Harry said it made him think you really wouldn't want to get ill because you might get a surgeon operating on you who'd not slept for a week. Then there was this bit where this man got brought into casualty. He'd been slashed across the face with a Stanley knife and there was blood pouring down his face. Harry said he was feeling a bit queasy and was reaching down for the remote which had fallen on the floor to change channels, find a quiz show or something, when he had this horrendous crushing pain in his chest, like as if someone had dropped a house on him. He couldn't breathe properly and he felt sick. Maureen had got a hell of a fright, he said.

"I shouldn't think it was a picnic for you either, by the sound of it." He gives me a weak-looking smile and says he's doing all right.

"It's good to see you," he says, patting my hand back. "I mean it."

He seems a bit vague and I can't tell if he's just dopey from his nap or a bit out of it. God knows what drugs they pump into you after something like that. Wouldn't be surprised if all the patients are coked to the gills as a matter of routine—keeps 'em quiet, need less nurses and that, like they do in prisons. Bromine, is it? Bromide? Something like that. Mega-tranquies of some sort anyhow.

It's weird visiting people in hospital. For a start, they're in bed in their pyjamas only you're supposed to chat away like everything's normal and you're surrounded by other blokes all in their pyjamas with their families all huddled round them. And you bring grapes and flowers and magazines and a card and so each patient's got like a miniature house round them with their vase and their cards and their wife sat next to them—only really it's just like playing house the way kids do when they're little because it's no more like being at home than having a picnic on the hard shoulder of the motorway is like having a relaxing barbie in your back garden. You can't relax 'cause there's all this equipment bleeping away or—worse—not bleeping all of a sudden, and there's tubes going in and coming out carrying God knows what, you'd rather not know thank you, and nurses bustling past and some poor sod mindlessly polishing the floor apparently twenty-four hours a day to make you think the place is clean as a whistle when we all know a hospital's the last place you want to hang out when you're ill because it's full of germs and diseases. The only thing you almost never see, if you think about it, is a doctor. You'd think chaps in white coats with stethoscopes round their necks would be two a penny in a hospital, but God knows what they do with them 'cause I didn't see a single one fluttering round Harry that whole first time I was there.

Well, Maureen comes back from her exciting trip to the toilet—every tiny thing feels like an event in a hospital because it's so sodding boring. I offer to go fetch her a cup of tea from the canteen because the trolley lady's bringing one for Harry and gone are the good old days when the visitors got one as well. Maureen says she thinks she might just manage a biscuit, too, but not to get the ones with the raisins in because they get stuck in her dentures.

One minute, her husband's at death's door, the next she's worrying about whether I might bring her the wrong kind of biscuit. But that's the way it is, isn't it? That's what we do. Tell ourselves everything's back to normal as fast as possible. Sweep it under the mat like it never happened if we can. Heart attack? What heart attack? Just a blip in our normal routine. Smooth it over. Right as rain again.

"Did Harry say . . . ?" Maureen asks as I turn to go.

"Say what?"

"Chris is coming." Her voice is proud, but her smile is shy, guilty-looking, like a kid who knows she's been naughty, like she knows that of course all she should be thinking about is Harry but she's so pleased her beloved son is coming from the other side of the world to be with them that she can't hide her excitement. "Said he felt he should be with his dad. Nothing could have kept him away." I bet. "Said he'd be on the first plane out. He'll be here tomorrow."

"Good. Of course he'd come. That's great. Right. Biscuits—no raisins. Rightio. I'm pleased for you."

I say it, because I know I should, but I'm not really pleased for her. I feel all tight inside, mean and sort of scrunched up and horrible. Chris will turn up and be welcomed with open arms and my presence will be unnoticed, unwanted even—I'll just be some bloke from work who's thoughtfully popped in for a few minutes. I tell myself I'm a sad, mean-spirited bastard and if I'm not careful I'll end up like my sodding father, then I stomp down to the canteen in search of some sodding raisin-free biscuits.

I realize I haven't had a bite to eat all day, so I splash out on a dodgy looking "all-day breakfast" sandwich, which is basically bacon and hard-boiled egg that's been steamrollered then stuck between two bits of bread, and a murky-looking coffee. They have those chocolate muffins and seeing them makes me think of Ella. I really want to speak to someone. Actually, I really want to speak to her. The canteen's practically the only place in the hospital where you can use a mobile, so I dial her number.

"Hello?"

"'s me."

"Hello you. Wassup?"

So I tell her about Harry and about Maureen and her biscuits and her knitting and about the return of the prodigal son from Australia. I take a bite of my sandwich because I'm starving then find that I can't seem to swallow. Gulp at the too-hot coffee to get it down.

"You OK?" Ella's voice, soft and close in my ear.

"Guess so." I pause, feeling myself start to well up. Stop it! I tell myself. Stop this right now! "I'm fine."

"Oh, Scott. You're not. I can hear you're not. I wish I was there with you. This must be hard—I know Harry's like a father to you. I'm so sorry. No wonder you feel a bit peculiar if this Chris is going to suddenly come back and be the golden boy for a while."

"It's OK. I'm OK. Chris is his real son, after all. I'm nobody. What's it to me? I should be pleased he's coming, pleased for Harry."

"Never mind what you should be or shouldn't be. You are allowed to be upset, you know. I don't think any less of you."

"I wish you were here."

"Do you want to come over? Maybe I can get Cora to take Jamie for a while."

I drop my voice.

"I could do with a cuddle."

"So could I. And, besides, I've got bosoms here going to waste. They need to be nestled in, so why don't you get your bod over here soon, hmm?"

"Oh, well, all right then. You talked me into it."

I know, I bet you think I sound like a pathetic bastard, some stupid cry-baby in the playground whining that it's not fair, that some bigger boy's pinched my ball. But that's about how I felt, like I was five years old and my best friend had gone off to play with someone else and I was left all alone, kicking at the tarmac and biting my lip so's I wouldn't cry.

Rosie

Mum said Uncle Harry's had to go to the hospital because he had a heart attack, but it is all right—he didn't die or anything. I'm supposed to be specially nice to my dad because he is sad about Harry. I made a Get Well Soon card and Mum bought one and Dad came and picked them up to take them to the hospital. Mum had to sign hers from Nat too because he was at swimming, then Nat was cross when he came back because he said he wanted to sign it and he was always being left out of everything and it wasn't fair and Mum should have waited for him.

Mum gave Dad a hug in the hall when he came round to make him feel better, but it does not mean that they are getting back together or anything because it was only a friendly hug. There was no snogging. Dad goes to see Harry every day at the hospital and some days he goes twice. He takes him a newspaper and tapes of old songs to listen to. I said he should get him a puzzle magazine because they are good when you are bored and they have the answers in the back for when you get stuck. And I told Dad he should buy some chocolates too because that's what you take people in hospital, but he said no, he didn't think it was a good idea because Harry was on a diet and was only allowed healthy things and no more cakes or doughnuts or chocolate or chips or anything and I said maybe he should take him a lettuce instead then and Dad said he thought it was a very good idea and it would give Harry a laugh and remind him of his allotment and that I was a genius. I'm not a genius actually in fact, but I'm glad I said about the lettuce.

Scott

We walk up and down the hospital corridors. Harry and me, arm in arm like a couple of old ladies taking the air along the seafront. You'd think that one good thing about being in hospital is you'd at least get plenty of rest. But not a chance—they say he's not to lay in bed all day, it's not good for him. Harry says he feels like a right wally walking about on his own in his dressing-gown, so I tag along.

"Here we go again," I say. "Nice day for a stroll, eh, Grandpa?"

"Cheeky sod. I bet this is more exercise than you've taken in years 'n' all."

As we walk, I tell him what's occurring at First Glass, what jobs we've got on, what's coming up, what birds Lee's knocking off now. I do impressions so he can feel like he's right there: Lee's side-to-side swagger, his cocky greeting—"Awwright?" Gary, tongue poked out in concentration like a kid as he peers close at the measuring rule; Martin, trying to talk through a faceful of egg sandwich. Harry laughs and nods, says he can't wait to get back to work.

"Hey—but no overdoing it, eh?" I tell him. "We can manage."

"How's that boy of yours doing?" Harry squeezes my arm.

"I don't see him enough to know. I'm still not Mr Popular in his book. Have to get reports from the front via messenger. Gail says his moods are up and down like a fiddler's elbow. I wish I could—well, you know."

"They can be awkward so-and-sos at that age, eh? Bet you were a right little tearaway yourself."

"You're not wrong, Harry. But ... I dunno. You reckon I should just let him alone, leave him to sort it out in his head—or what?"

Harry stops a minute, before we go back into the ward, rubs his unshaven chin.

"Talk to him. You don't want to leave things unsorted. Unfinished business. See, fathers and sons ..." his mouth tightens a sec and I know he's thinking about Chris. "'s tricky. Well, I'm no expert either—but I'd say you give it your best shot, eh?"

I nod.

"Yeah, I should have a crack at it."

"After all," he says, "we're all a long time dead. You want to get the good while you're still here."

He's a cheery old soul sometimes.

The first three days, by dint of luck and by sneakily finding out from Maureen, I manage not to coincide with

483

Chris at the hospital. I pop in to the hospital twice a day if I can. Harry says he's glad to see me but not to stay long because while the cat's away etcetera—and goodness knows what the little sods might get up to with only Denise to keep an eye. Maureen says she's not up to going in to work just now.

Then there's a conservatory to be done and it's a right bugger, frankly, so I have to go give Lee a hand and I don't make it to the hospital in the morning. It's gone two by the time I get there. I'm walking along the corridor, with my hands full: Harry's newspaper and a copy of *Auto Express*, a Nat King Cole tape—he's a right old softy is Harry—a bottle of lemon barley water, and a bag of satsumas. He likes those 'cause they're easy for him to peel in bed and it helps take his mind off his cravings for crisps and nuts.

There's two men walking ahead of me along the corridor. Suddenly, I click that the older one's Harry. That's his dressing-gown and I recognize his shuffle—it's them backless slippers of his. The other one must be Chris. As I watch, he puts his arm round Harry, then they turn the corner to carry on with their walk.

I should catch them up and say hello.

Yes, that's what I should do most probably.

*　*　*

I go in the ward and the nurse flashes me a smile and

greets me, "Hello there, you're late today. Harry'll be back in a few minutes I should think if you want to wait."

"It's OK. I can't stop now anyway. I'm, er—I've got—yeah—I'll just stick this lot by his bed. Tell him I said hi."

"I'm sure he won't be that long if you—"

"Nah. I'd better go. I'll come by tonight."

Eight o'clock. He should be gone by now, right?

He isn't.

Chris looks healthy and tanned and relaxed. I feel crap and pale and tense. Not a good start. I've met him twice before, when he came over with his wife and kids. Last time was about three years ago I think. You should have seen Harry, crawling about on the floor playing at being horsey for his little granddaughter. It was only the second time he'd seen her since she'd been born. He was gutted when they went back to Australia. I reckon in the back of his mind he kept hoping they'd decide to jack in their jobs and swanky house over there and come back here, that they'd see what they were missing. Problem was, they saw exactly what they were missing—mostly in the form of rain, rude service and lousy job prospects. Can't say I blame them really. But it was hard on Harry and Maureen.

Chris is an OK kind of bloke, I suppose, but he's got his own life and I don't think his parents figure much in it. He sends them a couple of cards a year and each time, Harry brings the card in to the office. It'll be a picture of a koala or a kangaroo or whatever and you can see Harry turning it over and over in his hands, looking at the picture, then reading the back, then looking at the picture again, before he says, ever so casually:

"Postcard from Chris. From Australia."

He always adds that and it's like he's telling me but really he's telling himself, like he's saying: see, he's sent a card from all that way away—as if Chris had strapped on a pair of wings and flown over with it personally instead of just whacking on a stamp and shoving it in a letterbox. I mean, to Harry's generation, getting something from Australia is still a big deal. Course, now flights really don't cost all that much, and Chris could come over three or four times a year if he wanted to. I guess he just doesn't want to.

Maureen writes them every fortnight. Harry's not big on letter writing. I told him he could e-mail them no sweat, but Harry's a bit of a technophobe ever since he lost part of the database. It didn't matter. Denise had a printout on file and she just keyed it back in again. Harry likes things he can pick up with his hands—like a sheet of glass or a piece of timber or a cutter—or a postcard.

*   *   *

Anyway. Chris. I'm here now and I don't see why I should have to go sneaking off again. Bollocks to it. It's fine. I'm cool with this, really I am. We shake hands and he says how's it going and I say fine and he must be relieved to see Harry's OK, but it must have been quite a shock when Maureen phoned him.

"Yeah, well I was due a trip over here anyhow."

"Business going well?" He has one of those jobs that you have no idea what he actually does all day. He's an Associate Executive Something-or-Other or an Executive Associate Director, something like that, for some food processing corporation. I don't know, I asked him about it last time we met and he said, "It's kinda dull, you wouldn't want to hear about it." And then proceeded to give me a minute-by-minute account of what felt like an entire year in the life of this mind-bogglingly tedious business—and, at the end, I still didn't have a clue what he did.

Maureen comes sidling up to us and says Chris is keen to come in to First Glass, take a look, especially as Harry will be having some time off. And I'm thinking, "Well, you sure as hell don't know how to cut a piece of glass, mate, so what use are you going to be?" Then it occurs to me that what he really wants is to have a good old snoop, probably find out what our turnover is, see how much his old man's worth. Chris goes off to the toilet and Maureen leans close like she's telling me a secret.

"Chris is such a love. Always takes such a keen interest in the business."

Er, hello? Takes a keen interest from umpteen thousand miles away by sending two postcards a year. Is she kidding herself or what?

"Er, yeah, right. And you're OK with him coming round work then?" Maureen looks puzzled and I feel like I've mishandled it.

"Of course. You'll show him how it all works, won't you, Scott? Whatever he wants to see."

"Rightio. No probs. He'll get the full guided tour."

Next morning I'm in at five to eight, but he's already there, sitting in Harry's car, waiting for me. He probably got here at 6 a.m. just to make sure he was here first. I feel like I'm being watched by an inspector from the Rev, and I fumble with my keys and bump myself hard against the counter as I rush to do the alarm.

"Two—seven—three—nine," he says out loud, watching over my shoulder.

Why don't you just fuck off?

"So . . ." he nods slowly to himself. "You don't have to have the alarm code written up somewhere to remember it?"

I can't tell if he's trying to take the piss or if he's actually serious. Please can I punch him? Just the once?

"No, even though I'm a bit of a thicko, I never forget it because it's Harry's birth date."

* * *

There is a pause. A definite pause.

"Hey—*I* know that."

Yeah, but you'd forgotten, I think. I *know* it.

Gail

I'm worried about Nat. I try to tell myself he's just being a teenager, but he seems so withdrawn and I can't seem to communicate with him at all. I ask him how things are going with Joanne and he just grunts. She seems like a nice girl, so maybe it's fine. And he's barely at home—when he's not at school or swimming practice, he's over at Joanne's or Steve's.

"So what do you get up to?" I ask him.

"Just, you know, hanging out."

"Oh. Right."

It could mean anything. I tell myself it means sitting around chatting and listening to music, maybe even discussing their homework. Not every teenager is off his skull on crack and beating up old ladies for their pension money, I remind myself. The papers are chock full of rubbish. I wish he'd talk to Scott. Or at least just see him other than when Scott picks up Rosie.

Cassie comes round and tells me not to get in a stew about it.

"Nat's basically a good kid," she says. "You know he

is and you've done a good job bringing him up. Don't keep beating yourself up and telling yourself you're a bad mother—you're *not*."

"I know, but he won't talk to me."

"Nat's not the type to talk about how he feels anyway, is he? Takes after Scott. He's a guy's sort of guy. I think he must miss his dad an awful lot."

"Yes, but I try to—"

The door opens and Nat lopes in.

"Yo," he says to Cassie, but it's a half-hearted sort of a "yo."

"Hey, it's my fave man." Cassie raises her glass to him. "How's it going?"

His face bobs up and down, like he's listening to music.

"'s OK."

I leap to my feet and say I'll fetch some crisps for us to have a nibble. I start fiddling about in the cupboards as if I'm not listening to them. Cassie's more likely to get him to talk if I'm not in his face being Nosy Mother.

"How's things with that pretty girlfriend of yours? Spend your whole time snogging, I bet. Or worse. Just don't get her up the duff. There's enough teenage pregnancies in this country without you two adding to the statistics."

"Get away!"

Cassie. For goodness' sake. Honestly. I clutch the crisp packet to stop myself remonstrating with her. He can't be having sex. Not at thirteen. *Surely* not. I mean, maybe they play around a little . . . I don't want to think about it. This is my little boy we're talking about. I hadn't even had my first kiss at his age. I dive back into the cupboard again, looking for some of those mini cheese biscuity things.

I sneak a glance round. Nat's leaning against the counter, his back to me. I clatter about, must just find a dish for these crisps, giving Cassie a bit more time.

"I hear your dad's got himself a new pad."

"Mn."

"Thought I'd go take a look next week. Rosie says there's a painting on her wall she wants me to see."

"Yeah, she's always on about it—'Natty, Natty— come and *see-ee-ee*!'—she drives me mad."

"Aaah. Sweet. It'd mean a lot to her if you'd go."

He shrugs.

"Go *on*. Humour your kid sister for once. She'll be tickled pink. Let her show off a bit."

"Mn."

"You know, your dad's not such a bad guy."

Nat jerks his head up, but says nothing. I plunge into the fridge and stand there like an idiot, shuffling things pointlessly from shelf to shelf. I take out the Coke and pour a glass for Nat. Now, ice. Nat's big on ice.

Cassie carries on.

"Still . . ." she says. "It's nice you're so happy to let Rosie have him all to herself. Pretty unselfish of you, I'd say. *My* big brother was always muscling in, but then he was my dad's favourite."

"Oh?"

"Yup." She raises her voice: "Ask Scott if it's OK for me to pop round and have a nose, next time you're talking to him, will you, Gail?"

"Sure. He'll probably phone tonight. I'll ask him then."

Nat is silent when I hand him the Coke but he has his thinking face on. He looks down at his drink and lowers two fingers in like tongs to pull out an ice cube, pops it into his mouth. Then, slowly, he crunches it, and very quietly I hear him start to hum.

Scott

You know how it is when your whole life is completely crap and you hit rock bottom? Maybe you don't. Maybe you're someone who's living a fairly normal sort of a life; maybe you and your partner, spouse, whatever love each other to bits; maybe you've got some fab career and you earn loads of dosh. If so, be grateful, you fortunate bastard, and enjoy it while you can.

What's my point, you're wondering? I've no idea. This is another thing that always drove Gail crazy. My inability to stick to the point. Ella thinks it's funny, though. She says I've got a butterfly-mind, she never knows what I'm going to say next, and she thinks I'm like a kid. Only she means it as a compliment. Maybe she's right. Anyway. Oh, yeah, you hit rock bottom, but gradually, if you're lucky, things start to improve: Your wife—ex-wife—stops looking at you as if you were something suspect on the bottom of her shoe. You start enjoying your Sundays. You even get yourself a girlfriend and you start to tell yourself maybe you're not such a bad person after all. You wake up and you dare—fool that you are—to look forward to the day ahead.

This is a mistake, of course. A mega-serious mistake. You think, "It must be someone else's turn by now. God's got bored of me and has settled on a new plaything to torment." So what do you do? You relax. Uh-huh. Bad move.

Because that's when God comes back to give you another poke in the eye.

They're selling First Glass.

I have worked at First Glass for over sixteen years. I know, you're thinking "Sad git, it's about time you moved on then." It probably is, but that's not the point. I'm not saying I've made a fortune or it's stood me in good stead if I should ever apply for the position of Prime Minister—but I've done all right. Better than my parents or my teachers ever expected me to for a start. I've earned a not bad living, learned a trade, had a laugh. And there was always Harry. He taught me the business, trained me like an apprentice, like he would his— like he would have with Chris. If he'd been here.

Thing is, I know Maureen's been wanting Harry to cut back on his days for the last couple of years in any case. I've even said it myself. And then his ticker went doolally on him, and it looked like he should definitely start taking it a bit easier. But not throw in the towel completely.

There's bigger companies who've been sniffing round First Glass for ages, of course. We've got a list of loyal customers that would stretch up the High Street and back, a nice mix of trade and private business. It's a good solid firm with a good reputation. It may not look much, but it turns a tidy profit, more than you'd think.

It's that Chris. One minute he's here, sporting a face the picture of worry for his old dad and a tan so even it looks like it's come straight out of a spray can, the next he's acting all concerned and saying Harry shouldn't be getting too stressed out. Then two seconds later he's snooping round the database and the invoices and poking his nose in where it's not wanted. He doesn't even know anything about the business. But Maureen thinks the sun shines out of his rear end. It's all: "Chris is ever so clever when it comes to business matters" and "Chris has the experience when it comes to handling finances" and "Chris knows best." It's utter bollocks. The man knows diddly-squat about glazing. He knows less than Rosie does and she's only ten.

Point is, I don't want to work for some sodding big anonymous company, having to bow and scrape to head office the whole time and be all yes-sir, no-sir, three-bags-full-sir. It's just not me and I'm not doing it.

Oh-oh, talk of the devil. Look who's here, rolling up in Harry's car. It's Chris—dah-dah, Saviour of the Universe. What a treat.

I've seen him approach, but I stay at my desk and don't look up when he comes in. The door's open but he should still knock. Acting like he owns the place already.

"Scott? Can I have a word?"

"Sure, carry on. Why not? You've had everything else."

"Hey, come on. There are no bad guys in this. I'm on your side." I notice he doesn't look at me when he says this. "I'm sure we can be adult about this."

I don't know if there's something in the air at the moment, but all I seem to have been hearing this whole year is people telling me to be grown-up and adult and mature the whole time. Frankly, I think I'm done with being grown-up. I'm no good at it and it hasn't got me anywhere. That's it. I am now officially tendering my resignation. I no longer wish to be a grown-up. As far as I can see, there are only two advantages of being an adult. One is you get to stay up late and eat as many sweets as you like—but that's out the window, because as soon as you hit about the age of twenty-five, all you can think of is what's the earliest you can go to bed without looking like a sad fuck—and you don't eat so many sweets because you spend your time worrying that your teeth are going to fall out and telling yourself that you really should be flossing every day and not just for one minute every six months while you're sitting in the car just before you go in to see the dentist. Two is—in theory— that you get to have sex when you're a grown-up. Per- sonally, I reckon I used up my entire allowance, mostly when I was about seventeen, and that's why I had, let's call it something of a fallow period, shall we? Still, Ella's helping me catch up again. She's considerate that way.

I don't feel very adult, sitting here, with Chris being all super-cool and casual, leaning in the doorway. I feel as if I'm about eight and he's some snotty, smooth smart aleck boy in the playground. I want to jump on his foot and give him a good smack.

Chris slips his hands into his pockets and suppresses a yawn. His tan is really annoying me now. He looks like he's leaning against the door of his cabin, out for a sail on his yacht. I don't know if he actually has a yacht, but you get my drift.

"I wanted to talk to you face to face," he says, still not meeting my eyes. "There's something important . . ."

I open the invoice file and flick over the pages as loudly as I can, licking my finger at intervals and poring over the fascinating figures in front of me.

"Scotty?"

"Oi!" He's got my attention now all right. "Only my close friends get to call me that. Don't push it, mate."

"Hey—sorry. OK, sorry. Look, I think we kind of got off on the wrong foot here . . ."

And then he starts talking about the new company and the sell-off and what would have happened to First Glass if we didn't seize this dazzling opportunity and how it means better job security for the guys and a decent lump sum for Harry and Maureen (and for you too, matey, I bet), which is good news because he won't have to worry about his retirement and Chris could invest some of the money just in case either of them get ill when they're older and need nursing care. He's got it all worked out. Probably had the whole thing planned for years and just took advantage of Harry's heart attack as an excuse to jet over here and put it into action.

"And the lads' jobs will be guaranteed?" I know for sure Harry wouldn't have agreed to anything less, but I want to hear it from Chris's own lips.

"Yes. Three full-time glaziers. With rotating shifts to cover Saturdays. And four days a week for the girl."

"She's not a girl. She's Denise."

"Yes. Denise. Four days."

"Right. And the price will cover all the stock as well as the lease and the goodwill and—"

"Yes. It's a fair price they're offering. More than fair, I'd say. But there's one—possible—sticking point . . ."

Why should I bother to ask him what it is when I know he's going to tell me anyway? He's desperate to tell me, you can see he is. And suddenly, seeing him there tilting forward, I know why he is. In that second, I know exactly what the sticking point is. It's so bloody obvious, I must have been blind not to see it before. Now it's as plain and clear to me as—as a sheet of glass.

But I want to make him say it. Why should I let him have it easy? I want to hear him say the words.

He coughs then and shifts from his casual-modelling-leisure-wear pose to something a bit more formal and upright.

"I'll be straight with you, Scott. The way they see it, they'd be looking to put in one of their own people as manager. It's standard practice."

What a surprise.

"And that would make me what exactly? The world's oldest tea boy?"

He looks shocked. Wrong-footed. He thinks maybe I'm serious, that I'd hang on for dear life and refuse to go.

"Well, I . . ."

"Don't worry. I won't stand in between you and your pot of gold. Just tell me what the deal is."

"Well, of course the overall terms of the negotiation are kind of confidential—family only—"

You bastard. You total and utter bastard. You know that's not what I meant, you arsehole.

"Yeah, that's not what I meant. I *meant* what deal am I being offered to trot off quietly into the wilderness without a fuss?"

"Um, your terms of agreement state—what? Are you on a one-month contract . . ."

"You're kidding me, right?" Harry and me have never gone in for all that rubbish. We've never needed it.

"I'm sure we could push it to three months, seeing as you've been here a long time—how long is—?"

"Sixteen years. Sixteen sodding years, with more extra Saturdays and unpaid overtime than you'll do in a lifetime. And you want to offer me three months' pay? Well, bollocks to you. Keep the whole lot, why don't you? Take it and buy yourself an extra case of fucking champagne for your fucking yacht."

"Yacht? What yacht?"

"Does Harry know about this?"

"Now, I won't have you bothering my dad about this. I'm sure you understand the doctors don't want him having any extra anxiety right now."

I want to call Harry. I want to call him now, this minute. I want to go knocking at his door, crying my eyes out and saying, "Dad, that big boy pushed me over—go and get him back." I don't want to deal with this on my own. I don't want to deal with it, full stop. Then I think of Ella. I look at my watch. In twenty minutes or so, there'll be the toot-toot of her horn and she'll pull up outside. I wonder if she'd mind closing the hatch and cuddling me in the dark of the back of the van. We'd be surrounded by sandwiches and crisps and cakes and people would be banging on the hatch demanding their lunch. But we would just stand there, holding each other, her eyes shining in the half-dark, her cheek soft against mine. Twenty minutes. I don't want that Chris still here when she comes.

* * *

I nod slowly.

"You're right. Give the old man my best."

I sense his surprise at my change of tone, but he's still standing there not leaving.

"Bye then." I smile and reach for the phone to show that our pleasant conversation is now terminated. "Great talking to you. Bye."

Nat

Dad's going to lose his job. Mum says it's not his fault but the business is being sold and the new owners want to have someone else instead of him. She says that but none of the others are going except for Harry and he's old anyway, so it's only Dad who's been sacked. He's always messing things up. Now we won't have any money for anything.

Mum says I should go round and see him, see his flat and everything, she says, "Go and see him, Nat, even if only for an hour or two. He's had a tough time recently, what with Harry being so ill and First Glass being sold. You know it'd mean such a lot to him."

Yeah, like he's hardly managing to get along without me. Rosie says they have a brilliant time on Sundays and Dad's girlfriend shows her how to do painting and make cakes and girl stuff like that. So they'll really be wanting me along. I don't want to make stupid cakes in any case. We have to in home economics class at school and that's bad enough, I'm not doing it on the weekends as well. The other night, Cassie was round seeing Mum and she was saying about going to Dad's flat as well.

Cassie's pretty cool though. So I dunno. Maybe I should check out Rosie's room. See this stupid painting that his *girlfriend* did. And make sure he's not spoiling Rosie or anything. He doesn't know about stuff like that.

Anyway, I'll only go if *she's* not going to be there.

There's a knock on my bedroom door. Rosie's knock—three little taps—not Mum's.

"What?"

"Natty?"

"Yeah?"

The door opens a tiny bit and her hand waves at me through the gap.

"Let me come in."

"There's not an elephant leaning against the door on this side, Rozza. No-one's stopping you."

She comes in and walks placing one foot really carefully just in front of the other, holding her arms out to balance like she's on a tightrope.

"Don't look down or you'll fall off, kiddo."

"I'm walking across the Grand Canyon," she says. "It's over one and a half kilometers to the bottom."

"Then you definitely don't want to look down."

"Sssh! You'll break my concentration."

I blow a big raspberry at her.

"I never asked for the Grand Canyon to be in my room."

She does the last few steps in a little run, then dives for my bed, and I clap like crazy.

"She's done it! And this is extraordinary, ladies and gentlemen, the atmosphere here at the Grand Canyon has been nail-bitingly tense, but this young wire-walker from Ashford in England has wowed the world with her incredible feats of daring . . ." I hold my pen under her chin like a mic. "Tell us, Rosie, what is your secret? Is it true you owe it all to your big brother, your personal trainer and manager?"

She punches me on the arm.

"No, Natty!"

She lays back on the bed and points her feet at the ceiling then starts bicycling in the air.

"Rozza?"

"What?"

"You still going to Dad's flat on Saturday night?"

"Yes. He said we could have pizza."

"Is it just you and him? Like, I mean, is he having anyone else round?"

"He might be."

"You don't know, do you? You don't know *any-thing*!"

"I do know. I do so. Ella and Jamie come most Saturdays and we all have breakfast on Sunday morning and Dad gets up and cooks it and I have mushrooms on toast. Or beans. Because I'm vegetarian."

"Yeah? Like so not. You had chicken nuggets only last week and I saw you eating fish fingers yesterday."

"Fish doesn't count. And nor does nuggets."

*　*　*

Who the hell is Jamie? I'm not asking Rosie. Bet I can get her to tell me though.

"Well, if you and Dad and Ella and Jamie are all going to be there, doesn't sound like there's a whole lot of room for anyone else. I mean, this *Jamie*—"

Rosie stops bicycling and stands up.

"You're being horrible again. You said you'd come and see the painting on my bedroom wall and now you're trying to sneak out of it, but I don't care and I'm going to eat your share of the pizza as well as mine."

She stomps across the room to the door.

"Oi, Rozza!"

"What?"

"You just fell down the Grand Canyon."

Scott

There goes my mobile again. It's been non-stop today.

"Yup?"

"Scotty?" It's Harry.

"Hello, mate. Not ready for your deathbed yet then?"

"Still struggling on. They'll have to knock me over the head with a mallet if they want to get rid of me. Thought you'd forgotten me. Been busy, has it?"

"Yeah, well, you know. That lot couldn't tie their own shoelaces if I wasn't there keeping an eye on them."

"Maureen said you were probably up to your eyes, and that's why you hadn't been round."

"Hang on a sec. That's not it. I've phoned at least three times, but Maureen said you were having a nap or were out on your allotment. And I didn't come to see you 'cause Chris said you'd been ordered not even to think about work and you could do without the stress."

"I see."

"This sell-off, Harry? It is *your* idea, right?"

"Come off it. You know me—if it was up to me,

they'd have to prise my cutter out my hand when I'm laying in my coffin."

"Yeah, true—but your box will wait, you don't have to rush."

I *knew* it wasn't his idea. Now what?

"Still, it's probably best, eh? You don't need the agg. of all that." Why am I trying to talk him into it? Shut up, Scott. Just shut the fuck up. "And you've got your bowls to stop you getting up to mischief. And your allotment."

"Scott. Do me a favour, will you?"

"Course. Anything. Name it."

"Come and see me. Not at home. At the allotment."

I've not been since last summer. Then Harry was falling over tomatoes—great fat ones that tasted of, well, tomato—which is something of a rarity nowadays. And courgettes. I took some home for Gail to cook. And runner beans, hundreds of them it looked like, hanging off these bamboo wigwams like dangly green earrings. Early potatoes, damp and sticky with soil. Lettuces with frilly leaves like the can-can petticoats in that awful show I saw in Margate one time. That was last summer, before my life became this thrilling rollercoaster ride, up and down, my stomach lurching into my mouth one minute, then down into my boots the next.

We fix on tomorrow morning. Harry's to keep active, the consultant says. Easy on the stress but no becoming a couch potato. He's been put on a diet and he's to take exercise. Gardening gets the thumbs-up.

It is a fresh day, sunny but cold, with snapping gusts of wind from the east. I clang the metal gate closed and make my way in a succession of right angles across to where I see Harry stooping in among his beds. He is wearing a pair of old black gumboots and a brown jumper with holes in the elbows.

"Ooh-arr," I do my daftest country accent. "'Ow goes it, 'arry-lad?" He smiles and claps me on the back.

"Weeds and slugs. My two great enemies. Whatever I do, they just keep coming."

"Need a hand?" Course, what I know about gardening could be written on the point of a toothpick. Can't tell a weed from a prize cabbage.

"You could get the barrow from the shed. It's open." He points to a small shed at the far end of his patch. "And my other shovel. The old one."

We begin moving a mound of soil from one corner of the allotment to another bed near the middle for some reason. It is the kind of pointless thing gardeners seem to like doing.

"Will you move it all back tomorrow?"

"Cheeky so-and-so." He taps the side of his head. "It's all in here, my son, all part of the plan."

And, although it's true I can barely tell one end of a rake from the other and I'm certainly not as fit as I once was, it's kind of fun, pottering about on the allotment with old Harry. Like making mud pies or messing around in the woods or on the gravel heaps when I was a kid—getting grubby and being out in the fresh air and not feeling like you're supposed to be somewhere else. I *am* supposed to be somewhere else, of course, but Lee and Martin and Gary and Denise are all in today and if they can't handle most things by now between them then God help them when they come to be working for the new lot. They won't know what's hit them. A big company's not going to be as easygoing as me and Harry, that's for sure. Besides, it's not my problem any more.

"I'm glad you came," says Harry. "I wanted to have a word here—not at home, you know."

He means away from Chris, away from Maureen even, but he won't say it.

"Course." I plunge the spade deep into the soil. "'bout time I did some real work for a change anyhow."

He stands astride one of the narrow beds and bends down to pull up some carrots, one by one. I'm not sure exactly what he wants to say, but whatever it is, he's finding it tricky. He's as bad as I am. Worse even. I feel a sudden rush of—what?—something like, no, it sounds bloody daft. Well, don't tell anyone, but sort of affection, as if, just for a second, our positions were reversed and he's my son, standing there struggling, not knowing what to say. It's so rare for me to be the one who's not at a loss for words that I figure I should help him out a bit.

"Harry. About the business. It *is* OK, you know.

Chris told me I'll not be needed. I'll manage. I can turn my hand to anything." I'm not half as confident as I sound. I can't just do anything—I need to earn decent dosh. Most of what I take home goes straight to Gail, aside from enough for rent and bills and to take Rosie out. It's tight enough as it is. I want to take Ella on holiday—she says there's a place in Ireland where you can even swim with a dolphin—or at least out to a fancy restaurant for dinner once in a blue moon, give her a chance to dress up a bit. She could do with a treat.

"If I'd had a whiff of that condition at the beginning, I'd never have let him go ahead with it."

"It's no sweat. Honestly. I should have been moving on anyhow. I can't be a sad old bugger like you, stuck in the same firm for forty years, can I?" He laughs and looks down at the carrots in his hand, rubs the soil off with his finger and thumb.

"I've come to a decision," he says. "About the money."

"It's OK. Chris told me. Three months' pay. It's all right."

"Shut up a minute. It is *not* all right and it's *not* up to him. He should *never* have said that, it was totally out of order!" He's practically shouting now.

"Keep calm. Watch your blood pressure. Come on, sit down for a sec."

He lowers himself onto one of the grass paths at the edge. I'm in my not-so-crap trousers because I've got customer calls to do later, so I squat next to him.

"If none of *this* had happened," he strikes his chest, "I'd have gradually taken a back seat anyway and made you a proper partner in the business."

"Harry, I—"

"No, hang on. I should have done it years ago. Let's face it, you've been running the place for years. Yes, you have—I know you like to make out I'm still in charge but any fool could see through that in two minutes."

"But I never—"

"Will you shut up?"

"Yes, Boss."

"And then when I died—"

"Who's talking about dying all of a sudden? The doctor said—"

"I'm saying *when I went*, you'd have got the business—with a share in the profits for Maureen, of course, and a bit to go to Chris too. But it would have been yours."

There is a silence. I don't know what to say. I never knew all this. I want to say thank you, thank you for thinking of it for even a second, even though it won't happen now. I want to say these things but I can't speak.

"But, because of *this*—" He strikes his chest again. It makes me think of King Kong in that old film, beating his chest, towering over the jungle. But this is Harry, a man old before his time, sitting on a grass path beside *his* patch, his beloved allotment with its funny little beds of fruit and vegetables. He's still trying to be strong, though, proud—on his own territory now, in charge again. "Because of this, my family ..." He pauses and I know he wishes he'd chosen different words, not the f-word, the one that excludes me. "Maureen and Chris have made me see I've got to have a decent nest egg for my retirement."

"They're right. You have."

"Still, I may be old and getting feeble, but I'll not be bullied. You're to have a share of the money from the sale."

"I don't want it. You may need it. What if you get sick or something?"

"There'll be enough. I'm not arguing with you, so save your breath. I've made up my mind."

Rosie

My dad says he's going to be a company director. What he's going to do is sell his car and have a van instead and it's going to have his name painted on the side and he'll be the boss. Only there won't be anyone else for him to be the boss of because it's just him, but he'll still be the boss and that's what matters. He says it was all Ella's idea and if it doesn't work out she's going to be in big trouble and he'll have to tickle her to death.

What it is is he's going to do people's painting for them and put up their wallpaper and their tiles in the bathroom, like he did in the flat. Ella says he's really, really good at it and he shouldn't be so modest. Actually, I think Ella is better than him because she can paint proper pictures and things on the walls, animals and butterflies or whatever you like, but Dad can only do plain.

Nat's coming to Dad's on Saturday. We're going to get pizza, proper take-out ones, not just the sort you get in the freezer. Ella's not going to be there though. Dad said she was seeing a friend. But Nat's coming and he's going to see my room and Dad said maybe we can both go with him to help him choose a van in a couple of weeks. I think he should have a blue one. I've gone off mauve.

Scott

OK, I did accept the money from Harry, but only once he showed me he'd have enough put by for himself. It'll help me get set up with a van and ladders and all the gear I need and tide me over for a while until I'm up and running. I told Harry any time he's bored and fancies a spot of work, he can come in with me because I'll still take on the odd glazing job alongside the decorating.

When Ella first suggested it, I laughed. Me, run my own business?

"Why not? You've got the skills, the trade contacts, you're used to managing things. You're not afraid of hard work, you're good with people, trustworthy . . ."

"Carry on, don't stop now you're getting up a head of steam."

". . . and you're also getting big-headed—but with good reason because you're lovely and sexy and funny and you've got this really gorgeous bit right here—" She lifts up my shirt and lays her cool hand on my back, just above my bum.

"It's no good me being gorgeous where no-one can see it. What about the rest of me?"

She gets these little curves at the corners of her mouth when she smiles. Not dimples, curves—like mini-smiles laying on their sides.

"Oh, the rest of you is just about bearable, I guess."

Nat's coming over on Saturday night. I had to tell Ella, ask her, you know, if she'd mind . . . She was great about it.

"Don't force him to meet me when it's probably taking him all his courage to come at all. We'll take it slowly. I don't mind. Let him go at his own pace."

I take her hand and rub it gently between my own.

"Yeah, you're right. Thank you."

She pulls me down to kiss her.

"Good luck."

I'm going to need it.

Nat

He thought he'd make me come round. Like he used to when I was just a kid. When I was really small—littler than Rosie even —if I was being naughty or cross with him, Dad would pick me up and turn me upside-down, then he'd tickle me or make like he was about to chuck me across the room until I started laughing and then he'd laugh as well and Mum'd come in and say, "What *are* you two up to? It's like running a zoo, this house. Come on, it's feeding time for the animals. Chicken and chips!"

He must still think I'm only about four and he can just tease me out of it. But there's nothing he can do this time. I don't want to see him again. Not ever. Never, ever, ever. That's what we used to say. Like if he was trying to get me to eat vegetables at dinner, he'd say, "Eat up your greens or you'll never be big and strong" and I'd say, "What, never?" Then he'd go, "Never ever" and I'd go, "Never, ever, ever?" until Mum would say, "Oh, for goodness' sake, give it a rest you two—you're driving me crazy." It was always "you two" then, like we were both her kids. Rosie was only little and she was never naughty all that much so she didn't get told off even half as much as me. Then I'd say, "But I'll never like greens. Never." And Dad would say, "What, never ever?" And we'd be off again, laughing and making slurping noises with our drinks and playing tabletop football with our peas, flicking them between the knives and forks as goalposts when Mum wasn't looking.

OK, what happened was this. First of all, you need to know that it's not like I'd made up with him or anything because I hadn't. You got that? But I kind of said I'd take a look at his flat, just a look right, mainly because Rosie was giving me earache going on and on about it, and Cassie said she was going to take a look, and Mum was nagging me, so I thought if I went maybe everyone would stop hassling me about it. Anyway, I said I'd go round, just to look. No big deal. For an hour or so. See Rosie's room and that. Maybe have some pizza. And Dad said OK and *she* wouldn't be there.

It's not all that far and it wasn't raining for once, so I roller-bladed round there. He's got this flat on the first floor. I rang the bell and he buzzed me in and I went up the stairs still in my blades. It's OK if you turn your feet sideways. I couldn't be arsed to take them off 'cause I wasn't going to be there long and the laces take for ever to do, but I had my trainers in my bag, anyway.

Course, at home Mum never lets me keep my blades on indoors because she says it crucifies the carpets and she keeps saying I'm going to crash into things and knock them over—which I don't. Anyway, I'm at the door and he opens it but he just stands there not saying anything and looking at me like he's never seen me before. Then I clock that we're looking at each other almost on a level, eye to eye, 'cause with my blades on I'm like nearly as tall as he is. He gives me this funny smile, with his mouth all weird and pressed together like he's scared to smile normally, then he goes,

"Hey!"

And I go,

"So, am I coming in or what?"

I'm waiting for him to tell me to take off my blades or something, but he doesn't. He just opens the door wide as it'll go, right back so it bangs against the wall. The hall's like really minuscule and it's got this funny matting stuff on the floor, not proper carpet. It's really rough and hard and if you kneel down on it for more than about a minute it makes all patterns on your knees, even through your trousers. I know 'cause this boy I used to hang out with, Ian, they had it all over the whole house. Point *is*, it's not the best stuff if you're wearing blades and what with that and trying to get round the door into the kitchen and round him all at the same time I kind of lose my balance and Dad grabs my arm. I don't need his help. Jeez, you'd think I was an old lady trying to cross the road or something the way he holds onto me. Then he squeezes my arm and makes like he's about to say something. So I give him a look, sideways on so's he can't really see and I'm not kidding, he looks just like Rosie does when she's trying not to cry. 'Cept this is my dad here, right? When Rosie does it, her eyes look all wet and she bites her lip on the inside. Mostly it works but you can see she's doing it. So this freaks me out like only a major amount and I kind of push past him and stagger into the kitchen, which has a vinyl floor. Excellent. So I'm gliding round that smooth as you like, pushing off from one wall to the other, even though it's only small. Dad gives me a Coke straight from the fridge and gets me a beer glass and puts about fifteen ice cubes in it, like you'd have in a restaurant. I love it like that, so cold it makes your teeth hurt.

Rosie shows me her room and I say, "Yeah, very nice." She's got loads of stuff there. She must be leaving things there each weekend. There's a couple of posters and her scruffy old bear she's had since she was about two years old and there's a board up with pictures of her friends on it, bit like her room at home really, and there's a picture of Mum and—Rosie!—a stupid one of me she took last year. It's not even properly in focus. There's an inflatable chair in the corner and she shows me some stickers she bought with her pocket money, little penguins and polar bears, and says how she's going to put them on cards and do speech bubbles so they're saying things and have I got any good jokes about the Arctic for her to use. Then she drags me over to the painting on the wall by whatserface. Actually, it's not that bad. It's got birds flying around and the clouds really look like clouds. The castle's dark but there's this one window lit up in one of the turrets and it really glows like there's an actual light on in there.

I've still got my blades on, so Rosie tries to tow me around the flat. There's two bedrooms, one for Rosie and one for Dad. No prizes for guessing where his *girl-friend* sleeps when she stays the night. I'm not stupid. In the lounge, there's a round table to eat at and a settee and a telly, CD player and stuff. And a couple of whack-ing great pot plants, big jungly ones. We never have plants indoors at home 'cause Mum says they always die on her and she can't be spending her whole life pick-ing up the dead bits off the carpet all the time.

I lay down on the settee with my blades hanging over the arm at one end and Dad says,

"Course, this opens out y'know, Nat. It's a sofa-bed. I got it specially. Case you wanted to come and stay. Some time. Any time. Whenever." He's looking down at the carpet which is like normal carpet, not like in the hall, and I could see all these grooves where my skates had been. I reckon he's about to say something about it, but then he says,

"I'd really like it if you came to stay. Your mum's cool about it too. So it's down to you now really."

"Mn."

"So, what do you think then? About coming to stay?" He's fiddling with his ear now, like he does when he's nervous.

"What, on this? How come I don't get my own room with a proper bed and works of art all over the walls then?"

Dad jingles his change in his pocket.

"Oh, Nat. I'm sorry. Really. But what was I supposed to do? I couldn't shell out for a three-bedroom house when you weren't even talking to me. But, if you want to come and stay, I'll get somewhere bigger, course I will. This new business is going to do well, I know it is, so I'll have a bit more coming in I reckon. Look, we'll do your room properly—however you like—with a hard floor so you can skate in there if you want. And you can put up your posters and stuff—we could take a look at some places this weekend—"

"Yeah, yeah, all right, keep your hair on. I haven't said I'll stay yet." He goes back to jingling his coins.

"But think about it, OK?"

"Mn."

"Anyway. Pizza-time I think. Pizza, pizza, pizza. You hungry?"

I nod. Course I'm hungry. Like, when am I ever not hungry? "Pepperoni Hot or have you switched allegiance?"

"No chance. Pepperoni Hot. Can I have a big one?"

"Rosie!" he calls through. Mum says you're not supposed to shout from room to room. She says Dad's got no manners, but it's a lot easier than running backwards and forwards the whole time. "What kind of pizza do you want, sweetheart?"

Rosie comes in balancing on her tiptoes, she thinks she's a ballet dancer. She gives us a little twirl, showing off.

"Cheese and tomato, please. No bits on it."

"Come on, Rozza." I stretch out one of my skates and give her a shove. "What's the point of a pizza with no bits on it? It's like macaroni cheese without the cheese."

"It's like a guitar with no strings," says Dad, taking her hand and twirling her round.

"A Ferrari with no wheels," I say.

"A ballerina with no tutu," Rosie joins in. Well, she's only ten, what do you expect?

"Shepherd's pie without the shepherds," says Dad, getting carried away.

"But there aren't—" starts Rosie.

"A bowling alley with no *balls*!" I bellow.

Rosie's giggling away like a mad thing by now and Dad goes off, laughing, to look for the number of the pizza delivery place. Rosie starts tugging at my arm.

"Come and see Dad's room. You haven't seen it yet."

We can hear him talking to himself in the kitchen. I reckon he's going a bit bonkers, it's his age most probably.

"I'm sure it was in this drawer. Where did I put it? I bet she's moved it. Women—they're always tidying things away so you can't find anything . . ."

* * *

Rosie pulls me into Dad's bedroom. Big double bed with a swirly red bedspread on it, not at all like he and Mum used to have. There's a chest of drawers with candles on top and a vase of flowers. Real ones, not plastic. On the shelves, there's some books. My dad hasn't got that many but there's others as well, ones I haven't seen before that I reckon must be *hers*.

And on the shelves, in front of the books, are two framed photos—one of Rosie and one of me. They're the crappy ones they do at school. Total rip-off. I look a complete nerd in my one 'cause they make you brush your hair so it's all smooth like a total dork and they keep telling you to smile so you can see my teeth. They are majorly uncool pictures. Rosie's is OK, I guess, because she's still a kid and sort of cute. Then on the shelf below that there's another two photos, but not in frames. Rosie points to one of them.

"That's Ella. See? She's pretty, isn't she?"

I ignore her. The other picture is of Dad. He's carrying a little kid on his shoulders. A boy with brown curly hair, wearing a bright yellow sweatshirt.

"That's Dad with Jamie. He's only two and a half."

"And who the fuck is this Jamie kid anyhow?"

"Nat! You're not s'posed to swear—"

"You can't tell me what to do. I guess you'll go running off to *Daddy* now."

"I wasn't! I'm just saying—"

"Yeah, yeah. Who is he? Don't look like that. It's

pathetic." She's doing her little lost kitten face, biting her lip.

"Jamie's Ella's little boy. I *tried* to tell you before, but you wouldn't listen. He's two and—"

"You said that already."

"OK! He's really clever. He knows lots of different makes of cars, just from the badges. Dad taught him. And he can—"

I give a big yawn, really exaggerating it.

"Mn. *So* interesting . . ."

Rosie stomps back off to her room. She is so easy to wind up, it's untrue.

I pick up the picture and look at it really hard, like if I look long enough I'll know everything in it. Dad's laughing and the kid is laughing too and he—Jamie's—got his hands half over Dad's eyes but you can tell they're only playing and joking around and Dad's holding both his legs. I guess *she* took the picture.

I can see it all now. It's so obvious I feel totally stupid that I didn't click before. He must think we're so dumb. I can tell Rosie doesn't know. But I know why he left now and all that stuff about him and Mum not getting on any more and needing to spend time apart is a load of crap. Everything he's said is lies. Mum knows. She must do, she's not stupid. So everything she said is lies too. She could have told me. I'm old enough. I could have kept it from Rosie. She should have trusted me.

But the more I think about it, and the more I stare at the picture, the worse I feel. My insides feel weird, like I might throw up, but my ears are burning like that time I had the flu and my legs are shaking as if it's freezing cold. I shove the photo in my pocket and stagger out to the hall again. Pick up my bag. I can hear him on the phone.

"No, that's one *large* Pepperoni Hot and one—"

I open the front door, click it closed quietly behind me, then clamber best as I can back down the stairs, practically breaking my neck in the process 'cause of my blades. I hoik my bag onto my back, then I'm out on the street and pushing off. I don't know where I'm heading, not back home, I know that much, but I don't care. As long as it's not back there, not with him. Anywhere else. Anywhere else in the whole wide world. I pick up speed, getting into a rhythm now, swerving round crumblies with their shopping as if they're obstacles on a slalom run. The wind is cold, slapping my face in sudden gusts, making my eyes water, and my hands are freezing without gloves but I swing my arms to make me go faster, faster and faster, wishing they were wings that would lift me up above all the people and the cars and the houses and then there would just be me and the air, blading through the sky. I imagine him calling me, shouting "Nat! Nat!" over and over, but the wind is loud in my ears and I don't want to hear him. A woman gives me a funny look, like as if I'm crying or something, but it's only the wind. I rub my eyes roughly with my sleeve and I skate on, on and on, gliding, wheels spinning along the pavements, taking me further and further away.

Gail

He hasn't come home. He left Scott's place over two and a half hours ago and he's still not back. It's dark now. Scott thought he'd come straight here. He's not at Joanne's or Steve's or Jason's. Steve's ringing round his other friends just in case. Joanne's mother said she'll call if they hear anything. I even tried his mobile but, of course, there's just a message saying it's out of service. I should have given him the money. He kept asking for the money and I didn't give it to him.

I want to rush out and look for him. I want to run through the streets calling his name until I find him. Scott brought Rosie back so he could go out looking but he says I must stay here in case Nat comes back. He's right. Greg has gone to the hospital to check the casualty department and he's promised to phone from there. I wanted to call the police too but Scott says he'll drop into the station in town, and I'm not to worry. *He* will find Nat. He's *promised* to find him. Mari offered to pick up Rosie and look after her, but I want her here with me. She's fallen asleep on the couch, wrapped in a blanket, so Cassie and I are speaking in whispers.

"Don't worry," Cassie says. "Nat's no fool. He's sharp as a razor. He'll be OK."

I nod shakily and try to drink my coffee.

Neither of us are saying it. I cannot say it out loud. If I do, maybe that'll make it true. But I know she's thinking it and I'm thinking it: *What if someone's taken him?*

I wish to God she hadn't used the word sharp, I don't want to think about anything sharp. I mustn't think it. I owe it to Natty not to think it. Not even for a second. I pray inside my head, "Please, God, let him be safe. I'll do *anything* you want. Don't let anything happen to him. Take *me* instead. Please let him be all right, *please*"—over and over in my head as I walk up and down, hugging myself with my own arms.

"I could go and look as well," offers Cassie.

I shake my head.

"Please don't leave me."

She gives me a long, long hug.

"I'm phoning Derek—Scott can't do the whole town by himself."

Scott phones and says he's spoken to his mate in the police, given him a photo so he can keep an eye out and they'll put the word out to the police on the beat. I give him Derek's mobile number so they can co-ordinate.

"Don't worry," says Scott. "I'll bring him back. I swear. You can rely on me."

Scott

I head for the station first, hoping like hell he hasn't got himself on a train to London or I'd never find him. It made me think of those programmes you see about teenagers, no more than kids really, living on the streets, getting into drugs, thieving, prostitution. Knowing Natty, he wouldn't have had enough money for the train fare on him, but he might have snuck on, hid in the toilet from the guard. I know a bloke who works there so I track him down and show him Nat's photo. He asks around and says no-one's seen a boy that age on his own and they probably would have noticed one—you did if it wasn't regular school time because you reckoned they'd be up to no good, vandalizing the toilets and what have you. I quell an urge to punch him one. Not my Natty, he's not like that. It's nearly half-ten now. I give him my mobile number and he promises to keep an eye out.

Then I drive round and round town, hoping I might just suddenly spot him, trying to think—where would he go? What would he do? Where would I go if I was

Nat? Derek's covering the park, the snooker hall, and the bus station. I check out the bowling alley, because I took Natty there a few times, but it's pretty much all families. Real families, you know, out together having a good time, not like the godawful mess I've managed to make of mine. The sports centre is just closing up—they have some late-night coaching and stuff going on on Saturday nights. I go up to the reception desk and show his photo to the two women there. The older one says, "Sorry, love. I don't remember him, but we get so many lads in that age. The courts and pool are closed. Only the main hall's still open—take a look if you like."

The other one, the young one, says, "Ooh, it's like on the telly. Are you a cop?"

What a moron. Normally, I'd have tried to come up with a cutting remark, something clever, but I don't care any more. I just want Natty back.

"No, not a cop. I'm a dad. He's my son."

The security guard comes with me to check the hall and the gents' toilets. Nothing.

Back into town and I park illegally to nip into McDonald's, knowing Nat can't keep away from food for long. The manager says no, he doesn't think he's seen him but they have so many kids in and they all look alike now, don't they?

"He was wearing a black padded jacket, black combat trousers and roller-blades."

"Exactly," he says. "They all are. Could be anybody."

It's not anybody, I want to shout at him, It's my son. He's my *son*, you idiot.

Still, getting angry isn't going to get me anywhere. I go back outside, shivering from the cold. I hope wherever he is that it's somewhere warm and safe and that he has a portion of chips to keep the chill off his hands. I could do with some myself because I'm freezing but I'm not getting any. It sounds daft but I can't stand the idea of me being warm in the car with chips and Natty being cold and chipless and alone. But it's the best way to keep your hands warm, holding chips, that's what I've always told him, that's the way we used to do it when he was little and we went fishing off the beach.

The—way—we—used—to. When—he—was—little. Hang on a sec. Hang on a sec. Would he? Could he have gone there? He'd have to have got the bus or hitched a ride. Dear God, don't let him have hitched with all these nutters out on the roads. I give Derek a call on his mobile, see if he's checked the bus station yet, and he says he'll go there straight away. It has to be worth a try—I'm going anyway, I'm all out of other ideas. I ring Gail to check if there's any news her end and tell her where I plan to go next.

"What do you think? Is it a long shot?"

"Go. Just go, Scott. I can't think of anywhere else."

"I'll call you when I get there."

"Thanks. Please find him. Promise you'll bring him back safe."

"I promise."

The phone rings a minute later and I jump, thinking maybe it's Nat. But it's Ella, calling from the flat, to see if there's any news. She'd offered to come round and stay in case he went back and turned up there. It's good to hear her voice, concerned but calm.

"Take care of yourself," she says. "And keep warm."

"I will. Get into bed and warm it up."

"It's best if I stay up. In case he comes back here. But I'll let you put your cold feet on me. Special treat."

"Ella?"

"Yup?"

"You know I love you, don't you?"

I can feel her smile shimmering through the phone.

"Yes. I love you too."

It's been a while since I've driven this road in the dark—not since I last went fishing with Harry. Years ago, when Nat was not much more than a tot really, that's when I first started taking him fishing with me, from the beach. You get a lot of blokes along this particular stretch, the occasional woman too, but mostly blokes—in ones and twos, mates or dads with their boys. Fathers and sons. I had this little wind-shelter tent and a tilley lamp and two folding stools and we'd go at night. You get there a couple of hours before high tide, stay three, four hours sometimes. There'd be a flask of coffee for me and a small one of cocoa or soup for Nat and we'd take along some sandwiches but we'd always go to the chippie as well because holding chips is the best way to keep your hands warm. And there's nothing like the smell of chips and vinegar and warm paper in your nose when the wind's biting your face off and the sea is grey and the sky is dark. And all you can see are the stars, the lights of the power station across the bay, the lamps of the men fishing and the red-hot dots of their cigarettes floating against the dark.

I park right on the front and scrunch down onto the shingle. Start asking the blokes who are fishing,

"Seen a young lad on his own?"

Showing them the photo. From one to the next I go, working my way along the beach. After about ten or twelve there's a bloke fishing by himself, with the same kind of tent that I've got.

"Yes, mate. I chatted to a lad. I'm not sure if it was this one, it's hard to see. Hair going forwards over his face like this? Dark padded jacket?"

"Yes, yes. That sounds like him." My heart's racing. Please let it be Nat, please let it be Nat.

"Yeah. I gave him some tea. He looked half frozen to death, mate."

"Did you see which way he went?"

"To get chips, he said. But it must have been over an hour ago."

I run along the beach then, stumbling on the shingle in the dark, calling out his name. The wind snatches my words and makes my eyes water, tears running down my face. "Natty! Na-a-t!" Running by the small shelter there on the promenade, I turn—and see a figure, a dark, hunched figure, almost invisible crumpled as he is right into the very corner.

I clamber up the beach, slipping and sliding, like trying to run up the down escalator, pull myself up onto the edge of the promenade. Stand up. Face him.

He looks up. Natty. I breathe out. I feel as if I've been holding my breath for hours.

"Oh," he says. "It's you."

"Natty."

"Why are you here? What do you want?" He looks terrible. Even in the dim light, I can see he's pale and cold, his eyes dark and bruised looking.

"Hang on," I say, not moving, not wanting to make him run again, though he looks defeated somehow, and weak as a half-drowned kitten. "Have a go at me in a minute. I'm ringing Mum before she has a nervous breakdown."

I phone Gail, tell her he's safe and well and she bursts into tears. Cassie comes on the line and says to call back in a while. I sit down further along the bench. Nat's holding a half-eaten portion of chips.

"Hands holding up OK?"

He shrugs.

"Chips have gone cold."

I edge a bit closer.

"Fish biting tonight?"

The ghost of a smile comes to his face.

"Stupid. Haven't got my rod, have I?"

"Natty?"

"Mn?"

"I—this is difficult—I don't know how to— Thing is, I guess I'm not much of a dad."

He shrugs again.

"Feel free to contradict me at any point."

A small laugh. Then silence.

"This little boy." He takes out a photo from his pocket, the one from my bedroom, with Jamie on my shoulders.

"What, Jamie?"

"Mn. Is he your kid?" He's not looking at me. He's facing dead ahead, staring out to sea.

God, is that what he thought? That all along I'd had another son hidden away?

"What? No, of course not. Where did you get that idea?"

"Thought that's why you left. What d'you need us for when you've got a whole other family all along?"

I slide closer along the bench.

"Oh, Natty. Shit. I can't bear it that you thought that. Not for a second. Listen he's Ella's son, that's all. I was carrying him because he's little and he was tired. You know what they're like at that age. Remember Rosie, eh? 'Lift me up, Daddy! Carry me, Daddy!'"

We laugh a bit at that.

"He's a nice kid, Natty. But he's not my son. *You're* my son."

"Mn." He scrunches up what's left of his chips and leans out to chuck them in the bin. "You going to have kids with her?"

"Nah. I'm too old and knackered." Then I think of Ella. Her calm face close to mine, her laugh, the way she moves around the kitchen, her hand reaching up to tuck her hair behind her ear, singing to herself as she cooks. "I don't know. We're not at that stage yet. But—Nat— even if I did, no amount of kids could ever replace you. It's not like getting a new battery and chucking the old one away 'cause it's no use any more. I mean, you're *Nat*. My Nat. There'll never, ever be another Nat."

"What, never, ever, ever, ever?" We used to say that when he was little, you know, all that parent stuff . . . "Eat your greens or you'll never get to be big." "What?" Nat would say back, "Never, ever?" "Nope. Never, ever, ever" we'd go.

"Nope," I say now. "Never, ever, ever, ever, ever . . . ever."

"Why d'you leave us then?"

I shuffle right next to him and put my arm round him. Feel him stiffen, his body tense.

"I didn't leave *you*, you dipstick. Jeez. How can I tell you? Grown-up stuff, it's so difficult, Nat. I don't understand it half the time. Mind you, your mum would say that's 'cause I'm not a proper grown-up—and she's probably right. But it was nothing to do with Ella—I hardly even knew her then. The thing is, I messed up big time and it was all my fault and then—your mum and I—well, we just couldn't be together any more. And, if I'd stayed, we'd have ended up rowing the whole time and maybe even hating each other—and that'd have been bad for us and bad for you and Rosie, too. Believe me, you and Rosie are the best things in my life, always have been. I'd do anything for you, you must know that."

I feel him give a little, his weight heavy against me. I give him a squeeze and pull him closer.

"You're my son. Nothing can ever change that or take it away—not from you and not from me. I love you, you big dipstick. I love you so much. You have to know that."

And I sit there holding him a while, the two of us looking out to the dark sky, the sea, the lights across the bay, the tilley lamps of the men and the glow of their cigarettes. We sit there, watching them, clutching their cups of tea, huddling against the wind, fathers and sons.

"C'mon then. It's cold." I pull him to his feet and give him a final hug. We stay like that a minute, then he pulls away.

"Leave over, Dad. You can't have blokes hugging along here. We'll get arrested."

One last squeeze then I let him go.

"All right. Fancy some fresh chips?"

He nods and we walk along the front together, just the two of us, father and son. Father and son.

THE END

Love is a
Four Letter Word

by Claire Calman

**also available from
HarperCollins*PublishersLtd***

ISBN 0-00-639187-7

Prologue

She sees herself fall in slow motion, the toe of her shoe catching on the edge of the paving-stone, her arm reaching out in front of her, her hand a pale shape like a leaf against a dark sky. The pavement swims towards her, its cracks the streets of a city seen from a skyscraper, the texture of the concrete slabs suddenly sharply in focus.

It is not a bad fall: a swelling on her left knee destined to become an outsize bramble-stain bruise, a stinging graze on the heel of her hand, a buggered pair of decent tights. Back at home, Bella balances half a bag of frozen broad beans on the knee and sips at a glass of Shiraz. She tells herself it is not a bad fall, but when she wakes the next morning it is as if a switch has been thrown, draining off all her energy in the night. She leans against the kitchen worktop to drink her coffee, not daring to sit down because she knows she will never get up again.

Overnight, London seems to have become a grotesque parody of a metropolis, no longer bustling and stimulating but loud and abrasive. Litter flies up from the gutters. Grit pricks her eyes. She feels fragile, a rabbit caught in the target-beam of headlights. Buses loom out of nowhere, bearing down on her. Cyclists swerve to avoid her, bellowing abuse. She tenses each muscle in her body when she crosses the road, imagines she can hear the thud-thudding of her heart. When someone bumps into her in the street, she thinks she will splinter into tiny fragments. In her mind, she sees her body shatter and the pieces shower through the air like the explosion of a firework, tinkling like glass as each one strikes the pavement. She imagines them coming to sweep her up so they could painstakingly reassemble her, but shards of her are left behind, unnoticed in the gutter, hidden by a litter bin or a lamp-post.

Her doctor is unsympathetic, sighing through his nostrils as she answers his questions. Months of overworking, he says. Prolonged stress. What else did she expect? Did she want to have a serious collapse? If so, she was certainly going the right way about it. No tablets, he says, no prescription. Time off. Rest. Rethink your life. That's it? she asks. That's it.

Her boss is unsurprised.

"You're no use to me half-dead," he says. "Sod off to the Caribbean for a month. Drink Mai-Tais till dawn and shag some waiters."

The Caribbean? She is so exhausted she'd be lucky to make it down the road to the travel agent. Perhaps they could administer her Mai-Tais via a drip.

*　*　*

Visiting her good friends Viv and Nick in the Kentish city where they now live, she wanders at convalescent pace through the web of narrow streets, past lopsided houses and ancient flint walls. She focuses on one task at a time, as if she were a stroke victim learning afresh each skill she had previously taken for granted. Then, meandering down a quiet side street near the river, she sees the For Sale board.

Compared with the London flat she had rented with Patrick, no. 31 is a delight. Sunny. Spacious. With a proper garden rather than a sad, overshadowed strip of concrete. Yes, says Viv, a fresh start is just what Bella needs. Plenty of companies would jump at the chance to have someone with her experience.

She seems to enter a trance then, dealing with the solicitor, the building society. Writing job applications. Forms, paperwork become a welcome distraction, tangible things to focus on—things she can solve. You take a pen, fill in the spaces in neat block capitals. The questions are straightforward: Name. Address. Bank Details. Current Salary. You do it all properly and you get the result you were aiming for. It feels like magic.

She moves smoothly through the weeks on automatic pilot, gliding through her notice period at work, her smile efficiently in place, her projects on schedule. Now that she knows she is leaving, she cuts down on her hours, and fills her evening with paperwork and planning, even relishing each hitch and setback—the vendor's pedantry about the garden shed, the surveyor's discovery of damp—as something she can get her teeth into.

In her neat ring-binder, sectioned with coloured card dividers, she can find any particular piece of paper in an instant. The rings click closed with a satisfying clunk, containing her, keeping her life in order. She transfers her accounts, her doctor, her dentist, sends out exquisitely designed change-of-address cards. This is easy: making phone calls, folding A4 letters into three and sliding them into envelopes, measuring for curtains. And it fills her head. She needs it to hold her, as if each stage of Buying the House is a sharp staple grasping together the sections of an ancient cracked plate.

**From *Love is a Four Letter Word*
by Claire Calman**